RUTHLESS
REIGN
MONICA KAYNE

Book Cover by Qamber Design

Book Interior by designsbycharlyy

Beta reading & line editing by Romance Editor, Nina Fiegl s.p.

Copy editing by Krista Dapkey

ISBN 978-1-7782704-5-1

First edition 2024

DEDICATION

This book is dedicated to all those who fantasize about a gorgeous 6'3 bratva leader pulling their hair and praising them in Russian...

May I introduce you to Roman Vasiliev...

AUTHOR NOTE

Ruthless Reign is a dark mafia romance with mature themes and profanity. Please check the FAQ section of my website for trigger and content warnings.

https://monicakayne.com/trigger-warnings

Please note: In Russian naming conventions, women often use a feminine version of their family surname. For example, "Ivanov" becomes "Ivanova."

CHAPTER ONE

LIZA

The bruise under my eye is definitely going to be a problem.

I gingerly touch the smudge of purple, wincing from the bite of pain. Digging in my makeup drawer, I find a long-forgotten peachy-coral lipstick tucked in the top right-hand side. According to a YouTube makeup tutorial I watched on concealing dark under-eye circles, peach shades work best to neutralize violet hues.

But it's not a late night that I'm covering up. It's a bruise my fiancé gave me at a party last night because I told the mayor his new public transportation plan was flawed. I was simply stating facts, but I should have known better. Anatoly hates when I talk politics. He hates when I have an opinion that doesn't align with his. And he really hates when I disagree with him publicly.

As soon as the words were out of my mouth, his face hardened. He said nothing as he seized my arm and led me to a dark corner of the veranda. His anger usually comes in the form of a berating lecture, so I wasn't expecting his fist. It happened quickly. He raised his arm and backhanded me. I cried out as the bite of pain jolted through my skull like a bolt of lightning. My hand flew to my face as tears welled up. My body trembled, not only from the cold air but from a raw, tangled knot of disbelief.

Disbelief and fear.

The glint in his eyes as my knees weakened is branded into my memory. He liked it. It made him feel powerful. There's nothing Anatoly likes more than power, especially over me.

A suffocating helplessness washes over me. Now that he's raised a hand to me once, what's to stop him from doing it again?

I wince a little as I carefully dab the lipstick over the bruise, patting it until the purple hue fades, before I add a final layer of concealer that matches my skin tone. I blow out a breath and angle my chin this way and that under the mirror's bright lights, making sure nothing shows through. Making sure I look perfect.

I startle at the sharp knock on my bedroom door.

Without waiting for a response, my mother sweeps into my room in a cloud of Chanel No. 5 and absolute confidence. As always, Anastasia Ivanova looks impeccable—her hair is styled in an elegant up-do, and her figure is sculpted from private workouts and draped in the latest designer fashion, thanks to Anatoly's deep pockets.

"I came to see if you need my help with your hair or makeup," my mother offers as sweetly as she can manage, but we both know why she's really here.

Her eyes flick over my face, assessing. She must have noticed the bruise this morning—not that she said anything. My parents very conveniently turn the other way when it comes to Anatoly because, to them, he's the white knight who pays our bills and keeps us in good social standing.

"I don't need your help," I say tightly. "Where's Sofiya?"

For some reason, my mother insisted that my sister come

home from boarding school for the dinner party we're hosting tonight. Even though I don't see why it's necessary, I'm always happy to see Sofiya. She's the one bright light in my world.

"She's in her room getting ready. You'll see her soon." My mother reaches out, adjusting one of my earrings. "I don't have to remind you how important tonight is."

Important to her, that is. This evening, we're hosting two of Moscow's most influential families: the Petroviches, my fiancé's family and owners of Russia's largest shipping company, and the Belovs, which includes my best friend, Kira, and her husband, Maxim Belov, who leads the country's most powerful bratva.

Funny how Mama never gave a damn about Kira until she married Maxim last year. Now she treats her like the Queen of England, and it drives me crazy. At least Kira has a sense of humor about it all.

I sigh and cross my arms. "It's a party, so don't make it out to be a state dinner. Everything will be fine."

She frowns. "Liza, this is your future family we're talking about. It's important for everything to go perfectly. Did you get the dress Anatoly sent?"

My lips flatten into a thin line. "I sure did."

This morning, an ornate gift box—courtesy of my asshole fiancé—was delivered to our house. Inside, there was a dress, a pair of designer shoes, jewelry, and an I'm-sorry-it'll-never-happen-again note tucked into a bouquet of roses. The dress is white, skintight, and, despite the designer label, trashy. It's exactly how he likes me to dress.

My mother went on and on about his generosity, but his so-called gifts are another way to control me. Everything about how I look tonight is calibrated to please him. My long dark-auburn hair is down and in waves. My makeup is smoky and sexy, the smattering of freckles across my nose covered up by a layer of foundation. I'm even wearing one of two acceptable perfumes he selected.

The girl I used to be—the one who prefers chunky jewelry, flowy dresses, and messy buns—no longer exists. She was traded in for a diamond ring and a monthly allowance.

"Now, if you'll excuse me, Mother, I really should get changed."

She ignores the not-so-subtle hint, gently tucking a strand of hair behind my ears. "You'll make a beautiful bride."

I stiffen. "One day. You mean I'll make a beautiful bride *one day*."

I've hoped and prayed that I could put off the wedding for as long as humanly possible. Once a date is set, the nightmare becomes real. It means moving in with Anatoly and eventually having his children. I'll be trapped with no way out.

Her eyes flash with irritation. "Darling, you're twenty-five years old and not getting any younger. Do you think a man like Anatoly will wait forever?"

"I'm not rushing into a marriage before I feel ready."

"Rushing? You've been engaged for a year." She grabs my arm, and her fingers dig into my flesh, shattering the illusion of a warm mother-daughter moment. "We need this marriage to happen, Liza. The monthly allowance Anatoly provides is generous, but it's simply not enough to meet our needs. And don't forget you're the one who insists on that hideously expensive school for your sister. If we didn't have to pay those exorbitant fees—"

"That's not up for debate," I say, my voice tight. Why is she bringing this up now?

Her eyes narrow. "You're engaged—a wedding is the natural next step. Once you're married, Anatoly will ensure Papa is given a lucrative position on the Petroviches' board of directors." She pauses, her expression hardening. "Think about the future, Liza. It's not only about you. This affects all of us. Sofiya as well."

There it is. My mother knows my weakness. Everything I do is for Sofiya. Without Anatoly's money, we'd be out on the street, and my sister's comfortable life and fine education would be ripped away.

My throat tightens, and anger burns in my gut. I'm tempted to remind her that if she had reined in my father's gambling and wasn't so obsessed with keeping up appearances, we wouldn't be in this mess. But I'm really not in the mood for a lecture on how "family comes first, no matter the personal cost," so I keep silent. She twists everything I say anyway.

I take a steadying breath and address her as calmly as I can. "Anatoly is busy running the family business while his father is getting cancer treatment. A wedding is the last thing on his mind."

My mother strokes my cheek, her expression blank. "You really should get dressed."

She turns to leave, and I try my best to ignore the uneasy feeling lodged in my chest.

An hour later, I'm slipping into a pair of dangerously tall Louboutins when my bedroom door swings open with a burst of energy. Without a glance, I know exactly who it is.

"Lizka, I've missed you." My sister smiles, wrapping her arms around me. "Honestly, this semester has felt never-ending."

Sofiya might be eight years my junior, but at seventeen, she's nearly my height, which always takes me by surprise. In my mind, she'll forever be the gangly girl with pigtails and a gap-toothed grin. But that's definitely not the woman in front of me now.

"I've missed you, too." I step back to take in her dark waves, so much like mine. "We have an hour before the guests arrive. Tell me everything that's been going on with you." I rub my hands in anticipation. "Spill all your secrets."

Sofiya rolls her eyes and flops down onto my bed with a theatrical sigh. "Secrets? As if. The nuns don't allow you to keep any secrets in that prison of a boarding school."

I toss a throw pillow at her and carefully perch on the edge of the bed, because that's all I can manage in this tight dress. "Oh, come on. They're not that bad."

I graduated from the same boarding school over seven years ago, back when my parents still had money. Kira and Anatoly also attended, which is where we all first met.

"They are! Alina Solovyova was suspended for a week because the headmistress found letters from a boy under her pillow." She smirks. "The letters did have some explicit details about the time they'd spent together over the summer, but still. It's none of their business what we do in our personal lives."

"Speaking of personal lives ... Have you met anyone special?"

She gives a little half-smile. "There's this one guy, Denis, from the boys' school. He's pretty cute, but it's not like we can see much of each other. The nuns make sure we're never alone."

I laugh softly. "Yeah, I remember how good they were at keeping us out of trouble."

She arches an eyebrow. "Like you ever got into any trouble. I bet you were a perfect student, just like you're a perfect daughter and a perfect fiancée."

"I'm far from perfect," I'm quick to say, but I'm well aware that's the façade I've maintained to the world, including her.

"Well, you're obviously doing something right." She scoops up my left hand, admiring the princess cut diamond ring on my finger. A ring that feels more like a ball and chain than a declaration of love.

She props her head in her hands. "I swear, you're so lucky to have found the man of your dreams."

The man of my nightmares is more like it.

Sofiya knows that Anatoly funds our lifestyle, but she doesn't know what it costs me. That I'm sacrificing my happiness for her future. And I hope she never finds out. It would only upset her.

"Want me to do your makeup?" I offer in attempt to change the subject.

"Ohhh, yes!" She claps her hands and takes the seat in front of my vanity mirror. "What's the deal with this lipstick?" She uncaps the tube and spreads a thin layer on the back of her hand.

I grimace and snatch it from her. "I was cleaning out my makeup drawer, getting rid of stuff I don't need."

"You can add that to the pile. Peach lips are definitely not in this season."

I give her a joking shove, then dig through my drawer for a smoky gray eyeliner and a golden eyeshadow to highlight her green eyes, identical in shade to mine.

As I finish applying the liner, she cracks a lid. "Oh, speaking of cute guys ... I heard Roman Vasiliev is coming tonight."

My heart stills, as it does every time I hear that name. "Roman?" I swallow hard. "I thought he was out of the country."

"He's back. Mama mentioned it earlier. I think she's trying to set me up with him, which is weird. I mean, he's hot and rich and all, but he's twice my age."

I grit my teeth. My mother has officially lost the plot.

Roman is a dangerous man, one of Maxim's right hands. Along with Pavel Fedorov, the three of them run the Belov Syndicate.

"She never mentioned he was coming to me, but if she had, I would have told her he wasn't worth the invite."

Sofiya gives me a knowing look. "Are you still holding a grudge against him? He was only doing his job."

Roman was Kira's "bodyguard" when she and Maxim married. In reality, Roman was spying on Kira because Maxim was suspicious of his new wife's reasons for agreeing to their arranged marriage. Every time Kira and I went shopping or grabbed drinks, Roman was there—watching her, but somehow always staring at me. Making me feel things I didn't want to feel.

I wish I could say my issue with Roman was a simple grudge—that would be easy enough to ignore—but the emotions he provokes in me are anything but simple.

I aggressively swirl a soft brush in a pot of eyeshadow. "Yes, well, I didn't appreciate being spied on. Everything we said was reported back to Maxim." I clear my throat. "I know it's in the past, but I still don't like him. He's so, so …" Sexy. Infuriating. Ridiculously handsome. "Full of himself."

My sister lifts an eyebrow suggestively. "Any man who looks like that has every right to be."

I press my lips together. It's true, though I'd never admit it.

"Trust me, steer clear of men like him. You'll have plenty of time for dating when you're older. For now, focus on school and having fun with your friends."

She eyes me like I'm crazy. "Why are you so obsessed with me getting good grades and going to university? I'd rather marry rich, like you."

"I swear to God, Sofiya, if you—"

"Take a pill, I'm kidding!" My sister snorts. "You know I'm practically top of my class, but there are other things in life."

"Of course. But education is power. It's independence, and I want you to have every advantage available in this world.

What happens if your husband drops dead one day or your marriage falls apart? You need to be educated to support yourself and any children you might have."

Sofiya looks thoughtful for a moment before her mouth draws into an impish grin. "I'll have to make sure my side pieces are rich, too."

She cackles, and I can't help but smile. My sister always jokes I'm more of a parent than our actual parents are, which isn't all that hard. Growing up, I was pretty much raised by the hired help while my parents jetted off to do whatever they wanted. When Sofiya was born, I vowed to give her the love and attention I never had. I'm the one who taught her how to tie her shoelaces and ride a bike. I know I can be overprotective, but it's only because I want the best for her.

"What about you? You never finished university," she points out.

Bitterness climbs my throat. "We couldn't afford it. That's why I want better for you. And I've continued to get an education on my own." I gesture to the stack of business and investment books piled high on the desk beside my laptop.

What my sister doesn't know—what no one knows—is that I've started day-trading stocks and bonds. I'm not playing with big bucks, just the few hundred dollars from my grandmother's inheritance that I managed to hide from my parents. It's this skill that I hope will one day grant me freedom.

"All done." I step back so Sofiya can see herself in the mirror. She beams, admiring her reflection, before she pulls me in for a quick hug. "We'd better go down. Everyone will be here soon."

"I need to take a selfie to send to my friends!" she exclaims. "I won't be long."

"Okay, *sestra*, see you down there."

I don't allow the smile to drop from my face until I'm gone from the room.

CHAPTER TWO

LIZA

Anatoly and his family are the first to arrive. My fiancé strides through the door with the confidence of a man sure of his place in the world. He's in his late twenties, with thinning dirty-blond hair and a growing paunch he disguises with sharply tailored suits.

Back in school, he was considered handsome, but his looks have faded along with any charm he might have had. The only one who can't see that is my mother, who's currently fawning over him like he's the second coming of Jesus.

Anatoly's parents are next through the door. Talya, his mother, offers me a quick air kiss while helping her husband, Stepan, shuffle forward. I briefly embrace him. Having recently been diagnosed with colon cancer, he's noticeably thinner and unsteady on his feet.

"I told you we'd be the first ones here." Anatoly's younger sister, Katerina, blows past her parents, looking around the foyer with disappointment.

It's hard to say who my least favorite Petrovich is, but Katerina and Anatoly are definitely in the running for first place. Much like her brother, she believes she's God's gift to the world.

"Katerina," I say in greeting, leaning in to give her an awkward half hug.

When she pulls back, she gives me a slow once-over, her disdain for my dress clear. Well, that makes two of us.

Looking every bit the socialite she is, she's paired a sparkly gold dress with thigh-high boots and enough bling to cause temporary blindness.

"So glad you could make it tonight," I lie.

She doesn't bother pretending she's happy to be here. Instead, she tosses her hair behind her shoulder and scans the foyer. "I heard Roman Vasiliev is coming tonight. Is that true?"

My eye twitches. If I have to watch Katerina hang off Roman's arm all night, I might gouge my eyes out. Not because I care who he gets involved with but because that would be … irritating.

"That's the word," I confirm. "News sure travels fast."

I'm not surprised she's interested, he's exactly Katerina's type. Rich, good-looking, and ruthless—like her.

Katerina offers me a tight smile before announcing she needs a drink and sauntering off.

Catching Sofiya's eye as she watches from the sidelines, I mouth, "Bitch." My sister giggles, fully aware of my feelings toward Anatoly's sister.

"Elizaveta. You haven't greeted your fiancé yet." I stiffen as Anatoly drops a kiss onto my cheek. His aftershave is too strong, and I hate the way his hand curls over my hip.

Well, tonight's off to a great start.

"Excuse me, Sofiya. Your sister and I need to have some words in private." He clasps my arm and pulls me into a quiet corner of the foyer.

After last night, I have to force myself to meet his eyes and resist the impulse to spit in his face.

His fingertips brush over my face, the very area he backhanded. "Good, no bruise. I knew I didn't hit you very hard." I bite my cheek to avoid telling him to fuck off. "You know I didn't mean it. I'm stressed out because of everything going on with my father."

Does he believe his own lies?

I can't hold my tongue any longer. "The reason you don't see a bruise is because I covered it with makeup."

He dismisses my words with a flick of his wrist. "I don't want to fight. Tonight's for celebrating. By the way, you look perfect."

His eyes trail down my body, and I squirm under his heated gaze. I hope he doesn't think I'll make time to be alone with him tonight. Honestly, I'd rather eat worms.

"Thank you," I say, to keep the peace. "The dress is …" Slutty. "Daring."

"With that sweet body of yours, you can pull it off."

Over Anatoly's shoulder, I see Kira and Maxim arrive fashionably late. Kira waves at me across the room while my parents rush to greet them.

I grin and wave back, then turn to Anatoly. "Are we done here? I have other guests to greet."

His mouth hardens. "This dinner is important. I expect you to act accordingly."

"I know what's expected of me," I say between clenched teeth.

Tonight, we're celebrating a new and very lucrative deal between the Petroviches and the Belovs. In short, Petrovich ships will be transporting illicit goods between the Belov Syndicate in Russia and the Brooklyn-based Kozlov Bratva, run by Kira's brothers. Essentially, US goods will be sold in Europe and vice versa.

Everyone but me is excited about this partnership. Because Anatoly going into business with my best friend's husband only tightens the ties that bind me to him, and that's the last thing in the world I need.

I look down at his hand still wrapped tightly around my arm. "Can you please let me go?" I hiss. "I need to mingle."

He releases me, but I can still feel the area where he grasped me too tightly.

"You know I only want the best for you," he murmurs. "The best for us, but you don't always make it easy."

Kira's weaving her way towards us, and I'm anxious to end this conversation. I attempt the sweetest smile I can muster. "Let's start over. You know I hate fighting with you."

He pats my ass. "I accept your apology."

I school my expression as Kira approaches and wraps me in her arms. She may be several inches shorter, but she has the presence of someone twice her size and hugs like her life depends on it.

Kira turns and greets Anatoly with forced politeness. She's no fan of his. She didn't like Anatoly when we were in school, and I can't say she likes him any better now.

In some ways, not a lot has changed—he was as much an entitled rich snob back then as he is today. Still, his good looks and family name had girls lining up to date him. Maybe it's because I wasn't interested in him that he pursued me. I brushed him off every time, but he was relentless. He'd corner me at school dances, send me unwanted gifts, and he even broke into our dorm one night with a bouquet of flowers. Kira, who was my roommate then, nearly pushed him out the window.

I should have known tigers don't change their stripes.

"It's so good to see you!" Kira exclaims.

"You too. And you look amazing," I gush as Maxim comes up from behind and wraps his wife in his powerful arms. "Pregnancy really agrees with you."

"I tell her that all the time," Maxim whispers against her neck, cradling her lower stomach with the palm of his hand, even though there's no bump to speak of this early in her pregnancy.

"Not sure you'll be saying that when I hit the third tri and am as big as a whale and can't tie my shoelaces."

"Sounds hot," he purrs. "I'll gladly get down on my knees and tie your shoes for you."

A sly smile spreads on Kira's face. "I'll take you up on that offer."

Not in a million years did I imagine Maxim—the cold-as-ice bratva leader—would melt for anyone, especially my wild-child best friend, but that's exactly what happened. Seeing them happy together is wonderful, but it also brings a twinge of sadness. It's a reminder that I'll never experience what they have.

Kira loops her arm around Maxim's neck and drops a kiss on his lips. "Why don't you menfolk go talk about business stuff? I need time alone with Liza."

Maxim gives me a wink and leads Anatoly towards the bar.

With a sneer, Kira watches my fiancé walk away. I can only imagine what she'd do if she knew about the bruise I'm hiding.

I link my arm through hers as we head into the sitting room, where most of the guests are mingling with champagne in hand. Soft jazz music wafts through the air, played by a pianist on a grand piano in the corner. I don't want to know how much my parents paid for that stupid luxury.

"I know you hate when people fuss over you," I say, "but how are you feeling? Really."

Not long ago, Kira survived an attack on her life. The incident contributed to her pregnancy being categorized as high-risk, which is why she needs to keep stress and worry to a minimum.

Kira groans. "I'm feeling great, other than my husband

driving me crazy. He has me on a schedule of prenatal yoga, tai chi, daily meditation, and massage. All this relaxation is driving me insane."

"Only you would feel that way." I shake my head with a grin. "In this case, I think you should listen to Maxim. He's a wise man."

"Sometimes," she concedes.

A server comes around and offers us each a glass of champagne. Kira shakes her head while I accept one and take a swig of the cool liquid. "Anyhow, tell me all about your time in New York."

Her eyes light up. "It was a whirlwind, but it was amazing to see everybody."

As she details her recent trip, a deep baritone laugh echoes through the room.

That voice.

A combination of nerves and excitement flutters in my chest. When I look up, my breath catches in my throat.

I always forget how damn attractive Roman Vasiliev is.

Piercing eyes the color of rich espresso and thick, tousled dark hair I have fantasized about running my fingers through more times than I'll ever admit. Not to mention his tall frame and defined muscles, evident even under the fabric of his clothes. Tonight, he's wearing a sharp dark-navy suit tailored perfectly to his body, tattoos peeking out of his collar. I'm not used to seeing him in anything but jeans, a T-shirt, and maybe a leather jacket, so this is a departure from his usual style. I'm definitely not complaining.

Too bad he's so stinking annoying.

Right now, he's chatting in the corner with Katerina, who's resting a hand on his forearm like they're friends. Or more.

Irritation flickers through me.

As if Roman feels my gaze, his attention snaps to me. Our

eyes meet, and a jolt of something hot and uninvited surges through me. A small smile plays on his entirely too full lips.

A man shouldn't have a mouth like that. It's practically … pouty.

I swallow hard and turn away, trying to douse the surge of heat I feel every time he's near.

"Oh, by the way." Kira's voice breaks me out of my fog. "Everything is set for London! I have every maternity store from Knightsbridge to Soho mapped out."

Kira and I are taking a trip to the UK this weekend. It's something I've been looking forward to for weeks.

I give her a faux stern look. "Aren't you supposed to be taking it easy?"

"Don't worry, we're going to take frequent high tea breaks. That's what London's about, right?"

"Never been," I admit, "but I'm excited for you to show me around."

Taking a sip of champagne, I savor the bubbles, hoping the drink will ease the tension that's built up inside me. There are several reasons for me to be on edge tonight, but watching Katerina fawn all over Roman is high up on that list.

He casually leans against the wall, his thumb brushing against his bottom lip. Katerina is talking to him, but his eyes remain on me.

This is our game. We're polite when others are around, but our sharp looks express everything we can't say. Except right now, he's not really glaring. He's staring at me with dry amusement.

Kira stops talking mid-sentence, her brows furrowed. "Is everything okay? You seem distracted."

"I'm a little lightheaded. Must've not eaten enough today." I shake my head and focus on gulping back the rest of my drink.

Before Kira can respond, my father's booming voice rises above the din, inviting everyone into the dining room.

Saved by the dinner bell.

"Just going to the ladies'," I tell Kira with a soft squeeze of her arm. "I'll meet in the dining room."

CHAPTER THREE

ROMAN

The Ivanovs do a great job pretending they're still rich.

I've just arrived at their ritzy Rublevka mansion, done up to the nines. A brand-new three-tiered fountain stands prominently in the driveway, the foyer is all sparkling Italian marble floors, and the walls are covered with rare art.

Boris Ivanov ushers me in with a warm handshake and pat on the back. "Vasiliev, it's been too long. What has it been, a year? Two years? It's nice to see you again."

"I saw you last month at the rare sports cars auction that Morozov hosted."

Boris pauses, searching his memory for that night. If I recall, he was already well into his cups by the time I encountered him. "Right, right. Well, it's nice to see you again."

I'm always amazed at how far someone born with everything can fall. Boris is the greatest example of pissing away money he didn't earn.

His wife, Anastasia, rushes forward and greets me like the social climber she is. If it wasn't for my association with Maxim, I doubt she'd give me the time of day. Sure, I'm rich and important now, but I come from nothing. She strikes me as the sort who would hold that against me. With a plastered-on smile, she escorts me into the sitting room, where the party is already well underway.

I quickly scan the room. Maxim is deep in conversation with Anatoly and his father, Stepan. I roll my shoulders, and search for a bar, requiring a drink or three before I join in any conversation with Anatoly Petrovich. He's got an ego the size of Russia and the social grace of a bull in a china shop.

If it were up to me, I'd steer clear of him, but fate, being the cruel mistress she is, didn't give me that option. I'm heading up this shipping deal for the Belov Syndicate while Maxim steps back to focus on his new family with Kira. With Stepan battling cancer, Anatoly has assumed the day-to-day management of the shipping company, which means he and I will be working closely. There's no avoiding it.

In truth, I work with plenty of assholes, but this one happens to be engaged to a woman I haven't stopped obsessing over since the day I met her.

Liza Ivanova is my every fantasy come to life, with a mouth that poets could write sonnets about, curves for days, and wide green eyes that could easily be my downfall if I allowed it. Which I won't.

At the bar, I order a vodka—well chilled and straight up—and the bartender seems disappointed by my choice, considering the extravagant cocktails on offer. As if I'd ever be caught dead drinking something with more than two ingredients.

Propped against the bar, I scan the room for a curtain of dark auburn hair—hair that has ignited many fantasies about winding it tightly around my fist and leading her to my bed.

Bingo. Warmth rushes my chest as I catch sight of her chatting in the corner with Kira.

The bartender slides the drink in front of me, and I pick it up without taking my eyes off Liza.

"You know staring is considered rude?"

I laugh into my glass and shrug as Pavel, Maxim's other right hand and one of my closest friends, settles in beside me.

"I'm taking in the room, enjoying the sights of this fine evening."

He smirks and orders a drink. "Real subtle, *bratan*."

I exhale sharply and finish my vodka with one large gulp.

I really thought I played it cool as far as Liza was concerned, but unfortunately, one of Pavel's deeply irritating superpowers is uncanny perception. Still, it's not like I'd do anything about this ... inconvenient attraction. She might make my dick hard, but she's strictly off-limits as Anatoly's fiancée.

Not that I give a shit about him, but I'm loyal to Maxim and the syndicate. Now that we're in business with the Petroviches and millions of dollars are at stake, I won't do anything to fuck up this deal. Especially not for a woman.

Liza turns to greet another guest, and tension knots my shoulders. Damn, that dress should be illegal. It's white and tight, with a slit down the back that makes me scheme ways to have her bend forward so I can get a better look at her fine ass.

"Still staring," Pavel reminds me, swiping a hand through his blond undercut.

"Well, she's giving me something to stare at." I motion to the bartender to get me another drink.

"You might want to check out Katerina instead; she's been making heart eyes at you since you walked in." Pavel's lips curl up in amusement as he takes a leisurely sip of his drink. "Fresh blood might be exactly what you need to get Liza out of your head."

I pull a face. "Hard pass."

I like Katerina about as much as I like her brother, which means not at all. They're both self-entitled snobs. I guess it's par for the course when you grow up stinking rich.

Maxim finally frees himself from his conversation with the Petroviches and heads our way. I can tell by the way he's loosening his tie that he's had enough of them for one night and is in need of a stiff drink. I ask the bartender for a Macallan neat and hand it to Maxim as he walks up to us.

He lifts the drink in thanks and takes a hearty swig, leaning against the wood-paneled bar. "Jesus, Anatoly likes the sound of his own voice."

"How long do you think we have to stay at this thing?" I'm already feeling itchy under the collar. It's all the bullshit small talk I can't stand, though I'd spend all night watching Liza if I could. Not that it would be wise.

Maxim and Pavel both laugh because they share my sentiment. We come from the same world, a much harsher world than this one. We've risen through the ranks of society, but at our core, we're still the kids from broken homes, raised on the wrong side of town.

My bond with both men dates back to my teenage years. Lost and still reeling from the devastation of losing my mother to my father's brutal hand, I was only fifteen when I made him pay for taking away the one person in this world who loved me the most. Whom I loved most. After that, I found myself hustling on the streets to survive.

Maxim was a few years older than me, already had a name in the underground fight scene, and was beginning to form his own gang. When I stupidly tried to pickpocket one of his men, Maxim intervened, stopping them from snapping my neck. He then gave me a choice: keep hustling or join his ranks. The choice was easy.

Maxim took a chance on me when no one else would. I was consumed by anger and didn't care about living or dying. Along with Pavel, who has his own tragic past, Maxim shaped us into his reliable right-hands. We're chosen brothers, and we'd do anything for him, including stepping up to run the syndicate while he enjoys his family.

Pavel raises an eyebrow. "It's a dinner party—it's usually considered polite to stay until the actual meal is served."

"Fine," I grumble, "but I make no guarantees about staying for dessert."

Maxim sips at his whisky, his eyes flicking over the crowd. "I'll make you a deal: stick around for the first few courses, and then you can excuse yourself."

I tilt my head, sensing there's more to this offer. "What's the catch?"

He sighs. "Remember that girls' trip to London Kira's planning with Liza? Well, she wants to go this weekend for five days."

I frown. Five days with Liza. Just fucking great. "Right … That."

Pavel looks like he's about to bust a rib holding in his laughter, and I shoot him a death glare.

Maxim lays a hand on my shoulder. "Listen, I wouldn't ask if it wasn't important. The baby will be here before we know it, and Kira really wants this time with her friend. I'd go, but Pavel and I have to wrap up the Crimea arms deal. You know I don't trust anyone else with Kira's life. Do this for me as your brother, not as your boss."

What am I supposed to say to that? If it's important to Maxim, I won't turn him down.

"I'll guard her with my life," I assure him. And try not to lust too hard after her friend.

"Appreciate it. Take care of Liza, too."

Maxim slams his drinks down on the bar top and wanders off to greet some new faces, leaving Pavel staring at me with a shit-eating grin.

"Live text me every detail of your girls' trip. Don't leave out anything."

It's amazing how my usually serious friend is practically giddy. Needling me is one of the few things that brings him genuine pleasure.

"Fuck off." I grip my glass so hard it may shatter in my hands.

"I want pictures."

"Do you enjoy my misery?"

Pavel pauses. "Yes. It seems I do."

I shake my head. "It's fine. Five days. What can happen in that time?"

Pavel doesn't even try to conceal his delight. "I can't wait to find out. And now I bid you adieu … and good luck."

Good luck?

He salutes me and casually strolls over to a pretty waitress.

That's when I spot the reason for his hasty retreat. Katerina is heading straight for me, stealthy as a cat stalking its prey. Sadly, I'm too late to dodge her approach—all I can do is brace for impact.

"Roman Vasiliev," she purrs, her voice laced with a not-so-subtle invitation. "I had no idea you'd be here, but what a pleasant surprise."

She leans in close to kiss my cheek, her lips practically grazing the corner of my mouth. I have to fight the urge to wipe the area with the back of my hand. Like most in her crowd, Katerina Petrovich is bold, brash, and endlessly seeking the spotlight.

I understand why women like her are drawn to me. They're after a thrill. Her life's been one of comfort, every privilege offered to her on a silver platter. I'm the taste of danger she gets to boast about to her friends.

Half the gossip about my sexual exploits are made up. Concocted stories for socialites to flaunt at their cocktail parties. It usually doesn't bother me, but I don't know … Lately, it's been getting under my skin.

"Really, you had no idea I'd be here? At a party to celebrate the deal between our syndicate and your family?"

She shrugs. "I don't pay attention to all the family business stuff. I have better things to do."

I hold back an eye roll. Does this woman realize how vapid she sounds?

"Speaking of which, there's this art event at the biennale this weekend. Why don't you come with me? It's supposed to be amazing."

I'll be watching over Kira and a certain forbidden fruit in jolly old London then. Which, truthfully, will be its own form of torture. Although not as painful as spending a few hours in Katerina's presence.

"Sounds like a good time. You should ask Pavel—he loves avant-garde art." Lie. "Unfortunately, I'll be working."

Katerina frowns and bites her bottom lip in a gesture she probably thinks is sexy but is actually just irritating. "Oh." Her gaze snaps to Pavel, and then back to me.

I'm man enough to admit that Pavel's a good-looking guy in a marauding Viking kind of way, but he lacks my charm. Not that he gives a shit, but ladies like a little flirting and banter. Still, neither of us is looking for a relationship. We know we're too messed up for anything beyond a fling.

Not long ago, I would've said the same thing about Maxim, but watching him fall in love with Kira has given me a new perspective. Still, if there's a woman out there for me, I haven't found her. And it's certainly not the one standing in front of me.

"Maybe another time, then?" Katerina asks hopefully.

I search the room until my gaze collides with Liza. She's shooting me eye darts full of poison, and her jaw is clenched so tight I'm concerned she might crack a tooth. Is she pissed I'm talking to Katerina? No. But ... maybe?

I decide to test this new theory by giving Katerina a big, flirty, dimple-flashing smile. "Sure, maybe another time." I cross my arms in front of me in a way I know makes my biceps pop. "What kinds of things do you like to do?"

She tilts her head in thought. "Shopping. Eating at the best restaurants. Going to the gym, obviously."

"Wow, you really don't limit yourself, do you?"

Katerina nods, oblivious to my sarcasm.

I'm barely paying attention to a word she says because I'm enjoying this stare-off with Liza way too much.

A thrill buzzes under my skin. My lips tip up at the edge in a hint of a smile, which she returns with a scowl.

I used to think this game we played was all in my head, but I'm not so sure of that anymore. She's as sweet as candy with everyone but me. I inspire defiance in her, and for some reason, that really turns me on.

Katerina continues to talk at me, but I'm still laser focused on Liza. Nothing good can come from this dance we do. I should probably end this now. Turn around and avoid her all night. But who am I kidding? That's impossible.

Does Liza know I'm accompanying her and Kira to London in a few days' time? Probably not. If she did, I have a feeling she'd make her displeasure crystal clear.

Honestly, what fun would there be in ruining her surprise? I want nothing more than to see her face when she walks onto the plane and realizes she has to spend five whole days with the man she despises.

We all get our kicks somewhere.

CHAPTER FOUR

LIZA

I EXAMINE MY REFLECTION IN THE BATHROOM MIRROR, SAYING A little prayer that my dollar-store makeup hack worked to mask the bruise under my eye.

Feeling the onset of a headache, I dig in my clutch and take out two painkillers, popping them into my mouth and chasing them down with a gulp of champagne. Between having to act like I enjoy Anatoly's presence and tolerating Roman and Katerina's flirty vibe, tonight already feels never-ending, and we're only in the second hour of the evening.

Swinging the bathroom door open, I step out, only to stop short.

Roman is there, looking all hot and annoying, casually leaning against the wall. A slow, teasing smile unfurls on his lips. "Liza. Funny running into you here."

A hand lands on my hip. "It's really not. I live here."

He chuckles, and the sound does something weird to my insides.

"True." He pushes from the wall and steps towards me. "Still, it feels like you've avoided me all night."

"Maybe you're the one who's avoided me, too busy chatting away with Katerina."

Damn. As soon as the words fall from my lips, I realize my mistake.

Way to show your cards, Liza.

He raises his dark eyebrows. "Yes, well, I was fascinated listening to Katerina talk about her many hobbies. She's a woman of varied interests—shopping, lunching, working out."

I cross my arms in front of my chest, but a small flicker of warmth spreads through me. Despite my intention to play it cool, a smile creeps onto my face. "She's certainly one of a kind."

Roman tucks his hands into his pockets as his gaze drifts over my face. He always looks at me like that, as if he's trying to figure me out.

I point towards the door I just came through. "Well, we're about to sit down for dinner. I imagine you wanted to use the restroom."

He doesn't move a muscle. I'm about to push past him when he makes a noise in the back of his throat. "You don't like me, do you?"

My gaze burns into the floor. What am I supposed to say? That I don't like how my body reacts to you? I shrug because it seems like the safest response. "It's not personal. I didn't like you spying on Kira and me."

"First of all, it's always personal when you dislike someone. And second, I was never spying on you."

"Doesn't make it any better."

He raises the drink in his hand and takes a long, lazy sip. I watch the tendons in his throat as he swallows. "Seeing as I'm working closely with your fiancé, maybe we can call a truce."

My chest tightens at the reminder that he and Anatoly are now on the same side. I purse my lips. "And what would that look like?"

"It would mean we're civil to each other. It shouldn't be so hard. You're perfectly agreeable to everyone else."

That's because everyone else is not Roman. Everyone else lacks his cool confidence, fast wit, and easy charm that fascinate me and get under my skin at the same time.

"I'm always civil to you," I point out.

"The looks you were throwing me across the room earlier were anything but."

I bite the inside of my cheek. That had a lot to do with Katerina hanging off his every word. "I have a resting bitch face."

Roman chokes out a laugh. "You only have a resting bitch face when it comes to me."

I offer a small smile. "All part of my charm."

"Does that mean we're friends?"

Friends? Roman and I have never been friends. Nor would I describe my feelings towards him as particularly friendly, but it seems safer to agree.

"Friends." I nod.

We seal it with a handshake, but the moment his hand touches mine, little sparks jolt up my arm like I've touched a live wire.

Damn him and his electric touch.

My throat goes dry as he brushes past me with a little wink on his way into the washroom.

It takes me a minute to cool off before I feel steady enough to join the other guests.

Like a circling hawk, Anatoly swoops down on me the moment I step into the dining room and offers his arm to escort me to my seat. He loves to play the doting fiancé when others are around.

"Tonight's a good night to celebrate, don't you think?"

Something in his tone gives me pause. I rub my temples, willing the painkillers to kick in.

"What do you mean?" I ask cautiously.

"Two powerful families united."

How much praise does this man require? "Yes, Anatoly, the deal with the Belovs is very exciting."

He chortles under his breath as he pulls out my chair and murmurs into my ear, "I'm not talking about the shipping deal."

Prickles of unease coast over my skin. I whip around to ask him what the hell he's talking about, but before I can get a word in, my father interrupts to consult Anatoly about the choice of wine. Something about our exchange feels off, but maybe I'm reading too much into it.

Wine is poured and gentle chatter floats around the room when Roman finally makes his entrance. Katerina tries to flag him over to where she's sitting, but he ignores her and takes the free seat beside Sofiya and, to my displeasure, directly across from me. I know we're supposed to be friends now, but I have no idea what that's supposed to look like.

"Sofiya, right? We've met before, but it's been a while." Roman holds out his hand to my sister, who blushes like a schoolgirl—as I suspect most women do when he pays them any attention.

I'm meticulously spreading a napkin in my lap and avoiding Roman's gaze when Anatoly lowers himself into the seat beside me and throws an arm around the back of my chair. I immediately stiffen.

"So, Sofiya, what kinds of things are you into?" Roman asks as a team of waiters serves the first course.

Sofiya's eyes light up. "I'm into the performing arts. I'm actually in the school play this year. We're performing *The Sound of Music.*"

"No one cares about a musical performed by a bunch of teenagers," Anatoly butts in. He tries to catch Roman's eye as if to say, *Aren't teenage girls idiots?*

Roman gives him a hard stare.

"Anyhow, Vasiliev. Have you had a chance to look at the schematics for—"

"What role are you performing?" Roman asks Sofiya, completely ignoring Anatoly's comment. Satisfaction washes over me at Roman's sharp dismissal.

Sofiya colors, playing with the ends of her hair. "I'm one of the von Trapp kids. Not the biggest role, but I'm still pretty excited."

Roman tilts his head as if he's genuinely interested. "Do you get to wear lederhosen?"

She giggles. "Only the boys do. I think I dodged a bullet—they don't seem to be very comfortable."

Roman gives my sister a little wink. "I hope I can snag an invite to the performance."

I know Roman is only being polite, but I appreciate the effort.

Roman's eyes travel across the table and land on me. "What about you, big sis, are you into performing as well?"

"Nope. Can't hold a tune to save my life."

"You can always take singing lessons," Sofiya suggests. "That's what we do at school, and it made all the difference."

"Maybe one day—"

I'm interrupted by Anatoly's snort of derision. "No wife of mine is getting on stage to sing or dance. That's ridiculous."

It's on the tip of my tongue to remind him I'm not his wife, but when his eyes cut to mine with a warning to drop the issue, I do.

"What's wrong with learning how to sing?" Roman's lips flatten into a thin line. It's clear he finds Anatoly as charming as a rodent rooting around in his garbage. "I bet Liza has a beautiful singing voice."

I can't tell if that's meant as a compliment or not, but my body reacts as if it is—a fluttering in my stomach that I try to dismiss.

"So, Vasiliev, there's a new route I've been meaning to

discuss with you, one that could expand our reach significantly."

Roman swirls the wine in his glass. "I'm sure Liza and Sofiya don't want to hear all of our business talk. Let's leave that for after dinner."

The sneer on Anatoly's face says it all, but he doesn't dare contradict Roman. Instead, he pushes back his chair and walks away, presumably to discuss something with my father, who's a much more willing audience.

Sofiya catches my eye and gives me a *Well, that was awkward* look, but I shake my head. I really don't want to give Anatoly any reason to get angry. Not tonight.

The clinking of a fork on glass catches the attention of everyone in the room, including my own. My gaze flicks to the head of the table, where I expect my father to rise and drunkenly give a gushing speech in honor of our esteemed guests—it's certainly something he's done many times before—but it's not him summoning the room. It's Anatoly.

All eyes are glued to him.

Unease drips down my spine when he holds up his champagne glass and angles his body towards me. I try not to look like a deer caught in headlights, but I know I won't like what he's going to say next.

"Anatoly, we're still eating. This is not the time," I implore.

He doesn't respond but waits until everyone has gone silent. "As you all know, Liza and I are engaged to be married." Murmurs of acknowledgement fill the room. "I'd like to announce that a wedding date has been set. A month from now, I'll walk Liza down the aisle and make her my bride." His eyes cut to mine, and I hate the possessive glimmer I find staring back at me.

Cheers erupt, my parents being the loudest. In fact, my mother practically sobs with happiness, spouting off her excitement, while the only thing I feel is cold, hard dread despite the smile I've plastered onto my face.

I knew this day was coming, but I'd prayed with every fiber of my being that it would be a long time in the future. But a month ... How is that possible?

I can't make eye contact with Kira, Sofiya, or anyone who may see through my thin veil of composure, but for some reason, my eyes land on Roman's. What I see confuses the heck out of me. He looks downright pissed, like he might blow a gasket, for reasons that don't make a lick of sense to me.

"Darling"—I fight to keep my voice steady as Anatoly approaches—"isn't this all a bit rushed? There's still so much planning and organizing to do if we're going to have the wedding of our ... dreams."

Anatoly scowls. "That's what money is for, Elizaveta. I'll hire the best wedding planner in the city. You don't need to worry about the details."

I stand, thinking I may throw up, but Anatoly takes that as an invitation to kiss me. His thin lips press against my own, and it's all I can do to keep upright.

When he pulls away, he whispers into my ear, "I can't wait any longer to fuck you, princess."

Bile rises in my throat, but I swallow it down. Although we've done other things, I'm still a virgin because he wanted me pure for my wedding night.

I'm keenly aware of everyone's eyes on me, including Sofiya's. I don't want her to worry or question why I look miserable at the prospect of this marriage. So, I push down my feelings, plaster on a smile, accept everyone's congratulations, and pretend I'm not dying inside.

CHAPTER FIVE

LIZA

Leaning on the cold marble of the bathroom counter, I suck in deep breaths in an attempt to steady myself. Anatoly's announcement still echoes in my ears.

I knew this day was coming, but I always secretly hoped I'd find another way to support my family and free myself from Anatoly's grasp. That was wishful thinking.

My eyes narrow on my reflection in the mirror. I've spent so much energy wishing I could go back in time and undo all my choices that led to this moment.

It all started two years ago when I bumped into Anatoly at a fundraiser. I was leaving the bathroom, chatting with an acquaintance, when he appeared in front of me. The first thing he did was apologize for his past behavior, for pursuing me when I clearly wasn't interested.

I hate that I fell for his asshole-turned-nice-guy routine, but men like him are chameleons. They draw you in with sweet words and grand gestures until you're in too deep to find your way out. That night he was charming, attentive, and surprisingly thoughtful. He seemed like a new man.

Not long after the fundraiser, he sent me a bouquet of my favorite flowers and asked if I'd go out with him. It had been five years since we'd graduated, and I figured everyone changes and deserves a second chance. That first date turned into another, and then another. I wasn't in love or even very attracted to him, but I knew those things could develop in time.

My parents were over the damn moon about the fact that I was going out with the future heir to the Petrovich fortune.

But everything changed about a year into the relationship. The attention and care he first showed me faded fast. I had been preparing to end it when my father lost a poker game to high-ranking members of the Kalinsky Bratva. By that point, we didn't have the money to pay his debt, not even close.

My parents sat me down and explained the situation. My father had already discussed a plan with Anatoly, and now they needed my buy-in. In exchange for my hand in marriage, Anatoly would cover my father's debts and provide our family with a monthly allowance moving forward.

I had no choice. If I said no, my father would be dead, and the rest of my family would be out on the streets. I did what I had to do, but it doesn't make wearing his ring any easier.

The bathroom feels like it's shrinking, the walls closing in on me, but I can't fall apart now. There's a dining room full of people who expect me to emerge smiling, ready to celebrate what should be my happiest news.

Sucking in a few final breaths, I smooth back a stray lock of hair, fixing the mask of composure that's become my second skin.

Stepping out of the bathroom, I'm immediately blocked by Anatoly.

He stands in my way, his cold presence trapping me again. "Everything alright, princess?" There's not a hint of softness in his tone.

"Everything is fine," I reply crisply. "I was taken aback. Most women appreciate a heads-up before an announcement like that." My hands land on my hips, and I don't bother to hide my irritation.

He sneers. "I thought you'd be pleased. Your mother certainly was."

Ice fills my veins. The meaning of my mother's visit earlier is now clear as day.

Anatoly steps forward, slowly backing me against the wall. "I don't think you fully appreciate everything I do for you. For your family."

My mouth goes dry. No matter what I say, he'll find a way to twist my words and use them against me, so I stay quiet.

He grabs my ass and pulls me against him, sending a wave of revulsion through me. "I'm the reason there's food on your table. I'm the reason your sister is getting an education. I'm the reason your father hasn't been killed by one of the many lowlifes he owes money to. And yet ..."—his expression darkens—"you act like marrying me is a burden."

I force the words past my lips. "It's not a burden. I just wasn't prepared. I need more time—"

"There is no more fucking time." He fists my hair and grinds his hips against me, his erection poking into my belly. "Do you feel that, Liza? I'm so hard for you. I'm sick of using your hands and mouth. This pussy is mine, and it's time I claimed it."

The thought of sex with Anatoly makes me sick. Putting my hands and mouth on him is bad enough. I hate the way he tastes. I hate the way he fists my hair to buck up into my mouth, making me feel like I can't breathe.

A wave of panic locks me in place as his fingers dig into the flesh of my ass while he lands a sloppy kiss on my neck. "I'm going to take you anytime I want, anywhere, and in any position. Your untouched pussy belongs to me and—"

"Get off of me!" My hands shoot out before I'm aware of what I'm doing, and I push against his chest with all the force I can muster.

My outburst surprises us both, and I use the opportunity to slip from Anatoly's grasp, my heart in my throat. But his hand darts out, and he grabs my hair to hold me in place. His eyes narrow to slits and his boozy breath wafts over my face.

"You better change your attitude, because if it's not you wearing my ring, your parents will have to find someone else to support your pathetic family. They might even be desperate enough to marry off sweet, innocent Sofiya, considering what a bitch you are."

My stomach drops, and tears roll down my cheeks, but I don't answer. I don't even know what I'd say. He knows Sofiya is the one person in this world I'd protect with my life. With my soul.

"That's right, Liza. You have no power here. No control. So shut your mouth and do as I say. That's all I want, princess. Unless"—his lips curl into a sinister grin—"you have a million dollars tucked away in some secret offshore account. You don't want to marry me? Pay me back every cent I've given to your family, and then we can talk about your freedom."

His triumphant look is like a punch to the gut. He has me exactly where he wants me—cornered, helpless, and indebted to him.

With a little shove, he releases me from his grasp and steps back, adjusting his cufflinks and patting down his tie as if he hadn't just torn my world apart and shattered any fragment of hope for my future.

He grasps my chin between his thumb and forefinger, forcing me to meet his intense stare. "Do we have an understanding?" I bite my lip and nod, tears still falling freely. "Good," he whispers. "Now pull yourself together. We have a party to get back to." He turns and heads back to the dining room.

I collapse against the cool wall, sliding down until I'm huddled on the floor with my palms pressed against my eyes. For one moment, I allow myself to feel the full weight of my despair.

CHAPTER SIX

ROMAN

I TAKE A FINAL DRAG, PULLING THE NICOTINE AND TAR DEEP INTO my lungs. Leaning my head back against the sidewall of the Ivanovs' home, I watch the smoke curl lazily into the night air. I rarely smoke, but I always keep a cigarette on hand for times like these—when I'm tense as a drawn bow, and there's no punching bag in sight.

Anatoly's announcement knocked the air out of my lungs. It shouldn't have. Liza's been engaged the entire time I've known her, so a wedding was always on the horizon.

It doesn't take an idiot to figure out that Liza isn't with Anatoly for his sparkling personality but for his flush bank account. The man is as rich as sin.

Whatever the basis of their relationship, it shouldn't be my concern. I'm not supposed to feel this way about a woman who is to be married to my business partner. But since I do, I need to put distance between us—at least for tonight.

Because lucky me, soon enough I'll have to spend five whole days with her in London. Fuck my life.

My mind made up to get the hell out of here, I stub out my cigarette and flick it in the bushes. I'll make up some excuse about work or my nonexistent dog needing a walk, or some shit like that.

"You have another one of those?" An unexpected voice pulls me from my thoughts.

Liza stands in front of me, her bright green eyes cutting through the night like searchlights. She must be fucking with me. Perfect Liza wants a smoke?

Something in her expression makes me keep my mouth shut.

Without a word, I reach into my pocket, pull out my pack, and offer it to her. She takes a cigarette and places it between her lips. I flick the lighter to life, holding the flame steady as she inhales. When she takes a practiced drag off the cigarette, I'm pretty sure my eyebrows hit my hairline.

"I didn't know you smoked."

She shrugs. "I didn't know you did either."

"I only smoke when I'm stressed or after— Forget it."

She gives me a wry look, exhaling a small puff of smoke into the night.

I take a moment to study her. Her hands are shaky, and her eyes are a little puffy. Whatever excitement I thought I glimpsed in her expression after Anatoly's announcement is long gone.

"I guess congratulations are in order," I say to test the waters.

She closes her eyes and tips her head back until it rests against the brick of the house. "Right."

Not quite the flush of bridal joy I was expecting.

I reach out, take her hand, and bring the cigarette to my lips for a drag. She opens her eyes and watches me closely.

"What's wrong?" I ask, no hint of teasing in my voice. There's something melancholy about her right now that I can't put my finger on.

"What do you mean?" She won't meet my eyes now, looking into the distance instead.

I let the smoke trail out between my lips as I scan her in the low light. "You're upset. What happened?" I ask again with a little more force.

She drops and stomps out her cigarette. "What does it matter to you?"

There's the lioness, fierce only with me.

"It matters," I growl. "Remember, we're friends now."

Friends, my ass.

Grasping her wrist, I draw her close until her chest brushes against mine. My palm lands on her waist, holding her in place, too close to be considered decent by any stretch of the imagination.

"What are you doing?" Her words are a puff of air against my lips, but she doesn't push me away or tell me to let her go, like a good girl would. She holds my stare as her pulse hammers in her throat.

Leaning down, I inhale her vanilla scent and bask in the heat of her body, committing it to memory because this is probably the closest I'll ever be to her. It's beyond reckless, but I can't find it in me to care.

"Tell me what's going on."

Her eyes narrow on me. "Nothing's the matter. At least, nothing that concerns you."

Irritation flickers in my gut, and just to provoke her, I lean down and whisper in her ear, "I think perfect little Elizaveta Ivanova wants to know what danger feels like before she's locked down for the rest of her life."

My words are a taunt, but she doesn't flinch or look away. She holds me in her steady gaze, daring me to continue.

"Maybe I already know what danger feels like." She flashes me a hard smile, one that doesn't come close to reaching her eyes, as she pushes away. "And I'm not always perfect, but it's easier if I pretend that I am."

Liza pops a piece of gum into her mouth, straightens her shoulders, and strides back inside, leaving nothing but an uneasy weight in my chest.

I light another smoke and run an agitated hand through my hair.

I'm full of shit, too. Here I am, lying to myself that I feel anything but an irrational sense of possession when I'm in Liza's company. This can't continue, pining over a business associate's soon-to-be wife. That's the kind of sin that blackens your soul. Worse. It's the kind of obsession that gets you killed.

There's only one thing to do.

I take my phone out of my pocket and text Tanya, one of my regular hookups. She has short blonde hair and deep brown eyes—the exact opposite of Liza.

Next time I see Liza, I'll have had so much pussy between now and then that she'll be nothing but a blip on my radar.

CHAPTER SEVEN

LIZA

Kira is already seated, waiting for me in a private booth at the back of the restaurant. She waves to get my attention as I enter, and I return the gesture. I walk over with a confident stride, keeping my back straight as I weave through the tables.

Kira insisted on lunch today, and I know exactly why. We didn't have a chance to talk privately at the party, but her worried looks following Anatoly's announcement spoke volumes.

"Did you have fun last night?" I try to sound casual as I pick up the menu, using it as a shield to avoid eye contact.

Her hand slams down on the table, capturing my attention. My teeth sink into my bottom lip as I lower the menu to meet Kira's intense gaze.

"What the fuck was that?" she hisses, leaning forward. "Anatoly can just decide you're getting married in a month and announce it to everyone?"

Tucking a piece of hair behind my ear, I choose my next words carefully. "He wanted to surprise me," I say evenly.

"We've been engaged for a year. It's not like I didn't see this coming."

An unsuspecting waiter decides to make his appearance at that moment. "Have you had a chance to look at the menu—"

My five-two dynamo of a friend shuts him up with one raised hand. "We're going to need a very generous bread basket, everything on the menu with carbs, a virgin cocktail for me, and a bottle of wine for my friend."

The waiter scurries away.

I reach for my water glass. "I don't need a bottle of wine. I'm perfectly fine."

"How is that? You're marrying a man you hate. Help me here. What am I missing?" Her intense eyes search my face for answers she's not going to find.

Sitting in my room for hours after the party, one thing became very clear in my mind—Anatoly holds my future in the palm of his hands. He wants ultimate control over me, and if I don't allow him that, my sister will pay the price. She'll be eighteen in a few months, and my parents will be able to use her as a bargaining chip.

I've thought about running away with Sofiya so many times, but what kind of life could I offer her? With no money and no university education, it wouldn't be much of one. And with the money and resources at Anatoly's fingertips, if he wanted to hunt us down, he could. We'd always be powerless.

"Okay, Earth to Liza. Now I'm really worried." Kira frowns, biting into a breadstick. "Why aren't you freaking out? Before I left for New York, you would have done anything to get out of the marriage."

"True," I say as calmly as I can muster. "But I've had time to think, and while Anatoly may not be my first choice, let's face it—marrying him takes care of a lot of my problems. It means security for my family, and you know ... He's not all bad."

Kira blinks at me warily. "I don't believe for one second you want to marry Anatoly. I know Maxim could help if you gave me the word."

I shake my head resolutely. I know Kira would do anything to help me, but last night was a reminder of how deeply connected the Belovs and Petroviches are. Asking her to choose between me and her husband's business partner would put her in an impossible position, and the stress would undoubtedly be bad for the baby.

No matter what, I won't drag her into this.

"Anatoly may not be my first choice, but I've accepted that this marriage is the best thing for me and my family." I lay my hand over hers, attempting to reassure her. "Maxim is in business with the Petroviches, so let's not complicate things between them."

Kira's face falls. "I'm not worried about Maxim, I'm worried about you." She's quiet for a moment. "Listen, if this is about money, I can help—"

"It's not," I cut her off quickly. I don't want her to know how deeply indebted we are to the Petroviches. It's not only humiliating but also complicated. "Anatoly is dependable, he's ambitious, and he's willing to put up with my parents and all their ... quirks."

She pinches the bridge of her nose. "Marrying for security might solve some problems, but what about love? Don't settle for a loveless marriage."

I wait until our waiter has finished pouring my wine before I continue. "Marrying for love?" I laugh. "You literally married Maxim to avenge your aunt's death."

She frowns and rips a piece of bread in two. "And now that I know what I could've missed out on, I don't want that to happen to you. Seriously," she pleads, "I had no idea what love was until I met Maxim. There's nothing better than finding your person, knowing they always have your back. You deserve that."

I hold back a bitter laugh. Love is not in my future. Now or ever. When I was younger, I truly believed we all had a soulmate and I'd find the love of my life one day. The funny thing is that Kira was the one who didn't give two shits about "all that romantic crap," as she called it. But life doesn't always work out the way we want it to. That's the harsh truth.

As long as Sofiya is safe and happy, that's enough for me.

"I'm thrilled you found Maxim." I force a light tone into my voice. "But honestly, it's not a priority for me. Some people marry for love, but plenty of others don't. I'm fine with it."

Kira sighs and looks away as a team of waiters descends, laying down a feast. The table seems to groan under the weight of pizza, pasta, and various other dishes. I haven't eaten all day, but my stomach is in knots. Not only am I lying to my friend, but in a month's time, I'll be walking down the aisle toward a monster.

When we're alone again, Kira sits back and crosses her arms over her chest. "It's not like your family ever considers what you want or your feelings."

I flinch. She's right, of course, but the reminder hurts.

"I'm sorry," she whispers. "That was harsh."

I swallow over the knot of emotion in my throat. "Don't apologize. It's true."

A shadow passes over her expression, a mix of disappointment and sadness. "I don't know what your parents did to deserve you, but they better realize what an amazing daughter they have." She twists her lips and picks at the food in front of her. "I truly hope you don't come to regret your choice."

"Forget about the wedding for now," I say, smoothing the napkin in my lap. "Let's talk about London."

She gives me a bittersweet smile. "I'm glad we get that

time together before life gets crazy—well, crazier than it already is."

I nod, feeling some of the heaviness from our earlier conversation lift. "I'm glad we do, too." I raise my glass of wine towards Kira, who lifts her drink. "Not to be lame," I continue, "but can we do all the touristy things? Like visiting the Tower of London and riding the London Eye at sunset."

"Hell yeah!" She raises her hand for a high five, and just like that, everything feels a little more normal. "I love doing touristy shit. I'm sure Roman will have a fit, considering those are some of the busiest spots in the city. But whatever, he'll have to deal with it."

"Roman?" I shake my head. "What does he have to do with anything?"

Kira pauses, her pasta halfway to her lips. "Well, he's coming as our bodyguard."

I kick off my heels under the table, an uncomfortable heat spreading through me. The thought of being around Roman day and night is enough to make a nervous rash break out on my skin. It seems like the universe's idea of a cruel joke.

I take a very generous gulp of wine. "Doesn't he have more important things to do? He's a busy man."

Kira cocks her head as if trying to gauge my reaction. "Roman and Pavel are the only people Maxim trusts to look after me when we're not in Russia." She shrugs. "I didn't have much of a choice in the matter, and you can't tell me you'd prefer grumpy Pavel." She makes a face.

"Pavel is perfectly lovely."

A smirk pulls on her lips. "Roman likes getting under your skin because you let him. The key is not to play his games."

Tension climbs my spine, settling between my shoulders.

Being around Roman puts me on edge. Remembering how his strong hand felt wrapped around mine bringing my cigarette to his lips ... Jesus. His rough touch lingers in my thoughts uninvited, but the more I protest his presence, the more questions Kira will ask.

"I'm fine with Roman," I declare. "We actually called a truce last night. We're friends."

Kira blinks in surprise. "That's good. Anyway, we're going to have fun, and Roman will fade into the background."

Yeah, right. Since when has Roman ever faded into any background? It's impossible.

Our waiter arrives, setting down plates of dessert with a flourish that momentarily distracts me from my thoughts. We didn't order dessert, but I think the staff has figured Kira out.

"Oh, is that opera cake?" She reaches for a fork.

Five days with Roman in a foreign city.

I swallow hard. It's fine. It's not like we're going to be alone, and either way, I'm an adult. I'll ignore Roman as best as I can. Not a problem.

"Wow, you need to try this cake." Kira moans, her mouth full.

I suck in a deep breath and open my eyes again, flashing her a bright smile. "Sure. It looks delicious!"

CHAPTER EIGHT

ROMAN

Steam swirls around me as I settle onto the wooden bench of the *banya*, the heat sinking into my muscles chasing away the chill of Moscow winter. The room is filled with the sharp scent of pine and birch sap—Russians believe it calms the mind as much as it cleanses the body.

If only it could cleanse my soul. But there's no cleaning something soiled and rotten.

The sauna door opens, steam billowing in as Anatoly and his father, Stepan, greet Maxim, Pavel, and me before settling onto the bench.

It's been a few days since the party at the Ivanovs', and Stepan looks even worse. The cancer treatment is probably kicking his ass, but I get why he showed up today. Just like Maxim is handing me the reins, Anatoly's father must do the same, allowing his son to take over the key aspects of the business while he focuses on his health.

When Maxim first made this deal a few months ago, it was with the belief that we'd be working with Stepan—a man not without his faults but respected for being a straight shooter.

But Anatoly lacks his father's respectability; he follows no code other than his selfish desires. Unlike him, I adhere to a code that I live and die by: protect my brothers, stand by my word, and uphold my honor at all costs.

"Gentlemen." I reach for a bottle of vodka from the ice bucket at my feet. Condensation beads on its glass like sweat. "I'd like to make a toast to celebrate the first of many successful shipments."

Yesterday, the first vessel of the Petrovich fleet arrived here from New York, filled with firearms from the Kozlov Bratva that we'll sell across Europe. The same ship is already sailing back to the US, full of counterfeit pharmaceuticals that the Kozlovs will then distribute stateside. If the first few runs go well, we'll soon expand: more ships, more ports, more products. And the end goal—more money.

I pour the vodka into shot glasses, handing them out one by one, and raise my glass. "To growth, prosperity, and a partnership that will stand the test of time."

I usually mean every word I say, but this toast is bitter on my tongue. The thought of a long partnership with Anatoly makes my skin crawl.

Still, I owe it to Maxim to suck it up and make this deal work. We've seen each other through the darkest of times, and Maxim has had more than his fair share. After the hell of losing a child in a brutal mafia hit years ago, Maxim deserves to focus on his life with Kira and their baby, and I'm determined to allow him to do that. He's put his trust in me to run the shipping division—one of the most important aspects of his business—and I won't let him down.

I inhale a deep breath and clink glasses with Anatoly, maintaining eye contact as custom dictates. I'm as naked as the day I was born, sharply aware of his gaze on my muscular, tattooed form. A small thrill moves through me, not because I enjoy a man's eyes on me but because I want for him to see the stark contrast between us. Let him take in every ridge, every curve of muscle, and every healed scar and bullet hole. Let him see what a real man is.

In contrast, he's pasty, sporting a generous middle, and his skin is unmarked by ink.

As the other men get lost in conversation, I take a seat beside Anatoly, watching the sweat bead and trickle down his forehead. He shifts uncomfortably, struggling with the intensity of the heat.

I may have asked the banya attendant to jack the temperature for this very reason.

"That was quite a surprise announcement you made the other night. A wedding in a month." I whistle through my teeth. "What's the rush?"

Anatoly wipes his brow and reaches for the ice-cold vodka, thinking that's what he needs to quench his thirst. Once he's downed another shot, his glazed eyes settle back on me. "A leader should have a wife by his side, don't you think?"

I shrug. "I don't think it's a requirement."

His eyes turn hard. "I'm sick of waiting for her pretty piece of ass. Back in school, Liza thought she was too good for me. Wouldn't give me the time of day. Well, now that bitch doesn't have a choice."

I'm under no illusions that Anatoly is an honorable man, but the words out of his mouth right now make me want to split his face in two.

"Seems like a stupid reason to get married," I grit out. He's too warped to pick up on the venom in my words.

"Owning that virgin cunt is as good as any reason to get married, as far as I'm concerned." He chortles, and it makes my blood boil even harder. "And the best part," he continues, "is her pathetic family does anything I say. I say jump, they ask how high. I say dance, they turn into dancing monkeys. Her mother would blow me if I asked her to."

"Charming," I spit out. "but I'm sure there'd be plenty of women willing to spread their legs. Why be tied down?"

Anatoly snorts. "Trust me. I fuck whomever I want, whenever I want, but none are as delectable as my fiancée," he slurs.

His words grate under my skin. Marrying Liza isn't about anything other than his need for control. Men like him are pathetic. My father was driven by the same dark compulsion, and I've seen the ruin it brings.

I crack my neck, battling to suppress the anger stirring inside me like a dangerous cocktail. "Make sure the wedding doesn't sidetrack you from our business. There's no room for fuck ups with a deal this big."

He makes a dismissive gesture. "Planning a wedding is women's business. All I need to do is show up."

With great pleasure, I notice his face has turned a sickly shade of green, and his thinning hair is wilting in the steamy heat.

Anatoly reaches for the vodka bottle again, sweat pouring off him in buckets.

"Might be time for you to take a break." I lean back against the birch wall, making it clear that I'm fine. "The heat can really get to you."

"I'm okay. Never been bet—"

He doesn't get the final word out before puking all over the floor.

Can't say I didn't warn him.

CHAPTER NINE

ROMAN

"Don't look so sour. This is going to be fun."

My eyes cut to Kira in the passenger seat, a broad grin stretching across her face.

I can't help but smile back. After all she's been through, she deserves to have a good time. I just wish her good time didn't include me and the woman I'd be happy to avoid for the rest of my life. But fate has a way of grabbing you by the balls and twisting hard.

Doesn't matter. Liza may be temptation personified, but I know better than to get close. Even if we're about to spend five days together like a happy little family.

I clear my throat, navigating Moscow's snow-covered streets on the way to Liza's family estate. "It'll be fun for you," I remind Kira. "Not for me. I have a job to do."

"Oh, come on. How hard is it to guard two women who plan on spending most of the time shopping and eating? Surely, this is not your toughest assignment."

"That remains to be seen." I wink at Kira. "It depends on how well-behaved you are."

"Usually, you'd have something to worry about, but not so much these days." She pats her belly to make her point. "Although ..." Kira leans forward as if letting me in on a little secret. "I'm going to make sure Liza gets to have some real fun. She deserves it, having to marry that *mudak*."

I'm not surprised by the acid in Kira's tone. Although we've never had a conversation about it, her occasional snide remarks make it clear she isn't a fan of Anatoly. She tries to be discreet because of our business dealings with the Petroviches, but Kira's not one to fake her feelings. I don't blame her; I can't stand him myself.

"You make it sound like Liza's being forced to marry him. There's not exactly a gun to her head." Yeah, she seemed a little off her game when she bummed a cigarette from me, but anything could've upset her.

"I wouldn't be so sure about that," Kira grumbles.

I flick a glance her way. "Why do you say that?"

She sighs. "It's just ... Forget it. What does it matter anyhow? The wedding's going to happen, and there's nothing I can do to stop it."

Something about her words gives me pause. "Why would you want to stop your best friend's wedding?"

Kira gazes out the window, turning her attention to the passing scenery. "She's marrying him to make her parents happy, no matter what she tells me—or tells herself, for that matter. She doesn't love him. She doesn't even like him."

My lips twitch as I shift up a gear. "That's 'cause he's a dick." There's no point hiding my feelings since Kira and I are on the same page. "But he's a rich dick. And you know the shit people are willing to do for money."

"That's not Liza," Kira huffs. "It's her parents. They have real sway over her."

A knot forms in my chest. Everyone knows Liza is with Anatoly for his deep pockets. But maybe there's more to the story than I originally thought. Not that it changes anything.

Because she still wears his ring, and in a month's time, she'll walk down the aisle towards him.

Beside me, Kira is quiet for a minute. When she finally speaks, there's a lighter note in her voice. "I'm going to show her the time of her life in London. If this is her last hurrah, I'm going to make it worth her damn while."

I smile over at Kira. "Shit. Maybe we should've brought more guards with us."

When I pull into the Ivanovs' circular front drive, there's no staff waiting outside to announce our arrival, but I do spot Anatoly's Aston Martin Valkyrie parked off to the side.

"I'll be quick." I leave the engine of the Land Rover running.

As I head towards the house, I slip a key between my fingers and press it into the pristine paint job of Anatoly's limited-edition sports car. I look back and take in the jagged, uneven line spanning the length of the vehicle, and suddenly, I feel a whole lot lighter inside.

CHAPTER TEN

ROMAN

Liza is completely in her element—hearts-in-her-eyes happy, with a huge smile on her face. She's practically skipping through the aisles, touching everything she sees, and we're not in Prada, Jimmy Choo, or any other designer store. We're in a quaint second-hand bookstore in Notting Hill, and she's glowing in a way that's damn near contagious.

I shouldn't notice every little thing about her, but I do. I notice how her eyes pop when she wears forest green and how she hums to herself when she's happy. How her lips tighten the moment her impending wedding is mentioned and how she furrows her brow in confusion at thick British accents.

It doesn't help that I haven't taken my eyes off her since we touched down in London two days ago. Sure, it's my job to be observant, but my attention is way beyond professional. Maybe it's just me wanting what I can't have. Either way, this attraction is highly inconvenient and a distraction I can't afford. The only thing it does is mess with my head and cause blood to rush to my dick.

I crack my neck and take out my phone to check the time.

Since we were able to shut down the store to the public, I told Bogdan and Feliks to grab lunch. Now I regret that decision; I hadn't realized how captivating it would be to watch Liza shop for books

"Check this one out," Liza says to Kira, waving another book about child-rearing.

Kira takes it from Liza and flips through the pages. "This is from twenty years ago. I really hope things have changed when it comes to raising a baby."

Liza giggles. Christ, that's my favorite new sound.

She's laughed more on this trip than in the entire time I've known her. Maybe it's being around Kira, or being away from her family and fiancé, but it seems this break is exactly what she needed.

Liza shrugs. "Why? I mean, making babies has been the same since the dawn of time."

Kira grimaces as she scans a page. "Oh my God. It says here that you need to wake up every few hours to feed the baby in the first few weeks. That can't be true, can it?" For some reason, Kira's eyes dart to where I'm standing a few feet away.

"Are you actually asking me for baby advice?" I blurt out.

"I know. What was I thinking?" Kira grumbles. "You're, like, the last person who'd know."

I shrug. "Isn't that what nannies are for? All those rich society women talk about having night nannies, day nannies, afternoon nannies … cocktail-hour nannies."

Kira rolls her eyes. "Well, I don't mind getting a little help, but we won't be hiring nannies for everything."

"I'll help you," Liza offers. "Okay, maybe not in the middle of the night, but what else do I have to do? I remember when Sofiya was a baby. I was a kid myself, but I swear I did more for her than my parents did."

Kira sighs. "You're going to be a newlywed by the time

this little one comes along. You'll be busy attending galas and lunching at the tennis club."

Liza shudders. "God, no. Are you trying to scare me? I'll always make time for you."

"Life is going to change," Kira adds softly.

Liza's expression falls, but she can't exactly argue the point.

Kira claps her hands. "I'm going to relax in that armchair and read this baby book. You hunt for that first edition of *Jane Eyre* I know you've had your eye on."

Liza nods and smiles, but I don't miss the crease between her brows as Kira walks away. I want to take my thumb and smooth it out.

"What exactly are you looking for?" I ask.

She eyes me thoughtfully. "*Jane Eyre*. Ever heard of it?"

"Do you really think so little of me?" I give her a smirk. "It's a book. A very old book."

Her lips quirk up at the corners. "Most people would call it a classic, but okay … 'Old book' works as well. Do you know what it's about?"

I cross my arms and lean against a bookshelf, noticing how her hair looks more auburn when it catches in the afternoon light. "No idea."

"As I thought." She purses her lips. "When I'm in a used bookstore like this, I like to dig around for rare books—collector's items, first editions. You never know what you might find."

"How do you know what to look for?"

She taps her temple. "I have a good eye." With that, she spins on her heels and heads towards a stack at the end of the aisle, scanning each row with precision.

When her face lights up with a find, she reaches up on her tiptoes, fingertips brushing the spine of the book she wants but can't grasp.

I'd usually position myself where I can see everything, but

since the store is closed to the public, I wander towards Liza. She's still reaching up when my body presses gently against her back, extending over her shoulder to grab the book she's after.

The warmth from her body sends a buzz through me. My hand closes around the spine, but I don't make a move to pull it down. Instead, I soak it all in: her soft curves pressed against my hard form; her scent—a blend of vanilla and spice; the rise and fall of her breaths against my chest.

"You smell good," I murmur.

My lips brush her ear, and she gasps softly. I have to fight the desire to wrap my hand around her hair and pull, exposing her neck to me.

Even though she's considered tall for a woman, she only comes up to my shoulder. She sways against me, and I steady her with a palm on her waist.

"Is this what you wanted?" Her mouth hangs open but understanding dawns when I hold the book out for her.

She's slightly flushed, the air between us charged with an unexpected intensity. "Uh, thank you."

I let my eyes travel down her body. She looks gorgeous in high-heeled leather boots, a snug gray sweater, and fitted jeans that do nothing to hide the delectable curve of her ass.

I shake my head, tearing my eyes away from her and ignoring the bulge growing in my jeans. *Down, boy.*

She bites her lip and gazes at the book in her hand. "Not a first edition, but that's okay. First editions are nearly impossible to find," she notes, her voice a little husky.

"What's the book about?" I ask. "In case a pretty girl wants to discuss it with me. I can impress her with my knowledge."

She narrows her eyes. "Why don't you read it for yourself."

"I'll take that as a challenge." I scrape my knuckles along my jaw. "What do you like so much about this book?"

Her lips twist in thought. "I read it when I was still in school, and it made me feel … I don't know. Hopeful, in a weird way. Jane has this really terrible beginning as an orphan, but she's able to rise above it. She becomes a governess, makes her own way in the world … falls in love."

Something flickers to life in my chest. "So, it's a love story."

"Yes and no. It's complicated."

I shake my head. "Everything's complicated."

Liza rests a hand on her hip. "Are you actually going to read it?"

"Damn right." I open my palm, and she stares at it for a minute before dropping the book in my hand. "I'll report back to you."

"I'll be shocked if you get through half of it."

Heat spreads over the back of my neck. "Prepare to be amazed, Liza."

"Oh, really?" She laughs, and the sound feels like sunshine on my face. "I guess we'll see soon enough."

CHAPTER ELEVEN

LIZA

"Here's to buying up half of that baby store." I hold up my pint of lager and clink it against Kira's glass of sparkling water.

"I did do some pretty serious damage, didn't I?" She smiles widely. "Poor Feliks has the pleasure of organizing the shipping back to Moscow."

"I think he can handle it," I quip, taking a sip of beer as Kira looks on enviously. It's not my usual drink of choice, but when you're in a cozy London pub, you might as well drink like a local.

Today has been what I consider a perfect day. In fact, the whole trip has been pretty awesome. The first few days, we were quintessential tourists, going from the Tower of London to the British Museum, doing some shopping and finishing the day with unforgettable meals. We spent today shopping in all of London's poshest neighborhoods. Kira has racked up quite the bill spoiling this unborn baby.

Tomorrow will be our last full day here, and I have no

idea what Kira has planned, but whatever it is, I'm happy to go along and enjoy it. Spending time with my friend has helped distract me from the ball of dread sitting heavy in my gut every time I think of what's waiting for me at home.

"So ..." Kira says cautiously, squeezing a lime into her soda. "Have you given any thought to wedding planning?"

"Not too much, actually. I hoped to leave it up to my mother. This wedding is for her anyway." I try and fail to keep the bitterness out of my tone.

Kira frowns into her drink, and I can sense all the words she's not saying. "Well, if you need any help, I'm here for you. Dress shopping, cake tasting, planning your escape from the church—whatever it is you need."

I laugh, although I'm not entirely sure she's kidding. "Thank you. If I need help, you'll be the first person I'll call. I was hoping for Sofiya to be my maid of honor, but unfortunately, Anatoly is insisting that it's Katerina." I scrunch my nose.

"That sucks," Kira says bluntly. "You can't even choose your own maid of honor?"

I stir my drink, my eyes traveling towards the fireplace beside us. "Doesn't really seem worth arguing over. I'm trying to pick my battles with my mother and the Petroviches, considering I expect many more ahead of me."

Kira sighs and reaches out, her hand resting on my forearm. "I don't want to sound like a broken record, but if you change your mind about anything, I'm here for you."

"Thank you." I know she has the best of intentions, but she has no idea how deeply tangled I am in Anatoly's web. Between the debt we owe him and his not-too-subtle threats towards my sister, I'm trapped. And really, her hands are tied now that the Belovs and Petroviches are inextricably linked.

Kira looks down, smoothing the napkin in her lap. When her eyes meet mine again, she masks her concern with a practiced smile. "I have an extra special surprise for you tomorrow. An experience you'll never forget."

I tilt my head to the side. "Should I be worried?"

"Please. You'll love it." She taps a finger against her lips. "Once you've had a few drinks to loosen up."

"Sounds like trouble."

Kira's expression turns mischievous. "Only the good kind."

"Well, that's not ominous," I joke, polishing off the final sip of my beer.

Kira waggles her eyebrows at me before she glances down at her phone. "Maxim is calling. Mind if I step outside to take this?"

"By all means."

She gives me a quick peck on the cheek, then jumps up and heads toward the front of the bar, Bogdan hot on her heels.

Man, her guards take their jobs seriously, but that doesn't surprise me. If anything happened to Kira, Maxim's wrath would be unimaginable. More than that, Roman is protective of Kira like a big brother.

I get the feeling his interest in me is anything but brotherly.

In the last few days, Roman has been an ever-present figure, discreetly standing guard wherever we are. I know he's only doing his job, but his attention often drifts my way, especially when we're alone. Despite Feliks and Bogdan's vigilance, I never *feel* them watching me. It's different with Roman—there's a certain intensity in his stare that seems to buzz under my skin.

It's a delicate balance, pretending indifference when every instinct is finely tuned to his presence. Like right now. I glance up and catch him checking me out from the bar. He looks effortlessly cool in his dark jeans and casual white tee that show off the tattoos crawling up his neck. He wears a blazer for the sole purpose of hiding the gun and holster strapped to his chest. Everything about him is sharp and defined—his jawline, his cheekbones, his strong profile. He oozes a raw, magnetic male energy that draws the eyes of every woman in the pub. But he doesn't seem to care about them.

My pulse flutters as he looks at me from beneath his dark lashes and lifts his glass in acknowledgment. It's filled with clear liquid, which I know is water and not vodka because he's on the clock. I bite the inside of my cheek as he rolls up the sleeves of his blazer, exposing his muscular and tanned forearms.

Squeezing my legs together, I try to relieve some of the pressure building in my core, but it doesn't do the trick.

I bet his fingers would.

Yesterday didn't help matters when he reached above me to get that book. He was so close I felt his body heat burning into my back. I was pinned in place, breathing in his scent; it took everything in me not to moan aloud, my body aching for more of his touch.

Lord, I really need to get a grip.

I can't keep getting all hot and bothered every time we make eye contact. Sooner or later, Kira's going to pick up on it, and that would be beyond embarrassing.

Trying to regain some semblance of control over myself, I dig in my purse for my phone and focus on checking my messages. I had hoped Sofiya would have texted back by now to let me know she arrived safely, but no such luck.

Earlier today, she messaged to tell me Anatoly was driving her back to school. The minute I read those words, a cold shudder ran through me. I know he's not driving her out of the kindness of his heart; like everything he does, it's to remind me that if I step out of line, Sofiya pays the price. He didn't like my attitude after he announced our upcoming wedding. He wants me sweet and submissive when I return home. It's the role I'm destined to play.

"Why the frown?"

Roman's voice startles me, and I press my hand to my heart. "Jesus, Roman. Maybe don't sneak up on a girl."

"I didn't sneak up. I've been standing over you for a full twenty seconds." A line forms between his eyebrows. "You need to work on your situational awareness."

"My situational awareness is fine." I slip my phone back into my purse. "You're the one who creeps up on people like a ninja."

An amused puff of air escapes his lips. "Want another drink?" He tilts his head towards the bar.

"No, thanks." For some reason, he takes that as an invitation to occupy the seat Kira vacated.

"You keep looking at your phone," he notes. "Expecting a call?"

"Been paying close attention to me, have you?"

"Always." My pulse flutters as he lets the word hang between us for a moment. "It's my job."

I shake my head and fiddle with my napkin on the table. "I'm not your job."

He arches a brow. "According to Maxim, you are."

"Right."

"I have something for you." He says this so out of nowhere that it takes my brain a moment to process his words.

I blink a few times. "Okay."

He reaches into his blazer and extracts a book covered in some sort of protective wrap, then lays it on the table between us.

"A book?"

"Not just any book. A first-edition *Jane Eyre*."

I'm momentarily speechless. "They're crazy expensive and

rare. How did you find one in less than a day?" I eye the book on the table, not even daring to pick it up.

He grins. "I know people who know people, and some of these people owe me a favor."

I shake my head as warmth curls low in my belly. "Kira and I were joking about me buying one. I-I can't accept this."

He leans in so close I can feel the heat emanating from his body. "Why not? You want it, don't you?"

I want it all right, but this gift is too much. If I accept it, what kind of message am I sending Roman?

A little voice in the back of my mind whispers that I could resell it for a lot of money. Last I heard, first editions of *Jane Eyre* go for nearly one hundred thousand at auction.

"How can I accept this? It wouldn't look right." I swallow down my emotion and whisper, "I'm nearly a married woman."

Roman runs a knuckle down his face in a way that suggests he's debating how to respond. Finally, he shrugs and slowly tucks the book back into his jacket.

I might be an idiot for passing on something I could resell for good money, but the idea of selling something so special curdles my stomach. However, after yesterday and the undeniable ping of chemistry between us, I can't let him get the wrong idea. It would be bad for both of us.

"Suit yourself." He clears his throat and leans back in his chair.

Disappointment weighs down my shoulders. I'm not sure if it's from turning down the book or because he's now looking at me with a coolness that wasn't there before.

"Did you have a chance to read it?" I ask, searching for a point of conversation.

"I'm about halfway through."

Oh, wow. I didn't expect that. "What do you think so far?"

"A little creepy, isn't it?"

I release a throaty laugh. "I guess it is. It's known as a gothic novel for exactly that reason."

"I don't mind it. I like the darkness."

"I think that says a lot about you."

"Maybe." He absently plays with a coaster on the table as his gaze searches my face.

"What?" I finally ask, feeling self-conscious.

"You've smiled more this trip than I've ever seen you smile."

I shrug, feeling a little defensive. "I'm on vacation with my best friend—I have a lot to smile about."

He leans forward and picks up an unshelled peanut from our table, cracking the outer layer with his fingers. "And you have a wedding to look forward to."

I trace the rim of my empty glass, not wanting to meet his eyes. "Exactly."

He pops the nut between his lips and chews, watching me the entire time like he can see through the mask I show the rest of the world.

"What about you?" I say, attempting to turn the conversation. "Any wedding bells in your future?"

He leans back, throwing one thick, muscled arm around the empty seat on his left. "None whatsoever. I'm free as a bird and like it that way."

I swallow, feeling a tightness in my throat. "That's right. From what I hear, you've never been with the same woman twice."

His eyes widen, and I immediately regret my words. It makes it sound like I'm keeping tabs on his life, which I'm not. But Roman is one of Moscow's most-eligible bachelors, and it's impossible to block out society gossip.

Instead of looking offended, he raises an eyebrow, intrigued. "You heard that, huh? What else are people saying about me?"

"Not from Kira," I'm quick to clarify. "We don't talk about

you. But, you know how it is ... Others talk." I wish I never opened my big mouth in the first place, but now it's too late to backtrack.

"Sure." He narrows his eyes. "We all love a bit of gossip. So tell me. I'm dying to hear what other people are saying about me."

I bite my lip, knowing I should put an end to this conversation, but curiosity has gotten the better of me. "That you slept with the commissioner's wife last year and then refused to see her again. That she was so distraught she threatened to hang herself, but you didn't care."

His expression turns dark, but he nods for me to continue.

"That you prefer to kill with your bare hands because you like to feel when someone's life drains out of them. That you have a dark side."

He runs a thumb over his bottom lip. "Well, I guess you know everything there is to know about me, then."

Guilt settles in my chest. I don't know why I feel bad, like I accused him of being a shitty person. "It doesn't mean I believe everything I hear," I say, as if that makes it any better.

His jaw tightens. "Seems like you do."

"Please, there's enough shit said about me and my family. Well, except some of those rumors are true, at least where my father is concerned."

His expression sparks with amusement. "So, you believe I sleep with everyone only once, unless I choose to torture the instead?"

I lift a shoulder, sucking my bottom lip between my teeth. "Like I said, not everyone. I imagine you're selective, at least about who you torture."

"I'm glad you think so highly of me." He strokes his thumb along the cleft in his chin. "You did get one thing right about me."

"And that is?"

"I do like to kill people. But I don't care if it's with my hands or not."

I blink up at him. That's the last thing I expected him to say. I thought he'd admit to sleeping his way through Moscow, and jealousy was already burning in my veins. But admitting he likes to kill people? I don't know what to do with that piece of information.

"The only thing I care about is that it's someone who deserves it. When you work in my world, that's the case more often than not." He leans in close and rests his hand on my knee with a possessive squeeze.

Sweet baby Jesus. All my senses laser focus on the place of contact.

"About the many women I've been with, all my conquests …" Under the table, his hand slides up my thigh, stopping just short of the hem of my skirt. "Don't believe everything you hear."

Panting, I look up at him and pray the flush creeping up my cheeks isn't too obvious.

He gives me a wink, pushes back in his seat, and saunters to the bar just as Kira comes waltzing through the pub's door and announces that I need another drink.

That's certainly not what I need.

I need a cold shower. And a new pair of underwear because this pair is soaked right through.

An hour later, we're back at the hotel. It's a big penthouse suite that we all share—for security purposes—but at least we all have our own rooms.

Phone in my hand, I'm pacing my bedroom nervously. I still haven't heard from Sofiya yet. It's nearly nine o'clock here, which makes it close to midnight in Moscow.

Lucky for me, Kira wanted to retire early, because I don't think I could hide my nerves any longer.

I've left voice and text messages for Sofiya, and there's been no reply, which is unlike her. Maybe her phone battery died or she fell asleep before checking her messages, or—worst-case scenario—they've been in a car accident.

Clutching my phone, I take a deep breath and hit Call on Anatoly's contact.

It goes straight to voicemail. Forcing the words out, I fight to keep my voice steady. "I haven't heard from Sofiya all day. I know you drove her back to school. Please call me when you get this. I'm worried."

I dial my mother next.

"Mama, finally!" I say when she picks up after the third ring. "Have you heard from Sofiya yet?"

"What do you mean *yet*?" she practically yells. The background is filled with the buzz of conversation and music. "Anatoly dropped her off hours ago. Why would I hear from her?"

I close my eyes, pinching the bridge of my nose. "What time did they leave the house?"

My mother huffs out a breath of annoyance. "I don't know. Who keeps track of these things? Anyway, the Petroviches were kind enough to offer us their private box at the opera tonight. I really must be going."

"Mama!" I cry in exasperation. "I asked Sofiya to call me when she arrived back at school, and I haven't heard a thing. I'm worried something happened to her."

"She's a teenage girl who hasn't seen her friends in a week. She probably got caught up chatting and forgot to message you back. You used to do the same thing."

I wasn't, but my mother has a selective memory that benefits her.

"Anyways, I see the Popovs. I must go and say hello. Try not to worry so much," she advises. "And try not to put on weight in London. You'll need to be fitted for a wedding dress as soon as you're home."

The line goes dead, and the familiar sting of rejection hits harder than expected. This isn't new. It echoes the countless times my parents favored glittering social events over spending time with me. There was the year they missed my lead role in the school play for a ski trip in Switzerland, and the time I rang in my fourteenth birthday with only the housekeeper for company while they mingled at a wedding overseas.

It's why I've embraced my role as Sofiya's protector so fiercely. Given our parents' track record, I'm determined to be the one person who always has her back.

I'm so wound up with worry that I storm from the bedroom to the hotel's terrace. The moment I close the French doors behind me and face the gusty wind, I unleash a deep, soul-cleansing scream, letting all my frustration pour out. My lungs burn with the release.

"Well, that's not a good sign."

Startled, I whirl around to find Roman leaning against the railing, a cigarette between his fingers and smoke curling from his lips. The moonlight casts shadows across his features, accentuating his surprised expression.

"I, uh, needed to let off some steam."

"Apparently." He holds out the cigarette for me to take a drag. "Seems you need it more than me."

I hesitate for a moment, but the raw edge of my nerves wins out. Stepping closer, I take the cigarette from him. The smoke is harsh against my lungs, a sharp contrast to the cool night air, but it grounds me. I exhale slowly, watching the smoke disperse into the darkness, and hand the cigarette back to him.

He takes a slow drag then looks at me, his gaze softer now. "Want to talk about it?" His question feels oddly intimate in the silence that stretches between us.

"I wouldn't even know where to start," I admit.

"Start with why you felt the need to scream like a banshee into the night."

I sigh and lean forward, resting my arms on the balcony railing. Normally, I guard my secrets fiercely, but tonight, I don't have it in me to hold everything back. Not after what he just witnessed.

"I haven't heard from my sister all day. Anatoly was supposed to drive her back to school, but it's late now and still no word."

His eyebrows pull together in concern. "So, it's unlike your sister to not call you back?"

"Definitely." A fresh wave of worry crashes over me.

"Have you called Anatoly?"

"Yes. He didn't answer. I left a message but haven't heard from him either."

He stubs out the cigarette in an ashtray and fishes his phone from his pocket. "She goes to the same boarding school you and Kira went to, right? I'll look into it."

My eyebrows shoot up. "I didn't mean you have to get involved."

He lays a hand on my back, the warmth of his touch immediately comforting. "It doesn't matter. I can help. Let me take care of this for you." Before I can argue, he brushes a hand down my cheek, his eyes gentle. "You don't have to shoulder everything alone, *milaya*."

Sweetheart.

My breath trips. Roman, with his criminal ties and tough exterior, is not a man I'd expect kindness from, and yet that's exactly what he's showing me.

I nod, feeling a tightness in my throat because I'm unused to accepting people's help. But this is bigger than me; this is about Sofiya's safety.

"Okay," I whisper.

"I'll be right back." He slides open the door and heads inside the penthouse, phone to his ear.

I turn around to look out over the city, alone with my thoughts and the boulder in my chest. I hate to drag anyone else into the disaster of my life, but I can't deny it feels good to let someone else help me.

When the phone in my hand rings, I'm caught by surprise.

"Oh my God, Sofiya," I blurt out when I see who's calling. My voice is thick with emotion. "Are you okay?"

The relief from hearing her voice is short-lived. "I'm fine, don't worry. My phone died, and Anatoly took me out for dinner with some of his associates before dropping me off at school."

"Wait, dinner with who?" I demand.

"I don't know. Some guys he's in business with. It was a long night. I'm tired." Her words are slightly slurred.

Alarm bells ring in my head. Something's off. "Sofiya, have you been drinking?" I ask, dreading the answer.

There's a pause. "Anatoly let me try some wine ... and maybe a shot of vodka. It was nothing. We were having fun."

My stomach drops, horror washing over me. "It's not nothing," I insist, but I try to sound calm, not wanting to upset her. "Drink a glass of water and try to get some rest, okay? Take an aspirin in the morning if you have a headache. It'll help."

"Sure, Lizka. Sorry I forgot to charge my phone."

"It's okay. I'll talk to you tomorrow. Get some sleep. And Sofiya?"

"Yes," she replies with a yawn.

"I love you."

"Love you too."

Heart in my throat, I slide down the terrace wall, hugging my knees.

Dinner with associates? Alcohol? What reason could he possibly have to drag her out later with a bunch of men? My chest tightens, a crushing weight pressing down on my lungs.

The terrace door slides open and Roman appears, kneeling beside me. "Whoa, take a breath." He takes my face in his hands.

I can't speak yet; I'm too messed up to even put my thoughts into words.

As if he knows, Roman's eyes lock on mine, concern evident in his features. Whatever he sees in my expression causes him to pull me toward him until my face is buried in his hard chest.

His fingers brush through my hair, and I tip my head up to breathe him in. Roman smells perfect, like the woods and a lingering smoky scent. He's only trying to comfort me, but my body reacts as if he's flipping a switch, igniting an electric energy inside me.

"Tell me what happened," he says after a minute.

I pull away and try to compose myself. "It's Sofiya. She called. She's okay, just forgot to charge her phone."

"That's good. I called her school and woke up some very confused nun." He smiles. "And I have a guard on the way to her school. He'll keep an eye on her dorm."

Tears sting my eyes. He may be a killer, he may live in a cold and dangerous world, but he's got a kernel of something good inside of him.

"What's wrong? This is good news." He runs a hand over the pulse point at my neck, and I have to bite my lip to keep from releasing a little moan. His calloused hand feels so good on my bare skin.

"Just overwhelmed, that's all."

He makes a noise in his throat and pulls back, tipping up my chin to make me look at him. "You'd tell me if things weren't okay, right?"

I lick my lips and force a small smile onto my face.

It's then that everything comes into focus: how close we

are—his face only inches from mine—how hard his chest is, and how good he smells. Seconds tick by, and neither of us moves.

Is he going to kiss me? It would take nothing for him to lean forward and press his lips against mine. His gaze flicks from my eyes to my mouth and back again, and I'm thankful for the cover of darkness hiding my blush. I'm no expert on the matter, but the hungry way his eyes slide down my throat suggests he's feeling it too.

I want him to kiss me more than I want my next breath.

But a kiss is dangerous. How could I stop at just a taste?

"I should probably go to sleep," I say, moving away, needing to pull out of his magnetic orbit.

Without a word, he steps back and sighs deeply, his hand sweeping through his dark hair—it's something he does often. I've noticed countless other things about him too, like how he rubs his neck when making decisions or checks his holster when we enter new places.

I suck in a few deep breaths to ground myself and then back up toward the French doors that lead inside.

"Can we not tell Kira about all of this?" I glance out over the city, praying that Kira slept through my banshee wail. "I don't want to worry her, with the pregnancy and everything, it would be stress she doesn't need."

He turns, and I notice a pronounced bulge straining against the zipper of his jeans.

Did I do that to him?

"We don't have to tell anyone about this," he assures me, sounding a little out of breath. "But I can leave my man to keep an eye on your sister for a few days."

I bite my lip. It's a generous offer, but a bratva bodyguard trailing Sofiya at school? That's not ideal. "Not necessary," I reply, "but I appreciate it."

I study him in the dim moonlight. I don't know what to make of Roman, willing to do whatever is necessary to put my mind at ease. He's gone way beyond acting as my bodyguard, and it's confusing my poor, dead heart.

He catches me studying him and raises an eyebrow. "What?"

I clear my throat. "Nothing, just … thanks for helping me. You didn't have to, and honestly, I would have lost my mind if I hadn't spoken with her."

He nods and turns away from me, looking over the city, both of his arms braced on the railing of the patio. "Good night, Liza." His voice is a pure masculine rasp, and it sets my lady bits on fire.

"Good night, Roman."

CHAPTER TWELVE

ROMAN

Liza backs off the terrace like my hair is on fire.

Fuck. Tonight didn't go as planned.

I only meant to comfort her, but the way her breath became shallow, her lips parted, and her face flushed when she looked at me with those big green eyes, I knew I was in trouble. Common sense screamed at me to get the hell off the terrace and lock myself in a bedroom with a bottle of whisky.

But did I listen? Nope.

She was scared and vulnerable, and instead of pushing her away, I did the exact opposite. I would have done a lot more if she hadn't come to her senses and scurried inside.

I pull out a cigarette and shove it between my lips, hoping the hit of nicotine will kill the lust pumping through my veins. I've been smoking too much lately, and I blame it squarely on Liza's presence. It's messing with my head.

Lord, the things this girl makes me feel. Desire is one thing, but I want to take care of her. Protect her and see her smile—the unguarded one where she looks truly happy, like she did in the bookstore.

When I'm back home, I'll screw my head on straight. I'll focus on work, the next Kozlov shipment is arriving soon, and I'm sure there's a shitload of other issues for me to deal with. I'll even volunteer for the next interrogation. A little violence should soothe my soul.

Taking my phone from my pocket, I dial the last number I called. Savin is one of my most reliable soldiers. He started with me a few years ago, but he's smart and ruthless—a combination I'm fond of.

Savin picks up after the first ring and announces, "I got here not too long ago. Sofiya's safely back in the dorm."

"Looks like it was a misunderstanding. The kid forgot to charge her phone or something like that."

He's quiet for a minute, his hesitation out of character. "Not sure that's the whole story."

"Oh?" I blow out a smoke ring and wait for him to continue.

"I was able to hack into the school's CCTV system to get a look at what happened. She got back to the dorms pretty late, but she wasn't alone." He pauses, weighing his next words. "Anatoly was with her. She was pretty unsteady on her feet."

The hair on the back of my neck rises. "Unsteady how?"

"A few drinks too many."

I hiss out a breath through my teeth. "That fucking pig. She's seventeen."

I know seventeen-year-olds experiment with alcohol, but it's typically not with their much older soon-to-be brother-in-law. He was supposed to drive her back to school, not take her out drinking. What the hell happened?

Anger bubbles in my veins. Either Liza doesn't know the truth, or she decided not to share it with me.

"What do you want me to do, boss? Anatoly left about an hour ago. The nuns wouldn't let him in the dorms," Savin adds with a little chuckle.

The sick feeling morphs into something darker and twisted. It makes me see red.

This is the piece of garbage I'm in business with? Worse, this is the man Liza is marrying?

"Stick around for a few days," I instruct. "Keep an eye on her, and let me know if Anatoly shows up again."

"You got it."

"Savin?" I grit my teeth, not wanting to ask but needing to know. "Did he touch her in a way he shouldn't have? Get handsy with her?"

He pauses. "No."

Thank fuck.

As much as I'd like to destroy Anatoly, my hands are tied because of our business dealings. Don't get me wrong—if he's a predator, I'll make sure he takes a trip down the River Styx. But I have to play it smart and lie in wait for the right moment to strike.

CHAPTER THIRTEEN

ROMAN

I take a final swig of the whisky left in my glass—my first and last of the night because there's still work ahead. The drink does little to distract from how un-fucking-comfortable I am in this tux and the shitstorm brewing inside of me.

My other hand holds a phone to my ear as I lean back in an armchair in a room in the penthouse suite I've commandeered as an office.

From the other end of the line, Pavel mutters a curse under his breath. I just filled him in on everything that went down with Anatoly last night. I usually stay out of people's business—less shit for me to wade through—but the minute I saw Liza upset, every protective instinct inside of me flared.

When I was fifteen, I failed to protect my mother from my abusive father. I vowed to never make that mistake again. If a man is sick enough to hurt a woman, then he deserves to have hell rain down on him.

"So this is the kind of man we're in business with?" Pavel snarls. "A man who thinks nothing of taking a teenage girl out all day without checking in with her family?"

My fingers tighten on the now empty whisky glass in my hand. "Until we find out what actually happened, our hands are tied. Savin's keeping an eye on Sofiya—we'll see if Anatoly makes a reappearance or if anything else happens, for that matter."

"What did Liza say?" His voice is as dark as mine.

"Nothing. Either she doesn't know about the drinking or she's keeping her mouth shut, but she was rattled—that much was clear."

"If he fucking put a finger on that girl, I'll take great pleasure in ripping him to shreds."

A vein in my temple ticks. As much as I want to see Anatoly pay for his every sin, he's currently in possession of a cargo ship full of our product. We can't go for the jugular … yet.

"Whatever skeletons he's hiding, we will unearth them. But we better have solid proof before we go to Maxim. He's got enough shit on his plate, and we can't mess with this deal unless what we have is ironclad."

"Whatever it is, I guarantee you it's shady as fuck."

"No arguments here," I agree. "Let's get eyes on him. See what he's really up to."

"I'll take care of it," Pavel vows.

We say goodbye, and I turn to face my reflection in the window, straighten out the lapels, and run my hand down the pant legs, smoothing out any creases in the tux.

This is our last night in London before we fly back to Moscow, and Kira has something special planned, though she won't tell me what.

As if sensing the dark cloud over my head, Kira comes breezing into the room, her eyes narrowing when she finds me staring hard at my reflection. "Why the brooding face?"

I meet her gaze in the window's reflection. "Who says I'm brooding?"

She steps fully into the room, closing the door behind her.

Kira looks as glamorous as ever in a gold evening dress, her blonde hair swept up in a loose bun.

"I know that look. You're not happy about something." She crosses her arms and leans against the wall. "Out with it."

I run my tongue over my upper teeth and turn to face her. "I know you want tonight to be a surprise for Liza, but I can't do my job properly unless I know where we're going." I gesture to my computer. "The club has no listed address, no website, and it's not on Google. It's like it doesn't exist. I need more to go on."

She blows out a breath. "Promise me you won't freak out."

My shoulders hitch. This woman is trying to kill me. "I make no promises. Just say it."

"Fine." She tilts her chin higher. "We're going to a sex club."

I literally choke on air. "Goddamn, Kira. What are you thinking?"

She laughs at my thunderous expression. "This is why I didn't tell you. Chill, okay? We're not going to do anything. It's only a show. We're there to watch, nothing more. Maxim and I have been there before, and he can confirm the security is top-notch."

"Why?" It's the only word I can manage. Another thought occurs to me. "So, Liza doesn't know?"

Kira shakes her head slowly. "All she knows is that it's a bit out of the ordinary." She gently nudges my arm. "Come on. Doesn't Liza deserve a good time? She'd never let loose like this in Moscow, but she deserves a crazy night at least once in her life before she's tied down."

I clear my throat. "A nightclub is cutting loose," I point out. "But a sex show—"

"Erotic show at a sex club," she clarifies. "There's a difference."

"Right."

Kira's face falls. "She should know what she's missing. Because sooner than later, she's going to be tied to that asshole for the rest of her life. And she'll never know what good"—Kira raises her eyebrows—"*you know what* is. Because Anatoly will be her first and last."

Jesus. My thoughts are diving straight into the gutter. If Liza's curious about what good "you know what," I'd be more than happy to show her. I know Anatoly prizes her virginity—the pig made that clear enough in the banya—but maybe I'm equally as twisted, because the thought of being the first man to spread her legs and push inside of her tight heat has me straining against the zipper of this damn monkey suit.

I hold up a hand to stop Kira. "Yeah, I get it. You don't need to spell it out for me."

She sighs. "I want to give her a wild night to remember. I know it won't change anything, but it might open her eyes a little." She gives me a hopeful smile. "We don't have to make this weird. You do your job, I'll make sure Liza has the time of her life, and we'll never talk about it again."

My knuckles whiten as my hands curl into fists, and my mind sinks to a dark place. I've killed, maimed, and tortured dozens of people without a second thought. But this might be my hardest job yet—watching Liza experience pleasure up close and personal for the first time and not being able to do anything about it.

Man, the universe has a messed-up sense of humor.

Actually, I shouldn't blame the universe, this is all Kira.

There's a soft knock, and then Liza pushes the door open.

Our gazes snag, and I instantly regret it. She's peering at me through those thick, dark lashes, looking like a goddess descended among mortals. Her gown is a bold scarlet that wraps around her curves like a flame, and a delicate gold necklace is looped around her elegant neck.

My hand would look so much better around that throat.

Just fucking great. My thoughts are already getting away from me.

I drag in a heavy breath, straighten my spine, and focus my attention on sliding my gun into the back of my waistband.

"Damn, girl." Kira whistles. "You look incredible."

Except that's an understatement. I look away because every illicit fantasy that's been running through my head is likely written all over my expression, plain for all to see.

A puff of air escapes Liza's lips and she holds her arms out. "All dressed up and no idea where we're going."

Kira links arms with her friend. "All will be revealed soon."

A fierce heat ripples through me. I graze my teeth with my tongue and stalk past Liza without a second look.

I'm here to do a job. Nothing more.

"Get your coats," I bark behind me. "I'll have Feliks bring the car around."

I can feel the uncomfortable silence as I storm from the room. I know I'm being a dick, but the alternative is losing control. I can't afford to let this reckless obsession continue. Even entertaining these thoughts is insane.

I need to make it through tonight, then I can keep my distance. Forever.

CHAPTER FOURTEEN

LIZA

Feliks pulls up to the curb, and the engine hums to a stop.

Peering out the window, I can barely make out the club's entrance. All I see is a large townhouse, its stately façade blending in with the upscale neighborhood.

I have no idea where we are or what we're doing here, but Kira is adamant about it being a surprise. Her only instruction for tonight was to look hot and leave my inhibitions at the door, whatever that means. I'm curious what she has in store for us tonight, but more than anything, I want our last night here to be special, so I do my best to go along with her plan and act excited, even though my mind is elsewhere. Hundreds of miles east, to be exact.

I don't know what game Anatoly is playing, but I fear he's using Sofiya as a pawn in his game of control over me. Anatoly didn't answer any of my calls today—not to his office, his cell, or even to his home. I know he's punishing me for going away on this trip, but I can't escape this nagging feeling that there's something more. Something I'm not seeing.

I glance down at my phone, scanning the text messages I exchanged with my sister earlier today. It did nothing to put my mind at ease, only opened up the door to a lot more questions, like who are these so-called associates, and why he would take Sofiya to dinner with them.

Me: pls call or text when yr up, I need to know you're OK

Sofiya: sorry was in class! bit of a headache this morning but I'm fine, don't worry

Me: I can't help it, what happened last night?

Sofiya: I already told you just a dinner, no big deal

Me: Anatoly had no right to give you alcohol at your age

Sofiya: all my friends drink! I promise, I wasn't even drunk

Me: that doesn't make me feel better. Just rest up OK?

Sofiya: sure, sis. Ttyl.

Simply reading over our text exchange sets my blood on fire. Sofiya clearly doesn't see the red flags, and maybe that's my fault. I've sheltered her from who Anatoly really is. She thinks he's taking an interest in her as his soon-to-be sister-in-law; she doesn't know the depth of his depravity. The scary thing is, neither do I.

"Better leave that in the car."

"Huh?"

My head snaps up to find Kira smiling at me.

She gestures to my phone. "Your cell. No phones allowed in the club."

I shake my head and try to come back to the present moment. "That's weird." I smirk and follow her lead, tucking my phone into the center console between us. "I wonder if this place is full of celebrities."

Kira shrugs. "Something like that."

I take lipstick out of my clutch and apply it, watching my reflection in a small compact mirror. When I finally look up, I catch Roman's intense gaze in the rearview mirror. My heart pumps a little faster in my chest.

He's been awfully quiet today, and I wonder if it has to do with last night, with the charged moment between us when my body confused his comfort with something more. But I can't deny the sparks that flare in my chest every time he's close. He poured a cup of coffee for me this morning, and I nearly dry humped his leg. And earlier tonight, seeing Roman in a tux was almost my undoing.

Two uniformed valets materialize from the night and open our doors, one gently helping Kira and the other assisting me to step out of the car.

Roman comes around the hood. With one arm resting against the roof of the car, he lowers his head to have a word with Feliks through the open window. I don't know what he says, but Feliks nods solemnly and drives off.

Roman straightens and pulls at each cuff of his suit. Tall, dark, and undeniably handsome, he looks like a broody James Bond. It's going to be a long night.

For once, Feliks and Bogdan aren't accompanying us inside. Kira said something about security already being very tight and the guest list exclusive. I don't think Roman is thrilled about any of this, but Kira is convincing when she wants to be.

Kira leads the way into the townhouse. The exterior's simplicity gives way to a luxurious interior, where burgundy velvet wallpaper lines the walls and crystal chandeliers cast a warm light.

A beautiful woman in a sleek black dress steps forward and takes Kira's hand. "Welcome back to Sanctuary, Mrs. Belov. Thank you for bringing your friends along."

Welcome back?

I raise my eyebrows, but Kira only offers me a little shrug.

"I'm Paulina, the club's manager." Tall, elegant, and poised, she reminds me of a former ballet dancer. She looks to be in her mid-forties, but I can't really tell because she's wearing a Zorro mask.

Interesting.

At the snap of her fingers, two muscular men wearing only leather pants and the same masks as Paulina enter the room to take our jackets.

My mouth goes dry. I mean, the view's not bad, but spending our last night in London at a high-end male strip club is not exactly what I pictured. I throw Kira a *what the fuck* look, but she doesn't seem fazed. She responds with a shrug and wink.

My eyes flick to Roman, but he won't look my way. He stands stock-still, jaw hard, focused on an unknown point in the distance.

I release a heavy breath. "The show will start in an hour," Paulina informs us. "Feel free to head inside, enjoy a drink, and make yourselves comfortable." A gentle smile grows on her lips. "The rules are simple: no using your real names, no phones, no cameras, and don't forget to mask up." She holds up a little black masquerade mask like the one she wears. "The rest is about enjoying yourselves."

Huh? This is getting weirder by the second.

Paulina, perhaps sensing my nerves, sidles up to me. "Turn around," she murmurs in my ear.

When I do, she takes the delicate masquerade mask and begins to tie it around my head. Her fingers brush against my skin with a deliberate slowness. I hold my breath as a shiver coasts down my back.

"This must be new for you," Paulina whispers, her breath caressing my ear as she secures the mask. "My advice is to let go. You might discover something about yourself here."

The masks, the half-naked guys, the advice to let go ... I'm definitely missing something here, but there's no point in asking questions, because Kira is already leading the way down a small hallway, which soon opens up into the main space.

Wow.

I stop in my tracks and take it all in. I expected more of an ultramodern club vibe, but no, this place is something different altogether. It's like stepping back in time to a 1920s speakeasy.

People are chatting at the bar with cocktails or in front of various nooks set up around the room flanked by fireplaces and bearskin rugs. There's no stage, which I find confusing because Paulina said the show starts in an hour. Like Roman, the men are all wearing tuxedos, though I can confirm that none look as good as him. The women's dress code is much more varied. Some are wearing dresses, like Kira and myself, but the rest are wearing ... Well, not all that much. Fine lace bras, thongs, garter belts, and super high heels.

I turn to Kira. "Is this ... a sex club?" I'm worried about the answer because if it is, what the hell is she thinking? I don't belong here.

Roman lets out a strangled cough, then grumbles something about keeping watch from the bar before he stalks off.

Kira chews the inside of her cheek. "Strictly speaking, yes, but that's not why we're here. We're here to enjoy the entertainment—like live theater, but sexier." When I grimace, she holds up her hands. "I get it. You've never done anything like this before, but it's only one night of your life. No one has to know. Just one night to see and experience incredible things."

I'm speechless. "Kira ... This is crazy."

Her gaze sweeps the room and then lands back on me.

"Why is it crazy to get a taste of what good sex looks like before you get married and lose your V?"

Jesus. I nearly cough up a lung. "Excuse me?"

"Anatoly will be the only man you ever sleep with for your whole life." She makes a face, unable to hide her distaste. "You won't even know if it's good or, let's face it, most likely bad. You'll think that's what sex is. At least see what pleasure looks like for yourself, up close and personal."

Her words burrow under my skin. Kira's heart is in the right place, but knowing what good sex looks like is the least of my concerns. Still, I can't help but be the tiniest bit curious.

So far, my experience of sex has ranged from okay to terrible. Before Anatoly, I dated a few guys. There was no one I was serious about, but I messed around with a few guys. Hands and mouth. Nothing mind-blowing. I always thought it was a nice idea to save myself for my future husband, which is very old-fashioned, but this was back when I was still a die-hard romantic.

Anatoly ruined that idea for me. The deeper my hate for him goes, the more repulsive it is having to go down on him or jerk him off. I picture a life of blow jobs where he holds my head still and thrusts brutally into my mouth with no regard for my pleasure. I imagine he'll roll on top of me, shove himself inside, and roughly take what he wants.

The thought of having to sleep with him, well, ever, leaves me dead inside. But I don't have to feel dead right now. Maybe tonight, I will do what Paulina suggested. Let go and enjoy myself.

Could I really do that?

Kira's hand lands on my arm, pulling my attention back towards her. "We can leave if this is really not your thing," she offers.

I swallow past the tightness in my throat. "I don't want to leave."

Her face lights up. "Really?"

"Really," I confirm.

"It's not gross. I swear." She bites her lip. "Maxim and I have been here before. Several times, actually." Her eyes glint as she links her arm through mine. "The spectacle alone is … Well, I guess you'll see for yourself."

A thrill coasts over my skin. It's one night. One night to be free, to forget the real world and live in the moment. Heat blooms at the base of my neck, and I turn around to find Roman leaning casually against the bar, a drink in hand. In that split second, something unspoken zips between us—electric and charged.

My heart skips a beat. I can't read his thoughts, but his smoldering gaze is intense enough to burn right through me.

To hell with it. If this is my one chance to experience something different, I'll be damned if I'm going to hold back.

I arch an eyebrow, daring him to watch me. Daring him to make the most of tonight.

The lights dim, and the music lowers to a simple electronic beat, indicating the show is about to start. But there's still no stage and still no clear performance area.

I give Kira a curious look.

She gestures all around us. "Just watch."

The lighting stays low except in a few places where a gentle spotlight falls, creating a halo effect on the floor and drawing all eyes to select areas around the room. The music changes to a hypnotic, sensual beat that pulses through the space, making the room feel alive.

Then everything happens at once.

Topless women in black tutus materialize from nowhere, spinning in pirouettes. As they whirl through the space, a white canopy bed suddenly appears as if it sprouted straight out of the floor. A handful of people are on the bed—both men and women in various states of undress, all wearing masks and undulating to the beat. There's no touching … yet. But the hint of what's next heats my cheeks and has my breath coming a little faster.

It's hard to pin down my emotions: nervousness, excitement, embarrassment, arousal. They all play a symphony along my skin.

I can feel Kira's eyes on my face, and when I look over at her, she leans in and whispers, "It's about to get a lot wilder."

A rush of arousal pools between my legs, and I'm acutely aware of the warm air on my skin—like my body has tuned into a new frequency.

A full-on orgy is taking place on the bed. One woman is lying in the middle, her legs spread wide as a woman and man take turns fingering and licking her pussy while another applies clamps to her nipples, sucking and kissing her neck. Her small breasts are turning red and swollen, but there's no question she's having the time of her life as she writhes and moans with pleasure. She comes hard, but her partners keep going, delivering orgasm after orgasm.

This is what true sexual pleasure looks like, and I want in on it.

I turn, stealing a look at Roman.

Holy shit, he's all coiled muscle and intensity. Despite everything going on in the room, his eyes are on me. He's leaning forward, both of his elbows on the bar as he runs a thumb over the cleft of his chin. I suddenly feel breathless as he raises an eyebrow, as if to ask, *What do you think?* I give him the barest of smiles.

On the other side of the bed, two men wearing only briefs are kissing and grinding into each other. The sight is more erotic than I ever imagined. A woman dressed in nothing but a white Venetian mask slips in between them, and then it's three bodies writhing and rubbing together, oblivious to everyone else in the room.

Behind me, Kira's breaths come faster as well; even with her experience, she's not unaffected. I turn in place to find a woman being bound to a chair with her legs spread open by rope, the knots intricate and precise.

My eyes must nearly pop out of my head because Kira leans over and explains, "It's called Japanese rope bondage."

After tying her up, he flicks a toy teasingly between her open legs, drawing the attention of partygoers who whisper and watch as her pleasure peaks. There's a smattering of applause when she throws her head back and cries out her release.

My heart beats in my throat.

Would I want to be touched like that? Certainly not by Anatoly, but … Would I want Roman to touch me like that? The thought sends a rush of moisture between my legs.

"Look around. Explore," Kira encourages me in a hushed tone. "I have to run to the ladies."

I nod but don't take my eyes off the spectacle. My guess is she's giving me space to experience the room on my own, without the awkwardness of a friend by my side.

But I'm not alone. I'm joined by about a hundred strangers and one man in particular, whose presence I am distinctly aware of.

The expression on his face is unreadable. I can't tell if he's aroused, angry, or something else entirely. The only thing that's clear is he's not watching the show. He's watching *me*.

When he sets his glass down on the bartop island and strides towards me, I turn back to the performance, the pulse in my neck pounding. He stops barely an inch from my back. The heat from his body radiates over my skin, teasing a shiver down my spine.

He draws a single finger down the bare skin of my back, and I nearly arch and cry out. His touch sends a rush of nerves throughout my body.

"You gonna stand here all day or make the most of your

time?" His warm breath brushes against my overly sensitive skin.

Trembling, I close my eyes to bask in his nearness. His heat. His smell. I don't turn around because his insinuation sends a bolt of pleasure to my clit.

He wants me to explore. He wants to see what turns me on.

It's reckless to be playing this game with Roman, my fiancé's business partner. A man I want but can never have.

I'm too far gone to pull back now.

I swallow and nod, unable to make eye contact with him as I slowly make my way closer to the performers.

I'm drawn to a young woman who stands against a wall wearing only white panties, illuminated in the crimson wash of a floor lamp. A stunning older woman dressed in a black corset and fishnets administers flicks to the other woman's breasts with a leather flogger. She picks up speed, focusing on the woman's nipples until both breasts look pink and sensitive, much to the crowd's delight.

Roman's eyes follow as I make my way towards a willowy blonde in bondage lingerie who's mounting something that looks like a carousel horse, but with a huge dildo where the saddle would be. She lowers herself on the plastic cock, writhing, rocking back and forth, and getting herself off as the crowd softly encourages her to keep going.

I notice that the room has thinned out. Couples, throuples, or various combinations of people slink off towards the area cordoned off for private rooms.

While classical music fills the air, two women clad in short black bobbed wigs and high heels lie down on a huge table. Select members of the audience step forward and cover the women's bodies in whipped cream, hot fudge, and ice cream—anywhere goes—before licking and sucking the sticky dessert straight off their flesh. The women scream out their delight, clearly enjoying the sensation of many mouths on them at once.

Out of everything I witnessed tonight, somehow this makes my clit throb hard, and my nipples tighten to sharp peaks. I've never had anyone lick me out like that, and frankly, I don't think I ever will. For the first time tonight, something like sadness weighs me down.

I'll never experience anything like this. I'll never know what it feels like to be with someone I desire who desires me for the right reasons. Someone who would take pleasure in my pleasure.

Someone like Roman.

"You can do more than watch. You can have a taste." Paulina's voice is a low murmur in my ear. She appears beside me, her eyes glued to the show but all her attention on me.

I let out a sigh. "I don't think that's for me."

"You never know until you try it," she purrs. Her eyes travel up and down my form, drinking me in. "Don't take this the wrong way, but I'm going to guess you haven't experienced much. That this world is new to you. Sex is new to you."

I hide my grimace as shame slides between my shoulder blades. "Am I that obvious?"

Paulina lets out a small laugh. "It's not a bad thing, love. I doubt it's obvious to most, but I have a trained eye."

I can't help but look over at her now. What the hell does that mean, a trained eye?

She cocks her head to the side. "Despite being stunningly beautiful and well over eighteen … I think you're a virgin. Am I right?"

My cheeks flame red. I don't know why she's asking me this, but there's no point denying it.

I nod and bite my lip. "My life is complicated."

"Oh, I'm sure. It always is." She takes a breath and skims

her hand down my arm. "Please forgive me for being so forward. We rarely recruit for this sort of thing, but you're an exquisite beauty. One our elite members would appreciate. I'd kick myself if I didn't say something."

I gesture to the women splayed out on the table. "I'm sorry, but I can't do … do that."

Her lips tip up at the corners. "Not that, exactly. We conduct auctions here, where women sell off their virginity to the highest bidder. It's very, very lucrative. It's not unheard of for a woman as lovely and innocent as yourself to take home a number close to six figures. American dollars, that is."

My mouth falls open. Auction my virginity? That's depraved … even if she's offering up a mind-blowing sum.

I shift uncomfortably. "I couldn't do that."

She huffs out a breath of amusement. "Everyone says that … at first. But I'll tell you this. We have a rigorous screening process, and we've never had a problem with any of our patrons. The act happens here, on-site, immediately after the auction, with very strict safety measures in place. We've never had a complaint. And we wire the money to you that very night."

My heart pounds fiercely in my ears. What she's suggesting is unfathomable, but so is the money she's offering.

Money that would be available immediately.

Money I could grow quickly through day trading.

Money I can use to free Sofiya and myself from Anatoly, and if need be, my parents as well.

It's a crazy prospect. In no other circumstance would I consider this, but if I do this right, this could be my ticket to freedom.

From the corner of my eye, I see Kira enter back into the performance space.

"I'll think about it," I say to Paulina.

I mean it. I don't know if I could actually go through with it, but it's an opportunity I need to consider at the very least.

She drops something that feels like a business card into my hand. I quickly slip it into my clutch.

"I know this is happening very quickly, but there's an auction at midnight. You have my number. Call me when you've made your decision." Paulina starts to turn away but then pauses. "Just so you know, I'll reserve the prime slot of the night for you. I think you'd fetch a very pretty penny, my dear." She saunters off, leaving me to pick my jaw up off the floor.

My eyes scan the crowd, landing on Kira heading toward me, and Roman in the distance. I try not to read too much into it. Even if he saw me and Paulina talking, he has no idea what was said.

Kira approaches me, giving Paulina a quick glance as she makes her way around to the other patrons. "What was that about?" she asks.

"Oh, nothing." I pray I have a decent poker face. "She wanted to make sure I'm enjoying myself."

Kira raises her eyebrows. "Are you?"

"It's wild." I grin. "But no complaints."

"Good. That was the point of tonight. The point of this whole trip." She gives my arm a squeeze and drops a kiss on my cheek before wandering off to take in the show.

A shiver coasts down my back when I hear the familiar deep rasp in my ear. "What did Paulina say to you, milaya?"

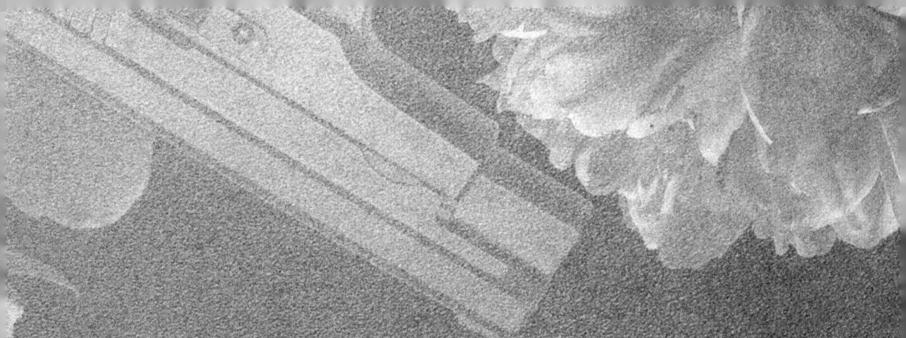

CHAPTER FIFTEEN

ROMAN

A whisper-soft breath escapes between her lips. Her body stiffens, but she doesn't turn around to face me, even when I pull her into the shadows. I keep her back to my front so we look like any other guests enjoying the show.

Most of the other patrons, including Kira, are now on the other side of the room, watching the final performance of the night. It's a multi-person orgy in a giant inflatable pool, with everyone naked but still masked. This place is something else.

But it wasn't the show that got to me. No, I was only half paying attention to the performances. Every single ounce of my focus was on Liza. Watching her breaths come faster, the slight flush of arousal turning her face and chest a beautiful shade of pink, dragged me to the edge of self-restraint.

I don't want to hold on any longer.

My hands land on Liza's tight waistline, and I pull her against me. If she's not going to look at me, she's sure as shit going to feel me. Every inch of me.

"She wanted to make sure that I-I'm having fun."

Bullshit. Paulina is attracted to her. I could sense it the

moment the manager tied on Liza's mask. While, on the surface, the idea of the two women together is hot, jealousy flares beneath my skin.

Despite Liza's casual explanation, I can sense her nerves. See them in the way her throat works to swallow and the flutter of her pulse at the base of her neck. She's equally affected by me as I am by her.

What I'm doing is very un-bodyguard-like, but I don't have it in me to care right now. Just like I don't have it in me to care that she's engaged to my so-called business partner. Rational thought has left my mind because she's softened into my touch, her body flush against mine.

"Really?" I rasp. "Because I think she wants you. Not that I can blame her." I brush one of my fingers down her arm, like Paulina did.

Liza's breath catches in her throat.

"Did you like her touch?"

She's quiet for a moment. The unfiltered sounds of other people's pleasure fill the space between us. I'm sure she's going to come to her senses and shut this down, but she doesn't. She very deliberately leans back and wiggles her ass against my crotch, causing me to hiss out a Russian curse.

"N-not as much as I like this." Her words are so low they're almost inaudible.

But I know what I heard, and I'm floored by her brazenness. Floored, but really fucking turned-on.

"Oh yeah, milaya? Would you like to experience the same pleasure that you saw tonight?" I slide my palm up the side of her body and stop just underneath her left breast. Her ribs expand against my hand with every quickened breath she takes. "Because I can help with that."

When she remains silent, I thread my fingers through her hair at the roots and pull, drawing a moan from her. She purposefully grinds her hips back, against my painfully hard cock that's now leaking pre-cum.

"I'm not a man to play with. If you want me to make you feel good, you need to use your words."

"Please," she hisses. "Yes."

The moment the word leaves her mouth, I'm on her. "Watch the show."

I drop small kisses along her neck, inhaling her intoxicating scent, as my left hand covers her breast, molding and shaping it to my delight.

A groan escapes her lips.

I lift her long dress from the back, my palm running lazily over her hips until it dips between her legs. Her panties are already soaking wet—the culmination of a night's worth of arousal.

It's not like anyone can see us, bathed in the shadows, but I still make sure to arrange the front of her dress so it hangs low, covering what I'm about to do to her. From behind, I push her panties aside and run two fingers over her silky slit.

We each release a deep groan at the first whisper of my touch. She squeezes her thighs together, and from the way her body reacts to my barest touch, I know she's going to come beautifully all over my fingers.

"This is wrong," she murmurs, eyes closed, as wet heat gathers between her thighs, dripping over my hand.

"So wrong," I agree with a gentle circle of her clit that has her mewling and biting her lip.

She's thirteen years younger than me and, according to her fiancé, a virgin. As much as I'd love to sneak into her bed tonight and make her come on my face before taking her on my dick, she'll come to her senses the moment we leave here. Which is why I'm going to enjoy every delicious moment of tonight.

I drag my teeth across my bottom lip. "I'd love to find out if your tits taste as sweet as I think they will."

"Roman." She groans when I pinch her nipple over her dress while the pads of my fingers circle her tender clit.

I suck on her neck, taking care not to bruise her. As much as I'd love to see my marks on her golden skin, there'd be no way to hide it from Kira—or Anatoly, for that matter.

Her breathing shallows, and I know she's close.

"Watch the show," I instruct. "Imagine it's me doing all those filthy things to your body." I suck one of her earlobes into my mouth as I slide a finger inside of her.

She stiffens momentarily but then throws her head back and moans. Her pussy walls grip my finger, and the way her tight heat would grip my cock … Shit, I don't think I'd last more than a few minutes.

"That's right," I coax her, making sure my thumb is still pressing against her swollen clit. "Let yourself go. Come for me."

Holy crap, she's not the only one about to let go. My balls are tighter than a steel knot, and with the head of my cock pushing tight against the crook of her ass, I'm a man on the verge.

Her eyes fall closed, and she takes an unsteady breath as I hit the right rhythm. From not too far away, it sounds like we're not the only ones hitting our climax. Her pussy throbs against my touch, and soon after, I feel her body tense as her orgasm builds.

Hearing her little cries and feeling her squirm in my arms, I don't have it in me to hold off anymore. With a final flick to her clit, I bring her ass flush again my cock and rut into her with a groan. Feeling the cum trickling out of her and over my fingers sets me off. The tingling deep in my balls is the only warning I get before I flood my underwear.

"Motherfucker," I bite out.

I shut my eyes and struggle to steady my breath as Liza melts into my arms. I don't think she realizes she made me explode in my pants like a damn teenager. I should be mortified. I should be repentant—after all, I made my business partner's soon-to-be wife come all over my hand.

But I'm neither of these things. In fact, I feel like a million bucks.

The show is still in full swing, which means we have a few more minutes before we need to find Kira. Liza turns in my arms to look up at me, her eyes wide and confused like she can't believe what she's done.

But I can.

"I just came from rubbing myself on your perfect body."

Her jaw swings open.

I reach my hand in my pants and swipe a finger through the pool of cum gathered in my underwear, then smear the wetness over her lips.

She looks startled but doesn't move, doesn't even dare to breathe.

"You look perfect with my cum on your lips," I whisper and then hold her head in place to run my tongue over her plump, beautifully parted mouth.

She pulls away. "We can't— This was … a mistake."

"Don't worry, milaya." I give her a cold smile. "This will remain our little secret."

She won't look at me while she smooths down her dress and runs her fingers through her hair to put herself back together again. A beautiful pink flush stains her cheeks, but I'm sure many people will mistake it for the glow of arousal that most of the patrons are sporting.

"Find Kira," I instruct. "I'll meet you both at the front."

She nods and scurries away.

I know I'm playing with fire in a situation where I can't afford to get burned. It's fine; this was a one-time thing. A loss of control for both of us. If you go to a sex club, you are sure to sin.

I send Feliks a text to bring the car to the front entrance.

I need to get back to the hotel, shower, fix a fucking drink, and do everything in my power to forget the sound Liza makes when she comes and the taste of my seed on her skin.

CHAPTER SIXTEEN

LIZA

I don't sleep a wink. Instead, I sit by the windowsill, staring at the drizzly, empty streets below. My mind races, stuck on a loop.

What the hell was I thinking, letting Roman touch me like that? It was reckless and impulsive—a result of getting swept up in the night's debauchery—but it was also crazy hot. Before last night, no man had ever made me orgasm.

His gaze as I walked around the club was its own form of foreplay. When he dragged me into a dark corner and whispered his desire against my neck, I couldn't resist him. I was keyed up, primed, and so ready for his touch.

The instant his body pressed against mine, everything else ceased to exist. There was only the electrifying connection between us. Even if it's a connection we can never act on again.

I lean my forehead against the windowsill, trying to cool the heat of my sins, but nothing will erase tonight from my memory. The way he pulled me against his hard body and let his fingers wander between my legs. His strong hands kneading my breasts. Him using my body to get off, wiping the proof of his possession on my lips afterward.

I should have been horrified; instead, I was ridiculously turned-on.

Thank God Kira was lost in her own lust-fueled haze. I'm pretty sure she spent the ride back to the hotel sexting Maxim, then she vanished into her room as soon as we got back to the penthouse.

I also disappeared before I could exchange a word with Roman. What would I say? He knows as well as I do that there will never be a repeat performance. It was a moment of weakness for both of us, and I hope like hell we'll never speak of it again.

My one consolation is that Roman has as much at stake as I do. He won't jeopardize the deal with the Petrovitches. It would be foolish.

We'll both take this sin to the grave.

Roman isn't the only indiscretion keeping me awake. There's also Paulina's offer.

Two things have become clear to me over the last twenty-four hours: first, I'd do anything to escape Anatoly, and second, I'm more gutsy than I realized. If I can take pleasure in a dark corner of a sex club, I can sell my virginity to the highest bidder.

It's crazy to even consider, but desperation has taken root, and I can't pass up what may be my only chance at freedom. For my future, my sanity, and my sister, doing nothing is not an option.

Sure, the idea of sex with a stranger—one depraved enough to bid on someone's innocence like it's a prize to be won—twists my stomach. But what's one night of selling my body compared to a lifetime with a man who sickens me?

Am I naïve to believe Anatoly will allow me to leave him?

Possibly. But maybe he'll realize I'm not worth the trouble, that I'm too much work. He could take the money and be done with me. There are plenty of other women who would worship the ground he walks on, but I'll never be one of them.

I reach for my cell and pull up the investment app I have hidden on my phone. I've been trading in hundreds of dollars, but if I go through with the auction, I would have so much more to work with. Could I turn $100 thousand into a million dollars in under three weeks?

It's a long shot. A very long shot, but I have to at least try.

Officially giving up on sleep, I prop up in bed and spend the next two hours crunching numbers and strategizing. Day-trading—rapidly buying and selling high-risk stocks—seems to be the best way to make a lot of money quickly, even though it's risky. I could lose everything. But as the saying goes: the bigger the risk, the bigger the reward.

I'm willing to take my chances.

If this works, I won't have to walk down the aisle toward Anatoly. I'll gain my freedom and independence without dragging Kira or anyone else into the nightmare that is my life.

But if I fail? I'll have no choice but to go through with the marriage, given how much money we owe his family. If we can't repay them, I have a terrible feeling he'd set his sights on Sofiya and my parents won't stop him.

The only way for the plan to work is to keep it under wraps. I'll invest in secret and hope like hell I can make enough money to free myself before the wedding.

Anatoly is abusive. I've hesitated to use that term because it's hard to admit, even to myself, but there's no better word for it. I need to confront the fact that his abuse—whether emotional or physical—will only get worse.

Staring at Paulina's business card, I see a sliver of light in the darkness for the first time in what feels like forever.

Kira is sitting at the dining room table, having breakfast, when I join her around eight. I've showered and changed, and hopefully, I don't look as ragged as I feel because I need her to believe the story I'm about to tell.

"Good morning," I greet her, flashing a big smile as I sit down at the table.

"Coffee?" She holds up the carafe.

"Definitely." I nod, grateful.

Feliks and Bogdan are nowhere to be seen, but Roman is in the next room, a phone pressed to his ear. His back is to us, and he's staring out the window, speaking in a hushed tone.

"How did you sleep?" Kira eyes me carefully.

"Fine, actually." I reach for a croissant. "You?"

"Like the dead." She takes a minute to stir milk into her tea before her eyes meet mine. "I hope you weren't weirded out about last night. I wanted you to experience something different. Once we leave today …" She shrugs. "Everything will change."

"Exactly," I say emphatically, "which is why I think we should stay one more day. What do you think? We could visit that little shop in Kensington you liked and check out Covent Garden Market." I hold my breath, eager for her to agree.

Kira's face falls. "I'd love to, but I can't. Maxim and I have a fundraising event tonight that we can't miss." She pauses in thought, then her eyes widen. "But you can stay! The suite is yours for as long as you want it, and I'm sure one of the men can stay and guard you."

I shake my head. "That's entirely unnecessary. I'll be fine without a guard," I insist.

Kira looks like she's about to argue, but another voice fills the space between us.

"Who's going without a guard?" Roman steps into the room, looking extra delicious. His dark brown hair is still wet from the shower, curling slightly over the top of his collar. He swipes a muffin from the tray on the table and lowers down beside me.

My heart beats triple time when I get a whiff of his aftershave. Memories from last night come flooding back.

Roman's gaze travels over me as heat rises to my cheeks.

"No one is going without a guard." Kira sends me a pointed look, and it takes me a minute to remember what we're talking about. To Roman, she says, "Liza's going to extend her holiday for a few days. Who can stay with her? Feliks?"

Roman's jaw hardens. "I don't think so. He'll be busy overseeing a shipment coming from Italy."

Kira's eyebrows pull together. "Okay … Bogdan, then?"

"Mmm, nope. He'll be with you and Maxim at the fundraiser." Roman takes a big bite of the muffin in his hand and blinks at Kira blankly.

"It's fine," I say to my friend. "Really, I'm good."

Kira looks unsure, but she can't force a guard on me. I'm about to call the matter settled when Roman scrapes his chair back, the sound echoing off the walls in the small room.

"I can't leave you without a guard," he says plainly.

Irritation blazes up my spine. "Says who?"

"Says Maxim Belov. I was put in charge of your safety. As a soon-to-be Petrovich, you're a high-value target."

I'm sure Anatoly will be furious to learn I'm spending another day in London, but I have no intention of giving him advance warning. I'd rather ask for forgiveness than permission. But it seems Roman might be a thorn in my side.

My fingers tighten around the handle of my mug. I give Roman a warning look, but he continues to eat his muffin, completely unfazed.

Kira sighs. "In that case, surely we can clear Feliks's sched—"

Roman clears his throat. "I'll stay."

My breath hitches. Roman is going to stay here with me … alone? My brain scrambles to make sense of what that means.

Kira tilts her head. "Really?"

I'm still too shocked to respond.

Roman lifts a shoulder. "Why not? What's a day or two more? The shipment is not due for a few days, and I can coordinate everything from here."

I try to be casual. "I'm sure you have better things to do. I'm happy to plant myself in the hotel spa for a few days. Security in the hotel is top-notch, so you won't have to worry about me. I don't want to inconvenience anyone."

"It's not an inconvenience." He takes another huge bite of his muffin, watching me as he chews.

I shoot Kira a pleading look.

She throws her hands in the air. "I don't mean to be a mother hen, but what does it hurt to have a guard?"

This is not good, not good at all, but arguing it any further would be suspicious. Not that I believe Roman's casual I've-got-nothing-better-to-do act.

Is he staying because he wants something more to happen between us? A shot of something hot fills my veins. While that idea is thrilling, I'm here for one purpose only.

With just him and me alone in the suite, slipping away unnoticed won't be simple. I'll have to be crafty.

"So it's settled." Kira pats her lips with her napkin, looking from Roman to me. "You'll both stay for another day or two. I'll send the plane back so you can use it to fly home when you're ready."

Roman crosses his arms, looking way too smug. When I finally meet his eyes with a hard stare, he raises his brows.

"Thank you," I say with a bright smile. "Guess I'm not ready for the fun to end."

Kira narrows her eyes. "Does this have something to do with avoiding wedding planning?"

"That might have something to do with it," I mutter.

Kira stands and loops her arms around my neck. "I'm happy you're doing something for yourself. You deserve this, you know—a little more time, a little space."

Guilt pierces through my chest at how easily lies slip off my tongue. But I'm doing what I have to do.

"I'll make the best of my time here," I say and mean it.

CHAPTER SEVENTEEN

ROMAN

"ARE YOU AVOIDING ME?"

Liza's back stiffens, and she removes her palm from the suite's front doorknob. She was trying to make a getaway before I noticed.

She turns around slowly, her expression giving nothing away. She's dressed in yoga pants, a cropped T-shirt, and sandals, and her hair is in a messy bun. A gym bag is slung over her shoulder.

Definitely avoiding me.

"Not at all." Liza straightens her shoulders. "Like I mentioned earlier, I'm spending the day at the hotel spa."

I cross my arms and lean against the wall beside her, enjoying the way her eyes dip and travel over my inked biceps. "In case you forgot how this works, I'm your guard. Where you go, I go."

She swallows thickly and tucks a strand of hair behind her ears. "Security is tight in this hotel—you said so yourself. I don't think a man would be appreciated in the women's-only spa area."

"Let's cut the bullshit. You're avoiding me because of last night."

From the moment Kira left with Feliks and Bogdan an hour ago, Liza hasn't said a word to me. She's been hiding in her room. But if it's going to be her and me for the next couple of days, we need to clear the air.

Her hands land on her hips. "Fine. You want to cut the bullshit?" she challenges. "Why are you here, alone with me, when you could've arranged for anyone else to take over from you?"

She's too smart for me to lie to her, so I don't bother trying.

I take a step forward, and she instinctively backs up until she's plastered against the wall.

With an arm braced on either side of her, I narrow the gap between us. "Because I don't want anyone else looking after you. Not Feliks, not Bogdan. No one."

Vulnerability flickers across her face before her hands slowly raise until they're both pressed flat against my chest. My heart pounds against her palms.

"We can't," Liza says. "You know that. I think we can both agree that we were caught up in the moment. It shouldn't have happened, and it can't happen again."

I grit my teeth, painfully aware that we can't risk another repeat—too much is at stake. Letting Maxim down by messing up our deal with the Petroviches isn't an option, but I can't seem to convince myself to wash my hands of this woman. Knowing you're an idiot and doing something about it are two different things.

"What's the real reason you don't want to go home yet?" I ask. "Scared you won't be able to look your fiancé in the eye?"

She closes her eyes and tips her head back. "You have no idea what you're talking about."

"So tell me." I lean in so close that my breath grazes her cheek, and I run the pad of my finger over her pulse point.

She shivers but closes her eyes, attempting to block me out.

"Tell me if I got this all wrong. If you never want me to touch you again, say it, and I'll never touch you again."

Her mouth opens and closes. Unable to meet my gaze, she looks past me. "You're wrong," she finally whispers. "After today, I'll happily go home and start planning my wedding to Anatoly. Like I said, this was a mistake. We were both swept up, but"—she swallows thickly—"we need to put it behind us."

I push off the wall and give her space.

I don't believe her, not for one minute. But it doesn't matter. Whether I believe her or not, it won't change a thing. If anything, she did both of us a favor by shutting down the possibility of more. I should thank her, but I'm not feeling that generous.

A beat passes. Silence hangs heavily between us.

"Understood," I say in a clipped tone. "I'll escort you downstairs."

She eyes me warily before shaking her head. "Not necessary."

"That's not your call to make. I'm still your guard. Once you're in the spa, hotel security can take over."

She nods, and I gesture for her to walk ahead of me. But I don't miss the tremor in her hands, nor the way her eyes stay glued to the floor.

I'm in a foul mood for the rest of the day. I try and fail to get any actual work done. When my phone finally rings, jolting me from my racing thoughts, I realize I've spent the last hour pacing aimlessly around the suite.

"Privet," I growl, seeing Pavel's name flash across the screen.

"So, you're staying in London. Alone. With Liza." He doesn't bother hiding the amusement in his tone.

Jesus. Word travels fast.

"Can't leave her without a guard, can I?"

"Definitely not. And you definitely couldn't have rearranged Feliks's or Bogdan's schedule either."

If I could shoot my hand through the line and strangle Pavel, I would. He may be my bratan, but I don't appreciate the reminder that Liza is off-limits.

"Did you call to give me shit, or do you actually have something to say?"

"Both, actually."

"Well, save the lecture. Nothing's going to happen." Nothing more, that is. "Why'd you call?"

He immediately sobers. "I have an update. It seems Anatoly took Sofiya to Beluga the night he drove her back to school."

My eyebrows pull together in confusion. "The restaurant?"

"No, the whale."

"Fuck off."

Beluga is a high-end restaurant in Moscow, with a private dining room that Anatoly likes to use for his business meetings. He's dragged us there several times.

"Our hackers were able to get CCTV footage of Anatoly's car parked around the back of the restaurant for hours. As far as we can tell, Sofiya was with him the entire time. The cameras didn't capture anyone entering or exiting the restaurant, but two other armored vehicles were parked near Anatoly's. They weren't civilian vehicles—not with armored plates and blacked-out windows—and they didn't belong to his guards. They were parked to the side."

I sit down on the couch, my fingers drumming impatiently on my thigh. "Assuming he was there for a business meeting, why bring Sofiya? She's a teenager."

Pavel pauses. "There could be a simple explanation for all of this. And Sofiya's seventeen, nearly the legal drinking age. We can't jump to conclusions until we know more. Our men have eyes on Anatoly. So far, nothing out of the ordinary to report."

I grind my molars. Something feels off, but it's possible I'm allowing everything I feel for Liza to color my perspective. Just because Anatoly's a shitty fiancé to Liza, it doesn't make him a predator.

I steer the conversation towards the many other syndicate issues Pavel and I need to discuss. With Maxim taking a step away from the business, Pavel has taken over our counterfeit operations, which range from art and wine to money, and even fake car parts.

As we discuss syndicate matters, I don't realize how much of the day has slipped away until I notice the sun going down over London. Liza should be back from the spa any minute now.

I've arranged for hotel security to escort her back to the suite. If I'm truly going to let this fucked-up obsession go, I need to avoid her as much as possible.

CHAPTER EIGHTEEN

LIZA

I wait until Roman is asleep. Or at least, I think he is. There's no way for me to know for sure, but I haven't heard a sound from his room after he turned off the TV, and that was hours ago.

It's almost midnight, which means I need to be in front of the hotel waiting for the driver in about fifteen minutes. I've taken a shower, curled my hair, applied makeup, and put on the dress that Paulina sent as a little gift. It's sexy, simple, and black. Really, the dress doesn't matter; as Paulina made clear earlier, it all comes off once I hit the stage.

The thought alone causes my heart to hammer so loudly that I can hear it in my ears. A flutter of nerves tickles my skin. I try to shake them off, but they cling stubbornly. This is easily the craziest, most daring thing I've ever done, but somehow the idea of not going through with it is even more scary.

I give myself a final once-over in the mirror, smoothing down the slinky fabric of my backless dress one last time. I covered the bruise Anatoly gave me with makeup, as I've been doing all week, but it's still tender—a reminder of why I'm doing this. What I need to escape.

I pick up my cell phone from the dressing table and see I have a missed call from Anatoly. It doesn't matter. I can't deal with him right now.

I power my phone off and leave it tucked away in a drawer. There's no point in taking it with me. While I'm confident no one can track me using my phone because of the security measures I have in place, I'm not taking a chance. Especially if Roman somehow discovers I'm missing.

An ache cuts through my chest at imagining how he'll react if he finds my bed empty in the middle of the night. Despite my earlier attempts to push him away, I know he'll tear up the city to find me. Not because he's my guard but because of whatever this is between us.

Was between us. I shut it down this morning. There was no other way.

I grab a small clutch, then drop my room key and a piece of paper with my bank details into it, along with a hundred-pound note for cash—credit cards are traceable.

A pair of high heels dangle from my hand as I quietly slip out of my room and down the dark corridor.

Paulina's driver is waiting for me in front of the hotel. It's a short drive to Sanctuary, and I spend the entire time trying to rein in my anxiety and not think about what lies ahead.

The driver pulls up to the back of the club, and somehow that makes everything feel real. Last night seems like an entire lifetime ago. When we were dropped off in front of the club, I had no idea what was ahead of me. But tonight, everything changes.

The driver opens the back door for me and leads me through the club's rear entrance. Inside, Paulina is waiting, dressed much like last night in all black, though tonight's dress is more glamorous. It's shiny, tight, and off-the-shoulder.

Without a mask, I can see her face for the first time. She possesses an elegant beauty with high cheekbones and piercing blue eyes showing a hint of fine lines at the sides when she offers me a warm smile.

Paulina guides me into what appears to be a lounge area. The room is dotted with sumptuous velvet chairs. There's a small bar and a cozy fireplace that casts a warm glow across the space.

"Drink?" she suggests, breaking the silence.

"Please." I lower myself into one of the chairs. "Nothing too strong." I need something to take the edge off, but anything too potent will ramp up my anxiety.

She pops a bottle of champagne and pours me a glass. "It's normal to be nervous. Everyone is. But I want you to know, the buzz about you has been off the charts. You're the star tonight, darling. You'll have Europe's richest men bidding against each other for a chance to be with you."

I'm not sure if that's supposed to be comforting, but I guess she's reminding me why I'm here—for the money.

I take a big gulp of my drink before asking, "How much money will I earn?"

"We'll start the bidding ..." She pauses for a moment as if trying to gauge my reaction. "How much do you need?"

I swallow hard. "One hundred thousand dollars."

Her eyes widen. "There are no guarantees, but we'll start the bidding a little higher than usual. We take a thirty percent cut, but I have a good feeling you'll still come out ahead."

She lays out the paperwork in front of me—a contract, including an NDA, and a form for my banking details. It almost makes me laugh that there's bureaucracy even in selling one's virginity.

"Do you have any hard limits?" Paulina asks carefully. "Things you don't want to do."

The question makes my head spin. How am I supposed to know what my limits are?

My mind wanders back to last night. The scenes weren't exactly beginner level, and I'll admit some acts shocked me, but I was more intrigued than anything. Still, watching is one thing while participating is something else entirely.

I imagine myself in place of those women last night, but instead of nameless, faceless men, it's Roman's gorgeous profile that materializes in my head—he's the one doing all those forbidden things to me. Licking between my legs, pushing me down, fucking me, flogging my breasts, watching me penetrate myself with a toy …

Holy shit. I've let my mind wander far off the path. But when I picture anyone else but Roman, my excitement evaporates into thin air. Damn, I need to banish him from my thoughts and focus on the task ahead. Because that's what it is—a job. A means to an end.

"I don't want them to hurt me," I say. "And only one man; I won't be shared." She nods, and I consider what else. "No toys or floggers, or anything like that. No restraints, and they need to use a condom." I pause. "I know I sound boring and inexperienced but … Well, I am."

"And that's the point." Paulina shakes her head. "These men don't want a vixen. They don't want the kind of women you saw last night. They're paying top dollar for your innocence. To teach you things, to be in control." She purses her lips. "To be the first man inside of you."

I reach a shaky hand for my glass of champagne on the table in front of me. "I'll know my limits in the moment. Will they respect them?"

"If there's ever a problem, security will deal with them immediately."

My shoulders lower an inch. That's reassuring, at least.

"Do you have any more questions?" she asks gently.

My breath catches. "I probably do, but nothing's coming to me right now."

She squeezes my hand. "I'll be with you the entire time. Do you want to see the lingerie you can choose from?"

I try to steady my breathing.

Paulina leads me to a wardrobe at the back of the room. She opens it to reveal a selection of delicate lingerie in various colors and styles. "Take your time," she says, stepping back to give me space.

My eyes scan the options. There's a bold red set with black lace trim, a sultry black ensemble with sheer panels, and a playful pink piece with ruffles. But my gaze lands on a white lace bra and panties set, designed to reveal more than it hides.

Paulina notices my interest. "White, as in virginal," she suggests with a wink.

I reach out and touch the delicate fabric. The bra's lacework is intricate, paired with skimpy, lace-edged panties. Transparent garters attach to sheer stockings with little jewels that will run up the back of my thighs. It's bold yet somehow feels right.

"This one." I hold it up.

"Perfect choice. Go ahead and change, and then come out to show me."

I take the outfit and step into a small changing room. As I slip into the white lace, I feel a mix of nerves and excitement. The fabric feels cool against my skin, and the jewels on the stockings catch the light as I move.

Taking a deep breath, I step out of the changing room.

Paulina's eyes light up as she sees me. "Look at you." She spins me around so I look at myself in the mirror. "You're stunning. You deserve to be worshipped, even if only for a night."

My eyes draw upwards, and I drink in my reflection. I've never considered myself anything special, but I can't deny that with my hair spilling down my back, my lips bold and red, and high heels that appear to give everything a lift, I am something special.

Maybe even something to be worshipped.

CHAPTER NINETEEN

ROMAN

I knew something was up the minute I received a call from the hotel manager, who informed me that several packages had been delivered directly to the spa for Liza, with a note that read, *For tonight*.

It didn't really take a rocket scientist to figure out she was preparing for an eventful night—one she conveniently never mentioned to me.

It's just before midnight when I hear Liza sneak out. I'm impressed by how quiet she is. The opening and closing of the front door to the suite is nearly soundless; I can just make out a small click as the door shuts behind her.

Standing, I look out the window with a clear view of the entrance below. Not two minutes pass before she appears, her silhouette unmistakable. Her dark hair flows over her shoulders, and her coat catches the breeze as she slips into a waiting limo.

Tension coils beneath my skin. Is this why she wanted to extend her trip? Because she's meeting someone? Maybe a man or woman she met last night?

Maybe Paulina.

Shit. I can barely stand thinking of her with Anatoly, but the idea that there's someone else pisses me off so thoroughly that I grab a pack of smokes from my drawer and light up, hotel's anti-smoking policies be damned. I inhale until my lungs burn and the nicotine spreads through my veins, calming my racing nerves.

I open my laptop and check the trackers I'd discreetly placed in her shoes, purse, and coat earlier, anticipating she might ditch her cell phone. My hunch was correct.

A blinking dot appears on the screen, heading towards Soho.

I stub out the cigarette and drum my fingers on the windowsill, trying to get a read on the jumble of emotions clogging my chest. I need to psych myself up for whatever I'm going to find.

Liza with another man or woman. Maybe both.

Traffic being light at this time of night, it doesn't take her vehicle long to arrive at its destination. I bite out a laugh when I realize where she's gone—back to Sanctuary.

Apparently, she didn't get enough of the show last night.

Well, if it's a show she wants, it's a show she'll get.

"I'm sorry, sir, but I don't believe you're on the guest list." A statuesque woman with sharp eyes and a tight bun, holding a clipboard, scans the sheet of paper in front of her again. "Tonight is a private event."

A private event? What the hell does that mean?

"I was a guest here last night. Paulina personally invited me." I pause then add, "Or I can call Aiden Donnelley, the owner. He's a friend of mine. I'm sure he'd be happy to clarify my identity."

She frowns and consults one of the giant bouncers behind her.

After some digging, I discovered that Sanctuary is run by the Irish mafia, the Donnelley brothers, who are associates of mine. If necessary, a phone call to them should secure my entry.

However, that turns out to be unnecessary as Ms. Tight Bun waves me through. After being frisked by security, I'm escorted into the main room by one of the topless ballerinas in a black tutu. She gives me some hot and heavy looks, but my only interest is in finding Liza.

"Can I get you a drink, Sir?" the ballerina asks as I scan the crowd for Liza, who is nowhere to be found.

"I need to see Paulina." I have a feeling that even if they're not together, Paulina will at least know where to find Liza.

The ballerina frowns. "As you can imagine, she'll be taking the stage soon and won't be available until afterward."

My brows draw together. "After what?"

She gives me an aren't-you-funny smile. "After the *proceedings*, of course. Good luck. Apparently, she's exquisite." She winks at me and saunters away.

Proceedings? Good luck?

Something about tonight is different in a way that puts me on edge.

It's then I take a good look around. It's not just Liza who isn't here, there are virtually no women in the room. It's all men, most of them decked out in sleek tuxedos with the unmistakable swagger and confidence that only radiates from the very rich.

What the fuck is Liza doing here?

An anticipatory buzz travels through the room. Uncertainty settles over me as the lights dim and a hush falls over the crowd. The burgundy velvet curtains part to reveal a stage erected at the front of the space.

Paulina steps onto a podium to address the crowd. "Gentlemen," she says with a practiced smile, "you'll undoubtedly agree that we've saved the best for last. It's not every day that we get to bid on such an exquisite treasure, especially not one all the way from Russia."

My blood goes cold, disbelief mingling with dread.

Bid. Exquisite treasure. Russia.

"I can assure you this treasure comes from a family of a high pedigree. She's a good girl, but for the right man here tonight, she wants to be bad for the first time. And one of you lucky men will have the pleasure of corrupting her."

An itch blooms under my skin and makes me feel like obliterating each and every man in this room.

Hearty chuckles and murmurs of approval spread through the audience, along with a smattering of applause. The men here are hungry—I can feel the predatory tension ripple through the audience.

"Are you ready to meet this fine jewel, gentlemen?" Paulina asks.

The man beside me yells out something about craving a taste of her innocence, and I shoot him a look so full of venom that he gets up and moves to the far side of the room.

"You all know how this works, so don't be shy. This sweet peach will go quickly … and for a pretty penny. The bidding for her virginity starts at fifty thousand US dollars. Let's see our rare beauty."

A platform lowers from the ceiling as hollers and jeers explode around the room. My lungs can barely draw in a full breath as the woman being auctioned off comes into full view.

Poison spreads through my veins. It'll be a miracle if I get through tonight without committing murder because they're all staring at Liza like they have a chance in hell with her.

They don't.

Blood will spill before anyone outbids me.

CHAPTER TWENTY

LIZA

Paulina warned me this would be the toughest part, and she was right. As the platform lowers onto the stage, and I feel all eyes on me, I think I'm going to be sick. The one saving grace is that I can't see any of the audience members because of the bright spotlight on me. Yet even without seeing them, I sense their presence—leering, judging, assessing.

The moment the platform touches down, Paulina steps forward and takes my hand.

"Ladies and gentlemen, here is our flower. A spring bloom, ripe and willing for the right man ... at the right price," she adds with a naughty tone.

A sour sensation fills my stomach, but she holds eye contact. Her words say one thing, but her eyes say, *Don't focus on what's happening out there. Look at me*. For that, I'm grateful.

She leads me across the stage to the right side of the platform, presenting me to the onlookers with a flourish that reminds me of those old car commercials where the presenter grandly reveals the new model. I'm the car in this scenario, and the audience eats it up.

I'm only half-aware of a man—the auctioneer—taking his place at the podium. "Gentlemen, as previously stated, bidding for the chance to take the virginity of this beautiful woman in front of you starts at $50 thousand. Kindly raise your hand to confirm your bid. Bidding opens now. Do I have fifty thousand? Excellent. Almost everyone in the room. Fantastic. Fifty-five. Can I get $55 thousand? Indeed, I can. Such enthusiasm."

God, this is humiliating. Although, not as humiliating as what comes next.

"Lose the dress. We deserve to see the ass we're bidding on," someone shouts from the crowd, sparking a wave of laughter that churns my stomach.

Paulina warned me of this. That they'd want to see me strip, and I'd have to decide how much I wanted to bare.

The room reeks of cologne and whisky, amplifying my nausea, but ... In for a penny, in for a pound.

I give Paulina a slight nod to indicate that she can help me take off my dress.

She moves behind me. Her hands are warm on my skin as she unfastens the hook of my dress at the top of the zipper. "You're doing great," she whispers, giving me a slight squeeze, before she slowly peels the fabric away, revealing the soft lace lingerie hugging my frame.

The dress slips down to the floor, and I step out of it with a mixture of reluctance and resolve.

The crowd breaks into applause, their eyes drinking me in as the barely there lace of my lingerie becomes visible, clinging to my curves and accentuating every line of my body.

I must be frozen in place because Paulina gently touches my arm, steadying me.

Her encouragement helps me lift my chin with newfound boldness.

She leads me to the other side of the stage, where I do a

little spin despite my nerves, showing off my body to a roomful of strangers. There are more catcalls and jeers, but I block them out. This may be humiliating, but a lifetime with Anatoly is far worse.

"Show us your tits. I want to see the shade your nipples will turn when I suck on them," a voice calls from the crowd.

I stiffen, hating the crude requests. Hating that they only see me as an object to be bought and sold, but what did I expect?

Paulina's hand runs over my back, landing on the clasp of my bra. She lifts her eyebrows in question. "I want you to earn top dollar," she murmurs.

Now is the time to decide how far I'm willing to go.

With my heart in my throat, I give a little nod, and she undoes the hook of my bra, letting the white lace slowly slide down my shoulders. For one long moment, I hold the fabric against my breasts, finding it hard to let go. Gathering my courage, I let the bra fall, revealing myself completely. I feel exposed and vulnerable as the crowd roars its approval. Despite being completely out of my depth, I know I have to give them what they want—a little show.

Shame coats my skin, but I push it down deep within.

Taking a full breath, I manage a seductive little spin and run my hands over my bare stomach. As my nipples stiffen in the crisp air, the yelling intensifies along with lewd remarks. The crowd's excitement drives the bids higher, reaching numbers beyond my wildest dreams.

Sixty thousand dollars.

Seventy thousand dollars.

Even more.

Two men compete, driving the price up over $100 thousand.

For this price, what will they expect from me? A sinking feeling drags in my belly like an anchor. Will the highest bidder respect my limits?

Before I can dwell on it, Paulina leads me to the front of the stage. "Turn around and touch your toes," she whispers. "You've gone this far; you might as well see it through."

I know she's right, but it's still so humiliating. My face burns with heat as I turn away from the audience and, with my back arched, slowly dip down to touch the floor. Holding in place, wearing only lace underwear and stilettos, I've never felt so exposed.

The crowd responds, and the bets go up over $150 thousand. A little spark of excitement takes hold. This wasn't for nothing. I've already made more than I hoped to.

"Take it all off. Show us your pussy already. We don't have all night … unless we buy you." A voice from the audience. I don't like how he sounds—aggressive and hungry, like I owe him something. Like he already owns me.

The auctioneer pauses the bidding, giving me a chance to decide. I freeze like a deer in headlights, caught between wanting to get this over with and make the most amount of money, and holding on to a thread of self-respect.

This time, when Paulina looks at me for confirmation, I shake my head. I won't be bullied into getting naked in front of an audience.

But the crowd doesn't care. It's not one voice anymore; now, it's a chorus demanding I take it all off, that I show them my pussy. That I touch myself and give them a little show.

The crowd grows wilder, more menacing. On instinct, I wrap my arms around my waist as my panic grows. Even Paulina seems unnerved by the crowd's fervor.

Feeling entirely out of my depth, I realize there's nothing to do but get through the auction and hope like hell that whoever wins me has a shred of decency. Because I'm in way over my head.

CHAPTER TWENTY-ONE

ROMAN

An ice pick lodges itself in my chest, cold and sharp, the moment I see her on stage. My blood seethes with a violent urge to kill every onlooker, but I'm also furious at Liza herself.

Is she so in need of money that she's willing to sell herself like a commodity on the open market for any man to bid on? She's engaged to a very rich man, and unless this gives her a little thrill, this makes no fucking sense to me.

But I'll get my answers in time. I have more urgent issues to contend with right now. Like the way every man's hungry gaze roams over her body. Their lust incites my rage.

Liza looks like a goddess fully dressed, but wearing nothing more than a few scraps of lace, she's perfection—smooth golden skin, flared hips, a generous ass, and perky breasts with rose-tinged nipples just visible through the delicate white lace hugging her curves.

A maddening feeling of possession pumps through my veins. She may not belong to me, but she doesn't belong to these mudaks either, and I'll make sure every man in this room understands she's not theirs to claim before the auction's over.

I can't stand the look of vulnerability that washes over her face with every crude jeer and whistle. It took raw nerve for her to step onto that stage, but any trace of that courage has vanished. The woman I see up there is drowning, in over her head.

But I won't step in, not yet. She needs to feel the weight of her mistake.

I stalk through the room, keeping tabs on the rowdy crowd and making a note of the more vocal ones—the men I'll have to kill before the night is over.

It's a long list, starting with the asshole in front of me.

"Show us your tits," he yells. "I want to see the shade your nipples will turn when I suck on them."

My muscles coil tight as Liza's cheeks turn crimson, and she stiffens. I circle the man who dares insult her and keep him within lunging distance.

On stage, Paulina whispers something to Liza. I'm going to guess it's a word of encouragement, because, with a small nod from Liza, the older woman unhooks her bra.

Fuck. Liza is going to bare all for these undeserving assholes. She hesitates—holding her bra in place, not ready to expose herself—but the moment is short-lived. Slowly, she allows the bra to fall forward, and her perky tits spring free with a little bounce.

Heat flares inside me. I didn't realize it was possible to feel such opposing emotions at once. On one hand, my dick aches. Her tits are perfect—the perfect size, the perfect color, the perfect shape—as I knew they would be. But on the other hand, having to share the view with the assholes in this room inspires violence. They don't deserve to breathe the same air as her, much less gaze upon her naked body.

The room breaks out in hollers and catcalls, and I snap, reaching for the Sig in my waistband, only to remember I left it at home, knowing I wouldn't be allowed in Sanctuary packing heat.

No bother. I've killed using my bare hands many times before. And I'm going to start with the motherfucker in front of me.

He's the loudest, the most demanding, and the crudest. He looks like your average finance douche, with a tightly pressed suit, a bad comb-over, and an air of smug entitlement. I'll take great joy in watching this mudak bleed out.

"Take it all off," the asshole yells. "Show us your pussy already. We don't have all night ... unless we buy you."

Liza can't hide her fear or intimidation at this point, but the crowd doesn't care. They're feeding off it. It turns these sick fucks on. They want her misery; they want to see her cry.

Even now, as her arms wrap around her slender waist and her nipples pucker in the cold air, it only serves to raise the bidding higher. She's already doubled her money, and the bidding is still going strong between two men in particular. They're both wasting their breath.

"I'm going win that bitch, and when I do, I'm going to fuck all of her holes raw," Comb-over slurs to his friend, rubbing his hands together. "She'll be so far from a virgin when I'm done with her she'll only be good for the whorehouse."

Something dark and dangerous crawls through my veins, and I can't hold back any longer. I had planned to keep the violence behind closed doors, but this man now signed his death warrant. It's time to put this shit to bed.

I reach for an empty champagne glass discarded on one of the tables. The crowd's raucous noise masks the sound of my next move. Gripping the stem tightly, I smash the glass against the edge of the table. It shatters, leaving a perfectly jagged edge.

A low burn smolders in my gut, growing hotter with each second as I wait for the right moment to strike.

"Come on, little Russian doll, I want to see the pink between your thi—"

He doesn't finish his sentence as I plunge the glass into his neck. Satisfaction roars through my system as he falls to the ground, crying out in agony. I kneel beside him. If I had the opportunity, his death would be much more drawn out and painful, but given the public venue, I keep it simple.

"This is what you get for being a sick bastard," I hiss into his ear as I twist the glass shard. Blood pours from his neck like a spout.

With one final look at his broken form, I stand, sensing the shock ripple through the crowd. The room collectively holds its breath.

Good. Let this serve as a warning to the others. The Donnelleys won't be thrilled that I openly shanked one of their clients, but I'm sure I can find a way to make it up to them. A gift basket of AK-47s perhaps. But right now, the only thing I care about is that Liza is spared this guy's abuse.

She squints into the crowd, a horrified expression growing on her face. Not that she can see anything down here, but she can hear the chaos unfolding, maybe even smell the metallic tang of blood in the air. The color drains from her face, and she looks ready to bolt.

There's nowhere for her to run. Nowhere for her to hide. No matter where she goes, I'll find her.

CHAPTER TWENTY-TWO

LIZA

"COME ON, LITTLE RUSSIAN DOLL, I WANT TO SEE THE PINK between your thi—"

He doesn't get the rest of the sentence out. Instead, the sound that comes from him can only be described as agony. It's part gurgle, part cry, but all pain, and then the thud of something—or someone—hitting the ground.

Just like that, everything seems to stop. The auctioneer goes silent, as does the crowd, with only panicked murmurs rippling through the room.

I squint into the audience to see what's going on, but I can only make out vague shapes. No one moves despite the sense of terror eclipsing the room.

One voice can be heard above all others—it's deep, gruff, and achingly familiar.

"She's mine for half a million dollars," he declares over the hushed crowd. "Anyone want to challenge me?"

There's not a peep from the audience.

"Going once, going twice … This auction is fucking over."

My blood goes ice-cold.

No, just no. Even for that wild amount of money, I can't.

The room falls into a stunned silence, the echo of his declaration hanging heavy in the air. The auctioneer stands frozen, his eyes darting to Paulina for guidance.

The expression on her face is pure triumph. "We have a winner," she declares. "For half a million dollars."

She thinks we've won, that we've hit the jackpot.

How very wrong she is.

Paulina is overflowing with excitement as she escorts me offstage.

"Liza, this is unreal," she squeals. "That's the highest winning bid we've ever had."

"You don't understand." My heart thuds like a hammer against my chest. "This isn't good. I know the man who won me."

Paulina gives me a confused look, but she has no idea who Roman is and what he's capable of.

Kira has always said Roman is an angel unless provoked—then, he's a complete psycho. Tonight was proof. I smelled the heavy scent of blood in the air and heard the chilling gurgle that followed. That was Roman's handiwork.

Paulina huffs out a breath. "Well … is that a bad thing?"

It is if it's your fiancé's business partner and a dangerous gangster.

"Yes." A fresh wave of anxiety rolls through me. "You need to void the contract. He's— He's dangerous."

"Sweetie." She grabs my shoulders like I'm a child having a tantrum. "That man, whoever he is, is paying half a million dollars for one night with you. That's life-changing money. Think of what you could do with it."

Right now, I'm not thinking of the money. I'm thinking about facing Roman's wrath.

I lied to him, snuck out of the suite, and worst of all, he knows my secret. That I'm hopeless enough to sell my virginity. Embarrassment coats my skin at imagining what he'll do with this information. Will he hold it over me? Threaten to tell Anatoly?

Roman has no reason to protect me. Not after I lied to him this morning, claiming there's nothing between us … that I'm looking forward to marrying Anatoly.

Another thought causes my breath to catch in my throat. Will he take my virginity for himself?

Blood thrums in my ears. Oh God, I'm in way too deep.

Gripping Paulina's arm, I force her to stop and listen to me. "I can't go through with it."

Her mouth flattens into a hard line. "You don't have a choice."

My knees threaten to buckle, and I have to hold the wall to steady myself. "You said I always have a choice."

She sighs and rubs at her temple. "Okay, calm down. I'll talk to him and figure out what's going on." She leads me to a room with a red door with the number five on it. "Wait in here. I'll be back."

I blow out a heavy breath. "Thank you." She gives me a final look I can't interpret before she shuts the door behind her.

Jesus, that was a close call.

With a tentative step forward, I take in my surroundings. The room is spacious and comfortable, reminiscent of what I imagine high-end suites in Vegas look like, with its red and black color scheme. A large, plush bed dominates the space, its black silk sheets reflecting the soft lighting. Opposite the bed, a framed gold mirror spans the length of the room, allowing for views from every angle. When I look up, I realize that includes the ceiling as well.

Oh shit. This is clearly a room designed for more than a good night's sleep.

As my gaze wanders, it catches the silver gleam of handcuffs and restraints discreetly attached to each corner of the bed. Realization lands hot and heavy on my skin. This is a sex room. The room where it all happens. There's a reason I'm in here.

Paulina has no intention of forfeiting the money. Why would she? The house takes thirty percent, and thirty percent of half a million dollars is a substantial amount.

I don't have a plan or a clear escape route, but I know without question I need to get the hell out of here. Now.

Swinging the door open, I take two steps forward before I collide with a giant boulder. A living, breathing boulder well over six feet tall, covered in tattoos, and goes by the name of Roman Vasiliev.

Shock steals my breath. I cry out and stupidly try to dart around him, but a band of muscle wraps around my waist and pulls my back against his hard chest.

"Where do you think you're going, milaya?" His breath is hot on my skin, his voice a dark rumble.

"I'm leaving. I don't care how much money you bid. I won't take it, and I definitely won't be doing anything with you," I hiss, fighting against his hold.

"That's really too bad because Paulina already processed my banking information. Which means …" He pushes me back inside the room and closes the door behind him. "You're mine for the night."

CHAPTER TWENTY-THREE

LIZA

Panic unfurls in my belly. "What do you mean by that? That I owe you my … virginity?"

He takes a step closer, his warm breath coasting over my skin. My bare breasts tighten under his intense gaze. I wish I had a T-shirt, a bra, or anything to cover myself.

"That's what I paid for. Isn't my money as good as anyone else's?"

A shiver rolls through me at the insinuation he expects me to go through with it, to sleep with him.

"No," I gasp. "This is different. You're my guard. You're in business with my fiancé!"

"About that," he says with a sneer. "Does Anatoly not give you enough of an allowance? You seem to wear nothing but designer clothes and jewelry, but apparently, that's still not enough for you."

I grimace, hating the implication that I'm money hungry. But it's better he believes that's the reason for my actions than discovering my true motives.

My eyes unintentionally drift downward, away from his

accusing gaze, and catch a splash of red on the cuff of his sleeve. It brings everything into stark focus.

Goose bumps prickle my skin, fueled by both fear and excitement. "What did you do?" I whisper.

Roman's eyes darken. "He needed to be taught a lesson. I hated those men looking at you, fantasizing about you. Thinking they had a chance when you were never going to be theirs. It drove me crazy."

I swallow hard. "Did you kill him?"

"There's a chance he lived." He brushes a knuckle down my cheek. "But it would be a miracle."

I must be as depraved as him, because instead of feeling repulsed, a low simmer of heat stirs in my belly. He killed a man to protect me in his own twisted way. I know Roman is rich, but he spent half a million dollars to end the auction for me.

"Are you going to hold up your part of the bargain?" His eyes scan the length of me. "Because I don't think I can stand here, with you half naked, for much longer without blowing a load in my pants." He smirks. "Something you seem to inspire in me."

My pulse races, mirroring the throbbing between my legs. I swallow hard and lift my chin. Would it really be the worst thing to have sex with Roman? He's hot and experienced. He's already proven he knows how to get me off. And sleeping with him is the best way to make sure he doesn't tell anyone else. That he keeps it our little secret. He has as much at stake as I do.

"Like you said." I force a confidence I don't feel. "Your money is as good as anyone else's."

His eyebrows pull together, and his mouth flattens into a hard line. "Is that the only reason?"

I shrug nonchalantly, even though nonchalant is the furthest thing from how I feel. "Let's make a deal. You take my virginity—right here, tonight, like any other buyer would

—and in the morning, we go home to Moscow and never speak of this again. No one can ever know," I stress.

He hisses sharply, and the sound vibrates up my spine like electricity. "Anatoly is going to figure out you're not a virgin on your wedding night, and there's going to be hell to pay."

"Let that be my problem. Your name will never come up either way," I assure him.

"Fuck, Liza." He breathes out harshly, his eyes darkening. "You're forbidden fruit, and I can't bring myself to fight against it." He reaches out and wraps a hand around the back of my neck, tugging me against him.

His lips crash against mine, and all thought evaporates as he urges my mouth open. I allow him entry, and his tongue slips inside, electricity coursing through me with every hot stroke.

My body is on fire. I had no idea a kiss could be like this—soft but strong, demanding and passionate. His kiss ignites my hunger in a way I never thought possible. He coils his tongue with mine, cupping the back of my head with his huge hands. He tastes faintly of whisky and mistakes. It feels as if I'm standing on the edge of a cliff, the ground crumbling beneath me, but I can't find it in me to care.

When we finally break apart, lust shines in his eyes. "Lie down on the bed."

For a moment, I'm frozen in place. Am I really doing this?

"I said lie down."

Lord, like anyone could say no to him. Not when he asks like that.

"Panties off. Blindfold on," he instructs.

It takes me a moment to register what he's asking. "Excuse me?"

"Oh, I think you heard me." He tosses me a leather blindfold that was hanging on the wall alongside a bunch of other kinky instruments, like a flogger and handcuffs. I'm not even sure what the rest of them are.

When I don't move fast enough, he takes over, lifting and cupping the back of my head to secure the blindfold for me.

A flush of perspiration settles over my skin. "W-why the blindfold?" I ask, my voice shaky.

He makes a rumbly noise in the back of his throat that I feel down to my toes. "I want you to feel everything. Every sensation that runs through this delectable body ..." His rough fingertips graze my nipples, and my body goes rigid with need. "When I pleasure you with my fingers ..." He drops a kiss between my breasts. "My tongue." He sucks a nipple deep into his mouth and circles the peak with his talented tongue. "And when you're ready, milaya ... with this." He grabs my hand and lays it over his straining cock still covered by his pants.

My lungs freeze. His every touch sparks a firestorm across my nerves. I've never felt desire like this, and it sends a rush of wet heat between my thighs.

I'm quivering with anticipation when he grabs both of my wrists in his huge hand. I don't have time to ask him what's happening—not that he'd tell me anyhow, with his insistence that I just *feel*.

The next thing I know, he binds my wrists firmly together, then pulls them above my head. I'm too shocked to move for a few seconds, but when I finally try to lower my arms, I can't. They're affixed to something.

"Roman," I warn, not sure if I like this loss of control.

"It's okay. I've got you." His hand brushes my cheek before I feel the warm, wet drag of his tongue as it glides from one breast to the other one, circling my hard nipple.

I moan loudly. I can't help it. My body is lit up like a Christmas tree, responding to his every breath, his every touch, and even the slightest brush of his fingertips.

Sex has always been something to endure and never about my pleasure. But everything Roman is doing is about making me feel good, and it's better than I could have ever imagined.

"Hold still." He hooks a finger over the edge of my panties and pulls them down my legs.

Embarrassment coasts over my skin, and I squeeze my legs shut.

Roman releases an amused breath. "I don't think so, sweetheart. Your pussy is mine for the night, remember? I want a good look at the treasure I bought."

Oh my God, he wants to look at me *there*.

"I can't," I squeal.

It's too much. How can I possibly show him more when I already feel so exposed?

But he doesn't give me a choice. His hands land on each knee, and he gently but firmly pulls my legs apart.

I freeze, growling out my unhappiness.

"Uh-uh, milaya."

I consider kicking him away, but when cool air brushes against my pussy, I suck in a sharp breath.

"Perfect," he breathes and swipes a finger through the center of my core. My body nearly arches off the bed, his touch igniting a rush of arousal.

He takes hold of me behind the knees and bends my legs until they're pressed against my stomach. I thought this would be my version of torture, being exposed and vulnerable like this, but a bolt of lust crashes through me instead. I've never been so turned-on in my life.

"Look at you. Untouched, unsoiled. Sweet pink lips and those lily-white thighs. Do you know how hard you make me?" He runs a rough hand down the inside of my thigh, and I can hear him work to control his breath.

As he runs a finger through my soaked center again, I mewl and bite my lip, drunk on his touch.

"Christ, the filthy things I'm dying to do to you. This right here was worth killing a man for. Now, hold still." He focuses on fastening my knees with restraints so that my legs are spread wide.

I attempt to wriggle out of his grasp, but once again, I discover I can't move more than a few inches. I swallow audibly. "Wh-what are you going to do to me?"

His voice, deep and seductive, drops an octave. "Anything I want, milaya." His fingertips drag down the inside of my thigh until they settle over my exposed pussy. "Fuck," he grits out in a low, deep voice.

His fingers dip into my pussy, making me shudder with pleasure. This is all new to me, and my body responds as if it's on fire.

"You're so wet. Is it just for me, or would you be this soaked for any man?"

"Just for you," I murmur.

He makes a pleased noise. "You're so responsive, so primed for my touch. Knowing I'll be your first makes me so goddamn hot."

The bed dips, and my pulse flickers, my skin burning up. What's he going to do?

His hands clamp over my thighs, and he takes a deep inhale between my legs.

"Roman, no." I try to close my legs but can't thanks to the bindings.

"Look at you, baby. This pussy is dripping with need."

My breath catches, and I swear my eyes roll back in my head. This need inside me is overwhelming and entirely new. It's too much but also so damn delicious.

"I'm going to give you exactly what you need." He drops a kiss above my slit and holds me down with one strong, calloused hand on my hip, ensuring I can't move.

A puff of warm air over my sensitive skin makes me shiver. This sensation is so raw and unfamiliar, heightened by my lack of sight. I nearly buck off the bed when his tongue finally reaches the place I need him most.

Holy shit. He circles his tongue around my clit, sucking it into his mouth before slipping one finger inside of me. With each slow, gentle stroke of his tongue from my entrance to my clit, my muscles clench.

This is … unreal. And all new to me.

I had no idea someone's tongue and finger working in tandem could feel this damn good.

"Do you like that?" he murmurs.

I don't need to answer. We both know I absolutely love it.

He doesn't stop. He licks me again and again. My lips part in pleasure, my breath coming in short pants.

"Oh my God," I gasp, pulling against the bonds. The logical side of my brain is no longer functioning—need has taken over. He wants me to feel, and more than that, he wants me to feel exactly how in control he is of my body.

I'm close, so damn close, and he knows it. But instead of taking me over the edge, like he did last night, he pulls away.

I gasp my protest. "Roman."

"No coming yet, pretty girl." His voice is thick. "I'm not rushing a moment of tonight."

CHAPTER TWENTY-FOUR

ROMAN

The foolish girl doesn't listen. When I walked in here earlier, I had no intention of actually fucking her. I only wanted to scare some sense into her—sense she's clearly lacking. But once again, she managed to get the upper hand.

She offers her body to me in hopes I won't reveal her little secret. Auctioning her virginity.

She's out of her mind if she thinks Anatoly won't notice. He values her virginity like a rare gem. A better man would have turned and walked away, but it turns out I'm not that man. Not after I've already had a taste of her and have been craving more.

I shrug off my jacket and unbutton my shirt with frenzied energy, letting it fall to the floor. She can't see my shirtless form, but the fewer clothes between us, the better.

The candles in the room bathe her body in light, flickering over her breasts with each breath. I'm desperate to get my mouth on her, to graze every inch of her glistening skin with my tongue, teeth, and lips.

"Roman, it's ... I need more."

I stretch her pussy open and dive in with my tongue, pushing as deep as I can go. Her soft whimper fills the air, and her squirming intensifies as her liquid heat fills my mouth.

"Do you know how hungry I am for you? No woman has ever made me this hard," I tell her, grinding my aching cock into the mattress.

I nip at the sensitive bud, circling my tongue in a steady rhythm around her clit. Easing a finger back inside her soaking wet hole, I feel how needy she is. Her pussy clenches tightly around my finger. My little innocent wants me to make her come.

She looks so fucking hot like this. Need glistens between her spread thighs, and she's ravenous for me—my tongue, my finger, and soon my cock—to take her over the edge.

I laugh quietly. "Half a million dollars, and you're worth every penny," I whisper against her folds.

God help me, I would have easily spent more. She could have all my money for all I care, because this is the most alive I've felt since—I can't remember when. Still, the idea that she was willing to sell herself to anyone sets my blood on fire. I want to fucking know why.

Time to take her to the brink.

I do it slowly, driving my finger in and out of her before slipping in a second digit as I lap at her clit, using the stubble of my beard to heighten the pleasure between her legs.

She's not the only one on a knife's edge. I want to savor her every moan, her every whimper, and every drop of wetness smeared on my face.

But I also want answers.

"Tell me what you really need the money for," I whisper against her inner thigh, my fingers gently working in and out of her.

Liza shakes and trembles. She's so close I can taste it.

She thrashes her head, refusing me the answers I want.

I'm keyed up beyond belief, my cock leaking pre-cum into my pants because I don't trust myself to free my dick, knowing my restraint is hanging on by a thread.

"Come on, milaya." My breath coasts over cunt. "You can tell me."

She moans, biting her bottom lip when I give her one more taste of pleasure by slipping my tongue inside of her. Her nipples pebble in response to my touch.

"Fine. I-I like to shop. I need the money for clothes and stuff."

Such a pretty little liar. She'll pay for that.

I run the length of my nose along her slit as I breathe her in one last time. Then I withdraw from her completely, hands and mouth. I even step off the bed, leaving her cold.

"Roman?" she mewls.

So needy.

"I know, baby. I know." I wipe the mist of sweat from her brow, comforting her with my touch. If she only knew how much this was costing me as well. "All you have to do is be honest with me. I deserve the truth, don't I?"

"Her lip quivers, perspiration coating her upper lip. Her body is protesting the loss of my touch, but her mind is holding firm—I can tell by the stubborn set of her jaw and the way she's lying rigid.

I know a hundred different ways to make a captive talk, but they all include methods I wouldn't dream of applying to Liza.

I'll never hurt her—for that matter, neither will anyone else—but I will toy with her, make her so crazy and delirious with pleasure she won't be able to hold back from telling me everything.

She doesn't know it yet, but I'm going to make her feel more than she ever thought possible.

LIZA

"Roman, please," I beg, teetering on the edge.

I desperately need his mouth and fingers to return to where they were before he started with his stupid questions. Despite my need, I won't spill a word. Roman might desire me, but at the end of the day, his loyalties lie with Anatoly—the man he's in business with. Not me.

His fingertips brush my right breast, sparking a cascade of unfamiliar, thrilling sensations. "You want me to believe that you were auctioning your innocence for spending money? Please." His voice rumbles beside my ear, the deep rasp doing nothing to cool the need firing through me.

When his tongue encircles my nipple and draws it into the warmth of his mouth, a shock of pleasure so intense it feels foreign crashes through me. Is it supposed to feel like this?

"Tell me what I want to know, and I'll make you feel so damn good you won't know what planet you're on."

I try to talk some sense into him. "You don't need to do this. It doesn't matter."

His chuckle is dark and sexy. "If it doesn't matter, why do you refuse to tell me?"

My instincts kick in, and I attempt to close my thighs, seeking some form of release, but the restraints hold firm. Exposed and at his mercy, I'm his to explore, tease, and deny.

"Forget it," I rasp. "Untie me, and let's get out of here. There's no point in any of this."

"I make the rules tonight." He drops a kiss on my aching clit, causing sparks of electricity to shoot through my body. "I decide when we're done, when I've had enough." He teases a lick between my folds. "I'm not even close to being finished with you. Maybe by the end of the night, you'll be ready to tell me what I want to know."

God, this man is frustrating beyond belief. He may be

stubborn, but I'm a damn mule when I want to be, and he'll soon learn that.

"Fine." I shift on the bed, willing my body to cool down to fight the torrent of need he's stirred inside me with his wicked fingers and tongue. "Do your worst. You'll get nothing out of me."

His voice is low and tinged with amusement when he teases, "I suppose we'll see."

This time, his mouth is insistent, sucking hard on that bundle of nerves, drawing a sharp gasp from my lips. His fingers make a come here motion inside of me, leaving me writhing with need.

For the love of all that is holy, what is this voodoo magic he's using on me? Never in my wildest dreams could I have imagined such raw intensity. He's the first and only man to make me feel this way. With every suck and lick, I'm falling under his spell, an orgasm building like an impending storm. But just as a deep, throaty moan escapes my lips … he pulls away.

I pant, helpless, and try to breathe through the loss of his touch. It's a good thing I'm tied down because if my hands were free, I'd throttle Roman—this is absolute torture.

Even though I temper my reaction, he's not fooled. Not one bit. He laughs at the way I bite my lip and grit my teeth, knowing how bad I need to come. "Ready to talk yet?"

I shake my head. "There's nothing to talk about. You're making something out of nothing."

He sighs loudly. "In that case, I have something else that might change your mind."

He rises from the bed, rummaging around somewhere—a drawer, maybe?—before settling back on the bed between my spread thighs. My body strains with anticipation, but for a minute, there's nothing. He doesn't move, doesn't say anything. He's totally still, which makes me tense.

Then there's a gentle buzzing sound, followed by the most

intense sensation I've ever experienced. If it wasn't for the restraints, I'm sure I'd buck straight off the bed.

"A vibe?" I force the words out. "That's a low blow."

"You want to come? You know what to do. Tell me what the money's for."

The soft head of the toy vibrates between my legs. Holy moly, his tongue and fingers are dangerous, but this? This is going to be the death of me, and he knows it.

"Roman, goddamn you!" I screech, tears pooling under the blindfold as the vibrations increase in intensity.

When I'm close to the edge, he removes the toy.

"Jesus Christ, you're impossible!" I explode.

"I'd say you're the one being impossible."

I grit my teeth, preparing for the next surge of raw pleasure. I've never felt such a powerful rush. Knowing it's Roman's touch stirs something fierce inside me—a deep, wild need I hadn't even known existed.

He starts the vibe, alternating between tonguing my entrance and swirling the toy around my swollen clit.

Can I handle another near orgasm? I don't even want to know. I'm sweaty, tired, and I really want to come already.

"Fine," I cry. "You want the truth? Take off my blindfold, and I'll tell you."

He pauses, then I feel him shift as he climbs up the bed and lifts my blindfold so we're eye to eye. I'm sure I look like a hot mess, with mascara smudged under my eyes and my skin glistening.

But when his eyes meet mine, they're soft and warm.

"I need something for me," I whisper. "Something that's just mine, that my family or Anatoly doesn't know about and can't touch. To be dependent on him for everything …" I shake my head. "That can't be my life."

It's a half-truth but an honest one.

He nods and runs his thumb over the apple of my cheek.

Does he believe me?

His expression is unreadable, but he doesn't push it. He doesn't ask for more details or specifics or probe my logic. He simply looks at me.

My heart is in my throat, my pulse a dull thud in my ears.

"You drive me crazy," he says. "I'm going to allow you to come now." The sin in his voice holds a dark promise of what's next. He slips the blindfold off and tosses it to the side. "What a pretty cunt you have." He leans in, burying his head between my thighs and licks me thoroughly.

This time, he's not teasing; he's out to make good on his promise. Slipping two fingers inside of me, he sucks my clit into his mouth, pulling on it with long, lazy strokes of his tongue.

"Come for me," he demands.

That's all it takes to set me off. Wetness floods between my thighs as my body spasms. I wish I could clench my legs together to absorb the intensity, but since I can't, I have to accept everything he gives. He continues until the pulsing in my core simmers down to a low heat, and I sigh in surrender.

Even with my climax still humming through my body, the sound of foil tearing snaps my attention back to the present.

I know what's coming next, and even though it will change everything, I'm ready. Circumstances may have forced me here, but with Roman, it feels entirely like my own decision.

Breathing heavily, he grips my legs and swiftly pulls me until my ass is positioned at the very edge of the mattress.

"I want to touch you," I say softly.

He nods and efficiently undoes my bindings, both around my legs and around my wrists. I flex my hands and stretch out my legs, enjoying this newfound freedom.

"Are you ready?" He strokes down my body, his eyes gently traveling over my face. The look he's giving me is almost too much, too intense. Full of emotion and meaning.

My body tenses in sweet anticipation, ready for him to surge forward and take me.

He slides his length between my folds, not yet pressing inside of me. I release a whimper. He feels so thick and hard as he lines himself up with my entrance.

"You're so goddamn beautiful like this," he whispers, sweeping his thumb over my cheek.

My heart squeezes at his words. I don't know how we ended up here after everything, but it's like all the pieces of a puzzle have finally locked into place.

Emotions tangle in my chest, and I haul in a breath, preparing to adjust to his size. "You're the first man to make me come, and now you'll be the first man inside me."

Roman doesn't move. Doesn't say anything. He cups my chin as his deep brown eyes hold mine, intense like a silent storm ready to break.

A low growl escapes him, vibrating against my skin. "Not like this," he declares, pulling back from me. "When I fuck you, it's going to be because you beg me too, not because I paid for this pussy. You'll give it to me because you can't breathe unless I'm buried nine inches deep," he rasps. "Keep the money; I don't care about it. When you're ready to be fucked properly, you know where to find me."

Disappointment sinks like a brick in my chest.

Is he serious? Doesn't he see how badly I want him—money or no money?

Something tells me nothing I do or say right now will change his mind, so I bite my lip and let him go without another word, leaving tangled feelings and unanswered questions hanging heavy in the air.

CHAPTER TWENTY-FIVE

LIZA

I GAZE OUT THE AIRPLANE WINDOW, SILENTLY URGING THE PILOT to defy international speed regulations to get me home faster. The tension in the cabin is off the charts, and not in a good way.

It's just Roman and me, sitting across from each other. We both keep sneaking glances at one another, only to abruptly avert our eyes.

I'd like to know the social etiquette for when someone goes down on you for the first time, gives you the best orgasm of your life, and nearly claims your virginity—the one he paid good money for—but stops short due to some personal moral code.

At least, that's what I assume the issue is. I wouldn't know for sure because Roman and I haven't spoken since last night. Even then, our only exchange was my request to fly home today.

There's a lot left unsaid between us, but it's better that way. What happened in London was insane and definitely a one-time thing. Considering Anatoly is his business partner,

Roman is probably feeling as awkward about it as I am. It's easier to pretend it never happened.

Which Roman is doing quite well. He appears to be buried in work, sending texts and staring at his laptop screen. Whatever he's doing, he's not paying attention to me or the phone in my hand, and I'm grateful for that.

I can't stop checking my bank app to make sure the money is actually there. That all this is real. Thanks to Roman, a cool $350 thousand is tucked away in an offshore account, set aside for trading. Turning that money into a million in three weeks is ambitious, but Roman's generous bid gives me a real shot at freedom.

An ache builds in my chest. Last night, I could only focus on the sting of rejection, but in the light of day, I see it differently. Whatever this incessant pull is between us—and I honestly don't have the words to name it—can't end well. It'll never be something more than it is.

Maybe he was saving me from making a decision that would always end in ruin.

"Roman," I say before I really know what I'm doing or asking. "What happened last night?"

His face tightens, and he blows out a ragged breath like hearing my voice is too much. "You know what happened. But let me put your mind at ease—no one will ever know. Go back to your fiancé and your pretty little life, and you can bury this secret with all the rest."

The metallic tang of blood fills my mouth, and I realize I've bitten down on my cheek. Hard. I should be thrilled he's promising to keep quiet, but instead, everything about this moment feels wrong.

"Um, well, thank you for …" Jesus, the words get trapped in my throat.

His phone rings, and I'm grateful for the distraction. He glances down to see who's calling. His nostrils flare, before his eyes meet mine again. "It's Anatoly. Have you spoken to him since the incident with your sister?"

Trepidation churns in my stomach. "No. I texted him to say I was staying in London for an extra day. I missed a call from him last night, but he didn't even bother leaving a voice message."

Roman nods, his gaze scorching my cheek. "I'll handle this." His voice is deep and authoritative as he takes the call. *"Privet."* He doesn't say anything more for the next minute; rather, he's listening to something Anatoly is saying. Whatever it is, Roman's face tightens with irritation. "Bad weather. Are you shitting me? The shipment's supposed to arrive tomorrow, and I'm only learning about this delay now?"

My back straightens as Roman's lips part in a growl. I can't hear what Anatoly's saying, but I can make out his "soothing" voice over the line; he's trying to placate Roman.

"I don't give a fuck if the North Atlantic is unpredictable," Roman grits out. "It was your job to build delays into the timeline. You know how tight our schedule is to get the product out to the buyers."

The silence that follows is tense. I've never heard anyone talk to Anatoly like that, and I find myself holding back a little smile, oddly pleased that someone put him in his place.

"Do whatever it takes to get the delivery back on schedule," Roman barks. "And keep me updated. I'll be back in Russia this afternoon." He's about to hang up the phone when Anatoly says something else. Roman's eyes flick up to me. "Yes, she's with me," he confirms.

My throat goes dry. I'm not ready to deal with Anatoly. I was going to feign illness when we arrived home so I could put off seeing him for at least a few days.

Roman's expression hardens as he extends the phone toward me. "He wants to speak to you."

I gather my courage and brace for the inevitable confrontation. Even though Anatoly didn't call me back for a full day after I left him a frantic message about Sofiya, he'll still be pissed I didn't take his call last night.

"Hello," I say, twisting my hands in my lap.

"I haven't been able to reach you. Why is your phone off?" he snaps.

"I was asleep when you called last night, and we're flying right now. Most people turn their phone off in the air."

"Is it also standard to deceive your fiancé?" A heavy knot forms in the pit of my stomach. Does he know? "I allowed you to go to London for one reason, and one reason only. Because you were with Maxim Belov's wife. Imagine my surprise seeing her at an event in Moscow last night. So let me ask you, princess, what's going on?"

Unease prickles along my neck, but I force a calm tone. "I wasn't deceiving you. Kira had to leave early, but I wanted to stay for another day. If you would have returned my call earlier, you'd have known this." When I look up, Roman's sharp gaze takes me by surprise. "And what about you,?" I huff, unable to stop myself. "Taking my sister to dinner without telling me. Don't you think I had a right to know?"

I expect his anger, but all that comes through the line is a cruel laugh. "Calm down, Elizaveta. It was a business dinner. As my future sister-in-law, she needs to learn how to conduct herself around my associates. You, of all people, should understand that."

"She's seventeen. You had no right to let her drink."

"Like you weren't drinking at that age? It was a glass of wine, for fuck's sake, and you should be less worried about my actions and more worried about your own. We're getting married in a few weeks, and sightseeing in London is your priority?"

"It was just a da—"

"Are you alone with Roman?" The edge in his voice sends an icy sensation trickling through me—a warning that I need to play my next move carefully. If Anatoly digs too deep into my actions last night, my entire plan could fall apart.

I switch to a softer tone, one I've perfected over time. "*Tolya*, don't be grumpy with me," I coo. "I was at the spa all of yesterday. I want to look my best for you when I come home. It was no big deal."

"I hope you enjoyed your freedom, because it ends now." His voice is an ugly snarl. "Let me speak to Roman."

My hand shakes as I reach forward. Roman's fingers brush against mine as I pass the phone back to him, and I have the distinct sense it wasn't accidental.

He scowls at the device in his hand before answering. "What is it?" His tone is even darker than before. "Don't worry about your fiancée, she's in good hands. Worry about getting me my shipment in time." He ends the call.

There's a brief moment where neither of us says anything. He doesn't need to; the look on Roman's face says it all. The air thickens around us, his composure as dangerous as a loaded gun.

Turning towards the window, I rest my head against the cool glass. From this altitude, the landscape is a distant memory, but watching the clouds pass by helps clear my mind.

Roman's sharp intake of breath through his teeth pulls me from my wandering thoughts. When I look up to meet his stare, his fists are clenched tightly in his lap, and a muscle in his jaw tics.

"What is it?"

"Who did this to you?" Roman's voice is dark as night.

"Did what?" I ask, genuinely confused.

A second later, he leans forward and runs his finger under my eye. What he's talking about comes into stark focus.

The bruise. The one Anatoly gave me the night of the dinner party.

I try to keep my expression flat. "Oh, that." I shrug like it's no big deal. "I was half-asleep heading to the bathroom in the middle of the night. Banged into a wall."

Even though the bruise has faded, he looks at it with such outrage I don't know how to process it. I had been covering it up with makeup the entire time in London, but with everything going on today, I forgot. Bad move.

His chilling tone stifles my breath. "Must have been quite a powerful wall to bruise you like that."

"It's fine." My face heats, and I seriously need him to drop it.

"Why?" he asks, dark energy rolling off of him in waves.

I stiffen. "Why what?"

"Why marry him? Surely, there are other rich men who can give you what you want."

I flinch, his words feeling like alcohol on a wound, but I shouldn't be surprised. I've led him to believe that money is the only thing important to me.

"Men like you?" I immediately regret my words.

"No, milaya, you should stay away from men like me."

My heart sinks—we're a story that ends before it even begins. I don't know how to process all these emotions, so I lean into anger instead. "How about you mind your own damn business?"

"After last night, you are my damn business," he growls.

My throat thickens with emotion, but I swallow it down as I always do.

Roman may have helped protect Sofiya, killed a man who disrespected me, paid a stupid amount of money so no one else could have me, and made me feel like I actually matter, but I need to end this now—before it threatens everything.

"Last night should've never happened," I say, unable to look him in the eye.

He releases a bitter laugh and rakes an angry hand through his hair. "Definitely not. Because an engaged woman shouldn't have been selling off her virginity." He leans forward so we're eye to eye and grabs my chin. Our lips are inches apart. "Aren't you sick of the hold your parents have over you? Isn't it time you put yourself first?" He lowers to his haunches in front of me. "Let me help you. All you have to do is say the word, and I'll do whatever it takes."

His offer breaks open a part of me that's been dead for a long time. Roman is no white knight—he's dark and dangerous and operates in the underworld—but I know he'd do what he could to protect me. My heart flutters at the thought, only to then clench in pain.

I can't accept his help because it would mean giving another man control over my life. In the end, what could Roman really offer me other than money? Protection, maybe. But he's tied to Anatoly, and with their business connections, ending things won't be easy.

Sucking in a lungful of air, I cross my legs and fold my hands in my lap. Emptying my expression of all emotion, I give him a blank smile. "I enjoyed myself last night, but it was a terrible lapse in judgment. I blame pre-wedding nerves. I'm grateful you stopped things from going too far because it would have been a mistake I'd regret. You don't owe me anything, Roman. From here on out, we go our separate ways."

"Bull-*fucking*-shit." His words come out sharp and pointed, like edges of a glass shard. "You enjoyed yourself? Understatement of the fucking year. You loved my hands on your body, my tongue in your cunt, and you were desperate for my cock. You may have done it for money, but there was nothing fake about the way you exploded on my tongue. And trust me, sweetheart, your taste is forever branded in my memory."

It feels as though I've been sucked in by the ocean's current, tossed around by the waves, and then thrown back onto shore, weak and disoriented. But despite the undeniable pull between us, the explosive chemistry, I can't let him believe we can be anything more.

I lower my gaze, hiding my breathlessness caused by his words. "Like I said … I enjoyed myself, but I'm not looking for a repeat. I *will* marry Anatoly. You might not understand it, but I'm committed to him."

His lip curls in disdain, and his hand tightens around his phone. If he squeezes any harder, I'm pretty sure it'll break.

"Whatever you say." He uncoils to his full height, straightens his leather jacket, and casually checks his watch. "Tell yourself whatever story you need to to sleep at night. It doesn't change anything between us."

CHAPTER TWENTY-SIX

ROMAN

The passenger door of my car swings open and then slams shut with a definitive thud as Pavel slides into the seat next to me.

"Fuck, it's cold." He blows into his hands while rubbing them together.

Outside the windshield, snow continues to fall, blanketing the neglected industrial area in a pristine white layer.

"That's what gloves are for." I spare him a quick look, noticing his checkered fleece bottoms. "Are you wearing pajamas?"

Pavel reaches forward and jacks the heat in my G-Class Benz. "It's the middle of the night."

"I would have gladly waited the extra five minutes for you to change," I say.

I keep watch on the silent building. About an hour ago, we got a call from the man Pavel had assigned to keep an eye on Anatoly. The Petroviches have plenty of other clients, but they're all respectable businesspeople for the most part, so a meeting like this—under the cover of night and in a derelict warehouse on the wrong side of town—raised a red flag.

"So, what did I miss?" Pavel jacks the temperature once again.

My patience already thin, I swat his hand away, lowering the temperature back to where it was. "Anatoly is still in the building. I can't tell how many are in there with him, but there are a few vehicles parked around the side." I pick up the binoculars from the middle console and scan the building once again, but there's still no hint of movement.

Pavel takes the binoculars from me and does his own visual sweep. "Seems pretty quiet." He gives me a look that I don't know how to interpret. "Did Liza say anything else about that dinner he dragged Sofiya to?"

My jaw clenches. "We didn't talk about it, to be honest." Because we had other matters to keep us busy.

In my bones, I know there's something deeply fucking wrong with Anatoly, and I'm going to get to the bottom of it one way or another. Preferably, before he marries Liza.

It's been less than a week since we came back from London, and Liza has been on my mind way too much. I keep replaying the night of the auction—her tied up and spread wide, just for me. How she tasted, and the way she fell apart under my touch. It took everything in me not to surge forward and fuck her like my life depended on it. She wanted it, too.

So what stopped me?

I needed to be sure she was spreading her legs because she wanted to, and not for money or because she thought it was the best way to keep me from spilling her dirty little secret.

"So, how was London Town?" Pavel tries to put on a casual tone and fails. "We never did get to talk about your time playing bodyguard."

I roll my eyes. "Nothing to report."

"Somehow, I don't think that's true." Amusement colors Pavel's tone.

I have to restrain myself from pulling a gun on him. "Nothing that concerns you," I say, irritated.

Pavel's lips twist. "Really? Because I'm gonna be honest, you've been a cranky bastard since you came home from London."

I grind my molars together, well aware he's right. I had hoped it wasn't so damn obvious that my head was a mess.

Liza can tell herself she's perfectly happy marrying Anatoly, but I know what I've seen—the way her hands shake when she speaks to him, the bruise on her face, or how she had to fight back tears when she told me Anatoly is her choice.

She has reasons for going through with the marriage, but they are rooted in fear and desperation. If she wanted my help, I'd give it to her, but I'm not a man who begs. And she's made her choice.

Beside me, Pavel releases a harsh breath, forcing my mind back to the present. "You're really keeping quiet about this, huh?"

I release a heavy sigh. "Trust me. It's not that interesting."

I'd also rather not be lectured on why getting involved with Liza is such a shitty idea. I know it is. Even if both Pavel and I suspect Anatoly is crooked, we're still locked into a multimillion-dollar business deal with him.

"If you say so."

"Shouldn't you be focused on finding Hope King rather than worrying about who I'm lusting after?"

That shuts him up for a good second or two.

Hope King is the daughter of Lai King, the leader of the Black Company, a triad we recently went to war with. During the attack on King's hideout in Switzerland, Pavel was stabbed by the young beauty. He could have easily taken her down, but he didn't. He couldn't bring himself to shoot her.

Lai King offed himself before he could face our wrath, but Hope vanished without a trace after the attack. She's a loose end that we need tied up, because as the heir to the Black Company, she could rise to power and mobilize against us. Who wouldn't want revenge after we took down her father?

Which is why Pavel is tasked with finding her and dealing with her—whatever "dealing" entails.

He runs his tongue over his front teeth. "Trust me, I haven't forgotten. She must be lying low because she's vanished like smoke. I have all our best people tracking her, but so far, not even a sighting." His mouth falls into a hard line. "She'll make a mistake eventually, and when she does, I'll be waiting."

"You better be. We don't need a second coming of the Black Company." Warring with them once was enough.

Pavel fiddles with the radio a bit. Checks his phone. Picks up the binoculars, looks around, and then puts them down again. "God, this is fucking boring," he announces. "Think this meeting has to do with the delayed shipment?"

I sit back in my seat, itching for a cigarette, but the glow would draw attention and that's the last thing I need. "Doubt it. This looks like something else entirely."

In the end, our shipment had been delayed a few days because of bad weather. Not unusual, but Anatoly had committed to a strict schedule. He was sure his team had secured the best shipping routes and could make up time if needed. I'd like to believe he oversold and underdelivered, but my gut tells me there's something more.

The doors of the warehouse swing open, and one by one, men exit into the dimly lit parking area. I recognize a few of Anatoly's guards, but the rest of the men are unfamiliar.

Pavel releases a low whistle. "Well, I'll be damned. It's a party."

He reaches for the binoculars, but I shoo him away. "Use

your camera," I tell him. "Get a few pictures while you're at it."

My focus sharpens as Anatoly steps out of the building, his presence commanding even from this distance. He clasps hands with a man I don't recognize. The guy is tall with dark hair, and well-dressed in a suit and finely tailored trench coat.

"Who the hell is that?" Pavel murmurs, focused on his phone.

"Beats me. We have connections with everyone worth knowing in this town, but I've never seen that guy before."

The hair on my neck rises. I don't have a good feeling about this.

Anatoly and the other man exchange a few words before they each turn and slip into separate chauffeured cars. Only two men remain, seemingly unfazed by the chill as they light up cigarettes. The orange tips flare in the darkness, puffs of smoke mixing with the steam from their mouths. They share a joke, their laughter reaching us despite the distance.

"What are these two up to?" Pavel squints into the dark.

"Not sure." I slip my gun from the middle console into the back of my jeans. "But I'm thinking we should introduce ourselves."

Pavel lowers his phone and smirks. "It would be inhospitable to do anything else."

I press the drill head tighter against the blond mudak's knee as beads of sweat pour down his face. Usually, I'd build up to the drill—it's more of a mid-negotiation kind of tool—but screw it, I'm not feeling charitable at the moment.

"Cut the shit," I say. "Tell us who the fuck you are and what that meeting was about, and we can all save ourselves some time."

"I-I don't know anything," he sputters. "I'm the runner,

that's all—I swear on my mother's grave. They don't tell me anything."

I grunt, irritated. "It's better if you don't assume I'm an idiot. A reminder: it didn't go so well for your friend over here."

His eyes dart nervously towards his counterpart, who's lying face down on the hard concrete floor of the warehouse. The asshole pulled a knife on me, which resulted in a shot to the head. Goddamn novice.

The man pales to a sickly green. I sigh, moving the drill from his knee to over his dick. I don't think I've ever drilled into someone's dick before, but hey, there's always a first.

"Are you fucking crazy?! Get away from me," he screams and struggles against the ropes binding him tightly to the chair.

From a few feet away, Pavel scrunches his face in distaste as the guy starts to whimper.

"You're young to lose your dick," I tell him, even though he won't be walking out of here alive. "You probably haven't used it much in your short life. I don't know who you're protecting, but it's not worth losing genitalia over."

"You don't understand." He's trying to keep his shit together, but he's shaking like a leaf, his bravado long gone. "They'll do way worse if they find out I talked. You might as well kill me."

Pavel and I exchange a look. Well, this just got a hell of a lot more interesting.

"What's your name?" I demand.

His eyes dart down to the drill and then back up to meet my hard stare. He swallows thickly, sweat pouring from his forehead. "Artem," he rasps.

"Nice name." Pavel nods. "This guy over here is Roman Vasiliev. Surely, you've heard of him."

Artem's eyes bug out, and he looks like he's about to piss himself.

"Yeah, that's what I thought. He's a little off on the best of days, but he's really lost his shit recently. You see, there's this girl he can't have, who he really, really wants—"

"Oh, for fuck's sake," I mumble.

Pavel only glances up at me with dry amusement. "As I was saying, he's got a really persistent case of blue balls, and it's making him pretty mean. So, if I can make a suggestion" —Pavel pauses, his light hair glinting under the fluorescents —"it would be not to worry about your future; worry about the here and now."

With that, my friend slips a pair of brass knuckles onto his right hand and lands a powerful punch to Artem's solar plexus, causing him to double over and wretch.

Good. Let him puke his guts out and rethink his stance on keeping quiet.

"My balls are fine," I whisper-hiss at Pavel. "So how about you mind your own fucking business."

I wish it was only a case of blue balls—that's easy enough to relieve. Getting laid isn't the issue; the issue is my dick will accept one person, and one person only.

Artem has stopped retching and is looking between us, head swinging side to side like he has no clue what's happening but is happy that our attention is off him.

"Since it seems you need a little motivation ..." When I turn on the drill to get started, he really loses his shit.

"Hell no!" Artem explodes. "You savage motherfuckers."

"That's exactly what we are." Pavel decks him again.

I take two steps back, the noxious smell of puke invading my nose. I much prefer the metallic tang of blood. "Get talking. Who do you work for?"

He spits blood onto the ground, but he won't raise his head to look at us when he mumbles a name.

"Speak up." I kick him.

"The Zhukov Bratva. I work for the fucking Zhukovs."

Pavel and I exchange glances. It's impossible that we've

never heard of a bratva operating in our territory. We reign supreme here, and all the bratvas answer to Maxim and the Belov Syndicate.

"Who the hell are they?" I pace on the spot.

"A gang out of St. Petersburg. Two brothers, Nikolai and Sergey. They're smart. Like, street smart. And vicious. Sergey has been running things for the last few years while Nikolai has been in jail, but they're expanding, taking over more territory."

"Why'd they meet with Anatoly Petrovich?" I snap, a bad feeling growing in the pit of my stomach.

"It was just Sergey tonight—no Nikolai—but I don't fuckin' know any of the details. All I do is stand guard outside and run errands for them." He gestures to his dead colleague on the floor. "Dymtro knew more."

Well, shit.

I turn the drill on and make a big show of finding the right place to start my dirty work. "You know more than you think." I smile at him, letting him take me in in all my unhinged glory. "Maybe you need a reminder."

Artem's shrill screams echo off the walls. He'll be talking in no time—no one wants to lose their cock to a drill.

CHAPTER TWENTY-SEVEN

LIZA

"Elizaveta, please focus," my mother chastises, her tone laced with frustration. We're at the wedding planner's office, deciding on the many details I have no interest in.

I huff out a sigh, my gaze darting back to my phone to keep an eye on a tech stock I picked up yesterday. The stock's price is climbing, so it's time to sell. "The lemon cream was my favorite," I offer, distracted.

"It's lemon curd," she corrects, as if I care.

"Right, curd. Tastes amazing either way. Perfect choice for the wedding cake."

Yeah, perfect for a wedding that's not going to be happening. At one time, I would have felt guilty over my mother going to such lengths for an event which will be canceled if I'm successful. But not anymore. My parents have never prioritized my needs or what's best for me. Roman is right—it's time to let them fend for themselves.

How long can I keep sacrificing my happiness for theirs? If left to them, it would be indefinitely. That's the problem. They will continue taking from me until there's nothing left.

"Maybe it's better to go with vanilla," my mother frets, worry creasing her brow. "It's usually safer to keep things traditional."

I barely suppress an eye roll. "Sure, Mama. Whatever you prefer."

I'm glued to my phone hidden under the table as the stock price steadily climbs. Shit, I'm going to need to sell soon.

"I can't decide on the tablecloths, though. White, off-white, or cream?"

My finger hovers over the sell button, ready to act as soon as the price hits my target.

"Liza, did you hear me?" my mother snaps peevishly.

With a quick tap, I sell, locking in a tidy profit of $20 thousand. It's been a week since I started trading, but the results are already impressive. I've made $200 thousand off my initial capital. It's a good start, but I'll need to pick up the pace if I'm going to make a million dollars before this wedding in under two weeks.

"Pick whichever, Mama. It's fine."

I glance up to find her frowning at me.

"I don't know what's gotten into you lately, but this is *your* wedding. The most important day of your life—of all of our lives—and your lack of interest is concerning. All of Moscow's elite will attend. You ought to prioritize planning over whatever it is you're constantly doing on your phone."

I sigh and make sure the trade has gone through before lowering my phone into my lap. "I was texting Kira." The lie rolls smoothly off my tongue. "She asked if I needed any help with the planning, but I'd say you have it under control. You and Mrs. Petrovich seem to be more than happy to handle the details."

"Speaking of which ... Talya and Katerina will be here any second, and I won't have you acting like a sullen teenager. Show that you actually want to be part of their family." She sniffs. "You have no idea what a privilege it is to take the Petrovich name."

An honor for *her*. The woman who doesn't actually have to marry Anatoly.

"I don't care about privilege and a good name. That's your concern," I bite back, unable to keep the anger from bubbling to the surface.

"How can you be so selfish?" my mother snaps, her low voice filled with indignation.

The wedding planner enters the room, but one look from my mother sends her scurrying away.

"Do you think I married for love? No. Marriages are unions. They're meant to strengthen families and secure futures. It's about duty, not personal happiness."

"That's not true. At least, not always," I point out. "Kira and Maxim are crazy in love."

Her eyes turn to slits. "Didn't their marriage start as a business arrangement?"

I gnash my teeth. I don't know why I'm bothering with this conversation because my mother won't be swayed.

"Your sister needs this union more than anyone." My mother slams her hand down on the table. "If we sink into poverty, do you think there'd be a chance in hell anyone would want to marry Sofiya?"

My grip tightens around my phone. "What if we don't need the Petroviches' money? What if I found a way to be financially independent from them?"

As if on cue, my phone buzzes with an alert for a promising stock. I ignore it.

The frown marring my mother's perfectly made-up face isn't what I hoped for. "What are you talking about, Liza? Have you lost your mind?"

What she really means is, *Where's my sweet, obedient daughter who never pushes back, never questions, and never wants anything for herself?* That's who I was for so long: the dutiful daughter, living her life to clean up everyone else's mistakes.

My mother continues to stare at me as if I'm an alien. It's my fault, in a way, because I've never stood up to her before.

"I insist that the maid of honor's dress be red, Mother. It's my best color." Katerina's whiny voice is heard before she even enters the room. Moments later, she steps in, greeting us with a frown. "Oh. You're both here."

My back straightens with irritation.

Talya Petrovich gives her daughter an admonishing look. "It's the bride and mother of the bride, so of course they're both here." The older woman steps forward, offering us both air kisses.

"I think red for the bridesmaid's dresses sounds lovely," my mother gushes as the two women sit down. "Don't you think, Liza?" Her kick under the table is a not-so-subtle nudge to agree.

"Sure." My grin lacks any genuine warmth.

Katerina flares her nostrils and flips her long golden hair behind her back. "I wasn't talking about the bridesmaid dresses. I don't care what they wear. As the maid of honor, I should be the only one wearing red."

"Red for a wedding? You'll look like a harlot." Talya frowns.

I have to bite my lip to keep in my laughter. I respect her bluntness.

"Maybe something softer," my mother jumps in. "Like a pink blush?"

"Maybe not." Katerina pulls a face and checks the time on her phone. "Anyhow, what do we need to do here? I have a facial in an hour."

"I thought you might want a say in the color scheme we choose, considering it will greatly influence the floral arrangements," my mother offers. "Your taste is impeccable, and it would mean so much to have your input."

My God. Could she suck up any harder?

While Talya and my mother discuss the merits of lilies versus white roses, I lean back in my chair and sneak a quick glance at my phone, checking on my trades.

"So, do you have your outfit sorted for the opera this weekend?" Katerina leans closer, putting on a falsely sweet tone that immediately has me on edge. She doesn't wait for my response. "I have a few designer dresses from last season, which you're welcome to borrow. You don't mind wearing last season's fashion, do you?" Her tone is casual, but there's a mocking undercurrent.

Like Anatoly, his sister loves to remind me how indebted I am to her family. How much less fortunate we are.

"I'm fine," I answer back cooly. "I'll wear something from my closet." I give her a blank smile and hope she takes the message to back off. I'm not interested in playing her power games, especially right now.

She gives a nonchalant shrug and examines her manicure. "I say that because my brother will expect you to look the part of a Petrovich. All of Moscow will be watching your first outing together since you announced your wedding date. It's important you look"—her eyes rake over me critically—"polished."

I fight a very strong instinct to push her face-first into the bouquet of hydrangeas in the center of the table.

"I'll manage with what I have," I respond, my voice frosty.

"Oh, sure, whatever you want." I can sense her eyes still on me, like a vulture circling before the kill. "I can send my aesthetician over to your place. She's amazing at threading, you know. She can help you with that facial hair." Katerina grins like the cat that ate the canary and motions to my upper lip.

I bite my cheek, not allowing her veiled insults to get to me. "Sure," I say. "How kind of you."

"I'll send her over to your house once I'm done. You probably don't know this, but guys go wild for a full wax—everywhere." Her eyebrows do a little dance to emphasize her point. "Considering who my date is, I'm aiming for silky smooth." Her tone drips with insinuation.

I do my best not to take the bait. She obviously has an agenda.

When I say nothing, her mouth tightens, and she leans in closer as if I'm hard of hearing. "Roman Vasiliev is taking me. He's been asking me out forever, and I finally agreed to a date." She shrugs, takes a tube of red lipstick out of her purse, and applies it slowly.

Her news hits me like a punch to the gut.

Roman and Katerina? Out on a date?

Envy flares like an itch under my skin. I don't like it one bit.

I reach for my water glass in front of me, trying to react like my heart isn't slamming against my rib cage.

"When a man looks like that," she purrs, "you know he'll be amazing in bed. So what if he's bratva. There's nothing wrong with a little danger."

My nails dig into my palms underneath the table. "Roman, really? I had no idea you were his type."

"Oh, you'd be surprised. Men like Roman—real men—are looking for a woman they know can rule by their side. They're not interested in"—she makes a flicking motion with her hand that is clearly aimed at me—"a meek little mouse. They want a woman who's confident and experienced. Up for anything."

My expression is brittle. "In that case, I hope your date is a success. Seems like you and Roman are a perfect match."

She gives me an indulgent smile. "You'll see for yourself, won't you." She checks her watch. "I must run. And here's a friendly tip: don't wear red. It makes you look sallow."

I fight the rush of jealousy flickering in my chest.

Katerina is despicable, and there's nothing to envy about her. Except for one thing—she'll be on Roman's arm, and I won't.

That alone sets my blood on fire.

CHAPTER TWENTY-EIGHT

ROMAN

When the foreman gives the signal, I step out of my car into the dark, frigid night alongside Viktor, our syndicate's head of security. I gesture to the vehicles behind me, and a dozen of my men quickly follow, moving toward the ship that docked minutes ago.

Ports are nasty places, especially this one on the edge of the Baltic Sea. It smells like dead fish and broken dreams, but I find it oddly comforting. This area of the port is Belov property, and no one in their right mind would mess with us here, including the authorities.

From the gangway, Viktor and I board onto the cargo deck, where the longshoremen are waiting on our instructions. They haven't started unloading because they know our men need to personally inspect each and every container, filled with millions of dollars of cocaine, as it comes off the ship.

It's not our usual operating procedure, but since the late shipment and Anatoly's secret meetings with the Zhukov Bratva, I'm being cautious. I don't trust the guy worth shit.

"I'm gonna go down and let the guys know what we're looking for," Viktor says, heading towards the crew.

I nod and make my way to the upper deck when something catches my eye. A single high-heeled shoe, scuffed and abandoned, sticks out from under a sealed container door.

That's fucking strange. I can't imagine a single woman has set foot on this ship, possibly ever. Maybe I'm overthinking things. I toss the high heel behind me and climb the stairs to find myself a better vantage point.

The heavy scent of salt and metal fills the air as I give a signal to my men to start. One by one, each container is lowered onto the ground. The clang and clatter of chains and machinery echo as the foreman opens the first container and our men step inside to confirm the delivery hasn't been tampered with. We'll weigh and test the product once we get it back to our warehouse, but I want to make sure nothing's been opened while en route.

Viktor comes up beside me, resting his arms on the railing. His black hair glints blue in the ship's artificial lights as both of us watch the proceedings below. As each container is checked and verified, my men step out and give us the thumbs-up.

I can feel Viktor's scrutinizing gaze on me before he speaks. "So far, so good. No sign of tampering on this shipment ... or the last."

I huff out a breath, which turns into a white cloud in the cold air. "I know, but something still feels off."

Viktor sighs and brushes a knuckle over his chin. "Is this about Anatoly's secret meeting with the Zhukovs or something else?"

A pang hits me square in the chest. If the "something else" is a dark-auburn-haired beauty I can't get out of my mind, then yeah. My distrust of Anatoly may have something to do with her and that bruise on her face, or the way she puts on a faux-sweet voice when she's trying to calm him down.

It reminds me so much of how my mother was with my father. How she carefully tiptoed around his temper, always trying to keep the peace in a house that was anything but peaceful.

I couldn't protect my mother, but every damn instinct inside me screams for me to take care of Liza, even though it's not in my own best interest.

Shit. Maybe I'm losing it.

When I don't answer, Viktor claps me on the back. "Got some intel on the Zhukovs."

My eyebrows raise. "You have my attention."

Since learning of their identity, we've been making inquiries into the Zhukov Bratva. It's headed by two brothers, Nikolai and Sergey. Although Nikolai, the older of the two, was in jail until recently.

"The short version is that Sergey, the younger Zhukov, has been stepping up to assert his control in St. Petersburg while Nikolai was in jail. He's been fighting gangs for larger territories and monopolizing the illegal arms trade in the city. He's got balls, but he's rash. It's the kind of shit that could easily spiral into a full-scale gang war."

"And the brother?"

"Word is Nikolai's the brain and Sergey's the brawn. Now that Nikolai is free and stepping back into his role as pakhan, there's definitely tension between the brothers."

"A power struggle always keeps things interesting," I comment. "Maybe that's why Nikolai wasn't at the midnight meeting with Anatoly, why it was only Sergey. Any more intel about that meeting?"

Viktor releases a frustrated sound. "Not yet. His inner circle is tight. No one's talking."

"Keep digging. Whatever business they have with Anatoly doesn't sit right." I frown, watching my men methodically go through each container. "I'm still suspicious about the delay of our last shipment."

Viktor huffs out a laugh like maybe he thinks I've lost the plot. "Everything was in order. None of the goods were tampered with." He shrugs. "I'm not saying the man's a saint, but delays because of bad weather are common in the middle of winter."

"That might be true, but I know what my gut is telling me." I flash him a devious grin. "And I found a way to get some answers."

"Which is?" he asks, pulling a beanie from his back pocket and lowering it over his head before blowing a breath into his hands.

"To use my body and charm to get what I want."

Viktor groans, but I'm not entirely kidding.

"You and your fucking plans," he grumbles. "What do you have in mind?"

"We only see the shipping logs that Anatoly's team sends us. Well, I have an insider at the company who will send us the originals. No questions asked."

"What's the catch?"

"I have to go on a date with Katerina Petrovich." I grit my teeth. "To the opera."

Viktor drags a knuckle over his jaw. "Seriously? You at the opera? I don't see it."

"Yeah, well, we all have to make sacrifices from time to time."

Katerina has been sending me flirty texts since the night we met at the Ivanovs' dinner party. I've been ignoring them, having absolutely no interest in her, but recently it occurred to me how short-sighted I've been. Katerina works in the family business—she has access to all sorts of company information.

So I made her a deal. I told her I'd misplaced the shipping logs that we had been sent and felt like too much of a dumbass to ask Anatoly's men to resend. She agreed to send me copies of whatever I wanted if I take her to *Carmen* at the Bolshoi this weekend. God help me.

Viktor shakes his head but can't suppress his amused grin. "You sure that's a good plan? Katerina might get the wrong idea."

"Nah, she doesn't care about getting serious. She only wants to be seen on my arm and fuck a man with bratva tattoos." Not that I'll be fucking her.

In fact, the one bright spot in all of this is Liza will be at the opera with Anatoly. I don't mind one bit if she feels a sting of jealousy seeing me with another woman.

Viktor winks and thumps me on the back. "I wish you luck." His smile drops as something in the distance catches his eye. "What the fuck is that?"

We both squint into the night and spot a dark van with no license plates rolling quietly through the shadows of the shipping containers. "An uninvited guest."

In a matter of seconds, I've reached into my waistband. My gun aimed, I shoot at the van, the crack of gunfire echoing across the port.

The van lurches, then suddenly revs its engine, barreling forward. The side door slides open, revealing men in balaclavas who open fire on our operations.

"Watch out, it's an ambush!" I shout as our men catch on to the action, drawing their weapons and returning fire.

We sprint down the ship's stairs, our boots clanging on the metal. Bullets fly in both directions. One of our guys goes down, clutching his shoulder.

The van door slams shut and the van peels off, tires screeching as it races toward the gate. Shots ring out as our men continue to fire, but the van crashes through the gate, metal crumpling and splintering under the force.

Viktor curses, slamming his fist into a crate as we watch the taillights fade into the distance.

"Goddammit!" I snarl, breathless. My pulse races, rage boiling.

If someone has a message for us, they should deliver it

like actual men. Make your presence known rather than staging an anonymous drive-by shooting in the dark of night.

Viktor is on his phone, barking orders to his hackers to use satellite imagery to track the van speeding away. When he hangs up, he looks at me for directions.

I roll my neck, tension knotting in my shoulders and down my back. "We find the bastards who did this," I command through clenched teeth, "and we kill every single one of them."

CHAPTER TWENTY-NINE

LIZA

"Sofiya, finally!" I say when my sister picks up the phone.

She's been impossible to get a hold of for the last week, and although that happens sometimes, I'm still uneasy after everything that went down while I was in London.

"Sorry, Lizka. I was at a dress rehearsal. It's been exhausting."

I put my phone on speaker and place it on the bathroom counter while I hover the eye pencil near my lashes, attempting a smoky eye.

Roman may be taking Katerina as his date tonight, but he won't be able to take his eyes off me. I'm going to look my best. Roman Vasiliev can eat his goddamn heart out because I'm not going to spare him a second glance.

"As long as everything is good?" I pause, pencil midair, and take a breath. "If something is bothering you, you know you can talk to me. About anything."

She sighs. "I know. You really need to stop worrying about me. I'm not a kid."

I give up on smoky eyes and press the phone to my ear,

leaning on the bathroom counter. "Listen, I don't want to keep bringing this up, but I'm still feeling uneasy about the night Anatoly dragged you to that business dinner."

She's quiet for a minute. "What about it?"

"I just … Who were the men he introduced you to?" Anatoly has refused to discuss the dinner with me, warning me to mind my own business, but for my own sanity, I need to know the details. I need to understand what happened.

"I dunno. Some businessmen from St. Petersburg. The only name I remember is the guy who seemed to be the boss, Sergey. He was nice enough, asking me questions about school and the things I liked to do. My plans after graduation." She gives a little laugh, and I can tell she was flattered by his attention. "But he's, like, in his thirties or something. He wasn't flirting, just being polite. I mostly scrolled on my phone because the whole thing was boring."

I pinch the bridge of my nose. "Was he the one who gave you the wine?"

"Ugh, this again?" she mutters.

"I need to know."

"I … I can't exactly remember."

Something about her confusion makes me feel sick. One drink shouldn't wipe a person's memory. Then again, as much as she claims her friends drink, I don't think she does.

"I'm pretty sure it was Anatoly, but it's hard to say. The drinks were flowing. I didn't want to make it an issue."

I have to bite my lip to keep from screaming in frustration. "Okay." I release a tight breath. "I'm not happy he did that, but it's not your fault. Please don't go anywhere with Anatoly again."

She sounds tired when she finally says, "Nothing happened."

"I know, Sofiya, I know. But you're my sister, and my loyalty will always be with you. Anatoly and I are working out a few issues at the moment."

"But the wedding is so soon!"

I press a finger into my temple. She has no idea how aware I am of that fact.

"It'll be fine," I tell her. "Time heals all."

What I really mean is, if luck is on my side, I won't be walking down that aisle.

I'm in a terrible mood after I get off the phone with my sister, but I don't allow myself to wallow. There's no time for that anyhow. Anatoly will be here to pick me up soon, and I need to appear as normal as possible.

I descend the stairs, retrieving my coat and clutch from the main-floor closet. Usually, Anatoly waits for me outside in his car, but when I glance out the front window, I can see his Jag parked to the side.

Strange.

Low voices spill from my father's study, and I turn, walking towards the closed door. As I approach, something about their conversation piques my interest.

"There's no more money until after the wedding. It's clearly laid out in the contract." Anatoly's voice is low and menacing, but it seeps under the door like poison.

Not daring to breathe, I press my ear against the door.

"With the wedding so soon, what does it matter? We'll be family in no time," my father points out. "The thing is ... I'm in a spot of trouble with the yakuza. You know how heated their poker games can get."

"That's your problem, not mine."

"I know I drink too much, it's my weakness, but these guys are serious. I only have a week to pay them back, or I'll lose an eye. How would it look for me to walk Liza down the aisle with an eyepatch?"

"Terrible." Anatoly laughs. "Maybe you should have

thought about that earlier. Tsk-tsk, Boris. You're a pathetic man, but your sins aren't my problem."

Dread seeps into my chest. I'm not surprised by Anatoly's cruel dismissal of my father, but it still chills me to the bone that the man who wants to marry me doesn't care a bit about my family's safety. That alone should set off alarm bells in my father's head, imagining his daughter married to such a man, but that's clearly not his first instinct.

Still, I know this wedding isn't going to happen. Either I'll have to pay my father's gambling debts using my investment money, or I'll have to ask for help.

Roman's face materializes in my mind, and with a calm surety, I know it's him I'd call to protect my father. To protect me.

Goose bumps rise on my skin at the realization. No one makes me feel like he does—warm, safe, and utterly protected. Even though I pushed him away, I know he'd be there if I needed him.

I draw a deep, shaky breath because, right now, I need to concentrate on what's happening on the other side of the door.

"But with the wedding so soon …" My father's voice carries a tone of desperation that makes my heart clench. Even though he's deeply flawed and selfish, at the end of the day, I don't want to see him hurt.

"Until it's official, we don't have a binding agreement. Unless … you find a way to sweeten the deal for me."

"I'll do whatever I have to, whatever you want."

My stomach churns with disgust to see how low my father has stooped, willing to hand Anatoly whatever he desires on a silver platter. The implication of "anything" sends a chill through me.

There's rustling inside the room, like Anatoly is rising from a chair. His voice drops so low I can't hear a word, no matter how hard I press my ear to the door.

Shit. What could they be saying?

A few minutes later, their voices go back to normal.

My father suggests a shot of vodka in celebration.

"Haven't you learned your lesson, you idiot?" Anatoly laughs, and it has a cruel edge.

That's my cue to back up.

I quietly shuffle towards the staircase as if I'd only just come down. When the door to my father's study swings open, I step off the last stair and feign surprise at finding my fiancé in the hallway. "I didn't realize you were here," I say to Anatoly.

"I came early. Took the opportunity to visit with your father."

My father and Anatoly exchange a look I can't quite read.

"Very well. I'm ready to go." I try to hide the quiver in my voice after everything I overheard.

His eyes rake over me, sharp and calculating, with an underlying heat that makes my skin burn. He looks at me like I'm a pretty object he's happy to have acquired, and truthfully, that's exactly what I am to him.

"You look stunning." He gives me a hard, possessive kiss that makes me want to puke in my mouth. He probably thinks I've dressed up for him, which is definitely not the case.

I'm wearing a sleek, formfitting fiery-red dress, paired with heels that add inches to my already tall frame. Despite her insult, Katerina isn't the only one who can pull off red. My hair is pulled back in a chic ponytail, highlighting the smoky eye I finally got right on the third try.

"Thank you." I try to keep my tone in check.

My father approaches and gives me a small peck on the cheek. "Have fun, dear." His averted eyes and hollow tone hint that he's signed a pact with the devil he can't escape.

Oh, Papa, what have you done?

CHAPTER THIRTY

LIZA

Anatoly leads me into the lobby of the Bolshoi Theatre, his hand possessively on my lower back as if I'm the most precious thing to him in the world. What a lie that is. To him I'm a sparkly accessory, something to show off.

Tonight is the big opening of *Carmen,* and the place is packed with Moscow's glitterati. I really wish Kira were here for moral support, but Maxim whisked her off to some tropical paradise. She hinted it had something to do with mafia business and Maxim being overly cautious. I hope it's nothing serious, but Kira didn't seem worried.

With a pompous smile on his face, Anatoly guides me through the crowd, soaking up the congratulations and excitement about our upcoming wedding. This is the only time he actually seems happy to be with me—when he's got an audience.

I've just freed myself from a conversation with the mayor's wife when Anatoly slinks up beside me, grabbing my arm. "My sister is here with Roman Vasiliev." He tilts his head towards the champagne fountain they're standing in front of.

"I see that," I say, struggling to keep my composure.

They look like the ultimate power couple. Roman is as handsome as ever, dressed in a tailored dark suit with his thick hair slicked back. Next to him, Katerina glows. I knew seeing them together tonight would be hard, but I hadn't anticipated the surge of raw, homicidal emotion I'd feel. Especially when Katerina plasters herself to Roman's side as they make polite conversation with a small group of people.

Glancing over, I'm surprised to see a frown on Anatoly's face. Since I got home, he hasn't mentioned Roman and me being alone in London, which I'm thankful for.

"I thought you'd be happy for Katerina to be dating your business partner," I say, testing the waters.

Anatoly's nostrils flare, and a cold flicker of something hard passes through his gaze. "I wouldn't choose him as a brother-in-law. Vasiliev's loyalty will always be to the Belov Syndicate, not to my family."

My forehead creases. I'm unsure how to interpret that comment.

Anatoly spots a business crony in the crowd and stalks off after him.

I'm pulled into another conversation where I pretend to be excited about being a bride and the joys of wedding planning. Meanwhile, warmth spreads up my neck. My gaze drifts past the woman I'm speaking with and locks with a familiar set of deep-brown eyes.

My stomach does a little dip, butterflies taking flight. Time slows, the crowd fades away, and for a moment, I remember what it feels like to bask in Roman's attention.

A figure steps in front of him, and the spell is broken. All I register is blonde hair and a red dress, much like my own, before his attention shifts to Katerina. She takes his face between her hands and brings her lips to his. It's not a chaste kiss, nor is it a first-date kiss; it's filled with tongue, heat, and passion—and it's all wrong.

Mine.

The thought echoes through my brain.

What a lie. He's not mine and never will be, but try telling that to my heart, aching with jealousy.

I didn't believe Katerina when she told me Roman had been pursuing her, but watching how she presses her body against his, their mouths still joined, I see I was wrong. He seems like a willing participant.

When she pulls away, the look of reverence he gives her is too much. His hand comes up and buries itself in her hair, then his eyes lock on hers as if she's the only woman in the room.

Screw this.

I can't watch anymore. I can't even bear to be in the same room as them. My heart feels like it's been ripped out of my chest, thrown to the ground, and trampled repeatedly. The worst part is I have no right to feel this way—Roman owes me nothing. I'm the one who pushed him away.

"Isn't it time to take our seats?" I cut Anatoly off mid-conversation.

He narrows his eyes, irritated at the interruption. "What's the rush? We have our own balcony."

"I just … I don't want to miss any of the show."

He sighs in annoyance and tells his companions he'll join them for a drink later.

Clamping a hand around my elbow, he leads me toward his private balcony. "What's gotten into you?" he snaps when we're out of earshot. "You look unwell."

"Only a headache," I assure him. "Nothing Tylenol won't fix. I have one in my clutch. I'll pop into the washroom to take it and meet you at our seats."

He grunts in response, his attention already captured by his phone.

It takes me a few minutes to steady my breathing and rein in my emotions. I expected to see Roman and Katerina together, but I wasn't prepared for that kiss and how he looked at her as he pulled away—like she meant something to him. Seeing Roman with Katerina feels like a slap in the face, a painful reminder of my gullibility.

How could I have been so blind? How could I let him fool me so completely?

Swallowing the lump in my throat, I take a deep breath and push out of the stall, fumbling in my purse for Tylenol because my headache is real.

"I see you didn't take my advice." That voice. Like nails on a damn chalkboard.

"I happen to think I look nice in red," I say, refusing to make eye contact with Katerina. Instead, I focus on my reflection in the mirror. Knowing she's watching, I take out a tube of fire-engine red lipstick and slowly apply it to my full lips.

"As long as you feel comfortable, that's what counts." She smooths down her already perfect blonde waves, admiring her reflection in the mirror. "Roman and I are sitting in the Belovs' box tonight because we want a little privacy." A slow, deliberate smirk spreads across her face. "Honestly, I don't even know if we're going to make it through the full opera with his wandering hands."

My shoulders stiffen, a tight smile fixed in place. She has no clue how I feel about Roman. For her, it's all about scoring one of Moscow's most eligible bachelors. He ticks all the boxes: handsome, wealthy, influential. And let's be real, the bad boy vibe only adds to the appeal. For a woman like Katerina, those are green flags.

"I'm so happy for you." I put the cap back on my lipstick and drop it in my clutch. "I'm sure the rumors about Roman going through women faster than tissue aren't true. I mean, I've never seen him with the same woman twice, but who knows. Maybe you'll be the lucky one to stick around."

Satisfaction zips through me as the smug look melts off her face, replaced by a pout. Part of me feels bad for leaning into Roman's reputation—a reputation I wasn't convinced of until tonight. Because I know what I saw. If he's into someone like Katerina, he's clearly not the man I thought he was.

I smooth down my dress, adding a little spring to my step as I pass her. "I'll say goodbye now, just in case I don't see you later. Oh, and don't forget to bag it up. I hear herpes itches like a bitch."

CHAPTER
THIRTY-ONE

ROMAN

I FUCKING HATE OPERA. TO ME, IT SOUNDS LIKE CATS YODELING after a few shots of tequila.

I might be the only one that feels that way, judging by the rapt crowd. Everyone's attention is on the stage, on the performance of *Carmen*, while my attention is wholly captured by the woman in the box directly across from mine.

She refuses to look my way.

I deserve her wrath, and I'll regret that kiss with Katerina until the day I die. It was unwanted and definitely uninvited. She tasted all wrong, nothing like Liza's sweet, sun-kissed flavor that's forever imprinted in my memory. I pushed Katerina away, but the damage was already done.

Hurting Liza was never part of the plan. The flash of pain in her eyes when her soon-to-be sister-in-law pressed her artificial, pillowy lips to mine made my heart twist.

Liza might wear another man's ring, but I'm the one she wants ... and the man she's going to get.

Truth be told, the plan to stay away from her shattered the moment I laid eyes on the bruise below her eye. Because I know a bruise is never just a bruise. First it's a bruise, and then a black eye, then a broken arm, and then it's your mother lying in a pool of blood while your father gets to move on with his life because you were too chicken-shit to stop him until it was too late.

I won't make that mistake twice.

I've spent my whole life making calculated decisions, thinking with my head and not my heart. In the time since London, my head and heart have finally gotten on the same page.

I'm not willing to stand by and watch Liza marry a man who doesn't deserve her and whose abuse will only get worse. But I have to restrain myself, because my ruthless actions will have major consequences. For me, for Liza, and for the Belov Syndicate.

Now, more than ever, I need to bide my time until the moment is right to make a move. Judging by Antoly's shadiness, that time might come sooner than later.

From across the opera hall, Liza finally turns my way, and damn, she's practically spitting fire from her eyes. If looks could kill and all that.

After a minute of death glares, she deliberately turns away. Despite her focus on the stage, I feel her energy directed at me like a silent storm across the divide. I nearly laugh to myself. She's fucking adorable when she's angry. But she has no need to be, and I'll set the record straight at the first opportunity.

Beside me, Katerina releases a little giggle as her hand creeps over my thigh, settling over my crotch. Her manicured talons run gently over the fabric of my pants in an attempt to get me hard. Like I could even get a semi for her.

I sweep her hand away and shoot her a warning look. "Like I said before, not happening."

She pouts—a move that's probably worked with many before me. I find it straight-up obnoxious. "We can find a back room somewhere." Her breath coasts over my ear, her sickeningly strong perfume invading my nose. "Or I can blow you right here. We're high up enough so no one can see."

She's saying that for my benefit. Katerina wants people to see us. It's all about making sure everyone knows she's the one on my arm tonight.

"Pass." I hiss out a breath of annoyance.

She can't take a hint. This was never a date; I came to her with a business proposal, nothing more. Being seen together tonight was part of her terms—she wants the world to think she's bagged a high-ranking member of the Belov Syndicate. It's far from the truth, but I have to hold up my side of the bargain.

I look up as Anatoly whispers something in Liza's ear, then stands and leaves their balcony. Once Liza is alone, her gaze drifts back towards me. She scowls, and I smile. Others might not take her hostility as an invitation, but I guess that's what makes me different.

"I have a business matter to attend to," I tell Katerina, then stand and button my suit jacket.

She frowns. "It can't wait until intermission?"

"It can, but I don't want it to."

Her friendly mask drops, and the real Katerina shines through. The one who's famously petty and bitchy. "Whatever. I don't care about this shit anymore. I'm going to find my friends at the bar." She stalks off, teetering in heels and her designer crimson dress swishing dramatically with each step she takes.

I don't know who told her she looks good in red, but they must have been color-blind.

Liza doesn't hear me enter her balcony. She doesn't notice when I close the curtain and take a few steps closer, the sound of my approach drowned out by the orchestra's crescendo.

But she does notice when my hand reaches around and

covers her mouth. Her body stiffens and she attempts to turn around, but I don't let her.

"Shh," I coax into her ear as I crouch down behind her seat.

With a hand wrapped in her hair, I force her to remain in place, taking this opportunity to breathe her in. Her subtle scent is like a breath of fresh air.

She squeals in displeasure.

I chuckle. "I know, milaya, you're pissed at me. I have to say I'm flattered by your reaction. You made it pretty clear you weren't interested, but I dunno … You might want to rethink your choice if I inspire that much emotion."

She attempts a response, but it comes out as a muffled noise of discontent instead.

Her anger only fuels my hunger. Maybe I won't clear up my involvement with Katerina but use it to my advantage. There's a thin line between love and hate.

"This is what's going to happen," I tell her. "You're going to be a good fucking girl, sit back, and watch the show while I make you come all over my fingers. Are we clear?"

This wasn't my intention when I walked in here, but knowing she despises me as much as she wants me has inspired a new approach.

She shakes her head and attempts a scream, but it's useless with my hand still covering her mouth. With my other hand, I fist her hair and twist her face around so she can see how serious I am.

"If you disobey or make noise, everyone will look up and see my hand up your dress. Is that what you want?" She freezes, her eyes locking onto me with a murderous glare. "I didn't think so. Anatoly is off smoking cigars with his buddies and being an obnoxious ass, so don't worry about him." I lick a long, hot trail up her neck, from the base of her collarbone to under her ear, before I wrap my lips around her earlobe and suck it into my mouth, savoring the contact.

Man, I've been obsessed with tasting her again, and she's just as delicious as I remember.

She inhales sharply through her nose, but instead of yanking away, she closes her eyes, enjoying the feel of my hot tongue on her smooth skin.

"You know I'll make you feel good, right?" Eyes wide, she nods vigorously. "Are you going to be a good girl and stay quiet if I take my hand off your mouth?"

Liza thinks for a moment before nodding again. Then she does something surprising. Her tongue snakes out between my fingers, the tip flicking over my skin, before she wraps her lips around a digit and draws it fully inside of her mouth. It feels like heaven, and I bite out a curse, my brain short-circuiting.

That is until I feel the sharp sting of teeth sinking in my flesh.

"Ouch," I whisper sharply.

She spits my finger out as if it's poison. Her teeth marks are evident on my skin.

Shit. She did not hold back.

"How dare you try to make moves on me when you're here with another woman!" she hisses, turned in her seat to face me. "A woman you couldn't keep your hands off a hot second ago." She shoots daggers at me as she pushes at my chest, trying to get as much space away from me as possible.

My lips quirk up. I'm pleased I inspire such fire in her. She's not as indifferent to me as she'd like to think.

I stand and calmly take the seat Anatoly vacated earlier. Now we look like two people simply enjoying the show side by side.

I lean in to her. "There's nothing between Katerina and me. It's business, that's all."

"Oh yeah, 'business.'" She angles her body towards mine, making air quotes. "Is that what we're calling it these days? I hate to break it to you, but that kiss didn't come across as all that professional."

"Liza," I say through gritted teeth. I cup her jaw in my hands so she's forced to look at me. "She kissed me. Trust me, I'm not the least bit interested, but I need something from her and taking her as my date tonight was the only way to get her to agree to my terms. If I knew she was going to be all over me, I wouldn't have agreed. She's nothing to me." I carefully run my thumb over Liza's lips. I don't need another set of bite marks. "You've consumed my every thought, my every breath, since we've been apart. Deny it all you want, but you belong to me. You were always meant to be mine."

The air crackles like a live current between us. I don't know who makes the first move, but the moment our mouths connect, she tilts her head back and matches my fierce kiss with equal passion. Our tongues dance together, and she moans.

I capture that sound, savoring her surrender as I explore her mouth, imagining it's more than my tongue pressing between her soft lips. Which it will be, soon.

But not now.

As much as I want to keep this scorching make-out session going, I also don't want to be caught—for her sake, not mine. Liza is the one with something to lose. Yeah, we're in the highest-level balcony, and it's dark except on the stage, but all it takes is one busybody with binoculars to see us. If we keep on going all hot and heavy like this, we're going to attract unwanted attention.

I break from our kiss, and she releases a little whimper that I feel down to my balls. She's not immune to my touch, just as I'm not immune to hers.

"Sit back in your seat," I whisper to her, "and lift your dress."

Still breathing heavily, she gives me an *Are you serious?* look. I give her an *I'm dead serious* look back.

Even in the dim light, she's so damn beautiful that my heart stops beating in my chest. With her wide, green eyes and high cheekbones dusted with the smallest collection of freckles that she can't completely hide, I could look at her forever.

But tonight, I'm going to do a lot more than look.

She's breathing hard, but her gaze doesn't waver from the stage. I lean towards her, reaching down to grab the hem of her dress, and flip it upwards so she's exposed to me. After seeing the white scrap of lace she wore at the auction, I didn't expect the simple cotton pair of panties she's wearing now.

My hand settles on her bare inner thigh, and I push her panties aside and dip between her legs, running a gentle finger up and down along her slit. Her mouth hangs open, her eyes fluttering closed with the barest touch from me.

My good girl has been craving this as much as I have.

"Fuck," I grit out, my cock straining against my dress pants.

Pavel might have been right about my blue balls, because no matter how much I jerk off with Liza in mind, my dick is craving the real thing. To be buried to the hilt inside of her.

"This is a bad idea," she whispers, even while gripping the armrests of her seat and parting her legs to give me better access to her entrance.

"Since when have I let a bad idea stop me?"

I sink two fingers inside her. Her eyes go wide, and she quivers, biting her bottom lip just in time to suppress a little moan of pleasure.

"We're … going … to be … caught," she barely manages to choke out.

"If anyone walks in, I'll shoot them."

Her eyes fly open, and she looks at me. Horrified.

I give a little laugh. "My guard is waiting outside and will stop anyone from coming in. Even Anatoly."

I hate having a guard shadow me, but since the attack on

the port a few days ago, I need someone watching my back. At least until we know more because the culprits are still out there, unidentified.

With that settled, she's moving her hips in little circles, attempting to get off on my fingers. Her pussy is so wet and needy. I let out a hiss when her inner walls clamp down on my fingers.

"Such a good girl," I praise her.

I hook my fingers forward to rub her G-spot, and even in the dark of the balcony, I see her eyes roll back in her head.

"Oh my God," she mewls, disguising her pleasure with a well-timed cough. Her breaths are coming fast and hard, and she's grinding down on my hand, chasing her release in a theater with hundreds of people.

Goddamn.

The only thing that would make this moment more perfect is if Liza was writhing on my cock, not only my fingers.

That's in the cards sometime soon. She just doesn't realize it yet.

CHAPTER THIRTY-TWO

LIZA

Roman Vasiliev and his magic fingers.

My breath comes out in sharp, needy pants. I must be drunk to go along with something so risky. Even in the dark, with Roman's guard at the door, anyone paying close attention could catch us. That realization alone should stop me, but it only intensifies the erotic charge building between my legs.

I'm way past the point of being able to stop. Not when Roman's scent—pine and leather—surrounds me and his fingers fill me. The stretch is intense but perfect.

From a distant place, I'm aware of the music soaring to a crescendo and filling the auditorium with its powerful climax. The opera singers on stage pour their souls into the final notes, their voices intertwining in a dramatic finale.

That's the moment his thumb coasts over my clit. With just a flick, I tip over the edge. My orgasm hits hard and fast, the peak of my pleasure timed with the peak of the finale, and I'm too far gone to hold back. I cry out, my eyes squeezed shut, and throw my head back, clenching the armrests like I'm holding on for dear life.

Oh, hell.

My thighs tighten around his hand, and he slows but leaves his fingers deep inside me, allowing me to ride out the final waves of pleasure on his palm. Wetness coats my thighs, and the satisfied growl that comes from Roman tells me he doesn't mind that I've soaked his fingers.

When my eyes open, he's looking right at me.

"Well done," he rasps, removing his fingers from my core.

Even in the dim light I can see how wet and shiny they are. He pops two fingers into his mouth and, holding eye contact, makes a show out of licking them clean like he's never tasted anything sweeter.

It's so hot, but that doesn't stop the horror from sinking in. Lights are flashing inside of my brain, reminding me of what a big mistake I've made.

Around us, the entire audience is on their feet, clapping boisterously, while Roman's focus is entirely on me.

"You did so well, milaya. How about you ride my face now?"

I smooth my dress down and flee the balcony without another word. Few times in life have I done anything so genuinely stupid that I'm afraid I completely lost the plot.

I've always been the sensible one. The reasonable one holding my family together. The practical one talking my friends out of their crazy ideas. When Kira and I were in school, that was my role. She was the wild one willing to take risks, but me? I was the one who kept her from doing the *really stupid thing.*

Yet here I am, a grown-ass woman with more to lose than I even care to think about, and I've done something really stupid. Again.

My pulse roars in my ears as I navigate the clusters of operagoers taking advantage of the intermission to grab a drink and gossip with friends. I slow my long strides, run a hand over my ponytail, and straighten my dress, trying to regain some semblance of composure.

What I did was reckless, but I don't feel a twinge of guilt. Because when Roman confessed his feelings and the reason for his involvement with Katerina, I had no fight left in me. I needed his hands on me. Needed to touch and taste him again.

It was just as good as I remembered—God, even better than I remember—but it was a moment of madness, a lapse in judgment.

Swallowing hard, I spot Anatoly near the bar and make my way through the crowd towards him, but he doesn't see me. He's focused on his sister, who's leaning against him, looking a little worse for wear.

"Is everything okay?" I ask cautiously.

He huffs out an annoyed breath. "It was, until this one came outside and decided to act like an idiot."

My eyes settle on Katerina. She's practically slumped against the bar, looking dazed, the glass in her hand tipping precariously in her loose grip.

"Roman, there you are!" She suddenly brightens, her eyes on something—or rather, someone—behind me.

Great, there's no escaping the man.

"Where'd you go, Kat? You told me to meet you at the bar at intermission," Roman says, playing it cool.

Katerina flutters her lashes and leans forward. "So ... are you gonna come home with me?"

Anatoly's nostrils flare, and I'm pretty sure he's about to blow a gasket. "The only person going home is you—right now, before you further embarrass our family." Anatoly may not want Roman as a brother-in-law, but he cares what he thinks. With barely a glance my way, Anatoly announces, "I need to take my sister home. I'll send a car for you."

Roman is quick to interject. "No need. I didn't plan on staying longer. I'll give Liza a ride home."

Anatoly's features tighten, and I'm sure he's about to shoot the idea down, but I step in before this becomes an issue.

"That won't be necessary," I assure Roman. "I'd like to stay for the rest of the performance, so—"

"If you want to stay, we can stay," Roman drawls. "I don't have anywhere to be. And you really seemed to enjoy the grand finale of the last act. I saw you get swept up in the rapture of it all."

My cheeks heat, and it takes serious restraint to not punch Roman in the throat. But I know better than to argue, because Roman is relentless when he wants to be.

"If you stay, I want to stay." Katerina's pleading tone grates on my nerves.

"That won't be happening. You're a mess." Anatoly's hand wraps around his sister's upper arm, and he starts dragging her towards the exit, then stops and turns around, glaring at Roman and me.

Something passes over his gaze, a look that I can't name, but it sparks a shiver down my spine.

"Get her home safely, Vasiliev. After all, Liza is going to be my wife very soon."

Roman doesn't answer; he just stands, tight-jawed and serious, watching Anatoly haul his sister away.

We don't speak in the car for a long time. In some ways, there's so much to say, and in other ways, it's best if we say nothing at all.

Surprisingly, Anatoly didn't put up much of a fight when I left with Roman. Then again, it wouldn't look right if he couldn't trust his partner to give me a lift home.

Neither Roman nor I have acknowledged what happened on the balcony. Other than Roman dismissing his guard for the evening, he's maintained a stoic silence. Something is on his mind, but I'm hesitant to ask what it is. We both have secrets we're holding tight to our chest.

I'm dying to know why he made a deal with Katerina, of all people. Sure, she flits about the office of the family business, but I don't think she does any actual work unless dressing up and looking hot count.

But who knows. It's not like Anatoly tells me anything, especially since I've come home from London. He's been busy with work, and I've been "busy" wedding planning—a convenient lie that has allowed me to avoid him as much as possible.

As long as he stays away from Sofiya, I can deal with him.

Roman's phone rings, and he takes the call through Bluetooth. "Privet."

"Get your ass to the office. You're going to want to see this," a deep male voice that I recognize as Pavel's says.

Roman hesitates. "I have a guest with me. I'll be another hour."

Pavel snorts. "Screw that. Pull over, put her in a cab, and get here stat. I looked over the files Katerina sent, and we have a problem."

My head snaps towards Roman, but he's too busy pulling a crazy-ass U-turn to look my way.

"Roman, are you serious? Call a cab? I don't even know where we are."

"I'm not putting you in a cab," he grits. "You're coming with me. You can wait until I finish my business, and then I'll take you home."

"Or you can take me home and then go on your merry way. My preferred option, in case you care."

"No can do." He hits the accelerator. "We're close to my office, and this matter we're dealing with is pressing."

"Fine." I cross my arms in front of my chest. "Will you at least tell me what's going on? Why Katerina?" I ask before I lose the nerve. "What business could she possibly help you with?"

He looks over at me before his eyes ping back to the road. "I like that you're jealous." A hint of a smile plays on his lips, making those damn dimples pop. "It shows you care."

I shrug. After my outburst at the opera house, I can't exactly deny how I feel.

"It's about our business with the Petroviches," he continues. "Probably best if you don't know, seeing as you're marrying Anatoly." He says those final words like a challenge, waiting to see how I'll respond.

Anxiety coils low in my gut. I'm strangely tempted to tell Roman the truth about, well, everything. How terrible Anatoly is. How indebted I am to his family. How he uses Sofiya to keep me in line. The urge to share my secrets and unburden myself of everything I've held so tightly has never been stronger, but I force the feeling down.

I can't afford to get sloppy. Not now. Not when Roman is in business with Anatoly. Not when my money is growing every day. I'm close to being free of Anatoly, but I have to see my plan through, even if I will always wonder what-if when it comes to Roman.

His gaze shifts to the rearview mirror. He frowns, checks his side mirror, and bites out a curse. Before I can ask what's going on, the high-pitched squeal of tires cuts through the air.

"Hold on." Roman's voice is tight, his eyes darting to the mirror again. "We're being tailed."

Fear nudges at my calm, my heart thumping against my ribs.

Even at high speed, Roman controls the wheel with practiced ease as he reaches under his seat. For a gun.

Oh, shit.

My grip tightens on the door handle. "What the fuck is going on?"

"Wish I knew."

The sharp crack of gunfire shatters the night, bullets pinging off the car's exterior.

Without a second's hesitation, Roman's arm shoots out, pushing my head between my legs. "Stay down!" he commands in a voice that no one in their right mind would argue with.

Squeezing my eyes shut, I swallow down the fear and terror lodged in my throat. I focus on breathing and not having a damn panic attack on the floor of Roman's car because that wouldn't help anything.

He lowers his window. The screech of tires is louder and more ominous. And then he's returning gunfire. Or at least, I think he is.

I peek up to watch him drive with his right hand and shoot out the window with his left.

"Let me take the wheel." A surge of adrenaline gives me a momentary boost of courage.

"No. I won't risk your life."

This is crazy. We're being shot at and chased by God knows who. Still, I don't think he'd take kindly to me defying him at this moment.

The sounds of the chase, the gunshots, and the shattering glass are terrifying. My heart is in my throat, and I'm praying like mad that this isn't how we die.

As horrible as this is, taking a quick glance at Roman single-handedly fighting off our attackers steals my breath. The man has skills, that's for sure.

With a sharp turn, he whips the car into a wild swerve. There's a final roar of the engine, a loud crash, and then … nothing. The car stops, and the world goes quiet.

Cautiously, I raise my head, my eyes adjusting to the dim light inside the vehicle. Roman sits still, both hands on the steering wheel even though the car is no longer moving, his breaths coming in sharp, heavy pants.

What in God's name just happened?

Beyond him, outside the window, I see the vehicle that was chasing us. Its front is crumpled against a lamppost, steam billowing from the shattered engine. I can make out silhouettes of bodies slumped forward in their seats, blood sprayed all over the windows.

Roman grimaces, and his right hand—the one that so expertly drove the car moments ago—now cradles his left shoulder. When he pulls his hand away, it's coated in red.

"Oh my God, you're hurt!" Horror rushes through me as the reality of the situation sinks in.

"Only a scratch," Roman insists, though I'm not entirely sure that's true. "Just a shard of glass that cut me." His attention laser focuses on me. "Tell me you're okay," he demands, his hands reaching out to pat me down for any signs of injury.

"I'm not hurt—you are!" Before I can stop myself, I'm unbuckling my seat belt and crawling over the console to settle into his lap, seeking the reassurance of his warmth and touch.

"We almost died," I whimper, throwing my arms around his body, careful to avoid his injured shoulder as I nuzzle into his neck.

He groans, and I don't think it's because of his injury; the blood in his body seems to have settled somewhere much, much lower. Wow. There's no question how he responds to my touch. Objectively speaking, it's a bad time to get it on but tell that to my suddenly needy pussy.

"Roman," I say thickly, hiking my dress up around my hips. "That was hot."

He chokes out a laugh, which morphs into a strangled curse as I grind against his straining dick. But it's true. It was terrifying in the moment, but now that we're here, alive while they're dead, and Roman kicked ass and kept me safe …

Do I have a danger kink?

No one is around—the streets appear deserted this time of night—and despite the orgasm I had not long ago, a new kind of hunger rises in me. One that will only be sated with Roman deep inside of me.

My virginity was always his—regardless of the auction, there's no one else I'd want to be my first.

Straddling him, I pull down the front of my dress to free my breasts because I need to feel more of him touching me. He gets the message, leaning in and sucking my right nipple into his warm mouth.

Holy hell. I've already come tonight, but the dual sensation of grinding my core against his hardness and his tongue roving over my sensitive flesh feels like heaven. I bite my lip and throw my head back, as he licks and sucks the peak before moving on to the other tit.

"You're so perfect. Have I told you that, milaya?"

I moan, arching into him, and bury my hand in his hair as he flicks my left nipple with his tongue, again and again until I can't think straight.

"You need to fuck me now," I demand. I've wondered how he'd feel inside me ever since London, and I suddenly can't wait another minute to find out.

I rock against him, frantic for more, but when I reach down to undo his belt buckle, he stops me with his hand over mine. With a final scrape of his teeth over my nipple, he leans back and closes his eyes for a moment to regain control.

"You have no idea how much I want to be inside you, but we have to get out of here. They might have backup on the way."

My face falls in disappointment, which only makes him laugh.

He brings his hands up and palms my breasts, making me shiver. "It's a temporary delay. I'm taking you back to my penthouse and fucking you silly."

His words slowly bring me back to reality.

"Wait. I can't go home with you."

His gaze thins. "Why not?"

"My parents, and—" I bite my lip, a jumble of worried thoughts invading my brain. "Anatoly will be furious you didn't take me home." I hate that this is what I have to worry about at a time like this, but I can't lose my head.

"We were just attacked. No one is going to question why I took you somewhere safe to lay low after what happened." He brushes a strand of hair away from my face. "We deserve this night together."

I gnaw at my lip, battling the internal tug-of-war of my desires.

Roman's eyes darken, but he says nothing for a minute, only captures my chin between his thumb and forefinger, demanding my attention. "Leave him to me."

"Okay," I whisper.

I have no more fight left in me. Only for tonight, I'll give myself to Roman. It might be stupid and risky, but if I don't, it's a regret I'll carry forever. Tonight will be for me. A memory to savor for the rest of my life.

Because once I'm free of Anatoly, once I'm free of this world, I won't be sucked back in by any man. For Sofiya's sake, I'll show her true independence and strength. What it really means to stand on your own two feet.

Roman's expression relaxes as his lips find mine.

This kiss is slow and seductive. His hands cradle my face as he slides his tongue against mine. I press closer, craving more, but he gently pulls away.

"We really have to go," he whispers against my lips. "But trust me, I plan on finishing what we started." With a final sweep of his hands down my body, he smooths my dress down and lifts me back into my seat, straps my seat belt on, and kisses my forehead.

This sweet, caring side of Roman makes my stomach swoop with need.

He makes me crave something real, something I've never experienced before.

CHAPTER THIRTY-THREE

ROMAN

It's goddamn cold out, but I ignore the howling wind ripping through the jacket of my suit as I step outside onto my balcony. I also ignore the dull ache in my shoulder as I swig from the bottle of vodka in my hand in an attempt to calm my racing nerves.

I've stared down the barrel of a gun countless times, but having Liza by my side amplified the fear to a whole new level. The thought of losing her because of my actions had my heart pounding relentlessly in my chest. Her life was at risk because of me. Dismissing my guard before driving her home was reckless, all because I wanted to be alone with her.

Swallowing a final gulp of vodka, I debrief Pavel on the situation via text, attaching pictures of our would-be attackers' vehicle that I captured before we fled the scene. They had no ID on them, and there was nothing in their vehicle to indicate who they're working for. Whoever sent them took pains to ensure they couldn't be traced.

I'll meet with Pavel in the morning. Whatever he wanted to share can wait another few hours. Hopefully, by the time we meet, our men will have some intelligence on tonight's attack.

Running one of the most powerful syndicates on Russian soil, we have no lack of enemies. Still, an uneasy feeling churns in my gut. Not many people knew the time our ship loaded with cargo was scheduled to dock.

Would Anatoly leak this kind of information to the Zhukovs? Anything is possible, but why? What's his motivation? Our partnership is mutually beneficial and making us all a shit ton of money. Until I have proof that Anatoly's loyalties lie elsewhere, I can't make a move against him. Too much is at stake. But I'm watching him closely; one misstep, and I'll take him down.

My professional restraint doesn't apply to Liza. Anatoly forfeited any claim to her the moment I saw that bruise on her. And I'm giving him a free pass for taking Sofiya out drinking with a bunch of his business cronies.

Stepping back inside my penthouse, I find Liza rummaging in the kitchen cupboard under my sink. "Looking for where I hide the bodies?"

She rises to her feet, smiling. "I was looking for your first aid kit."

"Why? What's wrong?" I ask, concern flooding through me.

"I'm fine. It's for you." Her lips press into a thin line as her eyes land on my shoulder.

"Right, that." I chuckle. "My first aid kit is in the bathroom."

I grab her hand and lead her towards my bedroom. As we step inside, curiosity lights up her features. She takes it all in —the stone fireplace, plush Persian rugs, natural wood finishes.

"This isn't what I expected." She releases my hand to wander further into my space. "I pictured some sort of swinging bachelor pad with mirrors on the ceiling. That kind of thing. But this is actually pretty cozy."

"I'll tell you a secret." I lean against the doorframe and watch her with a half-smile. "You're the first woman to step foot in here, other than my housekeeper."

She tilts her head and narrows her eyes. "Yeah, right."

"I have no reason to lie. This is my home; there was never anyone I wanted to invite into my space." I drag a knuckle over my chin. "I'm not saying I'm a saint, but I do have boundaries."

She flushes, and I can tell she likes the idea that I'm breaking new ground. That's when she notices the book by my bed. She thumbs through the dog-eared pages of *Jane Eyre*. "You actually read this?"

"Front to back." I straighten up. "I wanted to see what you found so compelling about it."

She sets the book down and raises her eyebrows. "And?"

I shake my head and bring a rough palm to cup her face. "The truth is, I read it to get in your head. To try and figure you out."

She licks her lips, unease flickering in her eyes as if she's afraid I'll uncover all her secrets. "Have you figured me out yet, Roman?"

"Far from it." My hand slides from her cheek to the back of her neck. "But I want to know everything there is to know about you."

She blinks up at me, her throat working hard to swallow. "We should deal with your shoulder."

I lead her towards the en suite, which is decidedly less cozy and more flashy. Marble countertops and a large, free-standing bathtub dominate the bathroom.

"Quite a tub," she murmurs.

"Could easily fit the two of us," I point out with a wink before I reach under the sink and pull out the first aid kit.

Liza wags a finger at me. "You won't be able to get this dressing wet. Now strip."

I shrug innocently. "I'm going to need your help."

She rolls her eyes, helping me take off my jacket. She then unbuttons my dress shirt and slips it off my shoulders, mindful of the wound. Her eyes linger on the expanse of my bare, tattooed chest. Heat creeps onto her cheeks as she drinks me in.

I grab her wrist and pull her towards me. "It's nothing you haven't seen before," I whisper against her lips. "Except, this time, you're free to touch."

"Tempting." Her voice is teasing. "But I have work to do first."

That doesn't stop her from leaning in and capturing my mouth in a deep kiss that's all kinds of magic. I'm ready to pull her down into my lap and ravage her mouth, but with a hand on my bare chest, she stops me.

"We have time for that," she promises.

I shake my head in an attempt to come back down to earth while she rummages through the first aid kit.

She studies my shoulder. "Looks like it's nothing more than a graze."

"How do you know how to do any of this?" I ask as she skillfully flushes the wound with saline before applying a disinfectant. "Your family's not even bratva."

She curls her lip. "Yeah, but my father got himself in trouble with the bratvas. His drinking and gambling addictions mean he's come home plenty of times with wounds far worse than this." She shakes her head, a frown overtaking her beautiful face. "You'd think he would have learned by now."

"Addiction is addiction. It's not easy to stop cold turkey."

"True. And it's not easy to stop when your wife insists on money coming into the household, no matter what. If my mother really wanted my father to get clean, she would have helped. Instead, she kept insisting that he gamble bigger to recoup his losses. Not that it ever worked."

"And that's why your parents need you to marry rich. To keep them afloat." Bitterness crawls up my throat as I think about all the shit Liza's family has put her through for their gain, never considering what's best for her and her life.

Her mouth tightens, and she doesn't say anything for a while. "Families are complicated, but everything I do, I do for Sofiya. My parents made their own bed."

The expression on her face tells me she's reached the end of her patience when it comes to her parents.

I release a sharp breath as she dabs at my shoulder with disinfectant.

"Sorry, this part always hurts," she murmurs.

"I like the pain," I joke. "Do what you have to."

"You need a few stitches," she says, threading a needle with a steady hand. "Want a shot of vodka?"

"Nah, I had some earlier. This won't be my first time getting stitched up without anesthetic. Helps that the nurse is so hot." I reach down and palm her ass.

She swats away my hand with a grin. "Behave." She leans in, her hands steady as she pierces the skin near the wound and pulls the thread through with precision. "Who would attack you?" she asks, focusing on her task.

"I work for the most powerful syndicate in Russia. Take your pick."

"There you go." Liza focuses on tying off the final stitch. It's adorable how seriously she undertakes the task, concentration etched in the furrow between her brows. When she finishes, she stands back and admires her handiwork. "Should heal nicely. You got lucky it was only a shard of glass."

"We both got lucky." I rise and pull her into me. "And now we're both going to get really lucky."

Her eyes darken as she picks up on my intent. I thought

she might lose her nerve, but when she leans in and closes the gap between us, her kiss is hungry and insistent. I grind my hips against hers, needing the friction. She feels too fucking good. But she would feel that much better if we were naked.

I pull away from her just long enough to drop my pants and kick my boxer briefs aside. Then my mouth is back on her as she runs her fingers over my taut chest and abs, pulling a deep groan from me. I need more.

"You look like a goddess in red." I strip the dress from her body. She laughs and brings her mouth to mine in a slow, erotic kiss. "Shit. What was that for?" I rasp. "Not that I'm complaining."

"Just 'cause."

I lift her, guiding her to perch on the edge of the marble sink. She widens her legs and I step forward, plunging my hand in her hair and pulling her mouth against mine. She makes a sound of need from deep in her throat, and I pull away to kiss and suck the delicate skin along the underside of her jaw. My straining cock presses against her, positioned at the entrance of her pussy.

With only one thrust I'd sink into her wet heat. I'd be the first man inside of her, taking what belongs to me.

"Are you sure?" I breathe against her skin.

"Yes," she gasps.

"Beg for it."

Her eyes snap wide, and she looks at me as if I had spoken in tongues.

I rub the tip of my cock over the length of her slit, paying extra special attention to her clit.

She releases a wanton hiss. "Roman, please."

"Please what?"

Her hand buries in my hair as she grabs a fistful and tugs. Shit, that feels good.

"You know what I want," she whines.

"In London, I said I wouldn't fuck you until you begged

me." I suck her bottom lip into my mouth, grazing my teeth lightly over her delicate skin. "I meant it."

Liza tips her hips forward, inviting me in. The movement causes the tip of my cock to brush over her clit repeatedly, and she shudders, her eyes closing in pleasure. Seeing how much she enjoys it, I do it again. Fisting my dick with one hand, I brush it through her folds, up and down over her slit, before rubbing it in circles over her clit.

"Jeee-sus! Fine, Roman. Please fuck me. I can't wait any longer."

Thank the lord she came to her senses. I can't either. She shimmies forward, spread out so beautifully for me. "Just because you asked so nicely," I say, and give a shallow thrust between her legs. Shit. My head rolls back because this feels way too good, way too quickly.

I'm by no means a small man, so I allow her time to adjust to my size. As I push forward, she cries out, and I capture her earlobe between my teeth, hoping the sensation cancels out the bite of pain in her core.

"Are you okay?" I rasp, my muscles tense as I try to hold still for her.

Her nod is frantic. "Oh God, Roman. Is it supposed to feel this way? Like it's too much?"

"Baby, it's only the first few inches."

"Are you kidding me?"

A laugh rumbles from my chest. "Deep breaths." I hold still as my lips explore her neck, sucking and biting at her skin. At my command, she fills her lungs with long steady breaths, her body slowly relaxing around me.

Even though I'm not fully seated inside her, my dick doesn't care. He's damn near ready to explode, and it's taking every ounce of willpower I possess to not press forward and impale her on my full length.

I kiss the corner of her mouth and drag my lips toward her ear. "I should put on a condom."

She pulls back and looks in my eyes. "Are you clean?"

I nod. "I get tested regularly, and I haven't been with anyone in a long time."

It's the truth. I tried and failed.

The night Anatoly announced their wedding date, I showed up on Tanya's doorstep and couldn't bring myself to ring the bell. I stood there for way too many minutes, trying to talk myself into going in, before I realized that Liza had me in a choke hold I wasn't going to escape anytime soon.

With arms around my neck, she pulls me forward and whispers in my ear, "Take me bare. I'm on birth control to regulate my periods."

This is a bad idea, underlined in red with a thousand exclamation points behind it. Because once I fuck her raw and fill up her tight cunt with my seed, no other high will compare.

But will that stop me? Definitely not.

"I can't say no to you." My hand delves between us, and I give her clit slow, sure circles to soften the pinch of my invasion.

"Don't hold back," she murmurs against my skin.

I groan as she wraps her legs around me to pull me closer.

Damn. Liza may be inexperienced, but I sense a freak in the making. The thought is hot as hell. I surge forward, giving her what she asked for by not treating her like a delicate flower. Trembling, I let out a hiss, the pleasure too intense to contain.

Her fingernails dig into my biceps, leaving little half-moons etched into my skin. I don't mind. I want something to remember this moment by.

"I love my name on your lips." I kiss down her throat, giving her short thrusts and sliding in a little deeper each time. "You can't imagine how unbelievably good your pussy feels milking my cock."

I kiss her like my life depends on it, relishing in her taste, in her surrender, as my thrusts grow more intense. As everything else fades away, I'm consumed by her and the primal needs she inspires in me.

She pulls back an inch. "Did I … Did I bleed? I don't want to look."

"Don't think about that right now. Focus on my lips and tongue." I suck the soft skin of her neck into my mouth. "Focus on my fingers." I cup one of her shapely breasts and pinch her nipples. "Focus on my cock rocking in and out of you. How I'm the first man to claim you."

And the last. But she's not ready to hear that yet.

CHAPTER THIRTY-FOUR

LIZA

THERE ARE NO WORDS TO DESCRIBE HOW IT FEELS TO HAVE Roman inside me, holding me close, making me feel safe, cherished, and desired. Yes, there's pain, but it comes intertwined with pleasure.

However I imagined sex would be like for the first time, this experience surpassed all my expectations. And that's because of one reason: Roman.

I can't get enough of him—the smell of his skin, the feel of his lips, the way he holds me with both command and reverence. I love how he grasps my hips as if his life depends on it, the ferocity of his groans in my ear, and how his thrusts become unsteady and urgent when my muscles clench possessively around him.

I'm perched on the edge of a bathroom sink, the cold marble pressing against my backside, but somehow, it still feels perfect.

"I am going to make you come for me," he declares between slow, drugging kisses. His fingers strum gently over my clit.

"I don't know if I can."

"You can, and you will."

He rocks into me steadily as my fingers tighten around his neck, my toes curling with every thrust.

"Open up," he commands. "You're going to get my fingers nice and wet."

Two of his inked fingers slide into my mouth. I swirl my tongue around them, enjoying the way Roman's amber-brown eyes turn dark as night.

"Perfect," he praises, lowering his soaked digits onto my overly sensitive clit. Instead of running them in neat little circles, like earlier, he pinches the nub. It's not a hard pinch, but sensation blasts through my body at the first touch.

"Oh my … Roman," I choke out.

"Roman or God." He smiles devilishly. "I answer to both."

If any of my brain cells still functioned, I might roll my eyes at his oversized ego. But as it is, I'm barely able to string a sentence together.

Whimpering against his mouth is all I can do. I grip him tightly as my body convulses. Everything around me vanishes, leaving only the raw hunger. I explore his mouth with my tongue, tightening my legs around his waist, as a groan rumbles from his chest.

His fingers dance over my clit, moving in time with his cock slamming into me, and just like that, the pressure builds in my core. I know I can't hold back even if I wanted to.

I squeeze my eyes shut, needing to get lost in the moment. "Roman, I'm going to—"

As my pussy clenches hard around him, he moves his hand from my clit and wraps it around my throat. His grip is light—he doesn't squeeze or cut off my airway—but his hold is so dominant and demanding that my body has a super-sized response.

I unravel, an orgasm ripping through me as he delivers a final deep, bruising thrust. His cock pulses, and heat fills me as he lowers his mouth against mine—not kissing, simply breathing in the same air.

"Holy shit, Liza." Roman's voice is thick as he touches his forehead to mine. "That was unreal."

He gives a final few pumps before he slowly pulls out of me. Wetness coats my thighs—proof of our shared pleasure.

"You must be sore." He doesn't wait for my answer; he wraps me in his arms and carries me into the bedroom. After laying me down on his bed, he kisses my forehead and returns to the bathroom.

I hear water running. I'm not sure what he's up to until he's back, easing my legs open to press something warm and soothing against my core.

"Is this okay?" he asks, concern lining his features when I sharply inhale.

It takes me a minute to realize he's using a warm washcloth to soothe me.

"It stings a little, but it was worth it." I flash him a smile.

Every muscle in my body throbs, but I've never felt so amazing. Like I'm still high off his touch.

He leans down and presses a kiss to my forehead. "I'm relieved to hear you say that."

Roman makes sure I'm tucked in under the covers, then joins me in bed, pulling me close, his solid weight warm and comforting at my back.

Despite everything, a small pang of something bubbles in my chest. "I wish it wasn't a one-time thing," I say into the dark.

Roman exhales loudly but stays quiet.

Is he disappointed? Maybe there's just nothing else to say.

He runs a hand down the side of my body. "It doesn't have to be a one-time thing."

I roll over to face him. "How can you say that? We both have too much at stake to risk"—I struggle for the right word —"*everything.*"

He stares at the ceiling, his expression not giving anything away. "Life has a way of throwing curve balls. Especially in the world I live in, where nothing is as it seems."

"I don't know what you mean."

He considers me for a second. Whatever is going on in that intense brain of his is a mystery to me.

When I think he's not going to answer at all, he releases a sigh. "Let's not waste the time we have together talking about this." He rolls over on top of me, his delicious weight pressing me down.

I allow myself to melt into the mattress.

"If we only have tonight," he says against my neck, "I want to make the most of it."

My eyes grow wide. "I didn't know it was possible to get hard so quickly after."

He snickers. "I won't take you again tonight, however tempting that is. I have other plans for you."

"Oh?"

My confusion melts away when he throws the covers off, crawls down my body, and settles between my spread thighs. Then his talented tongue gets to work.

CHAPTER
THIRTY-FIVE

LIZA

I WAKE TO SUNSHINE FILTERING INTO THE ROOM AND THE SMELL of Roman all around me. A smile forms on my lips as I turn to reach for him, but he's not there—only an empty spot, cool to the touch.

Oh. I had hoped we'd have one final morning together.

I push aside the sinking feeling as memories from yesterday come flooding back. Roman kissing me, on top of me, inside of me, and all the dirty things he said and did.

The bite between my legs confirms last night wasn't a fever dream; it was as real as it gets, and I don't regret any of it. How could I, when he made me feel alive, as though I was experiencing desire for the first time?

My first time with Roman is etched in my soul—a memory I'll cherish forever. But now, it's time to face the music.

Last night, I sent a quick text to my parents letting them know there had been an incident and I was spending the night somewhere safe. I turned off my phone before they could reply.

Anatoly must know by now, and I'm sure he's upset that I didn't call him myself. As much as I'd like to put off that conversation forever, I can't. But my story needs to be airtight, and for that, I need to speak with Roman to make sure we are on the same page.

The thought of powering up my phone and sifting through all the messages already has me stressed. Coffee first, then I can tackle the rest.

I stretch my arms overhead and hop out of bed, fully naked. Putting on last night's dress is unappealing, so I rummage around in Roman's closet for something to wear. In the first drawer I open, I find a simple white T-shirt. I slip it over my head, breathing in his clean, masculine scent.

We're almost a week away from the wedding.

Before leaving for the opera last night, I checked my account balance. I've done well, but I'm still $100 thousand short, which means I can't afford any more distractions.

I haven't allowed myself to dwell on what will happen if I can't come up with enough money to pay back our debts before the wedding. I could use the money I've made so far to take Sofiya and leave Moscow. Run away to New York or Paris or somewhere no one knows us. But that means living in hiding for the rest of my life since I have no doubt Anatoly would pursue us to the ends of the earth. Not because he loves me, but because he wouldn't be able to handle the blow to his giant ego.

And my sister … Would she hate me for ripping her from the life she loves? Would she believe that Anatoly is a monster, even though I've hidden that side of him from her?

Running away would also mean breaking Kira's heart. How could I even explain it to her? Who am I kidding? There's truly no winning in this situation, which is why I can't afford to fail.

On the flip side, I haven't allowed myself to think about what happens if I succeed. What I'd want my life to look like.

Hopefully, after paying Anatoly back, I'll have enough money left to continue investing and growing my income. Maybe I could even return to school for business administration or finance—a foundation for building my career.

The idea is so exhilarating that a shiver of anticipation runs through my body. Freedom. What a foreign concept—being able to do exactly what I want, whenever I want, with whomever I want.

In a perfect world, would Roman be part of my life? The answer is clear in my heart—yes, a thousand times yes—but there's no point in entertaining that possibility. Syndicate business will always come first for him. He's made that clear himself.

Indulging in a what-if fantasy will only break my heart.

No matter how this ends, I must stay away from Roman.

It might be hard, but it will be necessary.

After using the bathroom—blushing the whole time while staring at the sink ledge—I head towards the main living area, hoping to find Roman waiting for me with a steaming cup of coffee and a bare chest, because I didn't spend enough time ogling him last night.

I take a deep breath and pull my shoulders back. There's no point in lingering in here, not when we could be enjoying our final morning together. Maybe we can hold off the real world for a little longer and make use of that giant claw-foot tub in his bathroom.

When I step into the kitchen, I'm not greeted by the sound of clinking dishes or the smell of freshly brewed coffee. Only silence.

Did he go out to grab us breakfast? Probably not, considering the attack on his life. It's possible he's working out. He certainly doesn't get his ripped physique without time spent in the gym.

I wander through the rooms of his penthouse, first coming

across an impressive home theater and a cozy library. When I finally reach the gym, the door is open, letting in a soft morning light, but once again, it's empty.

A weight presses down on my chest. What did I expect? That he'd wake me up with breakfast in bed and poetry? I'm being silly. I told him this could only be a one-time thing—of course he left without saying goodbye. He probably thought it was easier this way, and frankly, he's right.

It still hurts, though.

I trudge back to the living room, knowing I can't put off the inevitable any longer. I need to turn on my phone and deal with the outside world.

My clutch is on the side table, where I left it last night. Sinking down onto the sofa, I open the shiny leather purse only to find it nearly empty. There's no phone inside, only a single handwritten letter.

Good morning, milaya,

I'm sorry to disappear so early. Trust me, if I had a choice, I'd be buried between your thighs all day, but duty calls.

Now, I need you to take a deep breath because you're not going to be happy with what I'm about to tell you.

You're locked inside the penthouse. There are guards outside the door and in front of all the entrances to the building. I also took your phone.

You're probably cursing my name right now, but I promise all of this is to keep you safe.

We don't know who attacked us last night. I was likely the target, but I don't know that for sure.

Until I get some answers, staying with me is the best option.

Hate me all you want but know I'll do whatever it takes to protect you each and every time.

I'll be back home as soon as I can. The kitchen is stocked with food, so help yourself. Wander around, snoop through my drawers, and find something in my closet to wear. I bet you'll look damn hot in my clothes.

Roman xo

What?! He locked me in his penthouse?

I try to throw the note across the room, but when it only flutters to the floor, I stomp on it with my foot. Then I pick it up and rip it into a million different pieces.

I appreciate that Roman wants to keep me safe, but it would've been nice for him to have checked with me first. Now, I can't contact anyone, and they can't contact me, and I have no idea when he's coming back.

Will my family worry? Will Anatoly be angry?

It's possible they'll think I was abducted or something bad happened to me, but that's no better.

Worry gnaws at me. At the very least, I have to find a way to contact Sofiya. But without a phone, I'm shit out of luck. Even if I find a computer, it's likely secured with a password.

But the worst part is that my phone has all the trading apps, all my financial information, and everything I need to manage my investments. What if Roman discovers it? I've gone to great lengths to secure my phone with encrypted passwords and multi-factor authentication, but there's always the chance that a computer whiz on his team could find a way in. Beyond that, if I can't monitor my investments, buying and selling at the exact right moment, I'm screwed.

Everything I worked so hard for is crumbling around me.

Fuck him, thinking he can play God with my life!

He has no idea what he's done, but he will find out soon enough when I take my revenge.

CHAPTER THIRTY-SIX

ROMAN

"She's going to fucking kill you," Pavel says as Viktor hands me back Liza's cell phone—the one his hackers broke into. "I amend that. She's going to string you up by your balls, damage your internal organs, and then cut off your dick until you bleed out."

"Sounds about right," I admit, cracking my neck. I'm fully prepared to deal with Liza's wrath because it's for her own good, even if she might not realize it yet.

Pavel settles into the seat across from me in our office tucked above a butcher's shop in the seedier side of town. It's the last place anyone would expect to find guys like us, which is exactly why we're here. And hey, if you need to make a body disappear, what's better than a butcher's shop?

I sip my coffee, but honestly, I don't even need the caffeine. It's barely dawn, and I've gotten almost no sleep, but I'm still riding high on the night I had with Liza.

Truth be told, I had to tear myself from my warm bed this morning. There is no better feeling than waking up beside her. Well, perhaps the only thing better is being buried inside of her. But I couldn't delay this meeting any longer.

"You're sure there are no tracking devices on here?" I ask Viktor, slipping Liza's phone into my pocket.

"Yeah, about that." He shakes his head, almost looking impressed. "We couldn't break into it. She has her phone locked down tighter than a nun's pussy."

"Jesus, I could do without the visual there." I shake my head. "So you're saying the hackers couldn't get into her phone?"

Viktor sighs. "I don't know what she's hiding in there, but whatever it is, she's gone to great lengths to make sure no one can access it. Which also means she's probably tech savvy enough to ensure no one's tracking her."

Apprehension pools in my gut. We all carry secrets, and considering her decision to auction her virginity, I'm guessing Liza has more than her fair share. But what else is she hiding? There's a nagging curiosity in me, a need to peel back the layers of her life.

"I thought you'd want to see this." Pavel hands me a stack of papers. "The police report from the accident. The cops got there before our men did, but our contacts at the station sent this over. They ran a trace on the plates. They're fakes, of course. Surveillance in the area showed nothing helpful. We're still looking into the identity of the drivers, but so far, their prints are coming up empty." He blinks, looking down at the gruesome photos of the two slumped bodies in the vehicles.

"You're lucky you walked away with your life." Viktor frowns. "I won't ask why you dismissed your guard when backup would've been helpful."

"I'm not sure if luck had anything to do with it," I grit out. "The only reason we're both still alive is because I'm a sure shot and capable of driving one-handed."

Viktor rolls his eyes.

I'm being an ass, but the truth is I did make a mistake. One that's still weighing heavily on me because every time I think that Liza could have died, a knot forms in my stomach. She's too damn bright of a light to be extinguished so young.

At thirty-eight, I've done most everything in my life I wanted to. I've seen the world, owned fast cars, drank fine wines, climbed mountains, and dived into the deepest seas. I never dreamed of having a family or a wife. Other than Maxim and Pavel, and now Kira, there'll be no one to mourn me in death. Knowing my death won't break hearts certainly makes my line of work easier.

But Liza is thirteen years younger than me and has her whole life ahead of her. She has Kira and Sofiya—people who love her and whom she loves. Dying beside me on a desolate stretch of Moscow's highway would've been cruel and unjust. Then again, this world *is* cruel. I know firsthand.

I run a hand over the scruff on my jaw, feeling a heavy weight in my chest. "It could be the Albanians. They've wanted to take us down for years."

"You're grasping at straws. We need to look a little closer to home." Pavel opens his desk drawer and pulls out a stack of papers. "This is what I wanted to show you last night." He passes me two separate files. "The first document is the shipping logs that Anatoly's men sent us. And the second is what Katerina sent you. Same shipment, same dates, but the logs don't match. They should be identical, but they're not."

What the hell?

I scoot forward in my seat and lean over the paperwork, my eyes darting between the two sets of logs. Anatoly's version has the ship waiting out the bad weather in the North Atlantic—the reason given for the delay. But the unaltered logs Katerina sent show that the ship stopped in Port of Rotterdam for a full day. The port is a major hub into Europe, and the gateway to Europe's underbelly. While it's not exactly on the route here, it's not a major detour either.

I look up at Pavel's stony face. "That motherfucker doctored the logs."

"Seems so." He cracks his knuckles. "The question is why."

My entire body radiates tension, like a coiled spring, and I slam my fist on the desk in front of me. "He's fucking up to something. I can feel it. Secret meetings with the Zhukovs. Forging the logs." I shake my head. "It doesn't make sense. Our men went through each and every shipment. It was all in order, nothing was missing."

The high heel I found on the cargo ship comes to mind. Is the crew bringing hookers onboard for a night of partying in Rotterdam? It certainly wouldn't be unheard of. Maybe they make a regular pit stop on the way here to get their rocks off. If that's the case, it would be a really bad reason to deliver cargo late. Or maybe I'm reading too much into it.

Viktor's forehead creases. "I'll have my hackers pull CCTV footage from the port of the day the ship was docked there."

"Good call." I check my phone. "A shipment left New York today. Let's send Savin to the Netherlands to watch the port in case there's a repeat. While he's there, he can make some inquiries."

Pavel releases a quiet, tense breath. "You think Anatoly was behind last night's attack?"

My lungs tighten. I walk to the window, gazing out at the streets below. "With Liza in the car? I don't see it." As far as I can tell, Liza is the only thing Anatoly cares to protect. Not because he loves her, but because he loves the control he has over her and her entire family. "But, damn, who knows. I'm assuming it's the same people behind the attack on the port and the attack last night."

I'm struggling to put together the full picture; it's like all the pieces are there, but nothing is clicking together.

"Maybe it was the Zhukovs," Viktor throws out, spinning

a pen between his fingers. "Revenge for killing their men at the warehouse."

I run an irritated hand through my hair. "There's no way for them to know we were behind their soldiers' deaths. Anyhow, they wouldn't mess with us unless they have a death wish."

Pavel crosses his arms in front of his chest. "Should we loop Maxim in?"

"I'll tell him when the time is right. I want him to know it's being handled, that he doesn't need to race home."

After the attack on the port, Maxim whisked Kira off to the Maldives to steer clear of any trouble. He's entrusted me to work out whatever shit is going on, and I don't want to burden him unless I know more. I already feel stupid enough that the Zhukovs slipped under my radar.

"Maxim is the only one we tell." I take a seat and rest my elbows on my thighs. "The less people who know what's going on, the better. Whatever bullshit Anatoly is up to, we need to catch him unaware. It's better if he thinks we're clueless."

"This may not be Anatoly," Viktor points out. "We've had him tailed since London, and after the meeting with Sergey Zhukov, there's been nothing out of the ordinary."

I shrug. "Only time will tell."

Pavel gestures to the documents on his desk. "And you're sure Katerina won't be a problem?"

"I had her send over a bunch of files at once. She doesn't know which one I was really after. Trust me, she's not that clever."

Pavel leans back, lacing his fingers behind his head. "Glad you're feeling so confident, but if it's business as usual, you need to return Liza to her fiancé before he gets suspicious."

My lips press into a determined line. "Not happening."

"How is that going to look?" Viktor frowns. "You know she wasn't the target of the attack. You were."

"We don't know anything yet." I shrug. "Until we do, she stays with me."

Pavel presses his fingers into the bridge of his nose. "Sometimes, I think you've lost your mind."

Over Liza, I definitely have.

Viktor squints at me. "How do you plan on letting Anatoly know you're keeping his fiancé hosta—as a guest?"

I smile and take out my phone. "Watch and learn, my friend."

I dial Anatoly's number and put the phone on speaker.

"Roman," he answers right away. "What the fuck is going on? Liza sends a cryptic text to her parents last night about some sort of attack on the way home from the opera, and then I can't get through to either of you all night. What the hell is that?!"

Funny how he doesn't sound all that concerned for Liza, only irritated that he wasn't able to get ahold of her when he wanted to.

"It was best to have no outside communication while we figured out what was going on. We still don't know who was behind the attack." I pause to let my next words sink in. "Although, we have our suspicions."

He releases a low grunt. "This is bullshit. Where is Liza now?"

"Don't worry. She's safe." I smirk, though he can't see it. "Maxim thought it best if she goes into hiding with Kira. We doubt she was the target of the attack, but it's better to not take any chances."

Maxim's word is law in this city, and Anatoly knows that. What he doesn't know is that Maxim and Kira are out of the country, and unless he has their private cell numbers—which he doesn't—there's no way for him to contact them.

"I'm perfectly capable of protecting Liza," he snarls. "We're getting married soon! She can't just disappear."

"We were nearly killed last night," I spit, "and you're

worried about a wedding? Delay the wedding for all I care. We have a bigger issue on our hands."

Anatoly's anger boils over, his voice rising. "She's my fiancée. I have every right to talk to her and to know where she is."

"Man, I wish I could help, but Kira's keeping tight-lipped. You know how protective she is of her best friend."

"I'm calling Belov!" Anatoly seethes.

"You do that." I think he'll find Maxim rather unavailable. "Might be smart for you to be careful as well. These days, it's hard to know who's your friend and who's your enemy."

"You don't need to worry about me, Vasiliev. I always watch my back."

"Trust me, I wasn't." I hang up before he can say another word.

I sigh and lean back in my chair, the weight of the last twenty-four hours pressing down on me.

"Does that sound like a guilty man to you?" I ask Pavel.

"He sounds like a man pissed off that you're keeping his fiancée."

"Screw him." I rise from my seat. "He doesn't deserve her anyhow." My shoulders bunch around my ears. "There was a bruise on her face. I saw it in London. She didn't admit he's the one who gave it to her, but I could tell. You can always tell." Pavel knows how broken my soul is. How watching my father beat my mother, unable to stop him, left scars on my heart that will never heal. What he doesn't know is that Liza is the first person to make me feel whole again. To make me feel something other than jaded and empty.

"Fuck me." Pavel rakes a hand over his face. "Listen, take Liza and get out of town. Lay low somewhere until we can figure out what's going on with that mudak."

Viktor's expression is equally dark when he says, "I promise to do everything in my power to uncover who is behind the attacks. Justice will be served. It'll be my pleasure to watch Anatoly burn in hell."

"Trust me, no one will enjoy that more than me." I crack my knuckles, feeling a fierce wave of determination wash over me.

Maxim taught me the importance of patience, to wait for the perfect moment to act. When that moment comes for Anatoly, I'll strike swiftly and without mercy.

But I won't sacrifice Liza's safety and well-being ever again. She is and always will be my priority.

"Gentlemen." I head for the door. "Call me when you have something. I'll be ready and waiting."

CHAPTER THIRTY-SEVEN

ROMAN

I PUSH THE DOOR TO THE PENTHOUSE OPEN, EXPECTING TO FIND Liza pacing and plotting a hundred different ways to kill me, but instead, I'm met with silence. I call out her name a few times, but there's no answer.

A cold dread settles in my stomach. My men are stationed right outside the door—there's no way anyone could have gotten in here undetected.

Could Liza have hurt herself to get back at me? The thought has me bolting through the penthouse, calling for her, but all I hear is the echo of my own voice against the cold, empty walls.

As I step into the shadowed living room, I feel the cold press of a blade against my neck. I'm ready to toss the assailant across the room when I realize who it is.

"Liza? It's me," I assure her. I'm so relieved to find her unharmed I don't immediately register she's the one standing in front of me, pressing a knife to my jugular.

"Oh, I'm well aware," she seethes. "Now, let me be clear about what's going to happen. You're going to give me my phone back, and then you're going to let me go." She presses the tip of what is clearly a kitchen knife against my skin, hard enough that I feel the sharp edge pierce the surface, and a sting of pain follows. "I don't know where you get off playing God with my life, but I really don't like it."

The edge in her voice could cut steel, but I can't help the smirk that tugs at my lips. I appreciate her bravado, even if I could disarm her in a heartbeat and turn the tables with a simple twist of my wrist if I wanted to. But I won't.

"My apologies," I say sincerely. "If you'd kindly remove the knife from my throat, I can give you back your phone."

She shoots me a fierce look. "Not until you tell me why you took it."

"I needed to check if there was a tracker installed. Nobody can know our location."

Her eyebrows lift, disappearing beneath her dark bangs. "And is there a tracker installed?"

"I don't know," I admit, my jaw tight. "Because, apparently, you're a secret computer whiz and no one could hack into your fucking phone."

She gives me a smug smile, but it doesn't last long. "That doesn't explain why you locked me up in your house. I can't simply disappear from my life. My parents are probably wondering where I am, and Anatoly …" She clears her throat but doesn't finish that thought.

Annoyance spikes through me. I hate how those meant to love and protect her simply don't care. They're only upset because this mess is unfolding right before her wedding—a wedding that won't be happening if I have a say in the matter.

I try to talk sense into her. "We were almost killed last night. Yeah, I was probably the intended target, but we can't assume anything until we have more information."

Her face falls. "Surely this is not about me."

"Probably not, but I'm not a man who takes chances when it comes to something I care about."

She blinks a few times, her expression softening. "I … I can't stay here with you," she pleads. "We had last night. Let's leave it on a good note." There's a hint of regret in her tone, but she covers it up with a fierce look.

It's then my gaze slides down her body. *Shit*. She's wearing one of my T-shirts and little else, as far as I can tell.

A warm sense of possession grows in my chest. "You look good in my clothes," I growl.

"Enjoy the view. Because this is the last time you'll see me in something that's yours. I'm leaving here, and you can't stop me."

My voice drops an octave. "I think we both know I can. Very easily."

"I'm serious, Roman. This has gone too far!" She twists the blade into my skin to make her point. "I'm getting married soon. Anatoly will send people to look for me. He'll ask questions. Don't put me in that position." Her eyes cloud with fear, and it makes me want to pummel that asshole's face even harder.

"I told you I'd handle him, and I did. He thinks Kira whisked you into hiding after the attack last night. Not that he's happy about it, but he believes you had no choice, that it was on Maxim's orders."

She bites her luscious lower lip, processing what I told her. Even Anatoly knows not to rise up against Maxim, at least not outwardly.

Her grip on the knife loosens, and I make a mental note to give Liza self-defense lessons at some point.

"But Kira's in the Maldives."

I smirk. "He doesn't know that."

Her mouth flattens into a thin line. "This is crazy. I can't stay locked up in here with you."

"We're not going to be locked up in here. I have other plans."

She shakes her head, her expression filling with anger again. "No, you don't. You don't get to make plans without asking me what I want." She juts out her chin. "There's enough in my life I can't control; I get a say in this." Her voice cracks with vulnerability, piercing through the ice encasing my heart.

"How about you lower that knife, and we sit down on the couch and discuss what's next."

She quietly considers it. "Fine, but first, give me my phone back."

"It's in my back pocket," I instruct. "Feel free to grope around while you're there."

Holding eye contact, she leans into me and fishes around until her hand wraps around her phone. I see the moment the insistent press of my cock against her stomach registers.

"Oh my God, you're hard. This turns you on."

"You turn me on," I clarify. "Although, I could do without the knife to my throat."

"Should have made different choices in that case." With one hand, she swipes at her phone, confirming everything is in order.

"You certainly know how to guard your secrets well."

She gives me a peevish look. "Maybe if the people around me had more respect for my privacy, I wouldn't have to."

"I don't care what's on your phone. I only care that no one can track you." The side of my mouth tips up in a smile. "Considering my hackers couldn't get into your phone, I imagine you've taken steps to ensure it's clean."

She notches her chin. "I've picked up a few skills along the way."

I'd like to know why, but with the knife awkwardly pressed against my skin, now's not the time for probing questions. "It's impressive," I murmur. "Just like everything about you."

She narrows her eyes. "Don't think a few sweet words will make me forgive you."

"I'm not looking for your forgiveness," I growl. "I'm looking for so much more."

I've finally had enough. I grab the knife from her hand and move it out of her reach. It takes everything in me to not throw her down and fuck some sense into her. Why she ever thought she could take me on is laughable.

Her eyes go wide as I wrap a hand around the base of her neck and haul her against me.

"I don't know what you're really after, but for whatever reason, you've decided to go through with your marriage to Anatoly." I lower my lips to her. "Let me have this time with you—a few days alone at my cabin while my men figure out who attacked us."

"It's only going to make saying goodbye harder," she says softly.

"I'll take that chance." I capture her lips with mine, and she softens beneath my hungry kiss. "Say yes. You can wear my clothes all weekend."

She laughs and pushes at my chest. "You might need a different approach if you're trying to convince me."

"Speaking of which, what do you have on under here?" My hand dips under the T-shirt, and I pause when I feel her bare pussy, wet and ready for me. "Oh, shit. Did holding that knife to my throat make you all hot and bothered?"

She blinks up at me innocently. "Maybe."

Damn. Does she have an unexplored knife kink? She feels so slick and perfect as I stroke through her folds before working two fingers into her cunt, right up to the second knuckle. Liza cries out and braces her hands against my chest.

"You still sore, angel? Or is this pussy ready for more?"

She drags an urgent breath into her lungs as I grip her by the nape and bring the handle of the blade against her opening. I move it around so it's coated in her slipperiness.

Her eyes nearly bug out of her head. "You've lost your mind!"

"Maybe." I chuckle darkly. "But you deserve it for daring to cut me." Deftly holding on to the knife's blade with my forefinger and thumb, I slowly work the handle into her pussy, watching her reaction closely.

Her pupils dilate and she fists my shirt, betraying a raw, unspoken need as intense as the look in her eyes. My good girl isn't so good after all.

"You might be sore, considering last night ..." I work the handle a little deeper into her cunt. "At least this handle isn't as big as my cock."

Liza arches into my touch, panting, the smell of her arousal—musky and sweet—filling my nostrils, and it's all I can do not to drop to my knees and eat her out. But she's enjoying this too damn much.

She closes her eyes and, with her head thrown back, allows me to fuck her nice and deep. The slick sounds make it clear how soaking wet she is.

I gather her heavy, dark hair in one fist and pull, which gives me access to the smooth skin of her neck. She whimpers, and I can tell from the way she's gasping and tensing against me that she's close.

"Rub your clit," I demand.

Without hesitation, her fingertips land on her nub, rubbing fast little circles. She lets out a gasp of delight, and holy hell if that doesn't makes all the blood in my body rush to my dick.

I twist the knife handle inside of her, and she moans like it's heaven. Shit. She really does have a knife kink. Unexpected, but definitely welcome.

"You're gonna get this handle glistening wet with your cum, and then you're going to lick it clean," I instruct her.

That's all it takes to set her off. Her eyes go hazy, and her head rolls back on her neck as her orgasm rushes up and overtakes her body.

I give her a few gentle pumps, letting her ride out the aftershocks, before I pull it out. The blade glints in my hand as I offer her the handle to lick clean, rubbing it over her full lips. She notches her chin and meets my gaze, running her tongue up and down the handle before sucking it deep between her lips.

Well, fuck me. I release a groan, my dick harder than ever.

"I can't wait until I can slide my cock down your throat," I announce. "Are you going to take it like the good little whore I know you are?"

Her shoulders stiffen, and she releases the handle of the knife with a pop. "I'm sorry. I don't like that—using my mouth."

My shoulders tense as I brush a finger over her cheek. "What did he do to you?"

She blinks hard and shakes her head, making it clear it's not something she wants to discuss. But I will get the story from her one day. I hate that Anatoly ruined that for her. It's one more reason to gut him like a fish when the time comes.

I cup her jaw, tipping her pretty face up to meet mine. "Trust me, milaya, you'll like it with me." I give her a gentle kiss. "I'll make it good for you."

"Well, you do seem to know exactly what my body wants, even before I do." She rolls her eyes in feigned exasperation. "That's the problem."

I lightly drag my teeth along the skin of her neck. "It doesn't have to be a problem. So, is that a yes?" I ask.

Liza lifts a shoulder. "That depends. Do you have Wi-Fi at your cabin?"

I bark out a laugh. "Yes, I have Wi-Fi. Are you looking forward to some Netflix and chill?"

She can't quite hide the smile growing on her lips. "Something like that. Only for a few days," she whispers. "That's all I can give you."

We'll see about that.

CHAPTER THIRTY-EIGHT

LIZA

We're about halfway to Roman's cabin when I realize I need to call Sofiya. Leaving my parents in the dark doesn't bother me, but I can't do the same to my sister. I won't be able to tell her everything, but of all people, she deserves to know that I'm okay.

It should have occurred to me earlier, but my mind was preoccupied, wondering if I'd just made the best—or worst—decision of my life. Although, it wasn't like I had much choice. Roman had already set the wheels in motion when he spoke to Anatoly.

I haven't been able to stop stealing glances at him since we got in the car. He's so handsome with his chiseled jawline and chin indent, and for the next few days, I can pretend he's mine.

Since I agreed to go away with him, an unfamiliar feeling has settled in my chest. It reminds me of what Kira described when she fell in love with Maxim—a thrill when he's near, and an electric charge at his touch.

But with Roman, it all feels different. There's something

deliciously selfish about hiding away from the world, spending days wrapped up in a man I'm so attracted to that the only thing on my mind is getting naked the moment we're alone.

Damn him. I don't know what kind of dick magic Roman has worked on me, but I am well and truly under his spell.

His eyes settle on me. "What are you smiling about?"

As soon as he mentions it, I become aware of the big, goofy grin on my face. "How maddening you are."

He purses his lips. "I've been accused of worse."

Roman pulls the car—an Audi with darkly tinted windows and license plates that he claims can't be traced—into a gas station somewhere along a quiet stretch of highway.

"Stay right here." He steps out of the car and locks the doors behind him, his gun tucked into his waistband. He conducts a thorough sweep of the gas station, ensuring we haven't been followed—a precaution he's maintained throughout our entire drive. He also insists that we don't need extra security where we're headed, claiming it's unknown to anyone but a select few.

When he's finally satisfied, he comes around the passenger side and opens the door for me.

"Bathroom's over there." He points to one side of the gas station. "I'll fill up the tank and wait for you right here." I start to push past him, but he stops me with a hand on my arm. "What's on your mind, milaya? Not having second thoughts, are you?"

I struggle to put my thoughts into words. I've kept so many secrets locked up for so long, it almost feels like I've lost the ability to be truthful. "A little nervous, that's all."

Nervous I'll lose my heart to you.

He gives me a little smile and runs his palm over my cheek. "Do you trust me to keep you safe?"

"Yes," I answer truthfully.

He leans forward to catch my lower lip between his, delivering a tender kiss. "Go. I'll be waiting right here. I won't take my eyes off that door," he promises.

As I lock the bathroom door behind me, a twinge of guilt surfaces because I've deliberately not told Roman I'm calling my sister from here. I was concerned that he wouldn't want me to contact Sofiya since he's worried about our location being discovered, but I have no intention of revealing our whereabouts. Truth be told, I'm not entirely sure where we are.

"Lizka!" Sofiya answers the phone in a rush. "Is everything okay? Mama told me something happened and you've gone into hiding with Kira."

"I'm fine," I assure her. "And yes. As a precaution, I am laying low for a few days."

"That's crazy," Sofiya blurts out. "Where are you?"

I bite my lip. I don't want to lie, but I can't tell her the truth either. "I'm out of the city until all of this blows over. Please, don't worry about me. Anyhow, I'd rather hear about you."

"Me? There's nothing interesting happening in my life except tomorrow I'm heading to my final dress fitting for your wedding." She pauses, as if the timing just occurred to her. "Wait, how are you going to prepare for the wedding? Liza, this is a disaster."

A lump forms in my throat as the lies slip through my lips, smooth as silk. "My dress fits like a glove, and I've approved the flowers, music, and color scheme," I point out, trying to sound upbeat. "Mama and Mrs. Petrovich are doing everything, anyhow. I'll make sure to be back for the rehearsal dinner the night before. It'll all be fine, you'll see."

I have it all worked out. Before the rehearsal dinner, I'll meet with Anatoly and lay it out for him. I won't be marrying him, but I will pay him back precisely what my family owes him—hopefully even the wedding fees, if he demands it. I'll offer to wire it to his account on the spot.

He might not like it, but if I repay what we owe him, our ties are severed. It's not like he can force me to marry him. Can he?

The discussion between Anatoly and my father before the opera lingers in my thoughts. What kind of contract were they referring to? Is it related to the debt we owe them, or is it something else?

"Maybe a little time away will be good for you." Sofiya sounds older than her years. "Last time we spoke, you sounded so stressed out. I know the circumstances aren't great, but hopefully you can take time to relax."

I smile to myself. "Good advice. That's exactly what I'm going to do."

"Really?" She sounds pleased. "Promise me you'll call again soon. I'll need updates."

"I will. Can you not tell anyone we spoke? I don't have the bandwidth to deal with our parents, but I wanted you to know that I'm fine."

She's quiet for a moment. "Sure."

"And, Sofiya?

"Yes."

"Anatoly hasn't come back to your school, has he? Or asked you to attend another business meeting?"

"No," she says slowly. "Why are you worried about that?"

From the window, I see Roman putting the pump back and taking his credit card out to pay.

"I want you to be able to focus on school and your friends without grown-up distractions. Anyhow, good luck with the play. Call me the moment after your first performance. I want to hear everything."

I say goodbye to Sofiya and take a minute to check my trading app. After getting my phone back from Roman, I'd made some quick buys. But checking now, only a few hours later, I see I've missed the sell-off peak.

Crap.

I close my eyes and lean my head back against the wall.

That's thousands of dollars lost. Quite literally, I can't afford to be off my game over the next few days. Even while I'm living in this bubble and playing house with Roman, it doesn't change what's waiting for me on the other side.

If I fail … Well, failure isn't an option.

I stomp up the stairs to the entrance of Roman's not-so-small cabin, the snow crunching under my boots. On the way up, we stopped for food and clothes after I insisted I couldn't actually wear Roman's too-big T-shirts and sweatpants. "I thought you said it was a cozy cabin in the woods."

"Did I undersell it?" Roman asks, each breath escaping as a visible puff in the crisp air while he punches in a passcode to unlock the door.

"Uh, yeah. This place is huge."

He winks at me and swings the door open.

Inside, the cabin feels much cozier with its rustic log walls and a commanding stone fireplace. I can only imagine how pretty it will look when daylight floods in through the expansive glass wall.

"What do you think?" Roman steps back to gauge my reaction.

"I like it," I admit, turning in circles. "It has a chalet feel. Definitely not the bare-bones cabin I was picturing."

"It was bare bones at one time." He drops our bags by the foot of the stairs and takes a quick assessing look around. "This place was in my mother's family for generations. I inherited it when she died."

"I'm sorry. When did she die?" I ask gently.

"When I was fifteen, but it wasn't until I was in my twenties and part of Maxim's crew that I had the money to renovate. Knocked the whole thing down and started from scratch."

Roman doesn't talk much about his past, and I don't want to pry, but I find this little glimpse into his family history fascinating.

"Do you come up here often?" I ask, leaning against the counter as he starts to unpack the groceries.

"Not really." His back is to me, so I can't see his expression. I realize I'm not being very helpful, so I busy myself opening the bottle of wine we brought with us and pour two glasses. "This place doesn't hold the best memories for me."

"Oh?" I swallow and take a sip of wine, waiting for him to continue, which he doesn't do right away.

Instead, he turns and braces his hands on the marble kitchen island, giving his head a small shake. "My mother died here."

A lump forms in my throat as I reach for him and rest my head between his powerful shoulder blades. Roman is stock-still, but his body softens when I nestle against him.

I know it's none of my business, but I can't stop myself from asking, "What happened?"

He releases a heavy breath before turning around to face me. My arms are still wrapped around his middle as I tip my head to look up at him.

"What happened is dark and ugly. It's not something I want to burden you with."

My heart squeezes. I don't want to leave him alone in the dark. I want to carry some of his story with me. I tighten my arms around him. "It's not a burden. Let me be there for you, even if it's just to listen."

Roman looks away, his expression conflicted as shadows pass over his eyes. After a long pause, he finally speaks. "My father used to beat on my mother and me. Not very original, huh? A drunk beating on his family." He scoffs. "I tried to step in … I hated to see my mother hurt. One day we were here, I was swimming in the lake, and when I came back to the cabin, it was obvious he'd roughed her up. She looked fine, certainly not worse than other times, but there was a bleed on her brain that led to her falling into a coma."

He's leaving out details, but I can read between the lines. My stomach drops to my toes, and my palms go clammy. "What a horrible thing to go through at any age, but at fifteen, you were only a kid." I lean my head against his hard chest. "I'm so sorry. It must be hard for you to be here."

He releases a bitter laugh. "Something like that."

I cup his face with my palms. "Look how far you've come despite everything."

"I run a crime syndicate. I'm not Mother Theresa." He cracks a smile. "I'm hoping we'll make some new memories together to erase the old ones."

His steady gaze sends a rush of nerves throughout my body. I reach up on my tiptoes and drop a kiss onto his lips. "Whatever you need, I'm here."

"All I need is you, milaya."

He sweeps my hair aside and plants kisses along my throat, trailing downward slowly. I tilt my head to give him access, and a moan slips through my lips.

From the back of my mind, a voice reminds me that I can't be his, but I ignore it. That voice isn't welcome here.

"You have me." I turn my head to brush my lips against his.

The kiss starts slow but soon deepens. Every stroke of his tongue against mine sends a flurry of shivers down my spine.

Breathing heavily, he pulls away, his eyes at half-mast. "If we keep going, I'm going to fuck you here on this table, and that's not what I had in mind for tonight. You deserve better than that."

"I have no problem with where you fuck me, only that you do."

He releases a breath in a long, slow hiss. "At least let me feed you first."

Roman claims he can cook and, considering there's no hope in hell for me in the kitchen, I'm happy to let him try.

"In that case, I'll go upstairs and unpack."

He crosses his arms in front of his hard chest. He's wearing a V-neck Henley, his tattoos peeking out the collar, and my throat immediately goes dry.

"No, you won't. Stay here. I need a sous chef."

I wrinkle my nose. "My cooking skills are pathetic."

He smirks. "I'll put you to good use."

He throws an apron my way, and I tie it around my waist.

"We're having wild mushroom pappardelle. Good with you?"

"Good with me." I shrug and reach for the glass of wine I poured earlier.

"You can start by cleaning and slicing the mushrooms." Roman hands me a clean kitchen towel and lays a paring knife on the counter.

"I think I can manage that." I turn my attention to the array of mushrooms before me.

"Gently wipe the mushrooms with the towel. They don't need to be cleaned in water," Roman instructs.

"Yes, sir. I'm impressed you cook for yourself," I admit, considering he can afford an army of private chefs.

He looks up from where he's started to boil water for pasta and gives me a smile. "In the name of full disclosure, I don't cook for myself very often. And I do have a cook—she taught me this recipe."

"To impress the ladies," I tease, even though it causes a little pang of jealousy to bubble up.

"There's only one lady I care about impressing." He

swoops down and lays a kiss on my neck. "And she's right here."

I roll my eyes even as my belly tightens with need. "You sweet talker, you."

"It's more like I craved the normalcy of cooking. My life has been anything but normal." He comes to stand beside me, taking the mushrooms I've cleaned, and begins chopping them with practiced ease. "My mother never did wake up from that coma."

The air is snatched from my lungs. I want to say something comforting, but I don't know what. He keeps his focus on the task in front of him.

"I can't imagine what that was like." I bite my lip. "Was it just you and your father afterwards?"

"No. I killed my father the day I found out my mother was gone." Sorrow knots my gut. I understand his actions, but it's a lot to process. "I spent a few years on the streets afterwards. I was a bit of a loose cannon. Fighting, running scams, trying to get myself killed because I didn't have the balls to do it myself."

I force down the lump lodged in my throat, but Roman seems unfazed.

"I learned early not to rely on anyone but myself. Things changed when I met Maxim and he took me under his wing. He gave me a purpose. He and Pavel, they're my family now."

"It certainly explains your loyalty to him."

"I owe Maxim my life." He gathers the cut mushrooms and throws them in a hot pan with garlic and thyme. The sound of sizzling fills the room, followed by a rich, earthy aroma. "Now, I have a chance to pay back his loyalty."

"How is that?" I lean back against the wall.

"By allowing Maxim to step back from his business. Pavel and I will run the syndicate while he lives his life." His voice softens, but shadows linger beneath his words. "When

Maxim lost his young son, I didn't think he'd ever smile again. Since marrying Kira, everything's changed."

My heart does a nosedive in my chest. I'm thrilled Kira's found her soulmate, but sometimes I feel a twinge of self-pity, realizing I may never experience that.

In another life, Roman and I could be more. More than this one time, more than a forbidden affair. Because even after I free myself from Anatoly, I need to break free from this life. From this city. No matter how safe Roman makes me feel, it doesn't change the fact that he's partners with Anatoly and part of the world I'm trying to escape, for me and Sofiya.

I rub the back of my neck. "What about you? What happens when you meet the woman of your dreams and want to settle down and make babies?"

His eyebrows pull together while he focuses on stirring the mushrooms. "I don't see that happening for me."

"You might feel differently in the future. With the right person." I don't know why I'm pushing the issue. Imagining Roman with another woman—and even worse, imagining another woman carrying his baby—makes me feel sick.

"I'm not exactly marriage material. No one in this life is. It's why Maxim is taking a step back from the business. Because the life we lead will never be safe for those we love."

"Is that why you've been single for all the time I've known you? Well, I *assumed* you were single," I'm quick to correct myself. "Maybe you weren't."

He tilts his head, eyes fixed on me. "Like I said, you're the first woman, other than those I employ, to step into my bedroom. And the only person I've ever brought here."

I chew on my lip. Am I only interesting to Roman because I'm off-limits? Maybe a brief affair is perfect for him. Great sex, no attachments, and at the end of the day, I'm marrying someone else. He probably gets off on how forbidden this all is. All that talk of needing me earlier was just that—talk. Of course, he doesn't mean it.

"If I found the right woman," he muses, all of his attention focused on me, "maybe I'd feel differently. Maybe I'd even leave this life."

Bitterness fills my throat. "The right woman, huh? Someone like Katerina?"

Roman dumps the cooked pasta into a colander in the sink and turns to face me, his hands gripping the edge of the counter tightly. "Is that what you think? That Katerina is my type?"

I lick my dry lips. I don't know what I think other than I need a reaction from him. "I get that your date was 'business,'" I say, using air quotes, "but Katerina is gorgeous. Sure, she might be a bit shallow, but she's in your circle, right? Marrying your business partner's sister would strengthen your alliance."

Roman stalks toward me, a scowl marring his handsome face. I feel like a trapped animal with nowhere to run. Why is he mad at me? I'm only stating facts.

He stops inches away from me. His hand grips my hair, and he tilts my head back so I'm looking up at him. Our lips are so close we're breathing the same air.

"You are deeply mistaken if you think, based on our conversation, that I want to be with Katerina."

I'm poking the bear, but I can't stop myself. The bite of jealousy is real, gnawing at me with sharp, insistent teeth. Anyways, he's the one who went on a date with Katerina and allowed her to kiss him.

My frustration peaks, and I open my mouth to push back, but he stops me with a sharp tug at my roots.

"Be very careful what you say right now, milaya, because I can't be held responsible for my actions. I'll claim temporary insanity."

A cocktail of fear and excitement blasts through me. I glance up at Roman through my lashes, and my voice comes out hoarse. "What are you going to do?"

"You know what happens when you tease a man like me?" I swallow and shake my head. "Push me, and you'll find out."

My nipples harden to little diamond points under my shirt, and my pussy damn near soaks through my leggings. What's wrong with me that I want to work Roman up? Make him so mad that he takes his anger out on my body?

My pulse races wildly as I poke a finger into his chest. "This is me pushing you."

"You were warned," he snaps. "Now get on your knees and beg for my forgiveness."

CHAPTER
THIRTY-NINE

ROMAN

Her confidence evaporates the second I demand she gets on her knees. Silly girl. Liza shouldn't provoke a man like me unless she plans on seeing the game through.

I don't make empty threats, and it's time for her to see exactly how serious I am. "I can see you're nervous." I run a thumb over her parted lips. "But you're going to suck my cock and love it, do you understand?"

Her bottom lip catches between her teeth, and she nods. Then she does something completely unexpected. Her warm palm cups me firmly over my jeans.

Shit. The sensation is incredible.

Holding eye contact, she slowly undoes my belt and moves on to unbutton and lower my fly.

"Take it out," I instruct her in a hoarse voice.

Her hand slides into my boxer briefs, and she wraps her fingers around my shaft, giving me a firm stroke. Her touch is unsure, hesitant, like she's exploring, but my dick doesn't care. Any contact with her body is enough to make my eyes roll back in my head.

"You feel good … smooth and warm." She rubs her thumb over the head of my dick that's slick with pre-cum.

There's nothing I want more than to see her on her knees, my dick sliding between her perfect lips, but I also want her to want it, even if she's going to pay for the way she teased me earlier.

Is she fucking serious wondering if Katerina is the woman of my dreams? The woman I'd consider marrying? Until I met Liza, marriage wasn't even remotely in my plans. After seeing the horror of my parent's union and considering the violence in my line of work, I was happy to opt out. But I happen to like the idea of my ring on Liza's finger.

"It won't take itself out," I remind her.

Her hands tremble as she pulls down my jeans and boxer briefs, finally wrapping her elegant fingers around my straining erection. I hiss out a breath, unsure of how long I can last once she takes me in her mouth. I'm already so on edge.

Most women look delighted when they see what I'm packing below, but Liza doesn't seem to share that enthusiasm, even if my size shouldn't be a surprise to her.

"How am I going to get my mouth around this-this monster cock?"

I nearly choke with laughter. "I'm flattered you think I'm sporting a monster cock, but I promise it's going to fit perfectly down your pretty throat, just like it fit in your pretty pussy. Now, I need you to listen to me." Her apprehensive gaze flicks to my face. "You pushed me because you wanted a reaction. You wanted to see what happens when you challenge a man like me—a dangerous man. Well, milaya, *this* is what happens."

She nods, and I step back from her to give myself a few strokes for her viewing pleasure. Her cheeks flame a scandalized pink—a reminder that this kind of intimacy is new to her. I don't have it in me to ask what Anatoly did to her.

Learning those ugly details would make me go apeshit. All I can do is make sure she loves this enough to erase the scars of her past.

"First, I want you naked, and then, I want you on your knees."

I don't wait for her response before walking into the living room and settling on the huge suede sectional. I pump myself a few times as I spread out like a king, watching to see what she's going to do.

It's too bad about dinner—the pasta must be limp in the sink and the mushroom sauce cold in the pan—but, fuck it, my dick can't wait any longer.

Liza joins me in the living room, standing right in front of me. Her breaths are quick and shallow as her hands move towards the hem of her shirt. Goose bumps rise on her skin as the cool air meets her bare breasts. They're a perfect handful with pretty pink-tipped nipples. I bought her clothes for the next few days, but I conveniently forgot to buy her bras and panties.

I run my tongue across my teeth, watching her closely as she hooks her thumbs around the waistband of her leggings, slowly pushing them down her thighs and letting them drop to the floor. She squirms as I take in the sight of her naked. Unlike the other night when it was dark, I can see everything now. My eyes roam over every inch of her, savoring the view.

A grunt of pleasure slips between my lips, and I have to ease off stroking my dick if I don't want to explode too soon. Which I don't want to. The only way I'm going to come tonight is down her throat.

"Come here." I point to the spot on the floor in front of me.

She looks unsure of herself as she lowers down between my spread legs. My mouth waters in anticipation. She takes me in her hand once again and gives the head of my cock a little flick with her tongue, like she's not sure exactly what to do with it.

I run a rough hand down the side of her face. "Do you like how it tastes?"

Liza hums her assent, and I sit back and watch the show. As much as I want her to take me deep, I also want her to get comfortable.

As she sucks, her eyes gradually drift closed. She's not moving up and down on my shaft but instead just cradling me in her mouth as her tongue works its magic.

"You're doing so good," I tell her. "You look gorgeous with my cock in your mouth."

She opens her eyes, and I see the gratitude shining back. Her body relaxes, surrendering to the sensation, cradled safely between my legs. Even though I told her this was payback for the way she'd pushed my buttons earlier, I want her to enjoy it as much as I do.

She becomes more brazen, licking me from root to tip as a soft hum of pleasure makes its way up my throat. I reach forward, capturing a nipple between my fingers and giving her breast a little squeeze as she continues to explore with long, deep licks.

"Wrap your lips around it, baby. I need to feel your hot mouth sucking me," I encourage, stroking her cheek.

There's newfound confidence in her gaze as she begins to run her tongue along the head before allowing my thick length into her sweet mouth. Shit, I have no idea how I'm going to last if the first few inches feel this good.

She looks up to gauge my response, and the view alone is nearly my undoing.

"You're doing such a good fucking job. Now keep your eyes on me and take me in a little deeper. That's right."

I cup the back of her head, applying the slightest amount of pressure, more as a guide than anything else. Whatever her past experience has been, I don't want it repeated with me.

She sucks me again, pulling me in deeper and taking more in her mouth every time she glides up and down. At the feel of her tits rubbing against my bare thighs and her throat closing around my thick length, my balls tighten with need.

My head falls back on the couch as I muffle a curse. "I don't have it in me to be gentle anymore," I rasp. "Can I use your mouth the way I need to?"

She holds my gaze for a few beats before nodding.

Thank fuck.

"Tap my thigh if I'm too rough." I grab a fistful of her hair and buck up into her mouth. I rock into her with a steady rhythm, sliding deeper and deeper between her lips with each thrust.

My grip on her hair keeps her in place as I slowly feed her inch by inch. Her eyes widen as she takes me further down her throat, determined to take me fully in.

When I push myself deep enough that it hits the back of her throat, she gags and pulls off my dick. She's staring at me, eyes wide and a little glassy. The sick, twisted part of me hoped to see tears form in the corner of her eyes, but not like this.

My voice is strained when I'm finally able to speak. "Is this what he did to you?" I ask, even though the answer will make me want to commit murder. "Was he too rough? Did he make you gag?"

She takes a shuddering breath. "All of that. And I hate how he smells, how he tastes."

Ice courses through my veins because even after all the pain he's caused her, she's still willing to marry him. I know she has her reasons, but I don't care what they are. She'll marry Anatoly over my dead body.

I run my hand softly down her hair and across her face, watching her closely to see how she reacts. Her breathing steadies, and her body gradually relaxes.

"I want to do this with you," she declares, her eyes brimming with emotion. "It feels different, and I want to overwrite the memories of— Can you teach me, show me what you enjoy? Don't treat me with kid gloves."

Her words turn me inside out, but I'll see it through for her.

"If this is what you want, milaya, I'll give you anything you want. Promise you'll let me know if it gets to be too much." She nods solemnly. "Good. Because you're going to stay right there on your knees and finish what you started. Understand?"

She gives me a small smile, and I reward her with a kiss on the head. I can tell how much she wants to please me. My breath escapes in a sharp hiss as she takes me back in her mouth.

I tuck a silky strand of her hair behind her ear. "Relax your throat, and breathe through your nose. Can you do that for me?"

Even with her mouth full of my cock, she gives a little nod, her half-lidded gaze firmly on me.

I rest my head against the couch and allow her time to get back into a rhythm. She takes me in deeper, dragging air in through her nose. The suction from her hot mouth and her hand gripping the base of my cock ... Everything works together to drive me to the edge.

I'm barely hanging on. I'm going to come in her mouth, and she's going to fucking love it.

"Look at me, Liza." When she does, I see a newfound confidence in her expression. "I'm going to come in your mouth, and I need you to swallow down every drop."

She nods as a bolt of white-hot pleasure streaks down my spine, and I erupt in her mouth.

It can't be easy swallowing my full load down, but she does her best. Her throat works hard, even as a little cum leaks out the side of her mouth. Her eyes water, but she doesn't lose eye contact with me. The raw, hungry expression she wears might be the best compliment I've ever received.

When she finally pulls off me, I don't waste a minute before I gather her in my arms and cradle her against my chest. "Was that okay for you?"

"It was a lot, but yeah." A smile breaks out on her beautiful face. "I liked it," she says, almost shyly.

I press my mouth to hers, my tongue working between her lips. She tastes amazing, even more so because I can taste myself. That thought alone nearly makes me hard again.

Working my lips down her throat and neck, she buries her hands in my hair as I suck and nip at her breasts. My dick should be thoroughly spent by now, but as she grinds on my lap, my erection makes a reappearance.

I grab her hips to still her. "That was one of the hottest things I've ever seen in my life," I tell her. "You, naked on your knees ... Absolute perfection. Even if you were a brat earlier." I smack her ass.

She yelps before fixing me with a stern glare. "Watch yourself, or that'll be the first and last blow job you get from me."

"Is that so?"

I cup her between the legs, chuckling as her eyes go wide and hazy, and a shiver works down her spine. She's so damn responsive.

"Well, I think it's time I ate my dinner," I tell her.

She turns towards the kitchen, but I shake my head.

"Not that. I think I'll skip straight to dessert."

I sink onto the couch, lift her with two hands, and slam her down on my face, a thigh on either side of my head. It's like I've died and gone to heaven. I'm hungry for her and eager to reward her after sucking me so good.

I don't waste time. I pull her clit into my mouth, giving it long, hard pulls.

"Shit, Roman, this is … Oh my God, is it supposed to feel this good?"

Only when it's done right. I don't say as much, because I'm rolling her clit between my lips, but she bucks her hips against my mouth, chasing her pleasure, and I want to applaud how fast she's unlocked her desires. I want to know everything about her. Every single fucking thing beyond what gets her pussy wet. I want to please her. I want to protect her.

I want to make her happy.

She grips a fistful of my hair as I tongue-fuck her hole to give her clit a break. As the pleasure overtakes, she can't hold herself up any longer. I take advantage, wrapping my arm around her hip and grinding her down onto my face. Her legs squeeze around me before her release makes her body go taut.

She cries out, soaking my mouth with her cum. I lap up every drop of her pleasure even as her orgasm fades, dropping gentle kisses everywhere but on her clit, which is too sensitive to take any more sensation.

When she's spent and sated and can barely move on her own, I scoop her up in my arms and draw a bath for her. She smiles up at me and nuzzles into my chest before I lower both of us in the warm water.

It's all the proof in the world I need that she belongs to me.

CHAPTER FORTY

LIZA

I wake up to the sound of … nothing. Not the usual roar of Moscow traffic, not the distant sirens or the city buzz. Peace and quiet, underscored by the steady rise and fall of Roman's chest with every breath he takes.

I take advantage of the moment to drink him in. His hard features are softened by sleep, his dark hair falls across his forehead, and he looks younger than his thirty-eight years.

Lord, staring at him like this is a mistake, because it brings out all the wrong feelings. Desire is one thing, but the tenderness invading my chest is dangerous. He's stirring something inside me that I can't afford to let loose—not with the tightrope I'm walking in my life right now.

Two days have passed in a blur of domestic bliss. We wake up late, have sex, eat, have more sex, and then attempt to be normal humans who do other things besides have sex. We've enjoyed saunas together, taking a break when we get too hot to roll around in the snow before going back inside. He's taught me how to play gin rummy, and I've managed to beat him twice. He built a campfire outside, and we bundled up to curl together and watch the night stars. I've taught him how to whistle and introduced him to the joys of '90s rom-coms. I know we can't hide away here forever, but I desperately want to.

As if Roman can sense my inner turmoil, he opens his eyes and gives me a knowing smile. "Good morning, milaya."

His muscular arm wraps around me, and he hauls me into his chest, sliding a hand beneath the hem of my sleep shirt to give my bare ass a squeeze.

"Good morning to you too." I chuckle.

"Why'd you bother to put on clothes?" he murmurs into my hair. "You know I'm going to take them right off."

I sigh. "I planned on waking up early and making you breakfast. Guess that didn't happen."

Truth be told, I also wanted to check on my recent trades, but I couldn't force myself out of bed this morning. Not when Roman's in it, pressed against me, his hands and smell everywhere.

"You needed the sleep. I kept you plenty busy last night." He drops a kiss on my forehead. "I thought you didn't know how to cook."

"Breakfast hardly counts as cooking. I can manage scrambled eggs and toast. Maybe I'll take cooking lessons someday."

He caresses my cheek and whispers in my ear, "I'll teach you."

His words kindle a flicker of hope in my heart, tempting me to believe, even for a second, that we could have something real. But I know better.

We won't spend lazy weekends together, him teaching me to cook, or cozy nights watching movies by the fireplace. In the end, he'll be a bittersweet memory of what could have been if my life were different.

Roman's breath grows ragged as he tightens his arms around my waist and grinds his erection firmly against my stomach. His grip constricts as he kisses me fiercely. Deeply. Relentlessly.

I weave my fingers through his hair and glide them down his neck, eliciting a deep, masculine groan from him. That sound, so potent and raw, is something I want to hear again and again.

"Are you sore?" he asks in a rough whisper.

I bite my lip. "But I still want it."

"Good girl," he growls, and my stomach dips with need. "How about you get on top so you're the one in control. Take as much or as little of me as you need."

I nod and rise up, peeling the T-shirt off over my head and throwing it into the corner of the room. His eyes, hungry and intense, follow the contours of my body as I straddle him. His palms trace my thighs, bringing me tightly against his erection.

We haven't been using condoms, and I don't want to start now. Maybe I've lost my mind, but I trust him when he says he's clean and that I'm the only woman he's gone bare with.

His pupils dilate within those deep-brown irises as he grips my hips, drawing me tightly against his length. My legs spread wider on either side of him as I lean in and close the distance left between us.

"Are you going to let me be in control?" I press my hands into his solid, inked chest.

Roman's eyes widen in surprise before a broad smile overtakes his face. "Go ahead. I'm going to sit back and enjoy the ride. This is your show." To make his point, he bends his elbows, folding his arms, and rests his head in his hands.

Exhaling, I sink down inch by inch. I stop about halfway and have to breathe through the stretch. This man is *thick*. I moan softly and close my eyes, but after a few moments, my body softens, and the bite of pain turns into pleasure.

Opening my eyes, I find him gazing back at me so

tenderly it causes an ache in my chest, but I can't go there with him. Instead, I offer something else. A show.

He leans back, eyes half-lidded and a lazy smirk on his lips, while I roll my hips in circles and grab my breasts, pinching my nipples as he swells inside of me.

"How's the show so far?" With an agonized sigh, I lift my hips so I can sink deeper onto his shaft. He groans when I'm fully seated.

"Never seen anything better." His voice is rough with need. "I could do this with you forever, and it still wouldn't be long enough."

I know those words should have me running for the hills, but I can't find it in me to correct him. To remind him I'm not his for the taking and never will be.

"You're the only one I want," I gasp.

Goddamnit, that's not what I meant to say, but the words tumbled out, lost in the rush of ecstasy as I work myself up and down his cock while his fingers dance over my clit.

When I open my eyes and meet his, they're shining with something I can't put my finger on. "Same, milaya. Same."

Roman pulls me against him and buries his face in my neck as we both unravel at the same time. He feels so warm and strong that, for a moment, I allow myself to sink into his arms and pretend this could be my forever.

We both lie there for a few minutes, recovering from not only the physical exertion but everything else he stirs up inside of me.

He repositions himself against the headboard, then lifts me onto his lap and holds me snugly against his chest. I can't help but trail my fingertips down his arms. A tattoo of an oak tree on his bicep catches my attention. "What's this for?" I ask.

The artwork is intricate, with roots that seem to dig deep into his skin and branches that reach for unseen skies. Beneath the tree, the ground is shaded with darker ink.

Roman's face shadows, the lines around his eyes tightening. "This tree is on the property here." He pauses, his voice dropping. "I planted it with my mother when I was a kid."

"Take me to see it," I whisper.

"I will. One day."

I'd rather not dwell on the fact that there's no "one day" in our future. Time is running out. Even though I'm still short of what I need to pay back Anatoly, the wedding is soon, and I'll have to get home to face the music—one way or another. I'm doing everything in my power to make sure I come home with a big, fat check and a see-you-never goodbye wave to Anatoly.

The conversation about leaving can wait until tomorrow. Today, I'm going to soak up all the happiness I can.

I press soft kisses against the sensitive flesh of his neck until a shiver rolls through his body. "So, what is there to do around here?"

"You keep on kissing me like this, and it won't matter what there is to do around here because there's only one thing we'll be doing."

I roll my eyes but can't keep the smile from my face. My eyes travel down his naked torso, and he leans back, letting me drink him in. He's not even subtle about it.

"Have you tried snowshoeing before?" He gives my thigh an appreciative squeeze.

"God, no. But I have a feeling that today will be my first time."

He winks. "So many firsts with me. I'm honored."

If he only knew—this is the first time my heart has thawed in so long.

I thought it was impossible to be bad at snowshoeing, but apparently, I was wrong.

When Roman suggested an outdoor activity this morning, I thought he was kidding. But no, he's a big fan of snow and, for some unknown reason, likes to clomp around in what looks like tennis rackets tied to his feet. He swore it was as easy as riding a bike, that everyone gets the hang of it—except me.

I'm lying on my back, starfished out in the snow after my fifth fall, and I don't have it in me to get up.

A shadow moves above me, but I keep my eyes closed, hoping he'll move on and leave me to my snowy grave.

"Need a hand, milaya?"

I pop open an eyelid. "Nope. I'm staying right here."

He smiles, and my heart stops for a moment. With the bright winter sun shining behind him—his thick, tousled hair peeking out beneath his hat, and the laugh lines crinkling around his eyes—he's the most devastatingly sexy man I've ever seen.

"If you're staying, I'm staying." He drops down next to me, tossing his snowshoes aside, and joins me on the snow-covered ground. "Good thing I got us waterproof snow gear."

I giggle. "Good thing."

Our eyes lock, and I can't tear myself away. Not when so much is conveyed in a single glance. I don't know what to call it, but I recognize it in my soul.

I have to break our gaze so I can catch my breath. "Why is snowshoeing so much harder than it looks?" I moan to keep the mood light.

"Is it though? Because I haven't fallen once."

"Asshole," I mutter.

His response is to pull me on top of him. We roll over a few times, him laughing and me squealing.

When he finally stops our roll, he buries his face in my neck. "You've got great rolling skills, though."

"Thanks. Such a high compliment." I'm still snuggled into his chest, watching his breath escape in small puffs. The stark branches of green pines tower over us. "I didn't take you as the outdoorsy type," I tell him.

"It's because you've only seen me in Moscow. When my mother and I would come up here during the summers or for winter holiday, she'd force me to play outside, probably to burn off my endless energy."

I smile, imagining a young Roman throwing snowballs and making forts. I hope it was a happy time for him. At least when he was alone with his mother.

"What about you? Did you grow up playing sports?" he asks.

A rough laugh breaks free from my chest. "Not exactly. My mother thinks a stroll in the park is braving the wilderness." I can't conceal the bitterness in my tone. "My mother didn't really care what we did, to be honest."

"Then why do you care about her? It seems you've lived life to make your family happy. When do you get to put yourself first?"

I bite the inside of my cheek. I hoped we'd never have to talk about my family history, but I don't think there's any way to avoid it. "It was the only way I knew to keep the peace when I was growing up," I say softly. I don't look his way but sense him hanging on my every word. "As I'm sure you know, the Ivanovs used to be a rich and well-connected family—the only reason, as far as I can tell, why my mother married my father. My father's never worked a day in his life. But when you're a bored-as-shit alcoholic, you tend to hang out with the wrong crowd. When he drank, which was often, he'd also gamble. Badly, I might add. The more money my father lost, the more my parents fought. So I learned to be the perfect daughter, the good girl who never caused any trouble or demanded attention, keeping my head down and my grades up. I guess I got stuck in that role."

Something strange passes through his gaze, like a dark storm cloud. He's angry on my behalf, but I'm not done with my story. I want him to understand why I've made the decision I have.

"After Sofiya was born, nothing else mattered to me. I finally had someone deserving of my love and affection. For the first time in my life, I felt truly loved back. I stepped in to be the parent to Sofiya that our actual parents could never be. Even now, everything I do is for her. To keep her safe and happy, to make sure her future is different from mine. That she can make her own way in this world, free to do whatever she pleases, not dependent on any man."

"Fuck, baby, you took on all that?" Roman is on his elbows, propped over me, his expression tense and serious. "And that's why you're marrying a man you hate?"

I stiffen, my face heating with shame as he looks at me with a gaze that feels like it's drilling into my soul.

"I bet my mother's losing her shit right now," I say, an obvious attempt to change the subject. "Both she and Anatoly are probably blowing up Maxim's cell phone. He won't know what the hell is going on when he picks up his messages."

Both my parents and Anatoly have called me repeatedly, leaving messages I don't listen to. I have nothing to say to any of them. They think I'm in hiding—that should be reason enough for me to not be in touch.

Roman chuckles. "Don't worry. I let him know what's going on. It's never a good idea to leave Maxim Belov in the dark."

Guilt works through me, knowing that Kira and Maxim are coming home in a few days specifically for my wedding—a wedding I hope never happens. I'm still $50 thousand short of the million I need, so after breakfast, while Roman was taking care of some work, I snuck away to keep up with all the trades.

I know in my heart that Roman would give me the money I need, but that would mean revealing everything. And then what? Would he break the deal with the Petroviches to protect me? Would he go to war for me?

Roman is bratva, first and foremost. When he took his oath, it was to Maxim and his syndicate. That's where his loyalties lie, not with me.

Roman sits up and stretches, then offers me his hand. "I'm freezing, and you must be too. We should go inside and warm up in front of the fire."

We're both quiet as we trudge back to the house.

"It's nice here." I look around. "I mean the property. It's peaceful. I'm glad you didn't sell it." I know I've said the wrong thing when his lips curve downward and a shadow passes over his features. "I know it's not all happy memories," I'm quick to clarify, "but I hope we're making a few new ones."

"With you here, I can almost forget about all the bad things." The pad of his finger trails over my cheek.

I can't breathe when he says these things to me.

"You've gone awfully quiet," Roman murmurs.

"Just cold." I rub my hands together and give him a smile.

He wraps an arm around my neck and pulls me into him. His voice is thick with promise when he whispers in my ear, "Then let me warm you up."

He lowers his head and drops small, drugging kisses along my jaw. He knows it's my weak spot. My insides melt, and my brain turns to mush when he runs his tongue along my jawline and starts talking dirty, telling me every nasty thing he's going to do to me.

Just when I'm ready to strip right here, freezing temperature be damned, a buzz in his pocket interrupts us. He groans and apologizes as he pulls out his cell from the inner pocket of his jacket. Whatever he reads causes him to frown.

"Something important?" I ask.

"I wish it wasn't. All I want to do is eat out that gorgeous pussy of yours and then drill you into the mattress. But first …" He holds his phone up.

I'm not sure what comes over me when I pull him towards me and whisper against his lips, "I'm going to get naked and wait for you in bed. Don't take too long. I'm already desperate for you."

He lowers my hand onto his crotch, and even through his many layers, I can feel his very pronounced hard-on. "Damn woman. Now I have to get on a business call hard as nails."

I laugh and pull my hand away because if I don't practice some self-restraint, this phone call won't be happening.

"Go." My voice is thick with need. "I'll be waiting for you."

CHAPTER
FORTY-ONE

ROMAN

I'M STILL HARD WHEN I GET TO MY SECOND-FLOOR OFFICE. Knowing Liza is in the bedroom only a few feet away, naked and waiting for me, is going to make this the longest phone call of my life.

If I could've delayed the call, I would have, but Pavel said it was important.

"I was hoping not to hear from you for at least a few more days," I quip when he answers the phone.

"Yeah, well, I think you'll want to hear this." The serious note in his voice catches my attention. "We got a fingerprint hit back on one of the men who attacked you and Liza in the car."

"And?"

"His name is Yuri Zhukov. A second cousin to Sergey and Nikolai."

A dark feeling slithers through me. "Fuck me. So it is the Zhukovs after us ... or after me. The only common denominator between the ambush at the port and the car attack is me."

Pavel sighs heavily. "It seems that way. We compared the tire treads from the port attack to the vehicle found at the shoot-out. Both sets are the same high-performance tires, nearly impossible to find in Russia. Only a few people would have the money or interest to import them. I think it's safe to say that both vehicles came from the same source."

"I'd ask why they're targeting me, except I think it's clear." I shake my head, pacing back and forth in a short, tight line. "I'm heading up the shipping deal."

"You think they want to mess with our deal?"

"More than that, I think they want to eliminate us." I roll my shoulders and groan. "We're the biggest fish in Russia. Take down the Belov Syndicate, and you clear the way to dominate organized crime in the country."

Pavel mumbles a curse under his breath. "Aligning with the Petroviches would certainly be a good way to consolidate their power."

The hairs on my arms stand on end. "Working together to crush us. Fucking ballsy, I'll give them that. Even if all they've managed to do is sign their own death warrant."

"We still need more to go on," Pavel points out. "Viktor has our hackers pulling all the logs and surveillance videos from the port, and Savin there now. Whatever shit went down, we'll soon know about it."

My jaw clenches, and a weight settles in my gut. "I'll loop Maxim in. Call me if you learn anything else. Whatever it is."

As soon as my call with Pavel wraps up, I text Maxim that we need to speak ASAP. Although I'd much rather have Liza on her knees, holding onto the headboard, I need to debrief Maxim—war is on the horizon.

CHAPTER FORTY-TWO

LIZA

I CAN'T BELIEVE IT. THERE'S A MILLION DOLLARS IN MY TRADING account. I've made enough money to pay Anatoly back.

I stare at the numbers on my screen. I check once, twice, refreshing the app to make sure it's not a glitch or my eyes playing tricks on me, but it's real. A one with six zeros following it sits in my account. Money I earned myself.

A day ago, I invested in a high-yield, high-risk tech stock that I sensed was going to soar, and it paid off in spades. Excitement courses through me. I could cut Anatoly a check today if I wanted to and walk away from him forever.

Freedom is within reach.

My chest explodes with something bright and happy, and my first instinct is to run and tell Roman. To fall into his arms and celebrate with him.

But I can't do that. At least, not about this.

I'm about to put my phone away when Sofiya's number flashes on the screen. A wide smile spreads across my face—she's probably calling to tell me about the play.

"Hey! How did it go?" I press the phone to my ear. "Did you wow the audience with your rendition of *Do-Re-Mi*?"

"What in the world are you talking about?"

My blood freezes to ice the moment I hear my mother's voice through the line.

"Mama?" I choke. "What's happened to Sofiya?"

"You selfish brat. I took Sofiya's phone because I knew you'd only answer a call from your sister. What kind of ingrate hides out days before her very high-profile wedding and refuses to take calls from her mother and fiancé?"

A cold sweat coats my skin, and a tight discomfort knots in my chest. "You know why I had to—"

"You expect me to believe you're hiding because of an attack you clearly weren't the intended target of? You're using this as an excuse to avoid wedding duties. Where are you and Kira? A spa in Budapest or skiing in Gstaad?"

"Nothing like that." I harden my voice. I refuse to let her speak to me like this, not after all I've sacrificed for her and my father. "I'll be home in time for the rehearsal dinner. You and Talya have done everything; you've never cared for my input, so I don't understand the issue."

"Anatoly is losing his mind," she scolds. "I honestly don't know what's gotten into you lately. You're acting like it's a chore to marry one of the wealthiest men in Russia."

Bitterness scorches the back of my throat, and I can't hold back the words that spill out. "It is a chore! Worse than a chore. He's terrible. I've tried everything to make it work. I did everything to make him happy, but it's never enough. And you don't care, as long as the money keeps flowing into your bank account."

My mother makes an irritated tsk in the back of her throat. "You sound like a whiny child. Well, consider yourself warned. If you don't come home now, Anatoly will marry your sister instead."

The air leaves my lungs in a steady whoosh. "No … you can't. She's seventeen! How could you agree to that?"

My mother's voice drops to an ugly hiss. "She'll be eighteen soon enough."

"Does she know? Have you told her yet?" I ask, breathless.

"No. We don't plan on giving Sofiya time to run, like her sister. She's at school for the time being, but if you have any hope in hell of fixing the damage you've done, I suggest you pack your bags and come home now. Honestly, Anatoly is beside himself. You'll have to do everything in your power to gain his forgiveness."

A crushing tightness grips my chest. Every instinct in my body is screaming for me to stop this madness right now. To set my mother straight.

"Listen to me, Mama. It doesn't have to be this way. I have the money to pay back the Petroviches what we owe them. We can finally be free. Don't fall for his lies anymore. This is our chance to cut ties and no longer be dependent on them."

My mother's cold, cruel laughter echoes in response. "Can you hear yourself? Do you actually believe what you're saying? You think Kira will just lend you the money to pay back what we owe his family? If that's the case, you really are delusional."

"It doesn't matter where the money comes from, but that I have it—a million dollars. We don't need to live under his thumb any longer."

"It's not only about the money! You should know that. His family is highly respected. The name Petrovich means something. I'm sick of being a social pariah. Taking the Petrovich name changes everything for us. If you won't merge our families, your sister will be forced to."

I sink to my knees, a cry flying from my lips, but I quickly muffle it with my hand.

How did I not see it before? I convinced myself that I had

a real chance at freedom. But now it's clear. There's no escaping him. Not when my family wants this union more than anything.

Anatoly always intended to use Sofiya to keep me under his thumb, and my parents, the sycophants they are, just played into his perverse games.

I should have protected my sister better, but I didn't. I've failed her.

"Please. Leave her out of th—"

"This isn't up for discussion. Be home by tomorrow if you want to fix the mess you've made." Those are her final words to me before she hangs up the phone.

Hot tears sting my eyes as I curl up on the floor. I tried so hard, sacrificed so much, and it wasn't enough in the end. They win. They always win. Because they know I'll do what I have to to protect my sister, even if it means marrying Anatoly.

Forcing several deep breaths into my lungs, I stand up and splash some water on my face in the bathroom. I'm still blotchy and shaken, but I do my best to pull myself together.

Roman can't learn the truth because I know in my gut he'll fight for me. For us. No matter what his business ties are to Anatoly, I know he'll do everything in his power to keep me safe.

That's why I need him to believe that our time is up. Even though it will tear my heart out, there's no other way.

CHAPTER
FORTY-THREE

ROMAN

Right after I say goodbye to Maxim, a gentle knock on my office door causes me to turn as Liza enters.

A smile instinctively forms on my face. "Aren't you supposed to be naked and waiting for me in bed?" I tease, but when I look up, her face is closed off, her eyes empty. "What's wrong?" In three quick steps, I'm in front of her, ready to pull her into my arms, but she steps back, out of my reach.

"I'm sorry, but our time is up. I need to go back home and deal with real life." Her words feel practiced, like she's speaking from a script.

My chest feels like it's caving in. Something is off.

"What's going on? Are you feeling scared about something? Whatever it is, you can talk to me." I fight to keep my tone even when I actually want to grab her by the shoulders and shake the words out of her.

She blinks back the tears forming in the corners of her eyes and takes a shuddering breath. "I-I can't," she rasps. "We always knew this would come to an end. I'm getting married in a few—"

"Bullshit," I snarl. "This is not about that. Something happened. What is it? Don't fucking lie to me. I deserve the truth."

She attempts to steady her trembling hands by clasping them in front of her. "We always had an end date. Something's come up, and I need to leave. Now."

I advance on her, needing to be close. Needing to look her directly in the eyes. "Tell me the truth. You've been hiding something from me—from the world—for a long time. If you want to end this, fine, but have the decency to be honest with me."

She shakes her head, grief flashing over her features. "Roman." She says my name like a plea. "Don't make this harder than it has to be."

I don't care that she wants to push me away; I refuse to let her. I haul her against me as my heart hammers in my chest. Good. Let her feel how very worked up I am. "You're not marrying him, and that's the end of the fucking story."

"How can you say that?" She tries to push me off, but I don't move a muscle. "This is not your decision, Roman. Accept that we're over. Accept that this was never going to be anything more."

"Screw that. I know how you feel about me because I feel the same way about you." I lean my forehead against hers, and my words come out in a low, gravelly tone. "If it's money you need, I'll give it to you. If it's a ring you want, you'll wear my ring. I'll do anything for you."

She shakes her head furiously, hot tears spilling down her cheeks. "How can you say that? You're just as tied to him as I am."

God, is that what she thinks? That a stupid deal means more to me than she does?

I drag a hand over the back of my neck. "Nothing is more important to me than you."

Her features twist with anguish. "This is crazy, Roman.

We can't throw away everything for this … madness. Please, listen to me. I have to get home."

"I haven't been completely honest with you." I grit my teeth, the words heavy on my tongue. "Anatoly is up to something. He's rerouted our ships without telling us, and he's taking secret meetings with a St. Petersburg-based bratva —the bratva we believe is behind the attacks on my life."

A shadow falls over her expression. "St. Petersburg?"

"The Zhukov brothers. Anatoly met with one of the brothers, Sergey, in secret. I don't fucking know why, but I do know they're violent and hell-bent on expansion. Whatever their business is, it's not good."

Liza pales as if she's seen a ghost. She dashes to the bathroom off the main bedroom, her hand clamped over her mouth.

What the hell?

When I hear the harsh sound of retching, I grab a bottle of water and a small towel, but as I reach the bathroom door, she opens it, still looking ashen and shaken.

"Enough secrets." I lead her to the bed and hand her the water. "Tell me the truth—right here, right now. What is this all about?"

Her eyes are heavy and haunted. "The night Anatoly took Sofiya to that business dinner, when we were in London … The associates they had dinner with were from St. Petersburg, and his name was Sergey." A tight knot forms in my gut. I don't like where this story is going. "Sofiya drank that night. I don't know how much or why, but Anatoly gave her alcohol."

My hands clench into fists. "I know," I admit.

"What?!"

"The man I sent to watch her messaged me that she seemed unsteady on her feet. Even though you told me it wasn't necessary, I had him stay there and watch over her for a few days."

She shakes her head. "This is so fucked-up."

"Did she give you any details about the dinner? Tell you anything that was discussed?"

Liza swallows hard. "She didn't remember that much. Maybe that was the point of giving her booze."

I swipe a furious hand over the back of my neck. "Shit. Why was she even there? What possible reason would Anatoly have to bring your seventeen-year-old sister to a dinner with bratva members?"

Pain flickers across Liza's face. "It's how Anatoly controls me. He knows how much I love my sister, how protective I am of her. He uses her to keep me in line, which is why I need to go home and fix this mess." She hugs her body as if she needs to protect herself. "My mother just called and made it very clear that if I don't come home and marry Anatoly as planned, he'll marry Sofiya instead, with my parents' blessing."

"Jesus Christ," I growl. "Sofiya is still a kid."

A fresh tear slips down her cheek. "She'll be eighteen soon."

Fuck me. Boris and Anastasia have sunk even lower than I thought possible, pimping out their daughters for money and power.

I grasp Liza's jaw, wanting her full attention for what I'm about to say next. "I will always protect you and your sister." I drop a tender kiss on her lips. "I won't let anything bad happen to either of you."

She swallows thickly, emotion swimming in her eyes. "How can you pull out of the shipping deal? Anatoly will fight you on it, and he doesn't play fair."

My laugh sounds callous and dark even to my own ears. "I'd like to see him try and take down the syndicate. We'll rip him from limb to limb." I deliver my next words with calm surety. "Anatoly is a dead man, milaya. He's fucked with the wrong people, and he'll pay for that." I brush a tear from her cheek with my thumb. "He'll pay for everything he's done to you. For every little hurt, every little bruise, he'll suffer tenfold at my hands."

The moment the words leave my lips, her gaze ignites, and her lips press against mine. It's the best feeling in the world. I kiss her back so fiercely I worry I might bruise her lips with the intensity, but I can't hold back.

When Liza pulls away, her eyes are still half-mast and hazy. "There's something you need to see." She reaches into the nightstand by her side of the bed and pulls out her phone, unlocking it and tapping on an app. After a few more taps, she hands it to me.

I scroll through the app filled with charts and numbers I barely understand. Then it hits me. I look up at her. "You're day-trading to make money?"

When she nods in confirmation, I continue to scroll.

"Holy shit! You've done really well."

"Yes." She gives me a small smile. "Look at the date of my first deposit."

I scroll back through her trade history, my eyebrows knitting together in concentration. "The first trade was the day we came back from London," I note.

She sighs. "You wanted to know what the auction at Sanctuary was about. There's your answer. My family is in serious debt to Anatoly; we owe him … a lot. I stupidly thought if I repaid him in full, he'd let me go."

I grimace as my chest constricts. "Don't you dare blame yourself for one fucking second. None of this is on you. This is all on your family and that piece of shit you had to call a fiancé. But it's over now. I'll burn down the world, I'll kill. I'll do whatever I have to to keep you and Sofiya safe."

Emotion swims in her eyes. "I know you will."

I pull her into my lap, her head resting against my chest. "You should be damn proud of yourself," I tell her. "Where did you learn these skills?"

"I taught myself," she admits, a slight hint of pride in her voice. "I just needed a little seed money."

My tone darkens. "I'm glad it was me providing the seed."

She smiles and shakes her head sadly. "I still need to get back to the city. Sofiya doesn't yet know what my parents and Anatoly have planned, but I don't trust them. I need to find a way to protect her."

"Where is she?"

"Still at school, as far as I can tell. I don't think she knows anything ... yet."

I brush a hand across her cheek. "We'll leave here first thing tomorrow morning and get your sister. You're both under my protection now, and there's no way in hell you're going back to that scumbag. And I'm including your parents in that category as well."

Her eyes roam over my face, studying me as closely as I'm studying her. "How did I get so lucky," she finally says, "to have found you in the chaos that is my life?"

"How did we both get so lucky," I correct her, running a thumb over the sensitive underside of her jaw.

It's on the tip of my tongue to tell her how deeply I feel for her, but I've already told her I'd fight through hell itself to keep her safe and happy. I'd lay down my life for her without a second thought. But I hold back from saying any more. Actions speak louder than words, and I'll show her what it means to conquer the world for the woman I love.

All that matters is this moment, us together; everything else is just noise.

CHAPTER FORTY-FOUR

ROMAN

I'm not sure how long we've been asleep when my cell phone rings. I fumble for it on the nightstand next to the bed. Liza is curled up on my chest—we must have both drifted off after the intensity of the day.

"Privet," I answer, trying to clear the cobwebs from my mind.

"It's Savin. I have something to show you. It can't wait."

"Give me a minute," I tell him. "I'll call you right back."

When I sit up in bed, the movement stirs Liza too.

She blinks up at me, confused. "What's going on?" Her voice is groggy but concerned.

"Syndicate business. I need to take a call in my office."

"Does it have something to do with Anatoly?" She frowns. "Because if it does, I want to hear it too."

I pause, running a hand through my disheveled hair. It's not common practice to let outsiders in on syndicate business, but she's right. This affects her as much as anyone, and she deserves the truth, even if it's ugly.

I nod. "Come with me."

Sitting in front of my computer monitor, it takes a few moments to understand what we're looking at. It's a livestream of the cargo ship, the one laden with Kozlov cocaine from New York, docked at the Port of Rotterdam at this very moment.

Savin's cameras reveal a grim scene under the cloak of darkness. Girls, young and disoriented, are being herded off our ship into two nondescript cargo vans parked on the docks.

"What the fuck is this?" I growl into my phone on speaker.

Objectively, the scene in front of me is very clear, but I need him to confirm that what I think I'm seeing is reality.

"He's trafficking women through Rotterdam. There were about twenty girls in the ship's hold," Savin explains. "I paid off a few port workers for the intel. Apparently, this happens every time our ships come through from the US."

My lungs freeze. *The high heel I found.*

Beside me, Liza releases a horrified whimper. I wish I could protect her from this ugly reality, but she needs to know what we're dealing with and who Anatoly really is. I knew he was ruthless, but even I'm taken aback that he's willing to get mixed up with this shit. The lowest of the low. I have a feeling human trafficking is at the heart of his business with the Zhukovs.

I haul Liza into my lap when I see she's gone pale. I won't hide anything from her, but it means she's going to learn some pretty grim truths about life in the underworld.

"Have one of your men keep an eye on the cargo vans," I tell Savin. "I want to know where they go and what happens to those girls."

"You got it."

My mind is racing in a million different directions. Anatoly played us, he lied to us, and took advantage of the ships we bought out to move human cargo. Drugs are one thing, but we don't touch human trafficking.

"The ship's already unloaded and will be moving out shortly," Savin says. "I'm told the stopover is an hour, max."

"Then what was that bullshit weather delay about?" I ask.

Savin grunts in disgust. "The girls died en route. It took extra time to deal with their bodies."

Liza stiffens in my arms, and I comfort her by rubbing her back in slow, calming circles. These are morbid details she doesn't need to hear.

"I want you on the ground here with us. Leave someone trustworthy in charge. We need eyes and ears everywhere."

"I'll leave right away," he confirms.

I say goodbye to Savin, knowing this is the start of a very long night.

Liza lifts her head from my chest and looks at me with such despair that my heart twists. "How did Anatoly get mixed up with human trafficking? I don't get it. His family runs a legitimate business. Why would he do this shit?"

"Power and money—the root of all evil in this world. His father never wanted to touch organized crime, but I think Anatoly likes dancing with the devil. And the devil comes in the form of the Zhukov Bratva."

Liza releases a heaving breath. "This is so much worse than I could've imagined. I have a bad feeling. Can we leave now to get Sofiya?"

Running my tongue over my teeth, I consider my options. "Baby, listen to me. It'll be faster if I have one of my men pick up Sofiya from school and bring her here. You'll both hide out here until we figure out what the fuck is going on. No one knows about this place other than my inner circle. It's safe. In the meantime, I need to go to St. Petersburg and meet with these Zhukov fuckers. Bratva to bratva."

Her eyes go wide. "You're going to leave me here alone?"

I smooth down the furrow between her brows. "I can't do what I have to and worry about you at the same time."

Liza nods, her face drawn and pale. She might agree, but the tightness in her jaw and the pinch between her brows speak volumes. We need to handle this matter now. I have a gut feeling shit's going to hit the fan real soon.

"Promise me you'll watch your back out there." The tremble in her voice tugs at my heart. "I can't lose you."

I wish I didn't have to leave Liza, but there's no other way. Our future depends on how I handle what comes next. "I promise I'll come back, milaya. No matter what, I'll keep you and Sofiya safe. Do you trust me?"

"More than anyone." She threads her fingers through my hair.

We both reach for each other at the same time. My hands cradle the back of her head as her lips meet mine in a sweet kiss that soon turns harder, more urgent, communicating everything we don't dare to say.

"I need to go," I say against her lips. "I'll check in with you when I can, and my man will stay and guard you."

Her face falls. "What about my parents?"

"You're too good for them. They don't deserve you." I trace the line of her jaw with my thumb. "It's up to them to choose sides. I hope you won't be too disappointed if they choose the wrong one."

"They've already done that. But I don't want them to die."

I nod, but I refuse to make any promises. "Just take care of yourself and Sofiya. I'll be back for you as soon as I can."

I brush my lips over hers one last time. Usually, I relish the moments before going to war—the adrenaline rush, the chance to unleash my savage side without restraint. But this time, it's different.

For the first time in a long time, I have something precious to lose—someone I can't bear to live without.

LIZA

It's the middle of the night when I walk Roman out to his car. It's freezing cold, but I don't care.

He draws me close, pressing me against his chest as his fingers rub soothing circles on my back. The uncertainty of what lies ahead is overwhelming, and I'm afraid if I look at him, I'll come undone.

My brain can barely process everything I learned tonight. Anatoly is mixed up in human trafficking, which is evil on another level. Do my parents know about this? If they do, are they looking the other way? I'm not even sure I want to know the truth; it's too sickening.

"I need to go." Roman plants a gentle kiss on my temple. "You're going to be fine. Feliks is on his way to your sister's school. He'll have to break into her dorm, but don't worry, it's what he does best. He promised he'd try not to scare the shit out of her. They'll be here in a few hours."

I trap my lower lip between my teeth. "Will you be able to call me?"

"I'm not sure when, but I'll do my best. I need you to lay low and try not to worry. Maxim knows what's going on. He and Kira are flying back soon."

I frown. "I don't want Kira to worry, especially with the pregnancy."

Roman smiles and brushes a piece of hair from my face. "Don't worry about Kira. She's a big girl and, frankly, one tough bitch." He gives me a pointed look. "You got this. I know you do. But in case ..." He pulls a pistol from his holster. "It's a little late to ask this question, but do you know how to use one of these?"

I shake my head. "No, never had a reason to learn."

"When this is all said and done, I'll teach you. There's always a reason to know how to protect yourself. For now, I'll show you the basics." I shake my head, a protest ready on my lips, but he continues anyway. "You'll have Feliks here, but I'm a big believer in *just in case*. Please. Do it for me."

A chill runs down my spine. I hate what he's insinuating. The idea is terrifying, but the thought of having no means of protecting myself even more so.

Roman holds the pistol out to me, his eyes locked on mine, ensuring I'm focused. "First, make sure the safety is off—then push this lever here to the side." He guides my thumb over the small metal switch. "Then aim, and when you're ready, squeeze the trigger." His hands are steady as he helps position mine with a calmness meant to steel my nerves.

I take a deep breath, feeling the weight of the cold metal in my hand. "I understand," I assure him, trying to match his calm. "I'll be careful."

Roman nods, his gaze serious. "Keep it by your bedside. And don't forget to set the alarm when you go back inside. Feliks has the code, and if anything happens, it'll alert me immediately."

"I'll be fine," I assure him. "It's you I'm worried about."

"Don't be." His eyes soften as he bends down and kisses me softly. "Go back into the cabin. I won't drive off until you're safely inside."

I'm afraid if I open my mouth I'm going to break out sobbing, so I simply nod.

From the window of the cabin, I wave goodbye, and he waves back before he climbs into his car and drives off into the night.

Feeling numb, I don't think there's any way I could sleep in the bed we shared, so I opt for the couch. With the gun on the side table within reach, I curl up in front of the TV, an old black-and-white movie on the screen.

Despite myself, exhaustion wins out, and I find myself on the precipice of sleep in no time, strange half-dreams filling my head before I fall into the grips of a deep, disjointed sleep.

CHAPTER FORTY-FIVE

LIZA

I WAKE UP TO ROMAN STROKING MY HAIR. I SMILE, MY EYES STILL closed, savoring the slow, gentle moment of us waking up together.

But something isn't right. It only takes me a few moments to shake off the remnants of sleep and realize it can't be Roman.

I open my eyes, and that's when my nightmare begins.

"You're so beautiful when you sleep, Liza."

I scramble to sit up, my heart pounding furiously as the room spins. "Ho-how did you get in here? How did you find me?" I demand, shock and horror slicing through the fog in my brain.

"I'm sharper than you give me credit for." Anatoly rocks back on his heels, looking too pleased with himself. "We had a trace on the phone when you spoke with your mother. You see, your parents are on my side. They're too in debt not to be. I own them, just like I own you. Although, it seems you need a reminder."

Rage builds up inside me at his words. He's more

disgusting than I ever thought possible, but also unhinged—a warning that I need to tread carefully because whatever he's doing here, it's not good.

"You triggered the alarm when you came in," I warn him, fighting to keep my voice steady. "Roman and his men will be here any minute. If I were you, I'd leave before it's too late. Roman won't take kindly to you breaking into his house and threatening his—"

"His what?" Anatoly's face, already puffy and red, contorts with outrage as his hand darts out, grasping my chin, his fingers pressing painfully into my skin. "His girlfriend? Are you dating now? In that case, you might want to tell your boyfriend that his high-tech infrared sensors and biometric locks can be jammed if you have the world's best hacker on your payroll." He tilts his head to the side with an ugly sneer. "Although, it's doubtful you'll ever see Roman alive. Maybe I'll pass on the message right before I blow his brains out."

Nausea crawls up my throat, but I swallow it down.

As if Anatoly can read my thoughts, he gives me a cold, callous smile and lowers himself beside me on the couch, trapping me. My eyes dash to the side table, but the gun is no longer there. I realize in horror that it's because Anatoly is holding it in his hand.

He holds up the weapon so I can see it. "Looking for this? Don't worry, I don't need to threaten you. You're going to do exactly what I say, without running that traitorous mouth of yours, because I have something you want."

My hands tremble, but I fold them to hide my nervousness and cast a glance around the room, looking for another weapon. "What could you possibly offer that would make me go anywhere with you willingly? I know what you're about now. I know what you're involved in. Human trafficking? How could you— It's sick. You're fucking sick."

He shrugs. "It's business. Don't act all high and mighty

when you've proven yourself to be an utter whore." He sets the gun down on the side table and reaches into his pocket to pull out his phone. After a few swipes, he turns the screen towards me.

A chill runs down my spine as I see Sofiya, tear-stained and gagged, bound to a chair in an empty room.

"We caught her on her way here. Unfortunately, the guard escorting her didn't make it out as well."

"You're a monster," I spit out, voice shaking, but my eyes are glued to the gun lying just out of reach. Getting my hands on it is my only shot at getting out of this alive.

With everything I've got, I throw an elbow into his ribs and make a frenzied dive for the gun.

He's faster, though, snagging my wrist and wrenching it painfully behind me. He yanks me back against him, pinning my arm so tightly that I gasp and kick out, panic surging as I try to get him off me, though it's useless.

He flattens his body against mine, his hard cock digging into my ass.

"Get off me!" I scream, twisting and turning in a frantic attempt to break free, but my strength is no match for his.

With a brutal yank, he pulls my head back sharply then forces me down, my face crushed against the couch's soft fabric.

"You're going to pay for giving another man your virginity. I'm warning you now—it's not going to be pleasant."

I claw at the cushions, every muscle straining as I fight to escape his crushing weight. I won't willingly give him my body. Ever.

"You don't even realize how depraved you are," I gasp. "I don't care what you do or if my parents agree. I won't be marrying you and neither will my sister."

He's panting, a sheen of sweat on his brow, as he grabs a handful of my hair again and forces me to look at him.

"Listen carefully to what I have to say next. You're going to forget about Roman. He'll be dead before sunrise anyhow."

Horror spirals through me, but I refuse to show Anatoly how much his threat hurts. Maybe he's lying, only saying that to scare me. Roman will be careful, he promised.

"You're going to shut your fucking mouth and marry me as planned. I won't be the laughing stock of Moscow, rejected by a stupid bitch like you. While I know you're a lying, conniving slut, you're useful to me. At least, for the time being."

I clamp my mouth shut. I don't know how I could possibly be useful, but there's no point in arguing. For whatever reason, I'm still valuable to him. When I stop being useful, I'm a dead woman. And while I can accept that, I can't accept that I didn't try to stay alive for the others—Roman, Sofiya, even Kira and Maxim.

"I'll do what you want. I'll marry you and be what you want me to be, but you have to promise to let Sofiya go unharmed."

"Unharmed? Well, that's up to you. I make no promises. But let her go? Unfortunately, I can't do that."

Panic constricts my breathing. Whatever is coming next won't be good.

"I was never going to marry Sofiya. Saying that was an easy way to control you. Sofiya is spoken for." He bares his teeth in an ugly smile, and my heart picks up speed. "By the end of the year, both of the Ivanov daughters will be married off. With your father's blessing, of course."

"What the fuck are you talking about?" The hatred in my voice is palpable.

"I'm talking about Sergey Zhukov. He's taken a real shine to your sister, likes them young and pure. At least one of the sisters knows how to keep her legs shut." With a twisted sneer, he pulls his hand back and slaps me across the face. My head snaps back, blood leaking from my nose. "Your ass better be untouched is all I have to say."

All the pent-up emotions from the past two years burst forth. I'm yelling, clawing at him, and unleashing all the fury simmering within me.

He grabs me, his hand tightening around my throat, threatening to cut off my air supply. Terror consumes me. I struggle for my next breath, the air wheezing out of me in short, desperate gasps.

"Listen, you fucking bitch." Spittle flies from his mouth onto my face. "You're going to marry me, and Sofiya's going to marry Sergey. We'll be the most powerful bratva in Europe, united by blood."

Horror curdles in my veins. This was his plan from the beginning. I was always a pawn, a means to an end. But to drag Sofiya into this ... and Roman.

Oh God, Roman.

Anatoly finally releases me, and I suck air into my lungs, trying to get my head on straight.

Sergey Zhukov. What kind of a sick monster wants to marry a teenager? Then again, what kind of sickos are involved in human trafficking? No matter what, I have to find a way to free my sister, even if it means sacrificing myself.

"You're delusional if you think this plan will work. If anything happens to Roman, you'll have the whole of the Belov Syndicate on your ass. I don't care who you're connected to—you don't want to mess with them. You're punching way above your weight."

"The Belov Syndicate won't exist in a few short hours," he hisses in my ear. "By this time tomorrow, everyone important will be dead."

Devastation rips through me. I can only hope he's saying this to scare me because the idea of a world without Roman, and possibly Kira and Maxim, is unbearable. I have to find a way to warn them, but I'm not sure how. The only thing certain is that I need to stay alive and vigilant for any possible opening.

He presses himself into me once again, his hands sliding up and down the sides of my body, making my skin crawl. I close my eyes and try to block out his touch, like I've done every time he's put his hands on me. I'm somewhere far away when I'm jolted back to reality by his phone suddenly ringing.

"Fuck," he grits under his breath.

Breathing hard, he pulls back from me and answers the call, his erection still pressed firmly against my ass. Whatever he hears on the other end of the line causes him to stand and wrench me up by my hair.

"Pull yourself together," he barks. "We're going now." He slips the gun Roman gave me into the back of his pants. "And remember: you don't behave, your sister pays. It's that simple. Understand?"

I nod.

I've never felt so helpless in my life.

CHAPTER FORTY-SIX

ROMAN

"This place makes our office look like Buckingham Palace," I mutter as we drive by the Zhukov Bratva headquarters—an abandoned storefront on the outskirts of St. Petersburg.

Viktor's men have been watching the building for hours. All their top lieutenants are inside right now, despite the early hour.

Pavel smirks. "Maybe that's the point."

From the back seat, Savin hands us Kevlar vests and comms. A quick glance in the side-view mirror confirms our men are in a van behind us, waiting for my signal to move. We're going in armed to the teeth and prepared to engage unless we get some answers. One way or another, the truth is coming out tonight.

Viktor briefly glances up from his computer. "You're clear to enter the building through the side door. Judging by the thermal signatures, only a handful of guards are patrolling the perimeter. Most seem to be in the basement."

"And both brothers are there?" I ask, sliding bullets into the magazine of my gun.

Viktor nods. "Sergey has been here for hours, and Nikolai arrived not long ago."

I check my phone again.

Pavel frowns at me. "What's wrong?"

I shake my head and slip the earpiece into place. "I thought I'd hear from Feliks by now."

Pavel's mouth tightens. "Give him a little more time. He probably has his hands full with Sofiya."

I shake off the anxious feeling pulling at my gut. Pavel is probably right.

I send Liza a quick message to let her know I'm okay, not that I expect to hear back. It's the ass-crack of dawn, so I'm sure she's sleeping.

"You boys ready to do this?" I ask my men. There's no point in waiting. It's time to go in before the Zhukovs get wind of us.

With a final gesture, we file out into the early morning darkness.

The building is quiet as we slip through the side entrance, each man peeling off to his position with practiced silence.

I'm the first one down the stairs when a Zhukov guard steps into my path. He curses, his eyes going wide, but he doesn't have time to raise his gun before Pavel steps from behind me and delivers two bullets between his eyes. Savin drags the dead man's body out of the way, and we continue our descent.

The air grows colder, thick with the musty smell of old basement and the faint tang of decay. It looks like this was some sort of underground social club at some time. We weave our way around cluttered tables and chairs, carefully navigating forward.

I stop in place when the sharp, heated exchange of angry voices pulls my attention. I signal to my men to flatten against the wall and listen as the argument escalates, voices ricocheting off the basement walls.

"... never should have involved us in that filth!" one roars. "I would never have agreed to this shit, and you know that. You went behind my back."

"Power at any cost, Nikolai. You taught me that!"

My fingers tighten around my weapon, the metal suddenly feeling colder and heavier. A glance towards Pavel confirms that he's equally surprised.

The Zhukovs are not a happy little family.

"Remember who you're talking to, Sergey. I don't care if you're my brother. I'll do what needs to be done. I lead this bratva. I make the deals, not you. If you've got a problem with that, I suggest you rethink your position, or you'll find yourself on the wrong side of my mercy."

"Really, brother? You'd threaten me? After everything I did for you and the brotherhood when you were in jail? I put the Zhukov Bratva on the map. Now you stroll in here and think you can take over, that you know better." Sergey scoffs, his voice dropping low and dangerous. "Why don't you see which of our men are still loyal to you? I have a feeling you'll be disappointed, *Pakhan*."

"Do you dare threaten your older brother?" Nikolai's voice is menacing. "I went to jail for you and our men. Because of me, others kept their freedom. How convenient that you forget."

The tension in the air is thick. They're like two wolves circling each other, waiting for the right moment to lunge.

I signal to my men to stay against the wall, but I want to see the Zhukovs' expressions for myself in order to gauge what's really going on here. I pull my gun from the back of my jeans and glide along the edge of the wall, closer to the area where the exchange is happening.

"I don't make threats. I make promi—"

Gunfire erupts around us, cutting Sergey off. Instinctively,

I hit the ground, the sharp echo bouncing off the concrete walls as my men exchange fire with two Zhukov guards who just burst into the basement, guns blazing.

Fuck me. I crawl, taking cover behind a flipped-over table. The air fills with the shouts of men, and the sounds of bullets whizzing and shells clattering to the floor.

With a well-aimed shot, Pavel takes down a guard rushing towards us. The guard collapses, his weapon clattering away from his outstretched hand. Adrenaline pumps through me as another guard aims at Savin. I sneak up behind him and silently slit his throat, leaving him to fall in a lifeless heap onto the ground.

A bullet grazes the air above me. I hunker down behind the table, squeezing off rounds until my magazine clicks empty.

Pavel inches toward me on his stomach. "Ammo," he says, hand outstretched.

I give him what I have and then radio Viktor. "Any more assholes heading our way?"

"You're clear, but the brothers and at least half a dozen guards are lying in wait in the other room."

Just as I expected.

I hand Pavel my gun. "I'm going in unarmed. Cover me."

"You're batshit crazy. They're going to blow you to smithereens the moment you walk in there."

"I doubt it. If it looks like someone is going to shoot, kill them first."

I hear Pavel grumble something that sounds like, "Crazy motherfucker," as we make ourselves known to the Zhukovs. My hands are in the air to show I'm unarmed.

In the center of the room, Sergey stands rigid, his pistol aimed directly at me. Beside him, Nikolai doesn't even bother to raise his gun. He leans against the wall, muscular arms crossed in front of him. He doesn't look the least bit surprised by my entry.

The guards scattered around the room stiffen at once, their fingers tensing on the triggers. No one moves; no one blinks. Except me.

"Morning, gentlemen." My voice cuts through the thick silence. "I think we have some business to discuss."

"Roman Vasiliev. I was wondering when you'd show your face." Sergey smiles, but it's not friendly. "Are you looking for your business partner, Mr. Petrovich?"

"Not at all. I'm looking for you, Sergey. Do you know why?"

He smirks. "I may have an idea. We're certainly overdue for a conversation."

"What the hell is this about?" Nikolai snaps.

From the shadows, I sense Pavel growing restless, his hand inching towards his weapon, but I subtly gesture for him to hold his position.

When Nikolai steps into the light, I'm taken aback by his appearance. Unlike his brother, who wears pressed suits and boasts a neat haircut, Nikolai has a shaved head and tattoos climbing his neck—a man toughened by prison. Sergey might look polished, but he's a treacherous rat.

I shrug. "This is about your brother and Anatoly abducting cats from the US to be sold in Europe, and using the ships that the Belov Syndicate chartered. For the record, that really fucking pissed me off."

Sergey rubs his hands together, that smug-as-shit smile curling his lips. "Don't get your panties in a knot, Vasiliev. If it's about money, we'll cut you in on the deal."

I crack my knuckles. "A bit late for that, but it's not about the damn money. We don't get involved in the flesh trade because it's disgusting. I think your brother agrees."

Nikolai's head tilts, and he erupts in manic laughter. "You crossed the Belov Syndicate? Brother, you've practically dug your own grave."

Sergey's face hardens, and his nostrils flare. "Fuck the

Belov Syndicate. And fuck you. The Zhukovs are going to reign over Russia soon, and there's nothing you can do about it. In fact"—his eyes glint with something feral—"this seems as good a time as any to announce my good news. Anatoly and I are going into business together. The Petroviches and Zhukovs will be business partners and brothers-in-law."

My blood turns cold. "What are you saying?"

His face lights up with malicious pleasure. It's clear he's enjoying himself. "I'm going to marry Sofiya Ivanova. I even have a contract signed by her father. Once Anatoly and Liza are married, the sisters will link our families."

My stomach drops. What kind of sick game is this? Boris Ivanov's depravity runs deeper than I ever imagined.

Sergey's eyes shift to his brother. "This will extend our influence and grow profits tenfold. You can't argue with that."

Nikolai goes stock-still, the energy around him swirling with intensity. "I can argue with whatever the fuck I want. You've overstepped, brother, and I don't appreciate it."

I look Sergey dead in the eye, so he doesn't miss a word. "What if I were to tell you that Anatoly isn't marrying Liza."

"I'd say …" A devious smile grows on his lips. "You're too late to stop him."

"What the the fuck does that mean?"

"Exactly what it sounds like."

Every muscle in my body coils and tenses as Nikolai stalks toward his brother, his face twisted in a murderous scowl. The guards exchange looks, unsure of their allegiance.

Nikolai's voice is soft, with a dangerous edge, when he speaks. "None of this was up to you. Not the alliance, not the trafficking, and certainly not your marriage. Don't you dare claim you're doing this for the brotherhood—we both know that's a lie. The only person you've ever cared about is yourself."

Sergey's expression sours. "I guess we'll see if that's true, won't we?"

"As much as I'm enjoying this conversation," I interrupt, stepping forward, "your marriage isn't happening. Liza and Sofiya are in hiding, and Anatoly is as good as dead."

Sergey scoffs. "I think you'll find that's not the case at all. Have you spoken to your beloved Liza recently?"

My head snaps back. Fear trickles through my veins like icy water.

He smirks. "That's right, you haven't, and you won't be speaking with her ever again, because you're not walking out of here alive."

That motherfucker!

I charge towards Sergey, my pulse thundering in my ears. As I close the gap, Sergey raises his arm. The dark barrel of his gun is aimed straight at my chest.

I dive, the world tilting as the ground rushes up to meet me, and the sharp crack of gunfire shatters the air. Time freezes as I wait for the pain and the darkness to follow.

My final thought is about Liza. That I'll never know what it's like to wake up beside her every day and go to sleep beside her every night. To do normal things like fight over the remote control, to lie in bed at night and talk about nothing, and to tell her I love her.

What a cruel fucking world that this is how our story ends. Before it even began.

CHAPTER FORTY-SEVEN

LIZA

Anatoly must have drugged me for the car ride because when I come to, the sky has lightened, and we're pulling up to a huge warehouse-looking space. As we approach, the doors open to reveal a private jet inside.

"What are we doing here?" I ask, although my mouth feels stuffed with cotton.

"What do you think?"

I'm not sure if it's a trick question, but I don't answer him. I'll find out soon enough.

With a rough hand on my arm, he drags me out of the car and forces me towards the small private jet. Even though I promised I wouldn't fight him, my natural instinct to survive kicks in.

"Get your hands off of me. I don't want to go anywhere with you." I struggle against him with all the strength I can muster, trying to escape his iron grip, but I'm still groggy. He tightens his hold even more, making it impossible for me to break free.

I open my mouth to scream, only to have his hot, sweaty

hand clamp tightly over my jaw. "I suggest you shut the hell up and get on the plane. You wouldn't want to leave your sister alone, would you?"

Dread stirs deep within me, and I'm sure I'm going to be sick. "Sofiya has nothing to do with you and me. I'll do whatever you want but leave her here."

A smug grin crosses his face. "No can do, princess. If you weren't such a whore and hadn't fucked that Vasiliev trash, we could've at least waited until Sofiya was eighteen. But you forced my hand, and now I'm forcing yours. With a little help from your father."

My heart pounds like a drum in my chest. "Please. Why hurry? In a few months, she can be married legally. We could put together a beautiful wedding and make a splash. Don't rush this because you're angry at me."

He wrenches my arm, and I cry out in pain. "Do you think I'm an idiot? If you know what's good for you and Sofiya, you'll shut up and do what I say."

My God, he's completely insane.

Inside, the hangar is surrounded by unfamiliar guards with big guns, making it clear that escape is not an option. Not that I would even try, knowing Sofiya is already on the plane.

We enter the private jet, where more guards sit stone-faced, waiting for our arrival. Muted sobs catch my attention. Sofiya is sitting at the back, her eyes closed and her head resting against the wall. She doesn't seem to register my entry.

"Sofiya," I murmur, feeling wrecked to have to see her like this. I wrench myself from Anatoly's hold and sprint to her.

Her eyes are red-rimmed, and she looks exhausted.

"Liza, oh my God. I don't know what's happening. Why is Anatoly doing this?"

I lower into the seat beside her and gather her in my arms.

Whatever explanation I give her won't make her feel better, so I say nothing at all.

"Roman's guard came to get me from the dorm, told me I was in danger, and then … Oh my God, he was killed right in front of me. Shot in the head before he started the car. Then they forced me out of the car, and—"

"Shush." I try to comfort her. "I'll explain later. Now is not the time." Not with Anatoly and his guards mere feet away.

I can't imagine what she went through today, and the worst part is that the day is not even close to being over. I have a terrible feeling that things will only get worse from here.

When I look down, I notice restraints on her arms and legs. Anger boils my blood. After everything she's been through, being tied down is the last thing she needs.

I'm about to take the matter up with Anatoly, when a member of the flight crew steps into the cabin.

"Air traffic control has cleared us for takeoff. If everyone is ready to go, you can take your seats, and—"

"We're not fucking ready to go," Anatoly seethes.

The first officer slinks back into the cockpit. "I'll wait for your order, sir."

Anatoly starts pacing in the aisle, looking agitated, phone pressed to his ear. "Where the hell is he?!" His frustration mounts as he repeatedly presses the call button.

I guide my sister's head to rest on my shoulder to shield her from the chaos around us. The only thing I'm grateful for is that Anatoly hasn't told her his plans for us. No good can come from her knowing what's next.

When Anatoly stops his pacing, the whole cabin seems to hold its breath. His expression morphs from anger to annoyance as he stands in place with his phone in hand.

"Sergey, where the fuck have you been?" he snaps. "We're waiting on the tarmac for you." My body goes rigid. I can't believe this is really happening. "And?" Anatoly asks. There's a brief pause before he nods. "Good. Vasiliev got exactly what was coming for him. I hope you made his death slow and painful."

Anatoly's stare bores into me, his lips curling upward.

The blood freezes in my veins, and a stone drops like lead into my stomach. A tortured scream rips from my throat, and my body shakes uncontrollably.

This can't be true. Roman can't be gone. The man I've fallen so deeply for ripped from my life by a sadistic madman. It's agonizing, like a blade has been driven deep into my chest and twisted ruthlessly.

"Liza, are you … are you okay? What's happening?"

Sofiya doesn't realize that they're talking about Roman, and I can't possibly explain it to her. Not now. Words are beyond me.

Seeing my state, she tries to comfort me. She can't hug me, but she starts humming a lullaby, one that an old nanny used to sing to us. I focus on the song, her voice, and the melody, and block everything else out of my brain as I burrow into Sofiya's lap while she strokes my hair.

I'm barely aware when Anatoly hangs up the phone and orders one of his men to restrain me like my sister. I don't have the energy to fight back. I don't have the energy to do anything but close my eyes and pray this is all a nightmare I'll wake up from soon.

CHAPTER FORTY-EIGHT

LIZA

I revel in the darkness, unable to muster the strength to even open my eyes. I can't focus. I can't think about what's next. I can't even talk to Sofiya. I just feel numb. Broken.

Less than twelve hours ago, I was in Roman's arms—the happiest and safest I've ever felt—and now, the worst possible thing has happened. The unimaginable. The life with him that I had only just started constructing in my head is erased—a one-time fantasy that will never be.

I knew he lived in a dangerous world with dangerous people—I had experienced that firsthand. But I wanted to believe he was invincible. Well, stupid me. It turns out no one is, only the superheroes in movies.

"Come on, Lizka," Sofiya whispers. "We've landed."

Huh?

I blink away the grogginess as the jet's engines wind down, their hum replaced by a deafening silence that seems out of place after hours of constant noise. My limbs are stiff, and my muscles are sore from the constrained positions and the cold metal of the cuffs that have kept me and Sofiya bound.

Anatoly stands in the open doorway of the jet, his silhouette dark against the blinding light spilling in from outside.

"Unchain them," he barks over his shoulder.

His men, two burly figures I've never seen before, move towards us. Sofiya flinches as they approach, but I tell her it's going to be okay. Not because I believe it, but because I need to say something comforting.

"Behave," Anatoly warns as the metal falls away from my wrists.

I rub at the red marks left by the cuffs, the skin tender and bruised. My hands tremble, not only from the pain but also from the rush of fear and uncertainty.

Somehow, I need to set aside my grief to figure out how Sofiya and I can escape from this nightmare. The thought of these two monsters joining forces at our expense is so terrifying it steals my breath.

As we step off the jet, bright sunlight stings my eyes. I have no idea where we are, and I doubt anyone will fill me in. The only thing I can say for sure is that the air is warmer here, scented with sea salt. We're somewhere far from Russia.

Anatoly leads the way to a sleek, black SUV parked on the tarmac. Another identical vehicle idles behind it.

I glance at Sofiya. Her face is pale and dark smudges rest under her eyes. Our gazes meet in a silent exchange, and I try to stay strong for her. I hope she knows I'm going to figure this out for us. I have no idea how, but I will.

If we can't break free, then Roman's death will have been pointless. I know he would have wanted me to fight tooth and nail to escape, and I am determined to not let him down.

A short time later, the vehicle we're traveling in comes to a stop. A blindfold has blocked out any view of the outside world since we left the airstrip. Rough hands guide me out of the vehicle, and the scent of sea salt mixed with dry earth fills my nostrils.

Anatoly's voice cuts through the silence. "Walk," he commands. His hand grips my arm, steering me with a force that leaves no room for resistance.

"Don't separate me from Sofiya," I beg. "Keep us together, that's all I'm asking of—"

"You're in no position to make demands," he snaps.

"I can make this easy for you, or I can make it hard. Give me this one thing—let me stay with Sofiya. Do that, and I'll cooperate," I bargain, hoping my words find some leverage.

Anatoly pauses then grunts a reluctant agreement. "Try anything, and I'll break your sister in before Sergey gets here." His voice takes on a dark edge.

"Why me?" The question escapes my throat before I can stop it. "You could have chosen anyone. Why pick Sofiya and me from the millions who would willingly submit to you? You know I've never loved you, and I never will."

"Oh, but the challenge of controlling you, breaking you when you resist—that's what I enjoy. Knowing your family is so desperate and willing to bend to my every whim only adds to the fun."

The delighted tone in his voice makes my stomach churn.

"You're sick," I say under my breath.

"Watch that sharp tongue of yours. Remember, Sofiya's fate is in your hands."

I clamp my mouth shut, happy that I got him to concede. Sofiya and I can't escape if we're not together.

Still blindfolded, I nearly trip over my feet as I'm dragged up a set of stairs and down a corridor. The sound of a key turning in a lock echoes as the door swings open, and I'm pushed inside with no further instructions. My sister is pushed through the door after me.

Once the door slams shut and I hear the click of the lock, I hastily remove my blindfold and tell Sofiya to do the same.

Blinking in the dim light, I scan the room—a stark, cold space with bare walls and a single barred window. My heart sinks. That's one less possible escape route.

The room has a table and a few chairs, as well as a mattress on the floor that makes my skin crawl when I think of how this room has been used. A windowless, bare-bones bathroom is the only room connected to this one.

The reality of our situation sinks in. This is nothing more than a holding cell.

Sofiya moves to my side. Her hand finds mine and squeezes it tightly. "Liza," she whispers. "What is going on? Why is Anatoly treating us this way?"

I shake my head and swallow hard against the secret I've kept from her for too long. "Anatoly is not the man you think he is." My voice cracks like glass. "When we first started dating, he wore a mask. He was charming and charismatic, and I thought he had changed from the boy I knew in school. But in truth, he's much worse than I could have imagined. I didn't want to worry you with my troubles, so I kept it from you. To be honest, I kept it from most people—the lies, the control, and even when he got physical with me."

"How could you keep this from me?" Tears well in her eyes. "I feel terrible. All this time, you were suffering, and I had no idea."

I rush to embrace her. "Because I truly thought it was best no one knew. Our family needed the money, and I didn't see another way."

"I'm so sorry I never realized what you were going through." She inhales a shaky breath. "You shouldn't have had to sacrifice yourself for our family. I could have helped. I wish you hadn't carried this burden alone."

My throat feels like it's closing in. "Don't feel bad, please. It was my choice, even if it was a foolish one. But there's more I need to tell you."

Sofiya wipes away a tear and takes a seat on the floor,

which is preferable to the mattress. "Does this have to do with your breakdown on the plane?"

"Yes." I sink down beside her, not knowing where to even start. "You remember Roman Vasiliev, Maxim Belov's right hand?" When she nods, I swallow past the brick of emotion in my throat and force myself to continue. "He guarded Kira and me in London, and that's when something first developed between us. He's everything Anatoly isn't. He treated me like I actually matter, like he cared about my thoughts and feelings. He even read *Jane Eyre* to understand me better.

"This past week, I was hiding out with him, not Kira, and just … I fell hard for him. It's strange how quickly you can feel so much for someone. I've never experienced anything like it, and it was the best feeling in the world." My voice catches, emotion bubbling thick and hot in my throat. "But he's gone."

Her jaw drops. "What do you mean, he's gone?"

"Did you hear Anatoly on that phone call? Roman is dead."

I'm overcome by a wave of emotion. Sofiya gathers me in her arms and lets me cry on her shoulder. This has never been our relationship. I've always been the one to look after her, but with my world crumbling, she's the anchor I desperately need.

When I pull away, I see my own sadness mirrored in her eyes. "You fell in love?" she whispers.

Tears continue to trickle down my cheeks, and I brush them away, only for new ones to quickly take their place. "I did, but I never got to tell him. Sergey Zhukov killed Roman, and he plans to kill the rest of the Belov Syndicate. I pray that Maxim and Kira are safe."

The possibility of losing Kira is too horrific to contemplate. I can't even allow my brain to go there.

Confusion crosses Sofiya's features. "You mean … the Sergey I had dinner with?"

"He's not just a business associate of Anatoly's—he's a vicious bratva leader, and they're partnering now on some … very dark deals."

"Oh my God." She clutches her knees, her body trembling with fear. "Is that why we're here? They're going to do something terrible to us, aren't they?"

My heart climbs into my throat, but I can't hide the truth from her any longer. "Sergey will marry you, and Anatoly will marry me, which will link their partnership through marriage."

"This … this can't be real." Sofiya's face drains of color. "Married? To Sergey? How can they force us to marry them?"

"Men like them can do whatever they want, and there's nothing we can do about it."

"I can't believe this." She stands up and paces the room frantically. "Wait." She comes to a sudden stop. "Did our parents have something to do with this?"

I bite my lip. "Our parents had *a lot* to do with it. I'm pretty sure Anatoly convinced Papa to sign a contract promising you to Sergey."

Sofiya clenches her fists, her expression showing how utterly betrayed she feels. "How could our own parents be so cruel?" she shouts, her anger boiling over. "They sold me like I'm nothing! Sold both of us!"

I shake my head. "I don't know. I honestly don't. But we can't focus on that right now." I grab her by the shoulders so she doesn't miss a word I'm about to say. "These men are depraved. They've been involved in shit I don't even want to tell you about. All that matters is that we get away from them. We need to save ourselves."

She walks towards the window to gaze outside. "How? There's nothing but cliffs and open water as far as I can see. We're completely secluded here."

"We need to scour this place for anything we can use as a weapon. Maybe if one of us pretends to be sick, we can distract them, and … I don't know, make a run for it. Try to get help."

Doubt creases her forehead.

"We're going to work together to find a way out of here," I insist. I need her to believe it as much as I do. "We can't afford to think otherwise."

She offers me a weak smile as her distant gaze shifts out the window. "If you say so, Lizka."

CHAPTER FORTY-NINE

ROMAN

Maybe I've died and gone to hell. It certainly sounds like it with the chaos everywhere—men yelling and boots stomping all over the place.

There's a sharp slap to my face, maybe from Satan himself, but when I open my eyes, it's Pavel kneeling in front of me, frantically patting me down.

"You died too?" I ask.

Pavel frowns. "The only dead person in this room is Sergey."

I force myself to sit up and find Nikolai's gun smoking, the barrel still pointed where his brother had been standing. Sergey is on the floor, motionless, with a pool of blood widening around him.

The Zhukov guards all look spooked. They draw their weapons, but Nikolai raises his hand, signaling everyone to stand down.

"Everyone in here, listen very carefully," Nikolai booms.

All eyes land on him, and the entire room goes still.

"My brother wasn't worthy of the Zhukov name. I am the

rightful head of this brotherhood. If any of you have a problem with it, speak now. You'll be free to go. But if you stay, I demand complete and utter loyalty."

He scans the room, but not one person makes a move to leave. Instead, all the guards lower to one knee, demonstrating their allegiance to Nikolai, the pakhan—the boss. He nods and makes a motion for them to rise. Then he turns toward me.

Thank you might not quite cut it in this situation, but either way, Nikolai doesn't seem like a man who wants to be thanked. In truth, he had his own reasons for killing his brother.

The air crackles with tension, but I stand and stride toward Nikolai.

His stare is piercing; he follows my every move, sizing me up and deciding if we'll move forward as friends or enemies. I hold out my hand, making it clear I'm leaning toward friendship.

His jaw ticks, and I can see the wheels turning in his head. But he's no idiot. Partnering with us is his best option, at least for now. He nods and steps forward to shake my hand.

"You want to help us take down Anatoly?" I look him in the eyes.

He shrugs nonchalantly, a sly half-smile playing on his lips. "Got nothing better to do."

Nikolai is either completely unhinged or an incredible actor because he seems completely unaffected as he kneels down beside Sergey's lifeless body and rifles through his pockets. He shows no remorse or emotion over the fact that he's killed his own flesh and blood.

Their power struggle was a long time coming, judging by what we overheard on our way in. With all his men watching, Nikolai had to assert his authority once again. I have no doubt Sergey wouldn't have hesitated to put a bullet in Nikolai's brain if given the chance.

"Get him out of here," Nikolai commands one of his guards. He stands, holding Sergey's phone, wallet, and a ring with what I'm guessing is the family insignia. "Let's take this to my office." He motions for us to follow.

I exchange a look with Pavel, who nods though his expression is wary. It's understandable, but we don't have time to hesitate, and we can use all the help we can get. Judging by what Sergey revealed, Liza is in danger and every second counts. Nikolai may be detached, but he's not without sense. That's more than I could say about his brother.

As we're heading upstairs from the basement, Viktor intercepts us, his mouth drawn into a grim line. It's a look I know well.

"What is it?" I snap.

"Feliks is dead. His body was found on the side of the road. Sofiya was taken from the car and ..." His hesitation tells me everything I need to know. "Liza is also missing."

"How is that possible?" I reel back, the air sucked from my lungs. "I would've gotten a security alert if anyone gained access to my property."

I pull out my phone to check my security cameras, but when I attempt to launch the live feed, there's nothing. Only darkness.

"Fuck me!" I roar.

How could this have happened? How could I have let this happen? My heart races, and panic zips through my system, but losing my shit won't help us find Liza or Sofiya.

Nikolai's face is grim when he says to me, "Let's go to my office. We need more information."

Fury radiates through my chest as I wonder if Liza is in pain, if she's hurt or worse, but I swallow down my devastation to plan our next move. Viktor, Pavel, and I follow Nikolai up another floor to an office that looks like the headquarters of some high-tech security company. Everyone takes a seat but me.

I can't sit; I'm too charged up. "I have the security footage right up until the moment she goes missing."

Nikolai sits before an expansive computer console, tapping buttons to activate his system. He reaches out for my phone. "Let me connect this, and we'll be able to display the various camera views on these screens." He nods towards the array of flat-screen TVs above his desk.

As soon as I connect my phone, I rewind the footage to right before I left in the middle of the night. It isn't long before we can see several dark sedans arriving at the cabin's main gates. A familiar figure emerges from one of the cars, surrounded by guards. I'd recognize Anatoly's silhouette anywhere.

An unfamiliar blip catches my eye on one of the screens. A small, flying object appears, moving swiftly across the sky.

"What the fuck is that?" I point it out to the others.

As soon as I do, the screens begin to scramble, displaying pixelated and indecipherable images. A second later, all the screens go blank.

"Motherfucker," Viktor curses as we all stare dumbfounded. "He's using a drone to jam your signals. But … that should be impossible."

"Are you fucking serious? How is he doing that?" I hit the desk in front of me.

Viktor shakes his head in disbelief, his jaw locked. "This is military-grade tech he's using. You can't even buy this shit on the market. He must have connections in special forces or something."

Guilt snakes its way up my spine. This is my fault. I was so sure she'd be safe—I promised she would be—and I was wrong.

As if reading my thoughts, Pavel lays a hand on my shoulder. "Don't blame yourself, man. You couldn't have anticipated this. None of us could. For now, we need to focus on finding Liza and Sofiya."

He may be right, but I'll never forgive myself.

Nikolai sits back in his office chair, a thoughtful expression softening his harsh features. From his pocket, he fishes out Sergey's cell phone. "Considering how closely my brother and Anatoly were working together, I think it's time we hacked into his phone." Nikolai chuckles as he taps the phone to life and shakes his head. "My idiot brother didn't even bother with biometric security. Sloppy as fuck."

The phone suddenly vibrates loudly in his hand, causing everyone in the room to glance sharply at one another.

He smirks, holding up the phone. "It's Anatoly. People say Sergey and I sound exactly alike. Let's test that theory." He puts the phone on speaker and drops it on the desk so we can all hear. "Privet," he answers.

"Sergey, where the fuck have you been? We're waiting on the tarmac for you."

As soon as Anatoly's nasally voice comes through the phone, rage erupts in my gut. I have to turn away, brace my hands on the windowsill, and focus on my breathing so I don't lose control.

"Something came up," Nikolai replies, mimicking Sergey's clipped tone. "Roman Vasiliev and his men paid me an unexpected visit. I had to take care of them first."

There is a pause on the phone. "And?"

"All taken care of. You won't have to worry about Roman and his lieutenants anymore. Or my brother." Nikolai smirks at the last bit.

"Good. Vasiliev got exactly what was coming for him. I hope you made his death slow and painful."

An anguished cry spills from the other end of the line. It's Liza—I'm certain of it.

A bitter cocktail of hate simmers in my gut, and I'm on the verge of going apeshit when Pavel and Viktor flank me, making it clear they won't allow me to jeopardize our chances of finding her.

But damn, it hurts. She's suffering because she thinks I'm gone, and there's not a goddamn thing I can do about it. I understand why Nikolai claimed that we're dead. If Anatoly believes I'm no longer a threat, he'll let his guard down.

"I don't have time to wait for you," Anatoly snaps. "Charter a plane and meet us there."

"I will." Nikolai pauses. "Text me the details again. Been having some trouble with my phone."

"Don't screw this up, Sergey." Anatoly's voice drops low and creepy as hell. "Your teenage bride is looking forward to you breaking her in."

"Can't wait." Nikolai's face contorts with disgust. "Guess I should pack my tux," he hedges.

"I don't care what you wear, only that we're united by the blood of these two sisters by the end of the day."

My muscles coil. I'm itching to punch something or wreck a room—anything to ease the relentless tension within.

Pavel slips Nikolai a piece of paper, who reads it quickly and then says, "What about Maxim Belov? Will he be a problem for us?"

Anatoly snorts derisively. "His plane is still in the air. As soon as he lands in Moscow, my men will be lying in wait for him. No one on his plane will be getting off alive."

"Good to hear it. See you soon." Nikolai hangs up and gives me a penetrating look. "You heard the man. He's got big plans for today. How do you want to handle this?"

My back snaps into a straight line as I pace through the room.

I turn to Viktor. "Warn Maxim, and make sure our men handle Anatoly's goons before Maxim's plane lands." He nods. "Savin will stay in Russia and coordinate everything here. The three of us will go after Anatoly. Any idea where the hell he's headed?"

Sergey's phone dings with an incoming message. Nikolai

swipes it open. After a minute, he announces, "Looks like we're off to Santorini. Lovely place to ruin a wedding."

My hands curl by my side. I can't wait to be the one to steal Anatoly's final breath.

"Any chance you can organize a private plane from here in under an hour?"

We've asked a lot from Nikolai already, but he's buzzing with energy. After years behind bars, he seems eager for action, and today won't disappoint.

"I can arrange something." His expression flickers with a hint of amusement. "As long as I get a turn to torture the fucker."

"I wouldn't dream of robbing you of a little fun," I say. "But I get first dibs. And I warn you, my vengeance will be thorough."

Nikolai's face breaks into a devilish smile. "Deal."

CHAPTER FIFTY

LIZA

I don't know how long we are kept in the room. Hours seem to pass. At some point, we are given food but no information. As the tiniest spark of hope takes root that the wedding might not happen today, a sour-looking guard barges into the room.

Sofiya immediately scrambles to my side as he unceremoniously drops a duffel bag onto the floor in front of us. "You have an hour to pull yourselves together," he orders.

"What do you mean? Pull ourselves together for what?" I scream at his back, but he doesn't bother answering, he only shuts the door in my face.

Sofiya rises from the floor where we've been sitting with our backs to the wall, trying to get some rest. Like me, she's tired. Neither of us has been able to eat very much, and other than a quick doze on the plane, we've barely slept.

"What do you think is in here?" Sofiya reaches into the duffel bag.

She pulls out a garment bag and lays it on the mattress. As

she unzips it, my stomach lurches. I know exactly what this is.

She pulls out two wedding dresses. My name is written on one hanger, Sofiya's on the other, as if our respective grooms had selected the perfect dress for their beloved bride.

Bile rises in my throat. The idea that we have to dress up for our farce of a wedding is sickening.

"I don't know why they care what we look like." Sofiya shakes her head, her dark brows pulling together. "Are we going to be taking pictures? Are we supposed to put on a happy face?" Her shoulders slump.

I wish I could say something to comfort her, but the truth is we don't have a plan yet. We've talked about possible scenarios, but it's impossible to know how this is going to play out.

Sofiya dumps the remaining contents of the duffel bag on the table. She frowns, holding up a cosmetic bag that appears to be full of makeup and hair accessories. From a shopping bag, she pulls two sets of high heels, towels, and stockings. The last item she finds makes her blanch.

"This is twisted." She holds up a lacy black bra and a barely there thong.

I rip the lacy undergarments from her hands and hurl them across the room. "Forget this. Sergey will never see you in these—not if I have something to do with it."

Her shoulders slump as she shakes her head. She looks so defeated it makes my heart hurt. "Liza, we need to stop pretending. We're in a foreign place with no money, no phone, and no idea where we are. We're surrounded by big, burly guards and men paid to keep us in line. I don't see how we can escape without getting killed."

"I know we don't have a plan yet, but we'll get there. Don't give up." I'm trying so hard to be strong for both of us, but I don't know how much longer I can keep this up.

Sofiya bites her lip and looks away, refusing to make eye contact. "Do you want to take a shower first, or should I?"

"You go first," I murmur.

She nods and takes the towels, shuffling away to the bathroom.

With the shower running, I hear her faint, muffled sobs. I slide down the wall and clutch my chest, sadness coasting over my skin. Maybe I'm deluding myself, believing there's a chance in hell for us to break free from here, but what's the alternative? Lying in wait and accepting whatever fate Anatoly has in store for us? That's not an option I can live with.

Leaning back against the wall, I remember Roman's promise to teach me how to fight—a promise he'll never fulfill. It's one of the many moments I'll never experience with him. Time was stolen from us.

Even without those skills, I can hear Roman urging me to use whatever means necessary to escape. He had faith in me, and it's time I find that faith in myself.

Pulling myself up, I dig through the duffel bag again in search of anything that might serve as a weapon. The makeup case offers little, but a compact mirror could be broken into a sharp shard. There's also a pair of tweezers and a metal nail file—used correctly, they can both inflict damage. I can't help but grin. Whoever packed this bag made the mistake of underestimating me.

Sofiya is subdued when she gets out of the shower. Wrapped only in a towel, she pads back into the main room, looking drawn and tired. "Will you do my hair for me, Lizka?"

"Don't worry about that," I tell her, buoyed by my findings. "I figured out a way to get us out of here." I wave my hands over the table to show her the items I've pulled aside.

Her lips part in confusion. "I don't understand."

"The mirror can be smashed in two and used as a blade.

The tweezers and nail file can be shoved in someone's eye. Hell, we can even get creative with the stiletto heels." Her look of genuine surprise coaxes a laugh out of me. "See, we can fight them."

She sits down on the edge of the mattress, her posture slumped. "I've never harmed a fly in my life, and those guards are huge. I'm sorry I can't be as strong as you. Trust me, this marriage is the last thing I want, but it's not worth getting killed for."

I drop to my knees in front of her. "After the wedding, Sergey is going to expect a wedding night. Your first time is going to be with a predator twice your age. I don't want you to experience something awful like that."

She hangs her head. "Neither do I, but nothing is worth us dying over."

Trying to conceal my frustration, I gently grasp her shoulders. I know she has every right to be fearful, but I still hate the idea of surrendering without a fight. "We're valuable to them alive, not dead," I point out.

I can tell from Sofiya's pinched face I'm not going to change her mind. "We need to get through this hell, and when we're home, maybe we can find a way out," she pleads. "If we can get a message to Maxim Belov, he can help us, right?"

My hands tremble, and a cold sweat breaks out on my skin. I won't tell Sofiya that their lives are in danger, too, because the thought pushes me to despair. It'll shatter any strength I have left.

I smile and nod, fighting to keep my face neutral. I grab her hand in mine. "You're right. We're strong. We need to get through today, and we can figure out how to escape later on." I'm not sure I believe my own words, but a hopeful lie is better than a brutal truth.

Sofiya releases a shaky breath. "We should get ready.

Promise me you won't do anything crazy. Please ... take care of yourself. Don't get yourself killed."

"I will. Promise me you'll do the same." With a half-smile, I add, "But if you have a chance to hack off Sergey's balls in his sleep, do it."

She releases a giggle. "I don't know how you're making me laugh right now, but I love you for it." Sofiya hugs me tightly, her embrace saying everything that words can't.

CHAPTER FIFTY-ONE

ROMAN

As our helicopter touches down on the secluded southern tip of Santorini, the island unfolds before us, awash in blue and white.

Viktor, Pavel, and Nikolai immediately set to work transforming our safe house into a command center equipped with laptops, satellite feeds, and monitors for our drone footage. The kitchen table is cluttered with various firearms and tactical gear that I should be sorting through, but I'm too worked up to focus on much of anything.

Thinking of Liza and what she must be enduring gnaws at my soul. I wish I had a better plan, a way to signal to her that I'm still alive, but I've got nothing. My only strategy is to obliterate Anatoly and anyone associated with him.

Fuck it. I need to at least make myself useful. I start organizing the arsenal we'll take with us, but when I miscount the rounds of ammo for the third time, Pavel casts a worried glance from across the room.

"We've got this," he assures me. "Go outside for a smoke.

We're moving out soon, and you need your head in the game."

Nikolai, who's been busy setting up a monitor, straightens up and fishes a flask from his jacket pocket then offers it to me.

"Thanks, man." I accept the flask.

Trust isn't something I give easily, especially to someone I've just met, but given the circumstances, I have little choice. We share a common enemy, and in this world, that's often enough to make someone an ally, at least for now.

Stepping into the brilliant Mediterranean sunshine, a deep ache fills me. Liza is somewhere on this island—so close, yet she might as well be a world away.

Anatoly will suffer for every depraved act he's committed, but if he's harmed Liza or Sofiya in any way, I swear I'll rip his throat out myself. I'll draw out the torture for days, savoring his torment like a cat playing with a mouse, until he's pleading for a mercy that'll never arrive.

Shit. My thoughts have turned dark again. I shake my head and take a deep swig from the flask, the liquor barely smoothing the jagged edges of my nerves.

Viktor steps out, holding a satellite phone. "Maxim." He hands me the phone. "He just landed in Moscow."

"Bratan," I answer, my voice tight with worry. "Are you and Kira alright?"

He grunts—a sound heavy with weariness. "We're fine, thanks to all of you. Our men took out every one of Anatoly's guards before our plane even touched down. It was a bloodbath on the tarmac," he reports with grim satisfaction. "I doubt we'll be welcome at the Moscow airport again."

I scratch my head and gaze out over the azure sea. "Is it possible that someone will alert Anatoly?"

Maxim scoffs. "There's no one left alive to report back to him, but either way, we're handling it on our end. Don't worry about what's happening here. Focus on what you need to."

Fuck, easier said than done. Maxim doesn't know everything that's gone down with Liza and me, and now is not the time to tell him. "How's Kira?" I ask.

"She's out of her mind with worry about Liza. I don't like it. It's not good for the baby."

"Tell her I'm not leaving this island without Liza. I'd die before I let anything happen to her."

"She knows that. We both do." There's a heavy silence on the other end of the line. "There's more to this story, I presume."

I close my eyes and pace the little stone path in front of the cottage. I don't know how or what he knows, but when the time is right, I'll need to fill him in.

"There is," I admit. "We have a lot to catch up on."

Maxim clears his throat. "Before I go, what's the deal with Nikolai Zhukov? Do you trust him?"

I pause, my gaze shifting inside to catch a glimpse of Nikolai setting up some computer monitors with Viktor. "I trust him enough to see this mission through. When this is all said and done, in his rightful place as the head of the Zhukov Bratva, he'll have to decide if he remains our ally or becomes an enemy."

"If he has half a brain, and it seems he does, he'll stay on our good side," Maxim points out.

Nikolai is definitely smart, but as far as I can tell, the man is devoid of emotion. Whatever his family history, Nikolai hasn't shown an ounce of remorse about blowing his brother's brains out, even though it was deserved.

"I'll let you go. Be smart. Don't let emotion cloud your judgment. You have a job to do."

My chest tightens with a deep, uneasy pain. This is no routine mission. Today, everything is on the line. If I pull this off, I walk away with the woman I love. But if I fail … Fuck, I can't even let myself think about that. So I won't.

I say goodbye to Maxim and stare at the flask in my hand. Vodka is not going to help. At this point, nothing will, except finding Liza and Sofiya safe and sound. I toss the flask aside and head into the cottage.

Nikolai looks up at me, his icy-blue gaze intense. "You came back at the perfect time," he tells me. "I messaged Anatoly to let him know I'm on the island."

"And?" I prompt, as Sergey's phone rings in Nikolai's hand.

He smirks. "I guess we'll find out." Nikolai puts the phone on speaker and answers.

"Where are you?" Anatoly snaps from the other end.

"Just arrived. Charming little island, isn't it?" Nikolai alters his voice to be less gravelly, like Sergey's was.

"We don't have all day. Hurry the fuck up. We need to get back to Moscow and take out any members of the Belov Syndicate still alive."

Nikolai sneers. "What, I won't get the wedding night I was promised with my young bride?"

Anatoly exhales sharply. "You'll have time to break her in after the ceremony if you make it quick."

Disgust rolls through me. He's talking about raping a teenager. He'll definitely be experiencing my drill through his dick for that one.

"Where should I meet you?" Nikolai rasps.

"There's a little chapel on the coast. I'll send you the coordinates. It's surrounded by nothing but cliffs and goats. If your bride gets cold feet, the only escape is a steep drop."

Nikolai forces a dark laugh. "Perfect." A *ding* sounds from his phone, and he swipes a few times. "Got it. I'll be there in half an hour."

"Good. Everything's set. Start without me. I need time alone with my soon-to-be wife first. She spread her legs for another man, and I think she needs a little lesson before she dares wear white in a church."

That goddamn mudak.

Tension locks my jaw, and my hands clench into fists. It's all I can do not to erupt in a rage. Fuck that. It's not only his dick that will experience my drill but every orifice in his body.

I turn to face the wall and press a palm above my head, struggling to steady my breathing. My teeth grind together so hard I could crack a molar, but it helps keep my anger in check for now. I'll unleash it when the time comes.

"Where are you?" Nikolai's voice cuts through the tension.

"Close to the chapel. Don't worry. You'll see me soon enough."

The call ends, and silence blankets the room. They're all waiting for me to get my shit together.

I take a final breath, turn around, and face them.

Nikolai crosses his heavily tattooed arms across his chest. All of us are inked up, but art covers almost every inch of his skin, adding to his menacing demeanor. "What's the plan, boys?"

I rub my chin. "You need to buy time with Sofiya while we rescue Liza."

His eyebrows shoot to his forehead. "How am I supposed to buy time?"

"His guards are mercenaries, guns for hire. They likely don't know what Sergey looks like. Show up at the chapel and find a way to stall without raising suspicions."

Nikolai swipes his palm over his buzzed head. "Got it."

Viktor settles in front of a computer, fingers flying over the keyboard. "Anatoly said he's near the chapel, so I assume Liza is close by too. I'll fly a drone in a circular pattern above the area. We might spot a clue that could be helpful in finding Liza—either his men or a vehicle."

"Good call." Pavel peers over Viktor's shoulder at the screens.

Nikolai steps out of the room and returns a few minutes later, dressed in a tuxedo. I can't help but raise my eyebrows. He's the last guy I'd expect to see in formal wear.

"A tux? Really?"

He holds his arms out wide. "I'm a man who likes to come prepared."

"Check it out. That's it!" Viktor points at a small white-washed structure on the screen with a cross on its roof. "That's the chapel." He flies the drone along the coast. "And check out this house with black SUVs parked out front."

I lean closer. From here, it looks like a run-down farm-house, isolated among rocky terrain. "You think that's where he's holding them?" I ask.

"I'd put money on it."

As we watch the screen, two burly men appear, flanking a slim, dark-haired woman. She could be mistaken for Liza if not for the shorter hairstyle. It's definitely Sofiya, her shoulders slumped and a bouquet hanging loosely from her hand.

Nikolai fixes his gaze on the screen, his eyes darkening with a fierce glint. "She's so fucking young," he murmurs, straightening abruptly and smoothing his lapels. "Gentlemen, if you'll excuse me. It's showtime." He reaches into his back pocket and flicks two sets of keys in my direction.

I catch them, eyebrows raised in question.

"Keys to the ATVs—the best way to get around this island." Nikolai strides towards the kitchen, where he arms himself, tucking a handgun into the back of his pants and a knife in an ankle holster.

I step up to Nikolai, extending my hand. "Thank you." It might be premature, but he's already taken risks for us, and I respect that.

We lock eyes as he grips my hand firmly, then he turns

and vanishes through the door. The growl of an ATV engine fades into the distance as I turn back to Viktor.

"How many guards are surrounding the house?"

Viktor frowns. "Looks like five or six guns for hire. No sign of Anatoly yet."

"We don't have time to wait for him to show up. We need to head out."

Viktor presses a few buttons on his keyboard. "I can control the drone from my phone."

"Good. Let's pull our shit together."

We hit up the table littered with guns, clips, and a few compact explosives—should the need arise. There's also tactical gear, like Kevlar jackets, binoculars, and night vision goggles.

Pavel gives me a grim nod. "You call the shots."

"Just bring Liza and Sofiya home alive. Nothing else matters."

CHAPTER FIFTY-TWO

LIZA

Sofiya and I are staring out the window, searching for any clue about what might happen next, when a key turns in the lock and the door swings open. The guard who dropped off the duffel bag earlier stands in the doorway, his imposing figure framed by the light. This time, he's not alone—a second guard accompanies him. He's bald and equally as intimidating.

Sofiya and I both turn as they enter, facing them in silence. My heart pounds against my ribs, the heavy beats echoing the gravity of the moment when everything changes.

The first guard points at Sofiya. "You're coming with us," he clips out in a gruff voice.

A panicked look passes between my sister and me. Why separate us now?

The idea of Sofiya facing today alone sends a wave of anxiety through me. Protecting her might be impossible, but I'm determined to try everything I can.

I step in front of Sofiya, blocking her path. "Anatoly

agreed that we wouldn't be separated. We're not going anywhere unless we're together."

The guard sneers. "You don't have a choice. My orders were clear—just her." Both men step further into the room, their intimidating presence shrinking the already stifling space. "Let's go. Now!"

Sofiya's eyes widen with fear, but she steps forward as if to go with him.

I grab her arm to stop her. "He's trying to scare you," I remind her. "They won't touch us. Anatoly wouldn't let them mark us on our wedding day." Even as the words leave my mouth, I'm not so sure of it. Gathering my courage, I challenge the guards. "I want to speak with Anatoly."

The bald guard glowers down at me. "We don't take orders from you. Now shut the hell up and get out of the way before I drag her out of here."

My sister puts her hand on my shoulder and whispers, so only I can hear, "Don't make trouble. It's not worth it."

Her hands shake, and her jaw is tight with strain. She's scared; of course she is. I am too, but I'm more scared about what will happen if we're separated.

Before I can argue further, Sofiya gently nudges me aside and steps forward.

"What are you doing? We can't give in so easily," I plead.

Her expression is filled with sorrow. "Let's not make this harder than it already is."

My sister is dressed up and looks every inch a beautiful bride. But waiting for her at the end of the aisle is a monster.

Instinctively, I lash out at the bald guard, my fingers clawing at his eyes. He curses, stumbling back, just as the second guard grabs me, his grip iron tight as he shoves me hard to the ground. A sharp pain shoots through my jaw as I hit the floor.

Sofiya's anguished cry is the last thing I hear as they drag her away. The door slams shut before I gain my bearings to sit up. This is some surreal nightmare. I'm alone, dazed, and trembling on the cold, unforgiving floor.

Tears prick the corners of my eyes, and a crushing sense of despair squeezes my lungs. I've never felt so powerless, so out of control. But I've already lost one person I love; I refuse to lose another.

As hard as it is, I drag myself off the floor and stand tall. Even though it feels impossible, I have to believe Sofiya will manage to take care of herself, just as I must focus on doing the same

Anatoly will be coming for me soon. And even though Sofiya is right—I can't overpower these men—I'll still fight back with everything I've got.

The wedding dress I'm wearing is not the one I was fitted for back in Moscow. It's over-the-top and princessy, nothing I would ever choose to wear. But on the positive side, it only takes me a few minutes to find hiding places within the ornate gown's layers of tulle and lace.

I slip the metal nail file into the delicate seam along the inner bodice, where it's hidden but easily accessible. The tweezers find a spot under a fold of lace near the waist. I tuck the shard of the broken makeup mirror into the padded lining of the dress's bustle, careful to place it somewhere it won't cut through the fabric or my skin. It's not much, but it's the best shot I have at defending myself.

When I hear footsteps coming down the hallway, everything inside me tightens in fear. The door opens, and there's Anatoly in a tuxedo. His twisted game of dress-up for this forced wedding sends chills down my spine.

His eyes rove over my body, not in a way that suggests he finds me desirable but rather like I'm dog shit stuck to his shoe. "Look at you, wearing white like a virgin." He tilts his head, his lips curled in disdain. "What a lie that is. I chose you because I thought you were pure, one of the few bitches who actually kept their legs shut until marriage. Turns out you're nothing more than a whore."

I flinch, and the tiny hairs on my neck stand on end. There's something unhinged about him. Violence simmers right below the surface.

He stalks towards me, and I instinctively retreat until my back hits the wall. I feel like trapped prey as he closes in.

"Now, I'll show you how I treat whores." His words are a venomous hiss.

"I've never been anyone's whore." My voice trembles. "I craved Roman's touch because he actually made me feel good. He cared about me and my pleasure. That's more than I can say for you."

Anatoly's expression morphs into something dark and menacing before he delivers a harsh slap across my face.

I cry out, my eyes watering, as I shove against his chest, but he catches my wrists, pinning them high against the wall. My body revolts as his fingers draw a calculated path down my neck, tracing the tops of my breasts spilling over the sweetheart neckline.

"You make me sick," I yell. "Get off me."

"I'll do whatever I want with you." He grabs my jaw roughly, lowering his mouth onto mine.

His kiss is vile, and a wave of nausea rolls through me. He forces his tongue in my mouth, plunging between my lips repeatedly—a glimpse of what I fear is coming next. I'm desperate to get him off me, but he won't budge.

Tears catch at the back of my throat, and as much as I don't want him to see my vulnerability, I'm powerless to stop them. He's laid me bare and made me face how utterly defenseless I am against him.

"You brought this on yourself. You're the one to blame for Roman's death. For everything."

I know his words aren't true, but a sickening pang of guilt

stabs through me anyhow. A part of me will always feel responsible for Roman's death.

Anatoly hurls me onto the mattress, climbs on top of me, and wraps his hands around my neck. I gasp for air and attempt to fight him off, but my head spins and white spots dance before my eyes. His face contorts into a monstrous expression as he tightens his grip.

When I think I'm going to black out, he releases his hold. I cough, and my lungs sear with each desperate breath. The relief is temporary, because he forces my dress up and settles between my legs. A fresh wave of fear ripples through me when I realize his pants are already down by his ankles.

Swallowing my pride, I beg, "Please, don't do this. Please. This is no—"

His hand connects with my cheek, hot and hard, before I even know what's happening. My head wrenches to the side in pain. Clawing at his face with one hand, I reach down with the other to wrap around the nail file. It's now or never.

I grip the file like a makeshift dagger as I jerk my hand back. In a swift motion, I drive the pointed end of the file into Anatoly's neck with all the force I can muster.

He roars and falls back, his eyes wild and unfocused, like those of an animal that's been shot. Seizing the moment, I kick hard to force him off me. He stumbles backward onto the floor, and I twist free from his grasp.

Heart pounding, I scramble to my feet and bolt through the unlocked door. My breath comes in ragged pants as I sprint down the hallway. Driven by desperation, I charge toward the first floor, silently praying I don't encounter a guard around the next corner.

At the bottom of the stairs, I pause briefly, considering which way to go. From the window of our room, the back of the property looked relatively quiet and deserted.

I suck in a deep breath and race towards what I hope is

the rear of the house. It might be reckless, considering my slim odds of escape, but the alternative is surrendering to Anatoly, which I will never do willingly.

As I slam the back door open, a racket from above tells me Anatoly is following. I hurt him, but not enough to keep him down.

Gasping for air, I scan my surroundings—no guards yet, but I'm far from safe. To my left, the land stretches into open shrubland, mercilessly exposed. To my right, the ground slopes steeply upward towards the clifftop. The climb is dangerous, especially in these ridiculous heels, but it's my best chance of slipping out of sight. If I get high enough, I can hopefully find a place to hide.

As I race upwards, Anatoly's enraged cries fill the air. He's losing his mind, calling his guards to the back of the property.

My heart pounds like a drum, but I shove Anatoly's shouts from my mind and push forward. Rushing up the slope, I stumble repeatedly, each fall harder than the last. After the third crash to the ground, I yank off my heels and toss them aside. Barefoot isn't much better; the jagged rocks slice into my feet, but I clench my teeth and endure the pain because there's no other way.

It feels like hours—realistically, it has only been a few minutes—when I risk a quick glance behind me. The sight freezes my blood.

Anatoly is closing in on me. Right behind him, at the foot of the incline, is a group of his guards.

"You better fucking stop running if you know what's good for you," Anatoly snarls.

Gasping for breath, I turn and force myself further up the steep hill. There's nowhere to run and nowhere to hide; the only possible escape is up. I have to keep climbing and hope like hell that I can outrun them or, at the very least, hide out.

My energy is fading fast. Even with adrenaline surging,

my body's reserves are depleted, and I can feel myself slowing down.

A quick glance back confirms my worst fears—Anatoly is gaining on me, his guards close behind.

"You think you can outrun me. That you can hide? You fucking can't! Stop right now, or this ends very badly for you."

Ignore him, ignore him, ignore him.

He wants me to surrender, but where will that get me? If he gets his hands on me, I'm as good as dead.

On all fours now, I force myself to scramble over the jagged rock, desperate to keep moving despite the exhaustion that threatens to overwhelm me. Hopelessness claws at my chest, but I push back against it fiercely. I can't abandon Sofiya to face this horror alone, and Roman would have expected me to fight to my last breath. He wouldn't give up, just like I won't. But I need rest.

My face meets the cool rock, and I catch my breath. As I begin to regain some strength, a deafening explosion rips through the air. Flames and smoke surge up from the house, and the shock wave that follows nearly topples me.

Holy shit! What the hell is going on?

Automatic gun fire splits the air.

Is this about me?

I don't have time to figure out what's going on because, despite the explosion, Anatoly is still coming for me. He pauses to shout orders to his men—something about securing the property and figuring out what happened—but he's still pushing forward.

"I told you not to run from me, you little bitch." His voice is full of venom. "I'm going to catch you and make you suffer more than you thought possible. Then I'm going to move on to your sister."

My stomach knots with fear, but his words shake me out

of my stupor. My breath saws in and out of my lungs as I push harder up the hill, and my muscles scream in protest.

Gunfire and shouts continue below, but Anatoly is gaining ground, close enough that I can hear his ragged breaths and curses as I try to stay on a straight path.

I make the mistake of looking back. In the span of a heartbeat, my toe catches on a rock, and I go down hard. Pain flashes through my toe, intense and piercing, as if it's been split open.

Gritting my teeth, I try to stand, pushing through the sharp jolt. I hobble forward, dragging my foot in the dirt, but it's useless. Fire shoots through my foot the moment I put weight on it. I try again and again to right myself. To move forward, even if I have to drag my foot behind me.

But there's no pushing through this. It's over for me.

The only thing I can do is curl up into a ball and cover my head with my hands to protect myself.

With a savage grasp, he flips me onto my back.

Jagged rocks bite into my skin, scraping across my back with brutal intensity.

He stands over me, his face a mask of fury. "How the fuck did you do it?" His hand finds my throat, squeezing as I gasp for air.

My eyes snap open, locking onto his dead eyes, as I try to figure out what he means. How did I do what?

"Are you working with Belov?" he continues. "Is that it? How did you get a message to him? Goddammit—tell me now."

His words confuse me, but I'm done fighting. I fought to the bitter end, but even I need to accept that it's over. He won.

Who knows, maybe Roman will be waiting for me on the other side. It's a nice thought at the very least.

"Tell me," Anatoly rages and squeezes harder, making it impossible for me to talk. Hell, I can barely breathe.

The edges of my vision begin to blur into darkness when, suddenly, a voice I never thought I'd hear again cuts through the air.

"It wasn't Maxim—it was me. Surprise, motherfucker. I'm back from the dead."

CHAPTER FIFTY-THREE

LIZA

The sound of Roman's voice is so vivid, so real, that my heart climbs into my throat and beats wildly. Maybe desperation makes you hallucinate?

Then I open my eyes.

It can't be. How is it possible?

The sight of him alive makes my stomach dip. Disbelief, joy, confusion—all of it—swirls inside of me.

Reality snaps back into place as Anatoly is torn off me. Roman wrenches Anatoly's head back by his hair, his face a cold, stoic mask as he drags him several feet away. Without hesitation, Roman cocks his fist and lands a heavy blow across Anatoly's cheek. He staggers backward, blood streaming from his nose.

Roman turns back to glance at me, his eyes shining with so much concern it floods my heart. I'm still in shock. This man—I honestly thought I'd never see him again—is here in the flesh, saving me. It's overwhelming and amazing at the same time.

I mouth, "I'm okay." My injuries can wait—killing Anatoly can't.

"You've really fucked up this time, Anatoly. You have no idea how brutal I'm going to make your death, but you'll find out soon."

Below, things have quieted down, but that doesn't mean Anatoly's guards won't be coming for us. "Roman, there are others," I call out to him. "We should get out of here."

He gives me a reassuring smile. "Pavel and Viktor are handling them. I don't know what kind of bozos Anatoly hired, but they were a joke to take down." His eyes swing back to Anatoly with a feral glint. "Let's not rush this moment. I think Anatoly should atone for his sins, don't you?"

"You're supposed to be dead," Anatoly shrieks, his face covered in blood. "What the hell happened?"

Straddling him, Roman slams his fist into Anatoly's jaw, and a brutal crack echoes through the air. Anatoly groans, his head snapping to the side with the force.

"I don't really think you're in a position to be asking questions, but since it's such a good story, I won't hold back."

Anatoly tries to fight back, swinging a desperate fist at Roman, but he's no match for him. Roman's bigger, stronger, and way more skilled as a fighter. Roman retaliates with a sharp elbow to Anatoly's gut, causing him to double over in pain and retch.

I prop myself up to watch Roman exact his revenge. Despite the cold air and my throbbing foot, the sight of Anatoly experiencing pain and humiliation is beyond satisfying.

When Anatoly finishes, Roman presses a knife to his throat. Anatoly's breaths come in ragged gasps, his once neat tuxedo now a mess with blood and puke.

"So, like I was saying," Roman snarls. "The man you spoke to on the phone earlier today, the one you thought was

Sergey, was actually his brother, Nikolai. He's with Sofiya right now."

Sofiya's not being married off to Sergey? I release a gasp of surprise.

Roman raises his head, his voice soft when he addresses me. "She's safe now. You don't need to worry."

My heart nearly collapses in relief. I know nothing about Nikolai, but if Roman trusts him, that's good enough for me.

Anatoly attempts to spit in Roman's face, which earns him a sharp headbutt that mangles his nose. My stomach turns, but I refuse to look away.

"The kicker is it was Nikolai who killed Sergey after he uncovered the disgusting shit you were up to. Trafficking women. Disgusting." Roman shakes his head. "Did you think I'm so fucking stupid I wouldn't notice you were working with that piece of shit, Sergey, on the side? You're a pitiful excuse for a human."

"Fuck you," Anatoly roars, his voice hoarse and broken. "And fuck her. I wish you'd both been killed in the attack after the opera."

Roman's eyes darken, and he whistles through his teeth. "You better watch your mouth. You're in enough shit as it is." Roman presses the blade against Anatoly's jugular. "Tell me, why did you want Liza dead after the opera? Is it because you knew I made her come all over my fingers as she enjoyed the show?"

Anatoly grunts loudly, his breathing ragged. "You were supposed to die that night. Liza was supposed to be scared shitless and fall in line. But the bitch didn't learn her lesson."

Roman's smile is so cold and twisted a shiver blasts down my spine. "Apparently, you haven't learned your lesson either."

In a swift move, Roman slashes the steel blade across Anatoly's cheek. Blood gushes from the wound—it's so gruesome I avert my eyes.

"I'm going to make you pay for each and every time you hurt Liza. Each and every time you put your hands on her when she didn't want it. She's too good for you. Always has been."

Anatoly thrashes his head side to side, blood seeping into the ground beneath him.

Roman grabs his chin and gets low to snarl in his ear, "I hope you go to the gates of hell knowing that Liza is going to wear my ring and carry my baby in her belly. While you're taking it up the ass by the devil himself, I'll be buried inside of her every night."

When Roman's eyes lock with mine, the raw emotion in them nearly breaks me. My heart leaps in my chest. After believing the worst, hearing him say that he wants to spend the rest of his life with me is more than I could ever hope for.

"It's probably best if you close your eyes for this part," Roman advises.

I bury my head in my knees, flinching at the sound of Anatoly's raw, primal screams. Whatever Roman is doing, it's fierce and utterly vicious, but no one deserves it more than my former fiancé. If I could stomach it, I'd deliver the last blow.

After a while, everything goes quiet, and Roman touches my back. "Liza," he murmurs, "it's over. Look at me. I need to know you're alright."

I lift my head, taking a deep breath. "I'm okay," I nod, tears spilling from my eyes. "I'm okay because of you."

Roman swoops down and picks me up to cradle me into his solid chest. It's the absolute best feeling in the world, even if he's covered in Anatoly's blood. I might be hurt, and we might be standing on a steep, rocky hill with the dead, mangled body of my former fiancé only a few feet away, but being held in Roman's arms like this is literally the best feeling in the world.

I run my hand over his face, marveling that he's real. That

this is Roman in the flesh. "I thought I'd never see you again. I believed you were gone. Forever. It felt like my soul was being torn apart."

His warm eyes search mine as he sweeps his thumb over my cheek to brush away my tears. "I'll never forgive myself for hurting you like that." He kisses me then presses his forehead against mine. "Anatoly had to believe I was dead, that I wouldn't be a threat."

He wraps his arms around me so tightly I can barely breathe. Roman looks torn up.

I hold his face and guide it to mine. "You did what was necessary, and I'll never hold it against you. You came for me. That's all that matters." I pull away and stare hopefully into his eyes. "Did you really mean what you said about us being together?"

"Believe it, milaya. From now on, it's you and me against the world. I love you so damn much, and I regretted not being able to say that to your face while we were apart. But it's true, and all I care about is making you mine."

My chest is a tangle of emotions. After everything we've been through, this moment is fucking everything.

"I love you too, Roman." It's the absolute truth. I feel it in my body, in my bones, and down to my very marrow. "More than I ever thought possible. More than I can put into words."

His mouth claims mine desperately. He kisses me like he's been starved for my touch. I kiss him back just as fiercely.

"Say it again," he demands. "Once isn't enough."

"I love you, Roman Vasiliev."

"That's music to my ears, baby." His eyes travel down my body to my swollen foot. "Fuck. You're hurt. We need to find a doctor."

I shake my head fiercely. "We can see a doctor when we get back home. I need to see my sister after everything she's been through today." My eyes go wide. "Kira, is she okay?"

"Kira and Maxim are fine. Everyone is fine, just worried

about you and Sofiya." He kisses my forehead and sucks in a harsh breath. "Did he viola—"

"He tried and got close," I explain, aware of how much it costs him to ask. "But I shoved a nail file into his neck. It didn't cause the same damage as your knife, but it allowed me to break free. Still, if you hadn't come when you did ..." I don't even want to consider the alternative.

"But I did come, and that's all that matters. Now, we have forever."

Warmth fills my stomach, and my eyes flutter shut as exhaustion weighs heavily on me. All I can do is nestle into his chest as he begins the slow walk down the hill. Keeping my eyes closed, I say nothing, reveling in the fact that Roman's holding me tighter than I've ever been held before.

Nothing else has ever felt this right.

CHAPTER FIFTY-FOUR

ROMAN

Liza and Sofiya fall asleep, curled up, as soon as the plane leaves the ground. Liza's injured foot is carefully propped up.

Seeing them so peaceful tears at me, especially after the hell they endured. But that nightmare is behind us now. I won't let Anatoly steal another second of my life.

I'd never known fear like when I watched Anatoly standing over Liza, his fingers wrapped around her throat, prepared to take her life. I'm not a religious man, but I prayed to every deity known to man that Liza was unharmed, that I had arrived in time to save her from certain death.

This nightmare has crystallized one thing for me: Liza is my future. I would give everything up for her. Nothing matters if she isn't by my side. Ever since she came into my life, she has filled every corner of my heart, my mind, and my very being. Now, nothing stands in our way.

Nikolai joins me, his gaze fixed on Sofiya's sleeping form. He removes his tuxedo jacket and carefully lays it over her, watching her with a tenderness I'd never expect from a man like him. A man who hasn't shown an ounce of emotion in the time I've known him. Which, admittedly, hasn't been very long.

A flight attendant approaches and hands me the cashmere blankets I'd requested. I drape one over Liza and another over Sofiya, leaving Nikolai's jacket still spread over her.

I then signal to Nikolai that we need to talk.

The cabin lights dim as we make our way to the back of the plane, where Viktor and Pavel are seated. As soon as we join them, the atmosphere turns tense. There are too many questions that need answers.

Starting with how Nikolai saved Sofiya.

"Can you explain to me what the fuck happened?" I lean back, arms folded across my chest, and fix Nikolai with a hard stare.

He blows out a casual breath. "Which part are you unclear about?"

For fuck's sake. "The part that explains why there's a wedding ring on your finger."

"Right. That." He rests his ankle on his knee and steeples his fingers together. "You told me to buy time. I was buying time. The Greek Orthodox ceremony went on and on—it was fucking perfect."

"She's seventeen!" I hiss.

He shrugs. "It was life or death. I was surrounded by a handful of trigger-happy guards who would have killed me on the fucking spot if they didn't believe I was Sergey."

Shit, this guy really is unhinged. But he does have a point.

By the time I made it down the hill with Liza, Viktor and Pavel had killed all of Anatoly's men and secured the location. Viktor took Liza back to the safe house in a car he stole from Anatoly, and Pavel and I continued to the chapel. From outside, it was all quiet, but we didn't know what we'd find inside. We busted through the door, guns raised, only to find all the guards dead and Nikolai and Sofiya missing. I was about to lose it when Viktor called to tell me that Nikolai and Sofiya had managed to escape back to the safe house by ATV.

Given the risks staying on the island posed, we thought it was best to fly home ASAP.

This is my first chance to debrief Nikolai. I wouldn't even know they'd gotten married if Liza hadn't asked me about it as we were boarding the flight. I thought she was kidding at first, but both Nikolai and Sofiya are sporting rings.

Viktor clears his throat as he stares at his phone. "I'm no lawyer, but from what I'm reading here, if marriage consent was obtained through force, duress, or fraud, the marriage isn't valid."

"There you go!" Nikolai throws his arms up.

I run an agitated hand through my hair. "Sofiya was probably terrified."

Nikolai's expression sours. "She knew I wasn't Sergey because she'd met my brother before. I tried to tell her that I wasn't going to hurt her, but yeah, she was fucking scared."

Pavel crosses his legs and glances out the window. Like all of us, he looks worse for wear after what feels like days without proper food, sleep, or a shower. "How did you manage to take out all six guards?"

Nikolai's lips tip up at the corner. "I told the guards they needed to witness our holy union from the pews. Idiots bought it hook, line, and sinker, and all lined up like ducks on the church benches. Didn't even think to post a lookout at the door." He shakes his head in disbelief. "Right after I kissed the bride, we heard your explosions, and I knew I had to make a move before they did." He dips his head to the side. "They were dead before they even had a clue what hit them."

My lips curl in irritation. He kissed Sofiya? I definitely didn't tell him to do that, just as I didn't tell him to marry her.

As much as I don't like his methods, he kept her safe, and that's the only thing that matters

"What happened to the priest who married you?" Viktor asks.

"He took off like the wind the moment I flashed my gun. Anatoly's goons forced him to perform the ritual. Can't blame the guy. He would have been dead if he hadn't agreed."

The flight attendants come around with whisky for all of us, and it arrives not a moment too soon. We down it like it's our last drink on earth.

"Why don't you leave the bottle with us," I suggest to the flight attendant.

After pouring another round, we all sit back, lost in our thoughts. But there's something I'm curious about.

I turn to Nikolai. "What's next for you?"

He scratches his chin. "I have a bratva to take back. Sergey brought in his own men while I was in jail—the guys who ran the trafficking with him. Even though they all pledged allegiance to me, I don't believe it. I'll weed out each and every motherfucker who kept Sergey's secret, and then I need to rebuild from the ground up." He takes a slow, thoughtful sip of whisky. "I hope I have the Belov Syndicate's support to take over St. Petersburg."

I tap my fingers on the tray in front of me. "You'll have to meet with Maxim and get his approval, but you've proved yourself to be an asset. If you play by our rules, there's no reason you shouldn't have our support."

I'm curious about Nikolai's time in jail and the Zhukov Bratva's history. Especially because they were relatively quiet until Anatoly partnered with Sergey. But fuck, that conversation can wait.

I thread my hands behind my head and stare out the window. My to-do list is endless—there are a million fucking things to deal with for the syndicate when we're back in Russia, and I won't miss a beat.

But there's only one priority: marrying Liza as soon as possible. She's broken down my walls, filled my soul, and thawed my frozen heart.

There's nothing more to say. I'm claiming her as mine forever.

CHAPTER FIFTY-FIVE

LIZA

I WAKE UP TO PURE BLISS.

When I open my eyes, I'm treated to the best view ever. My legs are thrown over Roman's powerful shoulders as he goes to town between my spread thighs. I cry out and grab a handful of his locks as he swirls his tongue over my clit before sucking it deep into his mouth. It's pure ecstasy.

And then a whole new sensation takes me by surprise.

His tongue dips lower, much lower. Wetness coats the crevice of my ass.

A surprised gasp escapes from my lips. "What are you doing?"

His answer is a low murmur. "Making you feel good."

I clench my cheeks together, feeling self-conscious as he explores this forbidden place for the first time.

"You were making me feel good," I squeak, but I can't deny his tongue running over my back entrance also feels pretty damn good.

"Patience. I'm getting you ready."

"Getting me ready for— Oh."

One of his fingers traces over the spot where his tongue was. Then I feel a gentle pressure at my opening as a finger slides in. He holds it there, keeping it shallow.

Okay, wow. That feels much more pleasurable than I thought it would. A shiver blasts up my spine as his tongue circles my clit, and he continues to do what he does best.

This is unchartered territory for me, but Roman seems confident he can make me feel good.

"Relax, milaya." He drops a slow, sexy kiss on my clit, in the same way he would kiss my mouth, just as he plunges his finger forward, both sensations working in tandem to heighten my pleasure.

I let out a long, low moan as I clutch at the sheets underneath me. He doesn't let up as his tongue continues to dance over my bud, and he twists his finger inside of me. Sparks of pleasure grow in my core despite the foreign sensation.

"You're loving this," he whispers huskily. "You've never been this wet for me before."

Is that true? I don't know because I'm beyond thought. Unintelligible words spill from my mouth.

When he sucks my clit between his lips, I arch my back and writhe like a woman possessed, unable to hold back the wild noises that break free from my throat. My pussy clenches, and waves of pleasure build into an intense orgasm that takes me by surprise. I'm not sure I've ever climaxed this hard, and it takes me a few minutes to come back down to earth.

Roman continues gently lapping at me until my breathing has steadied, and I let out a giant sigh. When he slowly pulls his finger out of my ass, I shudder. He releases a deep chuckle. "You seemed to enjoy that."

A slow satisfied smile grows on my face. Will I ever get enough of this man? "Unexpectedly, I did. It was … amazing."

His lips still glistening, Roman settles beside me and leans on his elbows, watching me intently. "Good morning, milaya," he whispers and drops a sensual kiss on my lips.

I can taste myself, and it sets my blood on fire. "Good morning to you too," I pant.

He leans in and sweeps the hair away from my face while I cup his cock beneath the sheets.

"Should we make it a really good morning?" I ask with a hopeful grin.

He groans but shifts away from my touch. "As much as I'd love that, Kira and Maxim will be here soon. Wild horses couldn't keep Kira away from you, and I'm not about to try."

"Probably better if you don't," I admit with a smile.

Since our return from Greece two days ago, we've been staying in Roman's penthouse. I've been laid up under strict orders from the doctor to rest, nursing a fractured toe. Thankfully, aside from that and some mild dehydration, Sofiya and I escaped without serious injuries, though we're both exhausted—mentally and physically.

But it's the mental scars that cut the deepest, especially for Sofiya. Her world has been turned upside down—she's gone from a high school senior to finding out her former brother-in-law for all intents and purposes was a maniac and learning her parents were ready to trade her to a lunatic for their gain. And on top of everything, she's married to Nikolai. Well, maybe.

Roman's lawyer is looking into whether the marriage is legally binding, but given the circumstances, it's doubtful

I was furious with Nikolai at first, but when Roman explained it to me, I understood Nikolai's reasons for what he did, even if I'm not thrilled with the result.

I run my fingers over Roman's faint stubble, and my heart skips a beat, as it always does, under his intense gaze.

His expression shifts to a sad smile. "I never apologized to you," he says softly.

"Apologized?" My eyebrows hit my hairline. "For what?"

His finger traces my cheek. "I promised you and Sofiya would be safe in my home, but in the end, you weren't. It's my fault you suffered, that you were assaulted and nearly forced by that monster."

I shake my head fiercely. "How can you blame yourself? The only one at fault here is Anatoly. Well, Sergey deserves some of the blame as well," I add, trying to break the tension.

Roman's gaze remains dark. "I'll never forgive myself."

I rest my forehead against his. "It's going to be a long life if you can't forgive yourself, Roman. Your job will always be dangerous, and I can accept that if it means I get to be yours. Forever. But can you accept it?"

He looks away, pain etched in the lines of his face. "Maybe it's time I made some hard decisions. Decisions like leaving the syndicate."

My eyebrows knit together as I softly cradle his face in my hand. "Is that what you really want?"

His hesitation is palpable. "I'll be happy with you no matter what."

I trace a finger down his arm, feeling the muscle tense under my touch. "You're not ready to retire. I'm sure of it. But there's a way for you to have it all. You can have me and the syndicate. It'll take some adjustments on our end. But don't give up—consider this a lesson. I want this life beside you, whatever it entails."

He lowers his head as if weighing my words. After a moment, he looks up with a bright smile. "In that case … I have something to ask you."

My nerves buzz with excitement as he opens the nightstand drawer and pulls out what is unmistakably a jewelry box. I hoped this day would come, but I hadn't expected it to be this soon.

"Open it," he rasps. "I know Maxim and Kira are on the way over, but fuck it, I can't wait."

My hands tremble as I sit up higher in bed to take the little black velvet box from him. My breath catches, and emotion stings my eyelids as I open the box to see a stunning pink sapphire ring. The stone is cut in a brilliant oval, set in a delicate rose gold band encrusted with tiny, sparkling diamonds. It's perfect.

"I thought it would look beautiful on you." Roman's eyes search mine. "So … is that a yes? Will you marry me?"

"Yes. A thousand times yes. Nothing would make me happier." I kiss him fervently, like I'll never get enough. Tears fill my eyes as he slips the ring onto my finger.

"Did I do good?" he murmurs.

"You did more than good." I swipe a tear from under my cheek. "I couldn't have chosen better myself."

"There's one more thing." He reaches below the bed. "I've been waiting a long time to give this to you."

He presents me with the first edition of *Jane Eyre*, the one I'd refused to accept in London. His eyes lock with mine—deep, intense, and brimming with emotion.

"You kept it."

"I knew you'd say yes one day. I was going to keep on trying for the rest of my life."

All the air *whooshes* from my lungs, and I'm about to tackle him back onto the bed, when Kira's voice carries from the other side of the door.

"Okay, love birds, time to get out of bed."

"Give us a second," I call out. "We're uh … in the middle of something."

There's a pause. "Jesus, how much longer is this *something* going to take?" To Maxim, she says, "I bet they've been doing a lot of *something* lately."

Roman and I exchange a smile. His eyes light up with affection as he leans in to kiss me. It's soft and sweet, and I know nothing will be the same again—not my life, not my future, and definitely not my heart.

Kira can't stop gaping at my ring. I don't know if it's the shock of learning that Roman and I are together, or if the pink sapphire is so dazzling it's made her dizzy, but she seems a little shell-shocked.

She clears her throat. "So, to be clear, things started between you two the night we went to Sanctuary?"

Roman smirks. "You took us to a sex club. What did you expect?"

Kira smiles like the cat that ate the canary. "Exactly that."

My eyes narrow as understanding sets in. "You planned for us to hook up?"

"You can't plan for that kind of thing, but I saw the way you two looked at each other from the start. I knew there was something there. I just created the optimal conditions."

My mouth hangs open. "Looked at each other? I disliked Roman intensely until we went to London."

Roman swoops in to kiss my neck. "You know what they say: there's a thin line between love and hate."

I'm still reeling from Kira's revelation. "You little she-devil. We are going to have a serious talk about boundaries," I jokingly scold her.

She lets out an amused huff. "Please. There was chemistry between you two from the start. We all noticed." She looks over at Maxim to confirm her point.

He holds up his hands in front of him. "I'm not getting involved."

Kira purses her lips. "I knew you were miserable with Anatoly, but you would never accept my money or help. I figured it was worth a chance to play cupid and see if my gut was right."

I look over at Roman, who seems more amused than surprised. He leans in to kiss my neck. "Well, Kira, you might have a new career as a matchmaker," he declares.

Maxim rolls his eyes. "Please don't encourage her."

She elbows him in the ribs. "Obviously, I'm amazing at it." She gestures to Roman and me curled up together on the couch.

I sigh and rest my face against his shoulder.

Roman kisses my head and rises from the couch. "Maxim and I have some business to discuss. We'll leave you two to catch up."

Kira scoots closer to me on the couch. While I've filled in Kira and Maxim on pretty much everything, there is something else I need to say.

"I'm sorry I lied to you. With the shipping deal, the pregnancy, and everything Anatoly threatened, I was too scared to ask for help. I only wanted to protect Sofiya and all of you."

She squeezes my shoulder. Emotion shines in her eyes. "Why are you saying sorry? I'm the one who's sorry you went through such hell. He was a monster, and you deserved none of the abuse he inflicted. It's hard to ask for help when the people who should be your protectors are the ones hurting you."

I bite my lip and nod. That's all I'm capable of at the moment.

Her jaw hardens. "Your parents enabled him, and they deserve to pay."

"They will," I say simply.

Sofiya and I have agreed that we want nothing to do with our parents. They can live on the streets for all we care. Roman won't kill them because I don't want to live with that cruelty on my shoulders. They made terrible choices, but I don't have to. Still, they'll live in poverty and be social pariahs, which to my mother might be worse than death.

Kira releases a little sigh and rests her head on my shoulder. "Now, we have a wedding to plan." She gives a little clap. "I never thought my little plot would end like this."

I release a throaty laugh. "We're not in any rush. I really

want to make sure Sofiya is settled before we start making any big plans."

"Does she know yet?" Kira gestures towards the ring on my finger.

I shake my head. "I'll tell her right after this. She's been hiding out in her room for days. I want to give her the space to process everything, but I also don't want her to close herself off from life."

"It's a lot to take in. She probably needs some time."

"She's trying to decide if she wants to go back to school, or if she'll finish the semester remotely." I shrug. "She has to make the decision for herself."

One thing I've realized is that I can't protect Sofiya from every bump and bruise life throws her way. She needs to make her own choices and navigate her path to learn what's right for her.

"She'll figure it out. And she's lucky to have you and Roman. We'll always be there for her as well."

I squeeze her hand. "You're the best. Even though I'm still kind of shocked you set Roman and me up at a sex club."

She winks. "You mean at an erotic theate'."

I snicker. "You're one of the good ones, Kira Belov."

EPILOGUE

LIZA

Later that day, I knock on Sofiya's bedroom door.

"Come in," is the mumbled answer.

I turn the doorknob and let myself in. Sofiya is lying in bed, staring out the window, which has been her go-to more or less since we got home. Just lying there, despondent.

"How are you feeling today?" I ask.

Sofiya shrugs. "To be honest, the same as every other day."

I know Sofiya is struggling. Her world was ripped out from under her. Her family, friends, and the comfortable life she believed was her future all went up in smoke in a matter of hours. She needs time and space, and probably a good therapist, to figure out what's next. Right now, she's mourning her old life.

"Is there anything you want to talk about? Anything on your mind?" Worry tightens my shoulders.

She sighs. "Nothing we haven't talked about before. Nothing that needs to be said."

I bite my lip. "Listen, I know now might not be the best

time, but I have some news." I raise my hand and show her the engagement ring that Roman gave me. "It's not going to be right away," I feel the need to explain, "but sometime in the future."

She smiles and gives me a hug, and it's the first time since we came home that I see a little spark in her eyes.

"I'm happy for you. I really am. Now that I see how you are with Roman, I realize you weren't yourself with Anatoly."

I brush a strand of hair from her cheek. "That's all behind us now."

She sighs and turns over to get a better look at me. "Roman and you fit together. You're right for each other. After everything, you deserve this happiness more than anyone."

The life I once considered a dream too far out of reach is about to become my reality, and I can hardly believe it myself. "Thank you." I lie down on the bed beside her and run my nails down her arm, like I used to when she was a kid. "It means a lot to hear you say that."

After a moment of quiet, she clears her throat. "I've made a decision," she says. "I don't want to go back to school. Everything's changed, and I can't pretend I'm still the girl I was before this all happened."

My eyes search hers, and I nod. "You don't have to be anyone but yourself. No one's asking that of you."

She clasps her hands behind her head. "Yeah, but you know how people talk. I don't want to deal with any of it. I'll finish school online."

I truly feel for her, I do, but I fight the urge to fix every little hurt. I'll be there for Sofiya, helping her through whatever comes next. I've arranged for a therapist to meet with her tomorrow, but I know firsthand that the only way to work through something is to allow yourself to experience your feelings, not stuff them down.

There's a lot I'm working through right now as well, but it helps to have Roman by my side.

"You're eighteen soon," I remind her. "You're an adult, free to do as you like. Maybe you want to spend some time traveling or, I don't know, take an acting class in London, or something like that."

"Maybe." She fiddles with one of her many rings. "Did you hear back from the lawyer yet?"

My eyebrows knit together. "About what?"

She takes a deep breath. "About the marriage. Am I still —" The words get caught in her throat.

I shake my head, annoyed at myself for letting it slip my mind. "The lawyers are confident that it's not legally binding. Either way, Roman and I will sort it out for you. Don't worry about it for one second."

A shiver moves through her. "Do I have to see Nikolai again?"

"I don't see why you would," I assure her.

I imagine the idea of seeing Nikolai again is disturbing—it would remind her of one of the worst days of her life. I've tried to talk to her about what happened at the chapel, but she doesn't want to go there with me. Maybe it's too fresh.

Roman taps lightly on the door, which is already half open, before stepping into the room. His eyes meet mine with an unspoken question. *How is Sofiya doing?* I give him a small nod.

"Dinner should be here soon. I ordered tacos, your favorite," he says to Sofiya.

Warmth floods through me. Roman has worked so hard to make Sofiya comfortable in his home. Even if it is an uphill battle, he's as dedicated to her recovery as I am.

"What do you say?" I ask my sister. "Ready to eat?"

"Sure. I'll be out in a minute."

I nod and plant a quick kiss on her temple.

In the kitchen, Roman hands me a glass of wine and

insists I perch myself on the counter to avoid putting pressure on my injured toe. His two powerful arms cage me in as he nuzzles my neck and plants a kiss at my pulse point.

A shiver works its way through my body. "That reminds me," I tell him with a saucy wink. "We didn't finish what we started this morning."

He pulls back a little so he can look into my eyes. "Don't you worry. I haven't forgotten about my marital duty."

"It's not marital yet." I smack him with a dish towel.

"Soon, baby, soon." He smiles. "How did Sofiya take the news?"

I take a thoughtful sip of wine. "Happy for us. But overall, still pretty down. She did make a decision, though. She doesn't want to go back to school."

"Can't blame her. Gossip about your parents' downfall will be all over the city."

I nod. It will always hurt that my parents were willing to sell off Sofiya and me as if we meant nothing to them, but I've made peace with the truth. For everyone's sake, I need to move on without them in my life.

"What did you and Maxim decide to do about the Petroviches?" I ask.

"We agreed to say Anatoly died in a tragic accident on vacation. We've paid off the authorities, and that's the story his family will hear." He grimaces. "I hate hiding that he was an abusive monster, but revealing the truth would bring unwanted attention to you and Sofiya. I can't risk that."

"I want to forget he ever existed." I shudder. "By the way, Sofiya asked about the annulment. I'm sure she's anxious to get it over and done with."

Roman drags a hand over his neck. "As long as the marriage license wasn't submitted to the authorities, there's nothing to annul. Either way, Nikolai is busy taking the reins of his bratva and securing St. Petersburg. But in the next few weeks, he'll be in Moscow to meet with Maxim and work out an arrangement between our organizations. If we need to deal with something, we can handle it then."

"Sounds good." I open my arms.

Roman steps into my embrace, wrapping himself around me, knowing exactly what I need. "When do I get to make you my wife?" he growls huskily against my neck.

"I'm yours forever, no matter what. But I have been thinking …"

His eyebrows raise.

"I don't want a big wedding. I only want close family and friends, and I was hoping we can have it at the cabin—a way to remember your mother."

He pulls away and looks at me, his eyes shining with emotion. "If we wait until summer, we can have it under the giant oak tree. It was her favorite."

I grin, my heart swelling. "I'd love that. I can't wait to share forever with you, Roman Vasiliev."

"Fuck, baby." He cups my head, his gaze intense. "I don't know how I got so lucky, but I've never been happier. No one else makes me feel like you do." His words take my breath away. "You complete me. You've turned my world around and made me a better man for it. This life isn't worth living unless you're by my side."

Damn. Tears fall unchecked. I never imagined I'd find a love like this—a love that is deep, real, and all-consuming.

"It's the same for me," I whisper as he brushes away my tears. "There's nothing else I want more than to be yours until the end of time."

Roman is my sanctuary, my protector—my everything.

Thank you so much for reading!

Want more of Roman & Liza?
Download the **BONUS EPILOGUE** from my website:
https://monicakayne.com/bonuses

OTHER BOOKS BY MONICA KAYNE

KOZLOV EMPIRE

Merciless Heir

Cruel Deception

Fierce Vow

Shattered Crown

BRATVA KINGS

Ruthless Reign

Savage Reign

Brutal Reign

ACKNOWLEDGMENTS

Ruthless Reign was my easiest and hardest book to write. The first draft was a breeze, but the second draft was like pulling teeth, trying to get Roman and Liza's chemistry to spark just right!

Nina and Sierra, thank you for your invaluable feedback in whipping this puppy into shape. It wasn't easy, but you were both encouraging and supportive, and I love you for it.

So much love and thanks to Chanel, Kalie, and everyone at Good Girls Author Services for your support and hard work. You always go above and beyond.

Jose, Keanna, Ashley, and Cassie, thank you for running my TikTok accounts (aka the slut phone, thanks for that, Cassie).

Thanks to Nana the Book Babe (and her boyfriend) who suggested *milaya* (sweetheart). I'm sure many readers will thank you!

Always, a huge thank you to my street team and the cheerleaders who are in my corner, making edits on social media and reaching out to let me know how much you enjoy my books. You have no idea how that fills my heart.

Lastly, love and many thanks to my family—including my parents and in-laws—who watched our kids during many 'working weekends'.

Love,

xo Monica

ABOUT THE AUTHOR

Monica Kayne is a former documentary TV producer turned proud romance writer. She writes dark and swoony romance novels with a liberal dose of sass and humor. Her favorite characters to write are sweetly possessive bad boys and the feisty, smart-mouthed heroines they can't resist. When she's not dreaming up sexy plots, she can be found searching for the perfect Negroni and her next K-drama fix. She lives with her family in Toronto, Canada.

Connect with me!
www.monicakayne.com

TikTok
@monicakayneauthor

Instagram
@monicakayneauthor

Facebook reader group
Monica's Mafia Queens

Printed in Great Britain
by Amazon

61561724R00221